DANCE OF THE PHOENIX

OTHER TITLES BY SAPIR A. ENGLARD

Cloak of the Vampire

Blood of the Gods

The Millennium Wolves

His Haze

Alpha of the Millennium

Ghosted Soul

Painted Scars

One Night

Desperate

CLOAK OF THE VAMPIRE

BOOK 3

DANCE OF THE PHOENIX

SAPIR A. ENGLARD

Montlake

This is a work of fiction. Names, characters, organizations, places, events, and incidents are either products of the author's imagination or are used fictitiously. Otherwise, any resemblance to actual persons, living or dead, is purely coincidental.

Published by Montlake, Seattle
www.apub.com

EU product safety contact:
Amazon Media EU S. à r.l.
38, avenue John F. Kennedy, L-1855 Luxembourg
amazonpublishing-gpsr@amazon.com

ISBN-13: 9781662532894 (paperback)
ISBN-13: 9781662532900 (digital)

Cover design by Faceout Studio, Addie Lutzo
Cover image: © Danielle Skinner / ArcAngel Images; © Nenov, © sanketb / 500px / Getty

Printed in the United States of America

To my readers, both old and new, whose love and support I deeply cherish.

PART I

CHAPTER 1
AILEEN

Miserable emptiness filled my stomach as I watched Tansy's face, serene in her slumber. She seemed far younger and more fragile than usual, with her long strawberry blond hair spread around her petite, pale body like a halo.

It had been a few days since the incident, and I'd spent all my time here, watching her. According to Leah, the nurse in charge of Tansy, my former suitemate hadn't awoken since the night the incident occurred. Since she was a vampire, and vampires shouldn't be able to go into a coma, Leah's thesis was that it was the result of psychological damage.

Leah had tried to make me leave in the first couple of days. She didn't say Tansy's state was my fault, but she sure insinuated it by showing her ire at my being in the infirmary. But at some point, it seemed the nurse took pity on me, as though she could feel my anguish, and let me be.

The sound of the curtain surrounding Tansy's bed drawing open made me turn around. Isora, my former suitemate from the Atalon League and a friend, stood there wearing her infirmary gown, a bottle of fresh blood in her hand. "Care for company?" she asked, giving me a worried look.

It was almost funny that *she* was concerned about *me*, considering she was still recuperating from being used as a blood slave. Yet she definitely looked better than she had when I'd rescued her, with her braided brown hair shining and healthy, her blue eyes no longer bloodshot, and her skin losing the last of its grayish tint and blemishes. It was only a matter of time before she would be released from the infirmary.

"Be my guest," I said quietly, returning my gaze to Tansy. I was glad Isora was doing well. While it didn't entirely relieve me of my guilt where she was concerned, it did lessen it a bit. Because even though I hadn't been able to stop her from being exploited by a vampire Lord who was supposed to care for her but instead misused her almost beyond repair, I'd managed to save her in the end.

Unlike Tansy, whom I had failed many years ago, and then again just recently—so much so that her mind had tried to protect her from everything, from *me*, by putting her into what could very much be an eternal slumber.

Isora grabbed a chair and put it next to mine, sitting down. "It's not your fault," she told me quietly, putting her palm gently on my fisted hand. "You're not responsible for me, Zoey, or this girl."

I tensed. Isora didn't know about my connection to Tansy, since both were my suitemates at different times, but I figured she guessed enough to understand there was one. But she didn't know everything. She didn't know about the darkest part of my past. The part that I was now 100 percent sure Tansy belonged to.

When I didn't respond, Isora took a deep breath and let my hand go, uncorking her bottle and sipping the blood. Part of her treatment, I knew, was to drink about seven liters of blood a day.

We sat in silence; the only sound breaking it was her drinking. I stared at Tansy, as if looking at her might wake her up and make everything better. What could I have done for her a few days ago that might've prevented this? Knowing there was nothing I could have done, really, made me grit my teeth.

"Aileen."

Isora's careful voice made me whip my head toward her and snap, "I'm fine, so stop nagging me."

She lowered her now-empty bottle and gave me a narrow-eyed look. "You're obviously not fine, so I'll keep on nagging you as I see fit." She rose from her seat. "But since it seems I can't get through to you, I'm going to call *Lord Rayne*."

I grabbed her wrist. "Don't," I said, glaring at her. "I'm *fine*."

Shaking my hold, she drew the curtain and stepped away. Irritated, I jumped to my feet and strode after her. She was somehow almost at the exit of the infirmary, but before she could leave, the door opened, revealing the very man she was going to call.

Ragnor Rayne, vampire Lord of the Rayne League, walked inside, his midnight blue eyes darting from Isora to me. His dark-brown hair was pulled into a messy ponytail, and his tall, muscular body was draped in black sweatpants, an indigo tank top, and his worn-out combat boots. His golden-toned skin was glistening with sweat, indicating he had just finished training before popping in.

I hadn't seen him since the incident with Tansy and our heart-to-heart that followed. He'd been so busy, he'd resorted to leaving me letters saying we would talk the next day. Unfortunately, every following day he would go AWOL again.

I didn't blame him for being busy. With the whole Lord Atalon situation going on, and the impending war between the Atalon and Rayne Leagues, I had no doubt he was up to his neck in work. I didn't even try to seek him out for that reason, and to be honest, after our far-too-painful conversation in which I spilled the beans about my past, the space between us was welcome.

Yet here he was now, walking toward me with an expression I couldn't quite decipher. I paused, watching him watching me as he drew to a stop a step away. "Come with me. We need to talk," he ordered, low voice taut with what sounded like anger. But why would he be angry at me?

Narrowing my eyes, I studied his face. He was as handsome as ever, this infuriating man, but there was something amiss in his eyes. He seemed to be on edge.

My first instinct was to refuse his command on principle, but since he seemed jittery, shifting from foot to foot, his broad shoulders tense and his hands curled into white-knuckled fists, I knew this wasn't the time or place for that.

Giving him a stiff nod, I glanced at Isora. She went back to her bed, watching us with big worried eyes.

Without another word, Ragnor turned around and walked out. With a flash of annoyance—and not just about his strange behavior but his general attitude—I took a deep breath, swallowed my ire, and followed him out.

Ragnor's office was a mess.

Paperwork, both printed and handwritten, covered the wooden desk and some part of the floor. The cabinets, their contents usually stacked in an orderly manner, were now wide open, folders and documents haphazardly thrown in. There were two large monitors, their cables twisted messily toward the computer itself, seated on the chairs. That, combined with the stifling smell of dust and barely dried ink, made the office feel like a storm had come through, leaving this disaster in its wake.

I stared, gaping, at the bizarre sight. This wasn't like Ragnor. I'd been inhabiting his private suite ever since I returned to the Rayne League, and it was so neat and orderly, I could hardly bear it myself, as a naturally unkempt person. This was so out of character, I was struck dumb.

Ragnor was a control freak. That also showed in his tendency to like clean and organized spaces. Out of all the Leagues I'd visited, the Rayne League was definitely the tidiest. Even the Atalon League, while polished and tasteful, always had dirt here and there from all the artsy stuff being moved around constantly.

I was about to speak, to ask what the hell was going on here, but Ragnor put away one of the monitors, took his own seat in the plush chair—the only furniture that hadn't had anything on it—and motioned for me to sit. Biting my tongue, I carefully tiptoed around the papers lying about and sat down.

Then, Ragnor spoke. "In three weeks, there is going to be a Hecatomb."

I wanted to tease him, to lighten up the air that had suddenly turned heavy with tension, but with his dead-serious gaze, I knew jokes would not be appreciated. Not now. So I warily asked, "What's a Hecatomb?"

He leaned back against his chair, jaw ticking. "A Hecatomb is a way for vampires to . . . 'war it out,'" he explained, voice foreboding. "Since all vampires are signed to the Secrecy Agreement, in which we vow to hide our existence from humans, when two Leagues go to war, they obviously can't do it out in the open. That's what the Hecatomb is for."

Pulling out a drawer in the desk, he retrieved a printed sheet of paper and set it on the desktop. With a pen in hand, Ragnor began writing something at the bottom of the page as he spoke. "The Hecatomb is a contest of sorts, gladiatorial in style. Each League brings ten members, five Gifted and five Common, to fight against each other, two versus two. The battles can only end in one of two ways: death or surrender. Ties are not possible."

Gifted vampires referred to humans with special talents that transformed into some sort of magical ability after the human received the Imprint. *Common* vampires, on the other hand, were regular vampires without any special powers whatsoever.

Ragnor stopped scribbling and raised his eyes to me. "Raking in victories is mostly for the League members' sake. Because, in truth, the final battle is all that really matters." He paused, lips pressed into a thin line. "It's a fight to the death between two Sacreds—or rather, the two Lords."

Sacred referred to vampires who'd lived for a few centuries and developed magic with age. Magic that had nothing to do with their talents, if they had any. To become a vampire Lord, one had to be Sacred.

A fight between two Lords who packed a lot of magical power was bound to be absolutely brutal.

Just the thought of it made my heart stop.

"The results can vary," Ragnor said, pushing the paper he'd just written on toward me. "Read this."

With trembling hands, I took the paper and read:

"In the event that League X wins more rounds, and its Lord wins the final battle, League Y's both Common and Gifted members will submit to be put in a special Hecatomb Auction.

"In the event that League X wins more rounds, but the Lord of League Y wins the final battle, League X members have three choices:

1. Remain as a League and appoint a member as a new Lord

2. Initiate a Hecatomb Auction and dissolve the League

3. Become Leagueless

"In the event that League X loses more rounds, but its Lord wins the final battle, League X will be considered the winner, and the Lord can then Auction off the Hecatomb participants, both Gifted and Common, who remain alive, in the next regular newcomer Auction."

In his cursive writing, Ragnor added below: *"In the rare case that both Lords lose their lives, the responsibility for the two Leagues' members is passed over to the Global Vampiric Association for ruling, regardless of which League won more rounds."*

I read the paper twice before I raised my gaze to meet Ragnor's. My head was bursting with questions. "This seems far too complicated," I said, reeling. "Who came up with this shit?"

Ragnor gave me a humorless smile. "The Hecatomb has been our method of war for centuries. It started when two Leagues in Europe needed to settle a score and were afraid of taking it out in the open air, in case they were exposed. They created the Hecatomb for that reason, and many other Leagues adopted this method from all over the world, until it became the official, legal way of settling a dispute of massive proportions."

Thinking it through, I hesitantly asked, "I thought the Vampire Society had a legal division."

Something softened in Ragnor's gaze for a quick moment before his face hardened again. "There *is* a court, but when it comes to one Lord against another Lord, the court dictates a Hecatomb—as long as appeal by the plaintiff makes legal sense." He paused, grimacing. "In this case, Atalon has been piling up serious grievances he twisted into plausible legal allegations against me for over two hundred years. Me taking you and Isora away was the final piece of evidence he needed to file for a Hecatomb."

"Wait," I said, trying to follow. "*Final* piece of evidence? What else does he hold against you?" But just as the words left my mouth, realization dawned. "The whole story with the Gifted fraud exchange."

The Gifted fraud exchange referred to an instance in the far past when Ragnor had duped Atalon. Atalon, being the arrogant prick that he was, wanted to give the Imprint to a certain human who both Ragnor and Atalon thought had the chance to become Gifted upon receiving it. He did that under Ragnor's nose, which then made Ragnor concoct a plan with said human, now a vampire, to get her into his League. So the vampire managed to trick Atalon into thinking she was a Common, and Ragnor offered an exchange: a Gifted member of his League in exchange for the allegedly Common vampire. Atalon agreed, and only after the deal was done did he find out that the Common vampire was, in fact, Gifted.

Despite the fact he'd gotten a Gifted vampire out of this deal either way, he couldn't forgive Ragnor for this, and it became one of the many contentious points between the two.

Ragnor nodded with a grave expression. "On paper, that case is not dissimilar to yours. In the legal eye, I *have* defrauded him when it comes to taking away his League members." He gave me an angry look I knew wasn't directed at me. "That, among other things, is what he presented to file for the Hecatomb."

I'd known Atalon was an asshole, and I knew he was preparing to go head-to-head with Ragnor. But the fact that Ragnor had to deal with this utter bullshit made me hate him even more than before.

Pursing my lips, I asked, "What's the Global Vampiric Association?"

Ragnor sighed. "Let's just say that they're like the high court. They don't get involved with regular League affairs unless something extraordinary happens."

He said it so calmly that if I hadn't been watching him like a hawk, I would've missed it. His face drew tight at his own words. If I thought he was capable of it, I would've said Ragnor was in a state of panic.

Heart ramming against my rib cage, I opened my mouth to speak when he interjected. "In any case, let's discuss the Hecatomb."

He pointed down to the paper before me, and I clamped my mouth shut and let him speak. "The Hecatomb is an official event. It's a chance for other Leagues to come as spectators and see what the participating Leagues are made of. One of the Leagues is also chosen to moderate the Hecatomb. A Hecatomb doesn't happen very often, so when it does, it turns into a whole-ass festival."

Hearing the disgust in his voice, I couldn't help but reel back. "Meaning everyone is treating it like some sort of a show rather than a fight to the death," I surmised. "It really *is* like the gladiators."

Ragnor didn't speak for a few long moments. He only stared at me with a torn expression that squeezed my chest so tight, it was hard to breathe. "What is it?" I asked, throat clogged as anxiety spread through me.

"There's one more thing," he said, his face contorting in fury. "The Lord who initiates the Hecatomb needs to give the main reason for the Hecatomb—one he can pick out of all his allegations—and in accordance with that reason, the League that moderates the Hecatomb can put in a demand."

A foreboding feeling spread through my veins. "Who is the moderator?" I asked, my heartbeat quickening as if my body knew what was coming before my mind did. "What did they demand?"

He sucked in a deep breath, eyes glowing neon blue, before he spit it out. "The moderator chosen is Lord Manuel Renaldi. And he asked to see you, Aileen, fight."

CHAPTER 2
AILEEN

"So let me get this straight," I said, thumping my foot restlessly, fear rising in me. "You and ten other vampires from the League will be participating in a life-or-death tournament, and I'm required to fight there as well?"

Ragnor's eyes followed me quietly, his jaw tight, as he reluctantly nodded.

My hands curled into fists. "This is infuriating."

"Infuriating it may be, but this is what's going to happen three weeks from now whether we like it or not," Ragnor replied in a tight voice. "Rest assured, though, that despite what you may think, participating in the Hecatomb is highly valued."

I folded my arms, glaring at him. "How so?"

He leaned back, folding his arms, too, as if to mimic me. "It's an opportunity for the chosen League members to rise above their current standing and gain recognition not just within their League, but in others too. It's considered an honor."

His words left a bitter taste in my mouth. "Honor?" I asked, narrowing my eyes. "There's nothing honorable about war."

"This is an unrealistic perspective, Aileen," Ragnor said in a patient voice, but his eyes locked mine in an unshakable hold. "Think about humans. All the wars humanity has been through in the past—can you really say the soldiers involved felt no sense of honor when they managed to represent their countries and win against an enemy?"

Logically, I knew he was right. But it didn't make me feel any better. "What does honor have to do with it anyway?" I asked, seething. "Per what's written on this piece of paper, if the League's members lose more rounds, depending on their Lord's triumph, they'll be forced into a Hecatomb Auction. So what does it all even matter?"

Ragnor's eyes turned wary. "Think about it, Aileen," he said quietly. "What's the purpose of the Auction in the first place?"

Giving him a filthy look as my chest tightened, my heart aching from a not-yet-fully-healed wound, I spit out, "To sell and buy vampires like objects for the benefit of the Lord."

He leaned forward slowly, cautiously, and said calmly, "It's not the complete truth." I narrowed my eyes, and Ragnor closed his, taking a deep breath and leaning back into his chair in something akin to defeat. "The Lords might give the final say in the Auction regarding who they would like to bid on, but we have Lieutenants for a reason. And that reason is to aid us in avoiding"—he paused with a tensed jaw—"emotional decisions."

Tense silence fell in the wake of his words. Staring down at my own hands holding one another on my lap, I knew he was giving me a choice. Either I could argue with him again about what happened three months ago, when he'd sold me to Atalon, or I could focus on the subject at hand.

And since we had far more pressing issues to discuss, I decided to drop it and instead vocalized what I realized. "So the Hecatomb can serve like a performance show for the participating members. To show the other Lords what they're capable of in real time, and not just as a talent show."

From the corner of my eye, I saw him nod. "Yes. It's a privilege the ten participating members have. The rest of the League members who would be put in the Hecatomb Auction, if it came to this, wouldn't have that."

This just emphasized, then, how important the choice of the ten participants was. Based on their winning or losing against the other League's members, they would decide their League members' fate—while also having this alleged "honor" to showcase what they could do, just in case. Which, in truth, made it balanced, considering they put their lives on the line.

"How are you going to choose the ten members?" I asked now, raising my eyes back to him.

Ragnor gave me a long look before he responded. "Each League can choose the members however it sees fit. In most cases, the Lord simply chooses the members and is done with it, but I decided to have all members of my League vote."

This seemed very un-Ragnor-like. But when I looked down at the paper he'd given me, I realized why he left the choice to a vote. The ten members were basically the representatives of all of the League members in the Hecatomb, meaning that if Ragnor lost, the ten members could rake in enough wins to help dictate the fate of the Rayne League participants.

"It's very magnanimous of you," I said quietly, for once not feeling cynical at all. I raised my eyes back to him, and for the first time since I entered the office, I could see beyond his supposedly blank face.

Ragnor was exhausted.

He was so exhausted that, even though he'd managed to hide it, I was suddenly aware of the dark bags under his eyes, the drawn skin of his face, and the slump of his shoulders.

And just like that, I felt like a dick. Because in the past few days, while Ragnor was extremely busy, all I had done was wallow in self-pity and blame myself for Tansy's current state. It hadn't even occurred to me that Ragnor might need me. He wasn't the type to exactly need anyone. Him being busy, leaving me to sleep alone in his private suite, not showing his face—I'd simply accepted it for what it was. I knew better than anyone about the extent of the mess I'd put him in, after all. It was a no-brainer that he needed to take care of things.

But I hadn't given a second thought to how *he* felt about everything. I had simply assumed he was fine, since he was the indomitable Ragnor Rayne. But seeing his face now, seeing through his indifferent facade into how tired he was, whether it be physically or emotionally, I realized I shouldn't have assumed anything.

Swallowing hard, I rose from my seat and went around the desk, careful not to step on the discarded paperwork. He watched me silently until I stood before his chair, and then, feeling a little brave, I sat down on his lap and wrapped my arms around his neck.

For a few tense moments, I was afraid he would tell me to get off, but then Ragnor's strong arms enveloped me, and he pulled me tighter against him, burying his face in my shoulder.

We didn't speak. We just held on to one another. And in his arms, feeling his warmth, his need for me, my need for him, I finally let myself feel how much I had missed him in the last few days. How much I truly needed him too.

And suddenly, I could no longer stay silent. "Is this the only reason why you've been so busy?" I asked quietly, not letting him go. "Or is there something else you're not telling me?"

He tensed for a brief second before he relaxed and leaned back just enough to look at my face. His hand cupped my cheek, and his eyes glowed neon blue as he replied, "I was looking for a way to not have you be there."

I froze, eyes widening. "What?"

He gave me a humorless smile. "Prior to Renaldi being chosen as a moderator, I made calls with all the North American Lords. I even managed to meet some of them in person. I needed to make sure they were on my side. That they understood the situation beyond what was written in the official Hecatomb application. I was hoping for anyone but Renaldi to be chosen as moderator.

"Unfortunately . . ." His smile disappeared, turning into a grimace. "The choice is always randomly generated, and Renaldi was picked."

I could see where this was going, but I didn't interrupt.

"Renaldi and I are not on the best terms at the moment," he told me quietly. "After our talk regarding Zoey, in which I told him I was going to take Zoey in and use it as the favor he owed me, he's been quite upset with me. After he was chosen as the moderator, I was basically chasing after him. I even flew to Vegas to meet with him in person. But when we met, Renaldi's mind was already set."

Zoey was another former suitemate of mine. She'd been sold in the Auction to Renaldi, and when attempting to escape, she was caught by a Jinni, an antagonistic entity that hated vampires. We saved her from the Jinn when Ragnor and I infiltrated their headquarters in Vermont, and instead of bringing Zoey back to Renaldi, as protocol dictated, Ragnor took her in as one of his own instead. Thus leading to Renaldi's inevitable falling-out with Ragnor.

He paused, giving me a searching look, before he murmured, "I tried to dissuade him from requesting you to be present in the Hecatomb. I told him the situation with Atalon was hardly about you, more about Atalon's hatred toward me. Renaldi turned a deaf ear, and this morning, I was told your presence is required."

His words didn't fully compute at first. But when they did, I leaned farther back from him and scanned his face, heart quickening in my chest as anger rose inside me. "Why?" I asked, trying to keep my voice calm, and failing. "Why did you try so hard to keep me away from it?"

Ragnor's hands grabbed my waist, his face darkening. "I don't want you anywhere near Atalon," he said with a sudden growl that made me tense. "Nor do I want you anywhere near the other Lords. I don't want any attention on you. I don't want everyone to realize that you were the catalyst for the Hecatomb." He paused, then added in a lower voice, "Or that you are the youngest Sacred vampire to ever exist. That you are . . . what you are."

He rearranged me smoothly so I was completely straddling him, and before I could say anything, his hands tore away my shirt, shoved off my bra, and grabbed my breasts possessively. I gasped, heat pooling at my abdomen. "If they realize what you mean to me, they'll do everything in their power to hurt you to get to me," he said, his glowing eyes suddenly hungry and desperate. "I don't know what they'll do if they realize what you are, and I refuse to let it happen."

Before I could speak, his mouth covered mine in a hot kiss that made rational thought impossible; all possible retorts left me in favor of a sudden wave of lust.

Losing common sense, I leaned into his hands kneading my breasts and moaned into his mouth as he tangled his tongue with mine, movements fast and furious.

Impatient, I pushed off his tank top, spreading my hands against his hard, toned chest, and he pinched my nipples, making me groan and undulate against his hard erection. I then fumbled with his pants, desperately looking to free his cock.

Before I could do that, though, Ragnor pulled back and, wrapping his arms around me, he rose from the chair, and put my ass down on his desk.

We were then wrestling, battling over who could undress the other first. It was a furious, maddening fight that made my desperation for him all too real, making me realize just how much I had missed him. Missed his touch. Missed his skin on mine. Missed *him*.

No words were needed when, with both my wrists tied in his hand above my head, he pushed his thick, long cock inside my aching pussy, filling me up so beautifully, it took my breath away.

Then, with mesmerizing power, Ragnor fucked me deep, raw, and hard, until we both found our release with screams and growls that shook the walls of his office.

Some time later, as we cuddled in Ragnor's bed (after we sneaked out of his office with barely any clothes on), satisfied from a few rounds of frantic sex, I said, "You know, you never took me out on a date."

His chest vibrated under my cheek as he chuckled, his hands twirling my blond hair, which I gave up on dyeing brown a while ago, playfully. "That's what bothers you right now?" he asked, amused.

I shrugged, grinning. "Well, it's the truth. You're still on probation, you know. You've already wasted a week out of the one-month limit."

He scoffed. "I thought we were past that."

My grin faded a bit before I braced myself on one arm, looking down at him. He gave me a lazy, heavy-lidded, smug look that made me frown. "I'm serious, Ragnor."

He studied me, his amusement dissolving, and he put his arm around my waist, making me lie on my back with him looming over me. "And here I thought I was out of the woods," he murmured, giving me a disappointed look. "In the next three weeks, I have to take care of the voting to choose which members will come with us to the Hecatomb. Then, we have the Hecatomb, which will take another week. In total, it's one month."

I knew what he was saying. I also knew I should let this go—the man was going to war for my sake, after all—but I couldn't let go of my fear.

Because the truth was, while he'd told me he loved me and had saved me more than once, he also knew that I was a Sacred. He knew I possessed a power he could utilize for his and his League's sake. A part of me, a part I wasn't proud of, was terrified that he only wanted me because of my Sacred status.

And even if it wasn't that, our earlier conversation had reawakened the pain from him giving me up once. Knowing he was capable of letting me go did not make me feel very secure.

"Then take me out after the Hecatomb business is done with," I said, forcing out a smile. "That means you've got to win this thing, you know."

He visibly relaxed. "Bold of you to assume I'll lose," he told me with a smirk.

I smirked back, pushing down my fears for now. After the Hecatomb was over, I could make Ragnor prove his love and devotion to me. At the moment, he didn't need to know I was skeptical. That I hardly believed him.

Because in the end, it was *my* issue, not his. And if I learned one thing from my relationship with Logan, my ex-boyfriend, it was that pushing my own insecurities and problems onto the man I was with would only drive him away, with no hope of return.

And I refused to do that with Ragnor. No matter how much my debilitating demons begged to differ.

CHAPTER 3
AILEEN

The Rayne League was abuzz with the upcoming election for the Hecatomb. Every time I visited the cafeteria with Isora and Zoey—both of whom were finally released from the infirmary after spending many days there recuperating from the ghastly, near-death state in which I'd found them in the Jinn headquarters—all everyone talked about was who they would vote for. Even in the Common residence lounge, where the three of us usually got coffee in the afternoon, no one talked about anything else.

"From what I can tell, the Troop Commanders are the leading candidates for the five Gifted representatives," Zoey told Isora and me a couple of days before the voting. We were sitting in the infirmary near Tansy's bed, which had become our private hangout spot ever since Ragnor announced the Hecatomb Election. Leah, the nurse in charge, had already given up telling us off, as though she were secretly hoping our voices might wake Tansy up from her coma.

"That's a no-brainer," Isora replied as she was braiding her chocolate brown hair. "Of course the League members would want the strongest vampires in the League to represent them." She paused thoughtfully before she asked, "Who are the Commanders anyway?"

That was a good question, and I had a partial answer. "I know one of them," I said, "but I don't know about the rest."

Zoey, who was combing Tansy's hair, looked up at me. "I thought your boyfriend would tell you these things."

Isora snorted, and I gave her a pointed look. "Well, my 'boyfriend' and I don't discuss such matters."

Both Isora and Zoey realized Ragnor and I had a thing going on, and when I remained tight lipped about our relationship, they resorted to calling him my "boyfriend" once they figured out we were trying to be discreet. That didn't sit well with me, though. The word "boyfriend" was far too light and precarious for my liking. Yet both of them delighted in seeing my scrunched-nosed reaction every time they said that word, and used it on purpose to get a rise out of me.

"What's he good for, then?" Isora murmured and winced when I elbowed her. Hard.

Zoey rolled her eyes at our teasing. "Well, there is a Troop show tonight in the auditorium. Want to go?"

"A Troop show?" I asked, frowning. Last night, when Ragnor returned to his suite, which I now shared, he had fallen asleep, barely saying hello to me. He'd been even more exhausted than before, with the Hecatomb coming up, and that meant we didn't really get to talk. So it kinda chafed that I learned about what was going on in the League through a friend rather than my "boyfriend," who was the actual Lord of this League.

Zoey released Tansy's hair and pulled a pamphlet out of the pocket of her jeans. "They handed it out earlier today in the Common lounge," she said, handing it to me. "Apparently, to help the voters, the Troop Commanders decided to put on a talent show, with our Lord's approval, to showcase both the Common and Gifted Troop members' abilities."

"That's interesting," Isora said as she leaned her chin on my shoulder, skimming the pamphlet along with me. "Does it mean the entire Troop is basically volunteering for the Hecatomb?"

"Most likely," Zoey replied. "After all, who's better equipped than the military division of the League, full of trained individuals, to fight for the League members' sake?"

Zoey was right, but then it raised another question: What was the purpose of the voting process, if the Troop members were the obvious choices?

Later that night, I got my answer.

The last time I'd visited the auditorium, or rather the Auction Hall, had been during, well, the Auction in which Ragnor had sold me to Atalon. Which, ironically enough, was what led to the most regrettable situation we were in now.

Instead of sitting in the front rows awaiting my turn to show off my talents and to be bid on, I was a spectator in the audience this time, eagerly waiting for the show to start.

Isora, who sat to my left, was talking with Zoey, who sat next to her, about what the show was going to include. According to the pamphlet, at the end of the Troop's show, there would be a chance for non-Troop members who wanted to participate in the Hecatomb to show what they could do. That part was bound to be interesting, if nothing else.

When the show started, a vaguely familiar man with brown skin and heavy makeup took to the stage, a cordless mic in his hands. "Hello, my friends and comrades of the Rayne League!" he called, causing the crowd to clap, shout, and whistle in almost bloodthirsty excitement.

Everyone was far too happy and excited about the upcoming Hecatomb, in my opinion.

"God, it feels like just yesterday Kaylon called my name in the Auction," Zoey murmured.

"Without further ado, show your love to the four Commanders!" Kaylon now said, and to a deafening cheer, four figures joined him onstage.

My eyes widened, shock thrumming through my veins, when Kaylon said, "Please welcome Haneul Kang, Oberon Grimes, Neisha Barnes, and Logan Kazar, our four formidable Troop Commanders!"

I knew Neisha. A beautiful woman with a toned, muscular body covered by unblemished brown skin, with extremely curly dark hair reaching her waist and almond-shaped chestnut brown eyes, she had quite the presence—especially since she was at least six feet tall. Wearing sweatpants and a sports bra, along with an anticipatory grin on her face, she looked ready to go.

Back at the Jinn headquarters, she had beheaded a Jinni with her bare hands. If I had to choose anyone to fight in the Hecatomb, she would be the obvious choice.

Haneul Kang, too, I vaguely remembered. More so, I remembered the pretty hawk resting on his slim shoulder. That hawk had gotten hurt back at the fight with the Jinn, and I remembered Haneul giving it a direct blood transfusion. I didn't know his name back then, but the sight of him caring for his hawk wasn't something I could easily forget.

However, Haneul didn't look like a fighter. Standing next to Neisha, he was evidently short and slimmer, with hardly any muscle on his stick-thin arms. With thick dark hair almost covering his eyes, he didn't seem very reliable in terms of physical strength. But his pretty hawk gave off the feeling there was more to Haneul than met the eye.

The biggest shock was Logan. He was my ex-boyfriend from when we were both human, over three years ago. With jet-black hair, turquoise eyes, and a tall and athletic body, he was an extremely handsome and capable man. Once upon a time, he'd been a soccer prodigy, and when he became a vampire, that talent of his became magical, making him a Gifted vampire.

What I didn't know was that he was a Troop Commander. Back in the Comprehensive Newcomer Course I took when I first became a vampire, he was our PE teacher. There had been no mention of him being a Commander. And since a Commander was the highest-ranking officer in the Troop, I realized his standing in the League was even better than I'd assumed.

The fourth and last Troop Commander, Oberon Grimes, I didn't know at all. He was the tallest of all the Commanders, at least six-five—taller than even Ragnor, I assumed—and he was built like a fucking tank, with tree-trunk arms and long, thick legs. As if to add to his intimidating aura, his face was covered in scars, some of which disappeared under his dark-blond beard. His hair, dirty blond and long, was half braided, half down, and reminded me of the haircuts the Vikings in TV shows sported. That, along with his cold silver eyes, made him seem like he belonged to the faraway fjords.

"Wow," Zoey murmured now, "this man is just . . . wow."

"Which one are you talking about?" Isora asked, amused.

Zoey scoffed incredulously. "Oberon Grimes. Who else?"

Out of the four, Oberon was definitely the most eye catching. It wasn't just his towering height and intimidating build. The entire air he emitted was extremely dangerous—that of a man one wouldn't want to meet in a dark alley.

"The show will go as follows," Kaylon now said, drawing everyone's attention back to him. "The four Brigades will fight one another two versus two, like the participants of the Hecatomb will. Each fight will take one minute. On the screen behind me, the names of the fighters will appear for your convenience, and each Brigade will wear different colors. Don't worry, though; the colors and which Brigade they belong to will appear on the screen at all times."

Said screen now blinked on, showing the colors along with the Commanders' names and the four Brigades they commanded respectively.

"After the Brigade members fight each other, it will be time for the Commanders to steal the show," Kaylon continued, smiling. "But for now, let's start with the first round!"

The Commanders and Kaylon emptied the stage, and four Brigade members took their place in front of the crowd instead, preparing for the mock battle.

"Good thing I'm right on time."

I jumped, heart booming in my chest, and whipped my head to my right. The formerly vacant seat next to me was now occupied by a cloaked figure with a very familiar voice. Midnight blue eyes peered at me from under the hood, and I gaped at him. "What are you doing here?" I asked in a whisper.

Ragnor gave me a tired grin and clasped my hand in his. "Watching the show, obviously," he murmured. "This counts as a couple activity, does it not?"

I couldn't help but chuckle. "That's . . . one way to put it, I guess," I muttered, then looked around me. Isora and Zoey, along with the rest of the audience, were transfixed by the mock battle. No one seemed to know their Lord was sitting right here, in the crowd, as if he were a mere League member.

Seemingly reading my mind, Ragnor squeezed my hand, and my gaze returned to him. "Don't worry," he said quietly. "Nobody is going to notice me."

He sounded so confident, it made me suddenly intrigued. "Are you using your powers?"

He grinned and pulled me closer to him. "Indeed I am," he said, his eyes now on the show. "All I want is to freely enjoy an activity with my girlfriend. If it takes magic to make it happen, so be it."

I grunted, huddling closer to his side. "Not you, too, with this boyfriend-girlfriend thing."

His rumbling laughter made my insides twist and turn in the best way possible. "What do you want me to call you, then?" he asked in a soft murmur, his lips at my ear causing me to shiver. "My lover?"

"That's . . ." I said, pretending to scowl. "It doesn't sound right either."

"Well, let me know when you decide on the best term for what we are," he told me in an amused tone that made me want to crush my lips against his. "Until then, shall we watch the show?"

"Yeah," I murmured, returning my own gaze to the stage. "Let's do that."

CHAPTER 4
AILEEN

The Troop's talent show was quite enlightening.

During the gala event and the fight with the Jinn over a week ago, I'd witnessed true supernatural phenomena on a scale I'd never known before. Those memories, like muddy waters in my head, were almost too fantastical to be my reality. Accepting the existence of vampires was one thing, but seeing seven-foot-tall horned giants battling vampires with unnatural force, and the responsive magic from their opponents, was another.

Looking now at the stage—watching the Troop members, starting with the Commons, fighting one another—was both unnerving and alarming. It wasn't that the Commons weren't good or that they fought badly—in fact, they were quite strong—but knowing Atalon and how much of a cunning asshole he was, I found their performance did not spark confidence within me. Not when their inexperience was so obvious.

When the crowd cheered after every mock battle, I couldn't help but look on in dread. Five Commons needed to participate in the Hecatomb. So far, the Commons who'd taken the stage would not stand a chance in a fight to the death.

Ragnor must've sensed my stillness because he didn't take his eyes off the stage, but his arm suddenly slithered around my waist, pulling me closer. "Keep watching," he told me, as though he read my mind.

Leaning into him, I obliged.

"And now, for the last battle of the Commons!" Kaylon, the pseudo host, now called into the mic from under the stage. "Please welcome onstage Commander Logan Kazar's Brigade members, Yelene and Sulien, versus Commander Haneul Kang's Brigade, Lynnea and . . . CJ!"

My eyes widened and my jaw dropped as I watched a familiar man taking the stage, along with three unfamiliar ones. That man, with his buzz cut and black skin over a lean and toned form, was wearing the battle uniform with his Brigade colors, his face set in cold anticipation.

Never before had I seen him wearing anything other than kitchen-assistance, dishwashing garb.

"What's he doing there?" I murmured to Ragnor, shocked. CJ was a second-timer Ragnor had taken under his wing for reasons unknown. As a second-timer, he was the lowest rank possible in the League, and his fate should've been far worse than working in the kitchens. Like Isora, for instance, who'd been bought as a second-timer only to become a blood slave for the Atalon League. Yet Ragnor didn't particularly like the whole idea of blood slaves, or slaves in general, so he put CJ in the kitchens, giving him a life better than what he could've expected in any other League.

But why was he in the Troop?

"Who are you talking about?" Ragnor murmured back.

"CJ," I said, turning to look at him. "I used to work with him in the kitchens." He and the other two dishwashing team members—Jada and Bowen—had been the first people to be friendly with me once I became a vampire. They held a special place in my heart.

"You should ask him yourself," Ragnor said and jutted his chin toward the stage. "Now, watch. Things are going to get interesting from here on."

I returned my gaze to the stage.

The pair from Logan's Brigade, wearing battle suits in turquoise, almost the exact same shade as Logan's eyes, launched an attack first, while CJ and his partner from the other Brigade, in bright yellow gear, were on the defensive.

Within the first ten seconds, it was obvious the pair in turquoise had the upper hand. They didn't just work together seamlessly—their punches and kicks were intense and, more often than not, they hit the mark. It almost looked like CJ and his partner were just there to act as punching bags for the turquoise pair.

But when it was almost thirty seconds into the fight, there was a turn in the tide. Suddenly, the pair in turquoise was retreating, while the yellow pair, CJ in particular, was on the offensive. The shift seemed so sudden, I had to blink twice to make sure I was seeing right.

CJ was throwing powerful punches, pushing the turquoise pair back to the edge of the stage. His partner acted as his shield, but she didn't need to shield him from anything; CJ was handling the entire battle on his own. He dominated everyone on the stage, at least for a few long moments . . .

Until the woman in turquoise suddenly grabbed CJ's wrist as he was about to punch her face, and while holding on to him, she sent a kick to his thighs, catching him by surprise and making his knees buckle. Using the momentum, the man in turquoise propelled himself by CJ and reached the woman in yellow, taking hold of her throat and shoving her to the ground, swiftly pinning her.

Just as CJ was about to regain his balance and reach for the woman in turquoise, Kaylon suddenly called, "Time's up! It's a tie!"

The crowd roared.

I let out a breath I'd held for the entire minute of the mock battle. CJ was good. Better than good; unlike the green Troop members before, he seemed to be a veteran. Same went for the pair in turquoise, Logan's Brigade members, but CJ in particular seemed seasoned in a way no other Common was.

"I'm glad this event's taking place," Ragnor suddenly said, and I turned to look at him. "Being able to see the progress my Troop members have been making is a rare opportunity I don't normally get."

I frowned. "How come you don't know what's going on in the Troop?"

He glanced at me briefly before returning his midnight blue gaze to the show. "It's not that I don't know," he said quietly. "I get weekly reports from Magnus, who's in charge of the Troop."

Magnus was one of Ragnor's two Lieutenants. "Not to sound judgmental," I said carefully, "but why aren't *you* in charge of such an important division of your League?"

Without looking at me, his lips twitched. "That sounds awfully judgmental of you, Aileen."

I rolled my eyes at his teasing tone. "You know what I mean."

He let out a breath. "The Troop requires constant surveillance," he said, face and voice both turning grave. "I have many enemies, and since I'm the face of the Rayne League, those threats are also true of the League by proxy. The Rayne League is one of the very few Leagues in the world that cultivates a military force, and there is a reason most Leagues would rather not have such a force in their midst."

Ragnor's hand suddenly crawled under my shirt, caressing the skin of my waist almost absentmindedly. "Historically speaking, many Leagues that had some sort of militia went through a coup d'état."

That, I didn't expect. "Why?"

Just then, Kaylon's voice suddenly came through the speakers. "We'll take a fifteen-minute break before the final rounds! Complimentary drinks and snacks are awaiting you outside!"

Isora and Zoey rose to their feet and turned to me. "Are you coming?" Isora asked, her eyes staying on me. Zoey didn't seem to notice Ragnor was right there next to me either. His hood might've hidden his face, but how could they not *see* him? Especially when his hand was fondling my waist?

"No, I'll stay," I said, confused. "Get me something to drink on your way back, though."

Isora gave me a mock salute, and the two left the hall along with most of the audience.

"You could go with them," Ragnor murmured in my ear, causing me to shiver.

Ignoring the sudden heat crawling over my skin, I said, "I'd rather you tell me why they can't see you."

His hand grabbed my chin and turned my head toward him. "Is that really what we should talk about?" he asked, eyes dropping to my mouth.

I licked my suddenly dry lips, and his eyes flashed neon. Feeling my nipples pebbling against my bra, I looked around me, saw we were relatively alone in our section of the gallery, and leaned closer to him. Heartbeat quickening in excitement, I sank my teeth softly into his lower lip, flicking my tongue against it.

A rumble vibrated through his chest, and he pulled me over so I was straddling him with my back to the stage. His heated, neon-blue eyes looked at me as if he could see me naked. His hands roamed over my waist and up my ribs, until they reached the sides of my breasts. My breath stopped as anticipation left me highly strung.

He cupped my mounds and squeezed them so hard, a loud moan escaped my mouth. Biting my lip hard, I watched as he kneaded my chest and grinned in savage satisfaction.

My eyes lowered to his crotch, where his cock tented his pants, hard and ready. Shuddering in sudden need, I freed his cock and grabbed it with both my hands. He bucked against my hold, and his hands left my breasts and lowered to my buttocks, squeezing them tight through my jeans.

I really wanted to have sex right there and then, but when I heard the murmurs of people returning to the hall, I paused, zipped him closed, and went back to my seat.

He gave me a disappointed look. "You know I made it so nobody notices us."

"Don't waste your magic on silly things like this," I chastised him.

He chuckled, squeezed my thigh, and leaned back. "Sex with you is never silly, Aileen."

Before I could respond—with what, I didn't know, considering he completely caught me off guard—Isora and Zoey returned, cutting off whatever it was I was going to say.

The next part of the show was the Gifted Troop members' time to shine. And shine they did.

Unlike the first part, this was more of a spectacle than anything else. Here, battle experience wasn't as important as it was with the Commons. Here, what mattered was pure, undiluted *power*.

One Gifted created a mini hurricane with the strings of his classical guitar to blow his opponent away, only the opponent held a flowerpot and used it to create vines that wrapped around her legs and the entirety of the stage, rendering her completely immobile—which worked against the storm. Another Gifted wore some sort of knitted hoodie the same color of his Brigade, and he was so fast, he was literally invisible to the naked eye, while his opponent was utterly still, closing her eyes as if in some meditative state, while his attacks skipped over her, as though she were wrapped in transparent titanium.

During the fights, the crowd was deathly silent, and only once the fights were over did they cheer, deafeningly loudly.

Then, it was time for the last mock battle. And this one featured another familiar figure—Cassidy Jones, my ex–best friend.

With her silky ebony hair in a ponytail and slim body in a battle suit colored turquoise—Logan's Brigade—she looked like someone else entirely. Her eyes, the color of emerald, were set somberly, her jaw locked tight in evident tension. She seemed angry, almost. Desperate, perhaps?

The last time I'd seen her, she was wounded from the battle with the Jinn. She looked no worse for wear, on the outside at least. Inside, I had a feeling it was a different story.

Cassidy's fight didn't last long. All she had to do was open her mouth, utter one strong note, and everyone onstage froze entirely. She walked around her partner to her opponents, and with a strange expression, chopped them at the back of their necks, knocking them unconscious.

Everyone waited with bated breath to see what would happen next, but when ten seconds went by, then another ten seconds, and another, and no one but Cassidy moved on the stage, Kaylon finally said into the mic, "Well, it seems the fight is over! Team Kazar wins!"

Cassidy murmured something, and her partner and opponents unfroze, finally able to move again.

Silence filled the hall for a shocked moment before everyone finally cheered far louder than they'd cheered so far.

And I could understand. Cassidy's power was frightening. If all she had to sing was one note for the enemy to freeze, then she was a force to be reckoned with.

"Your friend is doing well," Ragnor whispered in my ear. "As you can see, she's an asset."

I glanced at him. He scanned my face, as if worried that *I* was worried about Cassidy. "She's not my friend anymore," I informed him quietly, before returning my gaze to the stage. *And it's kind of your fault,* I couldn't help but add inside my head.

Though that wasn't fair to Ragnor. Cassidy had been on the Waiting List to become a vampire. Ragnor only did what he did because she wanted him to. With or without my intervention, our friendship would've ended either way.

"And now, for the final round—the Commanders!" Kaylon now called excitedly, and the four Commanders took to the stage, each wearing their Brigade color. "Oberon and Neisha versus Logan and Haneul!"

This fight was mostly a blur. The four of them were so fast, I couldn't help but simply watch, not understanding who was attacking whom, until Kaylon said time was up, and the blur cleared, showing all four breathing heavily and grinning at one another, still on their feet.

And just like that, the show was over.

Or so I thought.

"Now the Troop's show is over and done with; it's time to start the improvised show!"

Murmurs broke through the crowd, and I frowned, glancing at Ragnor. "What the hell is that?"

Ragnor's face became somber, and before he could say anything, Kaylon raised his voice and said, "If anyone in the audience would like to volunteer for a one-on-one mock battle with a randomly chosen Troop member, you have ten minutes to sign up! Find me near the stage to apply. Until then—have a final break, before this exciting final part of the show begins!"

Ragnor gave me a serious look. "This is your time to shine."

I blinked. "I beg your pardon?"

Ragnor gave me a humorless smile. "You must compete in the Hecatomb," he said, "however, nobody but you and me knows that."

Realization dawned. "You want me to showcase my abilities so I will be most likely 'chosen' to participate," I surmised, stunned. "Why didn't you tell me before? I would've prepared."

His smile dissolved. "Because you need to seem as authentic as everyone else who's going to come onstage after the break," he replied quietly. "I don't want anyone to know about you having to be there. Nobody needs to know about how deeply involved you are in the war."

I mulled it over. My relationship with Atalon, other than him being my former Lord and me his League member, was unknown to anyone in the Rayne League. The only thing the League members knew was that Isora and I had defected from the Atalon League for mysterious reasons and that Zoey had run away from the Renaldi League for quite obvious reasons. Only those who had been involved in the Jinn incident knew the truth of it all. No one else did.

Ragnor wanted to keep my involvement a secret. And so this was a good opportunity to keep up the ruse.

"Okay," I said, grimacing and rising to my feet. "I'll go sign up, then." Even though it was the last thing I wanted to do.

He suddenly grabbed my wrist, and I turned to give him a confused look. His returning gaze was dark. "Don't use you-know-what," he said, and I knew he meant my magic. "But feel free to use everything else."

I stilled, eyes narrowing as I studied his face. He was telling me to give it my all. It had to be convincing, after all.

But something in his intonation, in the unintelligible look in his eyes, made me feel like there was more to his words than simply that. A subtext I couldn't quite read. And that put me on edge.

We never discussed it, but Ragnor knew I could fight. He'd seen me fight, knew I was versed somewhat in mixed martial arts. But he didn't know the extent of my knowledge. He didn't know about one thing in particular.

And yet it almost felt like he was telling me to use that specific thing.

Or perhaps I was just reading into it?

Regardless, I gave him a tight-lipped smile. "Don't worry, my good Lord," I said, satisfied to see his nose scrunch in annoyance. "I'll do my absolute best."

CHAPTER 5
AILEEN

A couple dozen vampires now sat in the front row, awaiting their turn to show what they had. This shouldn't have surprised me, considering that vampires saw the Hecatomb as a stepping stone to climb up the hierarchy of the vampiric society. And yet I was still dumbfounded when I saw that that many people, who weren't even related to the Troop, were willing to put their lives on the line.

But the most surprising applicant was Zoey, who was sitting next to me.

"Are you sure?" I asked her for the tenth time since we'd found one another and sat together. "It's only been a couple of days since you recovered—"

"I'm sure," she cut me off, her jaw set stubbornly. "I'm feeling great. I can do this."

Seeing how sickly thin she still was, I had my doubts. "Just . . . don't overexert yourself, okay?" Though I doubted she was in any shape to perform well enough to be voted for, just going onstage and participating in a long mock battle was bound to take its toll on her.

For the improvised show, each mock battle would be five minutes long instead of one. And, as if word had gotten out about what was going on, the Auction Hall seemed even more packed than before, all the League members wanting to see their options, especially since the voting happened tomorrow, and a lot was at stake.

"It's just five minutes," Zoey now said. "I'm going to be fine."

Pursing my lips, I agreed to disagree in silence. Zoey was a big girl. She'd been through a lot ever since she was sold to Renaldi, then rescued from the Jinn manor. She was entitled to have free choice.

I just wished she wouldn't put herself in danger, especially after everything that had happened.

As the mock battles started taking place on the stage, I remembered a conversation I had with Zoey not long after Ragnor officially added her back to the Rayne League. I'd asked her why she'd been at the Jinn manor in the first place and not at the Renaldi League.

"When all hell broke loose at the gala, I used the chaos and ran away," she'd told me, sipping blood in her infirmary bed. "But the Jinn found me and captured me. They took me to their mansion, where you later found me. They used me as sustenance."

She'd talked about it with something akin to indifference. As if her fate at the Jinn mansion was far better than it would have been staying at the Renaldi League. While I knew from Isora and Eleanor, my former Atalon League suitemate, how bad the Renaldi League really was, in terms of how Lord Renaldi used his members for worse things than prostitution, I couldn't imagine being kidnapped by the Jinn was preferable.

But perhaps that's because I was used to doing those things Renaldi forced his female members to do—except for the prostitution part, that is.

Looking at Zoey now, eagerly waiting her turn to show what she'd got, stubborn determination etched in her face, I remembered her carefree, queen bee nature from before the Auction and couldn't help but feel sorry for her. She'd become a vampire with the hope of a better life than the one she'd led as a human.

And yet here she was, going through hardships she never could've imagined. Her brown eyes, once full of life, were now cold and detached.

"Just be careful," I said now, wincing as a Common Troop member kicked the non-Troop applicant right in the chest, sending him back with a cry of agony. It hadn't even been a minute, and the fight was already over.

Zoey didn't respond. So I stopped talking.

Half an hour later, it was my former suitemate's turn. When Kaylon called her name, she rose to her feet, adjusted her jeans and tee, and took the stage. Her Troop opponent was the woman who'd been CJ's partner in their mock battle earlier. Lynnea, her name was.

My heart rate picked up as I watched the two circling one another once Kaylon called "Start." I could only hope Zoey would be okay.

After a few long moments, in which the women seemed to size up one another, Lynnea made the first move. She jumped and shot a fist to Zoey's face, but Zoey cocked her head and the punch went flying over her shoulder. Using that momentum, Zoey grabbed Lynnea's upper arms and with almost no effort at all slammed her down on the stage with a loud *thump*. Lynnea groaned in pain but still moved her legs, trying to kick at Zoey, but Zoey used her thighs to pin her down, her hands around Lynnea's wrists.

Lynnea growled and struggled under Zoey's hold, but Zoey was immobile. It was such an odd sight, seeing Zoey, who was only now starting to gain weight after being skin and bones back when we found her at the Jinn mansion, holding down a taller, much more muscular woman who was also a member of the Troop.

Long seconds trickled by, filled with silence from the audience. No one cheered. No one clapped or called. In fact, I could swear I heard everyone's heartbeats quickening as the realization of what we were all seeing dawned on us.

Zoey had bested a Troop member in less than ten seconds.

When Lynnea finally surrendered, Kaylon said into the mic, his voice a shocked murmur, "The winner is Zoey Rittman! Remember this name, ladies and gentlemen."

After her display of absolute dominance in the mock battle, Zoey had just become a prime candidate to participate in the Hecatomb.

"Now, for the last mock battle of this wonderful show—Troop member Sulien versus Aileen Henderson!"

Déjà vu hit me when I climbed the stairs to the stage, only instead of an easel that dictated my entire vampiric existence, a man waited for me. This man, Sulien, had fought against CJ in the mock battle, I recalled. He had a lean, athletic build that was similar to Logan's.

If I were in shape, I could've bested him. But unfortunately, it'd been a few months since I last had any sort of training. In fact, my last true physical training had been during PE class with Logan. Since then, I'd been busier learning my newfound powers.

Basically, I'd neglected any sort of physical training. So I had to rely on muscle memory for this one, which did not give me a lot of confidence.

Once Kaylon called "Start!" Sulien rocketed toward me with fists flying.

I managed to block the first few punches, but when he feigned aiming at my midsection, I fell for it, and he landed a punch to my jaw. Staggering back, I ignored the pain and spit blood on the floor before bracing myself for another round of attacks.

Sulien wasn't as strong as others I knew, but he made up for it by being annoyingly relentless. He did not let me catch my breath or be on the offensive. He was attempting to dominate the entire battle.

And that, I couldn't let him do.

So as I avoided his barrage of kicks, I began preparing for my counterattack. Ignoring my aching, rusty muscles, I began to slow my movements. It was an extremely gradual process, so much so that Sulien didn't realize he was beginning to slow down as well to fit my pace.

I hadn't used Iovan's Imperium since that time during the first PE class with Logan. The main reason for it was that when one wasn't at their physical and mental peak, Iovan's Imperium could be rendered useless. To perfect this martial art, one needed to be in tune with their body and mind after a gruesome training that could last years.

My father had drilled these movements into my bones since I'd taken my first step. And while I was far from peak physical, or even mental, condition, muscle memory played a very big part in performing this martial art. It just wouldn't be executed in as deadly a fashion as it should be.

Iovan's Imperium included five Behests the practitioner needed to execute in order. The first Behest, *Gradus Diminutio*, was about lulling the opponent into a sense of false security, while in fact making them match your pace as you prepared for the next Behest.

The tricky thing was, the opponent had to be completely oblivious to the fact you knew this martial art, or this wouldn't work.

Unsurprisingly, Sulien was clueless. In fact, his face lit up in bored resolve, as if he couldn't bother giving his all to this fight anymore.

And that's what Iovan must've considered when cultivating his martial art: a play on the opponent's sense of supremacy.

We were moving at a far slower pace than before, and my muscles were screaming at me in pain. Gritting my teeth, I knew if I didn't move to the second Behest, *Propero Incrementum*, despite not entirely completing the first one, I wouldn't be able to continue. So I took a slow, deep breath and, with every ounce of strength I had, launched myself at Sulien with an explosive, accelerated movement full of power, backhanding him across his face so hard my knuckles groaned and shooting a fast kick to his ribs, knocking him down to the floor.

Adrenaline rushed through me, propelling me to move even faster than before. Before Sulien could even try to rise back up, I was straddling him, shooting a fast set of punches to his face, making his head bob from side to side. At first, he tried to struggle against my body, but I caged his legs between my thighs, rendering him utterly motionless.

Only when I felt the tension in his body leaving, telling me he was losing consciousness, did I stop, drenched in sweat and gasping for air, awful pain reverberating through my sore bones.

Panting, I saw Sulien had completely passed out, his face swollen. Grinding my teeth, I released my hold on him and pushed myself off his body, landing on my butt. I leaned my elbows against my raised knees, blinking drops of sweat on the floor. Drool of saliva mixed with blood trickled down my chin, dripping over to my shirt.

I had barely executed two Behests—quite poorly too—and I felt as if I'd been run over by a truck. I'd become so fucking weak, it wasn't even funny.

"And the winner is . . . erm . . . Aileen Henderson?"

Why Kaylon phrased it as a question, when Sulien had obviously lost, I had no idea. All I could hear was the crowd clapping, though it sounded quite reluctant—or perhaps I was imagining things. I couldn't even lift my head to see what was going on in the audience. I was that exhausted.

The lights on the stage were suddenly shut down and Kaylon cleared his throat and said into the mic, "That's it for the improvised show! I hope you all enjoyed it and have a better idea who to vote for tomorrow! Have a good night!"

A moment later, a familiar large, warm hand landed on my shoulder, followed by a soft murmur. "I'm going to carry you. Bear with it, please."

I couldn't have resisted if I'd wanted to, and, in all honesty, I did not want to. So when Ragnor slithered his arms under my knees and back and lifted me up, the remaining tension finally left my body, and I leaned my head against his chest, closing my eyes in relief.

"You never told me you knew Iovan's Imperium."

I didn't process Ragnor's words immediately. He was straddling my back, massaging my aching shoulders, back, and legs, and I was feeling so sleepy as he worked my kinks, it took me a moment to realize what he'd just said.

"Oh," I murmured into the pillow, moaning when he unknotted a particularly sore muscle in my thigh. "How . . . do you know Iovan's Imperium?"

He didn't stop massaging me as he spoke. "I studied it a few centuries ago," he said quietly, "from a martial arts expert. I could tell when you used the correct order of the Behests."

Surprised, I turned my head to the side and glanced at him. "It's not very common knowledge." To say the least. In fact, that he could tell it was Iovan's Imperium just from the few movements I'd executed, and not even in their fullest form, was quite the feat.

"True," Ragnor said, his hands sliding up my back to my shoulders. "Very few practice it nowadays. I didn't know you were one of them."

I sighed as his thumbs dug into my shoulder blades in slow, circular motions. "Iovan Heka was one of my ancestors," I said. "He was a Child of Kahil."

Ragnor said nothing for a few long moments as his hands moved to my sides, massaging my waist. "That explains a lot," he finally said after a while. "So your father taught you, I assume?"

"Yeah," I murmured. "He trained me every day from the moment I could walk until he was first put in prison."

Ragnor hummed in understanding. We were silent for a while until he finally finished massaging me and slapped my butt. I whirled my head toward him and narrowed my eyes. "What was that for?"

"For hiding that you were a Praefectus," he said with a frown, using the word for one who had mastered Iovan's Imperium. "I knew you had some martial arts knowledge, thanks to Logan's reports during your newcomer days, but I didn't know it was like that."

I leaned back, gently pushing him off me, and sat down, facing him. "Logan didn't mention that?" I asked with a frown of my own.

Logan knew Iovan's Imperium, since I'd taught some of it to him during my time at foster care with his parents. I'd even used some of it *on* him, in ways he would never forgive me for.

So why didn't he tell Ragnor, his *Lord*, about it?

Ragnor's face twisted, turning carefully expressionless. I tensed. It had been a while since I saw this kind of face on him, and it put me on full alert. "Why would Logan know about it?" he asked, midnight blue eyes locking mine in a dangerous hold.

It was then that I realized I hadn't told Ragnor about one thing in my past. One of the most crucial things in my past that actually pertained to the present too: the relationship I used to have with Logan. The fact that Logan's family had taken me in as a foster kid when my father ended up in jail. That Logan now loathed my very existence—and rightfully so.

Oh, fuck.

Just the thought of sharing that, telling Ragnor about Logan and me, made my heartbeat quicken and my mouth turn dry. Anxiety filled my insides, my stomach churning with sudden fear.

"No, I guess he shouldn't know about it," I said, hoping my voice was as indifferent as I willed it to be.

Ragnor's eyes scanned my face silently before he nodded and got off the bed. "I'm going back to the office," he said with his back to me as he slid his feet into his usual combat boots. "Take a shower and rest. The day after tomorrow, once the voting is done, you're in for two very intense weeks of whipping you into shape."

I didn't have the time to respond before he left the room and slammed his suite door shut.

And I had the nauseating suspicion that Ragnor knew I had lied.

CHAPTER 6
AILEEN

The moment Isora, Zoey, and I set foot inside the cafeteria the next morning, I felt an eerily familiar tingling sensation all over my skin.

I tried to shake it off, thinking it must be my imagination, and went about filling my plate with food and brewing my regular Americano with AB plus, but when the three of us settled at a table and murmurs broke out all around us, I knew it was not, in fact, just in my head.

Not when the gossiping vampires spoke just loud enough for me to hear.

"I heard the Lord personally carried her, as if she's someone important and not just a Common like us . . ."

"They said Sulien was still in the infirmary after their battle . . ."

"What is she even doing here? Isn't she supposed to be in the Atalon League?"

It threw me back to a couple of months ago, when I was still in the Atalon League, and Atalon himself was trying to make me his lover. Back then the League members had talked about how I didn't deserve to be with a vampire Lord, especially *their* Lord. That hadn't bothered me much, considering I had no interest in Atalon whatsoever—even before I knew he was the asshole to end all assholes.

But now, with the things they were saying about me, it was a different story.

"Wait until they learn you're our Lord's lover," Zoey muttered softly enough to not be overheard. "Their heads are going to blow up."

I snorted. "I'd rather their speculations remain just that." I paused, glancing between Zoey and Isora, who both seemed nonchalant about the whispers around us, before I tentatively asked, "Is Sulien really in the infirmary still?"

The two exchanged looks briefly before Isora turned to me and said with a serious voice, "Your mock battle yesterday was quite . . . intense."

"That's one way to put it." Zoey smirked humorlessly. "Did you really have to pummel his face like that? It was terrifying. Everyone thought so."

I hadn't thought about how my actions yesterday might've been perceived by the onlookers, but when I thought about it now, I realized that perhaps the hesitant clapping of the audience after my fight hadn't just been in my head. When I executed the second Behest, I had been so focused on keeping the power flowing through my muscles so I could best Sulien that I didn't realize I was going overboard with the punches to his face.

"Shit," I murmured, staring down at the still-whole omelet on my plate.

"Yeah, it was . . ." Isora said quietly, and when I raised my eyes to meet hers, she gave me an apologetic smile. "Terrifying, really."

Great. "Let's hope they'll forget it by the time the Hecatomb comes around," I said, slicing a bite of the omelet. "Though to be fair, Zoey, your performance was just as horrific."

Zoey chuckled. "Not really," she said with a voice full of pride and her shoulders squared. "I was commended on how swiftly I won my fight. In fact, I think people are going to vote for me."

Isora and I stared at her, incredulous. "Are you sure you want to be chosen to participate in the Hecatomb?" Isora asked, eyes wide. "It's not just about putting your life on the line—Renaldi is going to be there!"

"I know," Zoey replied with a somewhat beastly grin, her brown eyes flashing with excitement. "I'll be able to kill two birds with one stone."

I didn't like the way she said *kill.* "You know Renaldi is a Lord, right?"

"It doesn't mean he's invincible," Zoey retorted, anticipation in her voice.

I felt as if I'd never truly seen her before. "Well, color me impressed."

We didn't stay long in the cafeteria after that. The vampires around us kept on gossiping about me, some of them about Zoey too—though the tone of their voices about the latter was vastly different, more like awestruck, really—and neither of us could stand it. So we cleared the table and headed to the voting, which took place in my former Comprehensive Newcomer Course classroom.

It was a quick process. There were two boxes—one for the Gifted candidates and one for the Common—and we needed to write ten names on ten different notes.

Once we were done, we headed to the infirmary to visit Tansy. As Zoey brushed Tansy's hair, like she did every time we visited, we discussed who we'd voted for.

"All the Troop Commanders, obviously," Zoey said, "along with Cassidy—her Gift is even more terrifying than what you pulled, Aileen."

"Thanks," I said dryly.

"Same," Isora said, and then gave us both a smile. "As for the Commons, I voted for you two."

"You did?" Zoey and I asked simultaneously.

"Obviously," she said, shrugging. "You two were better than most of the Common Troop members who were on display yesterday. Especially you." She nodded toward Zoey. "How come you're so good at fighting?"

Preening at the compliment, Zoey smiled from ear to ear. "Well, I was always quite a good fighter," she said proudly. "I had to be, to survive the kind of life I had when I was human. When I was given the Imprint, I finally felt like I could use my full potential, you know?"

Isora sighed. "Lucky you," she said, leaning back against her chair. "I was never good at the physical stuff."

"Don't worry," Zoey said easily, "I can teach you once the Hecatomb is over with."

She was already talking as though she had been chosen. But to be fair, I could understand. Zoey was definitely one of the best fighters I'd ever seen. She would be an asset to the Hecatomb. Her pride was not misplaced.

But it chafed a bit, thinking everyone viewed Zoey as this surprisingly good, charismatic fighter, while they saw me as some sort of bully. I mean, it was a fight—a mock battle, sure, but still a fight. What did they expect me to do? Go easy on my opponent? What would've been the point in the whole damn show, then?

I remembered something Logan had told me what felt like a lifetime ago, when we were still human. I'd been struggling in my new middle school soon after moving in with my foster parents—Logan's folks—and ending up in Logan's class was the only solace. With him being a good-looking, straight A, friendly soccer prodigy, he was the most popular boy in school, so having him as a friend, and soon after as a lover, had given me protection from others without me even noticing it.

But once in high school, Logan was in different classes than me. Being a smart, studious guy, he had already taken junior year level classes while a freshman, and I had to fend for myself in the regular classes. We were still a couple, but my safety net was now too far away.

I didn't have friends other than Logan. Granted, I didn't even try to make friends, but my classmates seemed to avoid me like the plague. Everyone knew my father was in jail—though they didn't know for what, and the rumors surrounding that were quite interesting—and they took me for a would-be criminal as well.

They weren't wrong about that, though.

Logan realized what was going on and made sure to spend all his free time with me. He abandoned his friends to dote on me, eat lunch with me, and kiss me in public so everyone knew we were together. As if that would protect me.

Unfortunately, because he was the most popular kid in school, especially after he'd gone through a growth spurt between the last year of middle school and high school, half the girls in school liked him, and none of them could understand what he was doing with the likes of me.

When Olivia Garland, one of the popular girls, confronted me about my relationship with Logan, we got into a physical fight. She was the one who started it—and she was also a tae kwon do practitioner—so of course I retaliated. But when I used Iovan's Imperium on her, easily beating her without even fully executing the second Behest, everyone looked at me as if I were a monster. As if I'd beaten an innocent girl instead of defending myself.

I scared them so much, when anyone found themselves alone with me, they would burst out crying and run out in terror.

I'd been angry about it, especially since Olivia got a worse punishment than I did, which should've cleared my name to an extent or at least showcased her as an active part of this whole fight. I told Logan that. And Logan, who'd been there during the fight, trying to get Olivia and I off each other, told me something I would be able to quote until my dying day.

"Your face, Aileen. It was so disturbingly cold, as if you felt no emotion, while you beat her to a pulp. You didn't look human."

Had I looked like that yesterday, during the mock battle, too? Had I looked like that when I'd used Iovan's Imperium on Logan? Was this a piece of my father etched in my DNA that I would never be rid of?

The results came in the next morning, and they were printed on a plain sheet of paper and pinned to a board near the entrance of the cafeteria:

HECATOMB PARTICIPATION VOTING RESULTS

GIFTED

- Oberon Grimes
- Logan Kazar
- Haneul Kang
- Neisha Barnes
- Cassidy Jones

COMMON

- Yelene Yarnikova
- Sulien Salvador
- CJ Maron
- Zoey Rittman
- Aileen Henderson

PART II

CHAPTER 7
AILEEN

The fourth floor of the Rayne League compound was dedicated to the Troop's training facilities, top secret restricted areas, and one conference room.

When Zoey and I entered the conference room the morning after the votes, I was a bundle of nerves. It was one thing to know I was forced to participate in the Hecatomb but quite another to have everyone else think I was *chosen* for it.

Thankfully, the room was empty but for one familiar face. A smile broke over my face, and I walked over to my former dishwashing team member and sat next to him. "CJ."

He turned to me with a fond look. "Aileen."

"You know each other?" Zoey asked as she took the seat to my right.

"CJ was my mentor during my kitchen-duty days," I told her before turning to him and mock scowling. "You never told me you were part of the Troop!"

He put his strong arms behind his head and gave me a somewhat sad smile. "I was enlisted only last month. Some would even say promoted."

"But you don't think so?" Zoey jumped in with a frown.

"I think people's lack of regard for the kitchen staff and the importance of that job is quite demeaning," CJ retorted pointedly, almost defensively. I couldn't help but share the sentiment, especially since I knew not just CJ but Jada and Bowen, the other members of the dishwashing team, and how hard they worked.

"Either way," I said, smiling, "I didn't know you could fight. You gave one hell of a show."

He shot me a look. "I can say the same thing about you two."

Before I could reply, more people entered the room, taking their spots around the long meeting table: Logan, accompanied by Cassidy, along with the two other Commons selected, one of whom was Sulien, the Troop member I'd had a mock battle with.

"Hey," CJ said as the female Common vampire took the seat on his other side. She was quite pretty, now that I saw her up close, with pixie-cut platinum hair and bright quicksilver eyes. "Have you spoken to Jada?"

Yelene sighed. "She won't leave her room. I think you should come over later today and talk it through."

"What happened?" I asked CJ, worried. Jada was the first vampire in the Rayne League who had acted friendly toward me. She was a warm and funny woman, and I genuinely liked her.

CJ was about to speak when a few more people entered the room: the three Troop Commanders other than Logan, who was already here. Neisha was one of them, and she waved at me before plopping herself next to Zoey.

Once all ten of us were present, the doors opened once more, and Ragnor entered, followed by his two Lieutenants: Magnus and Margarita.

It had been some time since I last saw Margarita, and I couldn't help but feel bile rising up inside me at the sight of her petite form and the mane of her red curls. It might've felt like a lifetime ago, but I still remembered how she treated me when I was a newcomer. I was far from letting go of that grudge.

Magnus, on the other hand, I knew nothing about. I never really interacted with him, and all I knew was from what I could see: He was, most likely, the best-looking man I'd ever seen. With burnished-gold hair and honey-colored eyes, along with a tall and toned figure enveloped by bronze skin, he was like the incarnation of Adonis. But his type of beauty was like a sculpture's in a museum: gorgeous yet completely detached. Aloof and distant. There were a few occasions I'd seen him smile and act friendly, but only to Ragnor or some flavor of the day he took back to his room at the end of the day.

Ragnor took the seat at the head of the table, with his Lieutenants sitting at his sides. Everyone fell quiet when he began speaking. "Greetings, everyone," he said formally. "Starting today, you're going into two weeks of an intensive training regimen to prepare for the Hecatomb.

"You'll have both group and private training sessions for the first week," he went on, glancing at me briefly before he continued. "The week after, you'll train with your partners."

Zoey's hand shot up, and Ragnor nodded for her to speak. "What do you mean by partners?"

"In the Hecatomb, you'll participate in a two-on-two fight," Ragnor replied patiently. "The pairs consist of a Common and a Gifted. After the first week, which will be closely supervised by Magnus and myself, we will decide who to pair with whom."

Lowering her hand, Zoey's face turned contemplative as she mulled it over.

"Don't mind it for now," Ragnor said. "All you need to do is focus on bettering yourself as much as possible until the Hecatomb."

The meeting was adjourned soon after, and the training finally began.

The training room assigned to the Common Hecatomb participants was large and wide, reminding me of a martial arts training room. Mattresses covered the floor, two rings suspended from the ceiling and ladders scaling one wall.

The other four Commons and I were currently standing in a resting stance while a man called George, who looked like an actual tank—all muscle, no fat—moved slowly among us, silently sizing each of us up with dark, cryptic eyes.

I kept a blank expression on, impassively staring ahead every time he scanned me up and down. I didn't know what he was trying to achieve—it wasn't like he could tell much about our abilities with a simple deep stare—but whatever it was, all I could do was wait until he was done.

And minutes later he stopped in his tracks and clapped his hands together once so loudly, the sound echoed in the room. My eyes automatically snapped toward him.

"Give me jumping jacks," he said, folding his veiny tree-trunk arms.

There was a short moment of shock before all five of us started jumping. Thank God I had put on a tight bra that held my boobs in place; otherwise they would've been all over the place.

For the first few minutes, no one uttered a word. Everyone was simply doing what George had told us to, no questions asked. However, at some point, the sound of short breaths filled the air. It didn't come from Yelene, Sulien, or CJ, who seemed no worse for wear, what with their highly developed stamina. Rather it came from Zoey, who didn't seem like she was built for such a long, monotonous exercise. I, too, was suffering, but I'd learned how to breathe while doing such exercise, so my only problem was the sweat pooling on my skin.

When George raised his hand for us to stop, all of us stilled our movements and returned to a resting stance. His eyes then moved to Zoey, and he pointed at her and said, "Start doing laps around the room and don't stop until I tell you to."

Zoey's face was already flushed from the initial workout, but it seemed to redden even more at being singled out. But she didn't say anything and instead stoically nodded and did as ordered.

George returned his gaze to the four of us who remained standing before he said, "Get down to push-ups."

The four of us settled into position and began. And this time, I felt myself starting to fight for breaths while sweat dripped into my eyes. Biting my lip, I forced myself through every push-up, ignoring the uncontrollable shaking of my arms and the groaning muscles in the backs of my legs.

"Stop."

I climbed to my feet and found George's eyes on me. "Start doing laps."

Barely breathing, all I could do was nod just like Zoey did before I joined her.

This was how the first hour of training passed. As Zoey and I ran our laps, exhausted and sweaty, the other three did the exercises George ordered them to. It wasn't until the beginning of the second hour that he suddenly said, "Everyone, stop."

Zoey practically fell down on all fours, spitting as she fought to breathe. I sat down with my back to the wall, wishing the air conditioner was stronger.

George approached and looked down at us with disapproval. "You two. Take a fifteen-minute break before starting laps again."

This did not land well with Zoey. "Excuse me?" she said, perplexed.

His eyes narrowed as he looked at her. "You heard me."

She seemed furious. "I can hardly move my legs, and you expect me to run laps again?!"

He crouched before her, his expression suddenly dead serious. "You chose to offer yourself as a participant," he told her in a silky tone with an underlying edge. "You could've avoided it, pretended this has nothing to do with you, and gone on with your life. But you're here now"—his face darkened—"and I'm going to make sure to do everything I can so you will survive what's to come. The question is, will you?"

Zoey visibly gritted her teeth as she glowered at him, and, to my surprise, her eyes glowed a soft gold. "Yes."

"Then do what I say and be back here in ten minutes."

I cleared my throat, and both Zoey and George turned to me. "I thought you said we had fifteen," I told him with a shrug.

He gave me a humorless smile. "You will have even less if you continue to waste my time."

Zoey and I were immediately on our feet, running out of the room as if our sore muscles were figments of our imaginations.

"Damn him," Zoey bit out once we were in the small Troop-only kitchenette we now had access to. She aggressively uncorked her bottle of A-plus blood and took a long chug.

"He's right, though," I said, sipping my B minus. "You could've sat this one out and none would be the wiser." I paused and frowned when she glared at me. "Why did you decide to go up onstage a few days ago?"

Zoey's glare turned to her blood bottle, and that told me her anger wasn't directed at either me or George. "Doesn't matter," she said, her free hand fisting. "I'm here now, and I have to get stronger in the small amount of time we have."

I studied her for a few long moments. It didn't look like she was regretting her decision. Instead, her face showed a panicked desperation.

It made me wonder, not for the first time, about what she had gone through while at the Renaldi League. According to Eleanor, my former Atalon League suitemate, the girls at the Renaldi League were coerced into doing horrifying things. Acting as prostitutes while also killing Lord Renaldi's adversaries. I doubted any of them were unscathed by trauma.

I wondered what Zoey had been forced to do. How far had Renaldi pushed her in the few weeks she'd spent in his League?

But I knew better than to pry. If Zoey wanted to tell me, she could.

"What about you?" she suddenly asked, snapping me out of my thoughts. She gave me a penetrating look. "Why did you sign up for the show?"

And since I didn't want to tell her the specifics of the convoluted mess I was in, I gave her a wry smile and said, repeating her own words, "Doesn't matter."

CHAPTER 8
AILEEN

By the time the training session with George ended, I was more than ready to crawl into bed and sleep. Unfortunately, I had private training assigned right after, so sleep would have to wait.

I dragged my feet to the cafeteria to get a quick bite, and when I left, Ragnor was waiting for me outside. He was wearing his trench coat, jeans, and combat boots, silver keys held in his hand.

"Hi," I said, giving him a lame wave that made me feel deeply ashamed of myself. It felt like we hadn't spoken in far too long, which we hadn't—not since our strained conversation about my knowing Iovan's Imperium. He'd been busy, I was pretending to be busy, and so now there was this tension between us that hadn't been there before.

He nodded toward me, jaw locked. "We're going out."

"*Not yet*," I wanted to joke, but the humor dissolved into nervousness when I realized Ragnor refused to meet my eyes. He was still pissed about our last conversation, I could tell.

So I said nothing and simply nodded, following him toward the exit of the League.

He led me to a parking lot outside the warehouse where the entrance to the League was, and there he took me to his familiar SUV.

Once inside, he turned on the engine and reversed out of the lot, heading toward the main road to go into the city.

Soft music played on the radio, which made the silence between us more bearable but not less tense. I looked outside the window feeling somewhat stifled, as if a pair of invisible hands had wrapped themselves around my neck.

I knew I was the one at fault for this. I'd stupidly let out a hint that I somehow knew Logan and then lied about it. I knew I should apologize and explain what happened.

But telling Ragnor about my history with Logan . . . It scared me, even more so than telling him about my father and the horrors he inflicted both on and with me. Because with Logan, the things I'd done were of my own volition. My father hadn't been there to force me to do anything.

With Logan, the only monster in the room had been me.

And I couldn't face it. Not now. Perhaps never.

There was no way for me to convey this to Ragnor. He would press me to tell him why I refused to talk about it. It would turn into a constant point of contention between us.

"Aileen."

I tensed and slowly turned to look at him. Ragnor's eyes were on the road, but I felt his attention was solely on me. "Yes?"

His hands clenched on the steering wheel. "You're not asking where we're going."

Spine stiffening, I gave him a rigid smile and said, "Will you tell me if I do?"

"There is no reason for me not to," he replied coolly, and a chill spread through my skin, raising my hairs on end. There was a double meaning there. A dig at my hiding things from him again.

Swallowing hard, I returned my gaze to the window and clamped my mouth shut.

After a few tense minutes, he parked the car in a suburban area at the open garage of a modern-design town house. When I was about to leave the car, he suddenly grabbed my wrist.

Taking a deep breath, I turned to look at him. This time, he did meet my gaze, and his was aglow. "We need to talk."

I gave him a fake smile. "About what?"

"You know what," he said, his eyes narrow.

My smile faltered, and I averted my gaze. "Can we just forget it?"

"I've been trying to do just that for the last couple of days," he said conversationally, "and yet here we are."

"Please," I blurted before I could think twice about it, and to my horror, tears welled in my eyes. I shook his hold off and turned my head away so he wouldn't see. "Please, let it go for now."

He didn't say anything for a few long moments before he gave out a rough sigh and opened the driver's door. Shakily, I got out of the car, too, swallowing the tears, and followed him inside the town house.

The living room and kitchen area was almost completely empty. Everything was colored white, from the sofas to the islands, the ceilings, and even the stairs leading to the second floor, and it gave the place a washed-out, dreamy feel.

Ragnor led me to the backyard, which was filled with neatly trimmed grass that disappeared into a wooded area, before he stopped, took off his coat and threw it on the nearby chair, and turned to me. "Let's start with your training."

His face was impassive, his eyes midnight blue again, and I knew he was trying to respect my pathetic plea. So I acted as if nothing was the matter and gave him a smile I hoped wasn't as fake as the previous one. "I thought I'd be trained by someone else, so as not to have a conflict of interest."

Despite the heavy air between us, I saw his lips twitch. "I doubt my wanting you to live is a conflict of interest, so we're good."

I gave an inward sigh of relief. *Thank you, Ragnor, for letting me have this one secret.*

"Also," he added, giving me a much more relaxed grin, "who's better than a Sacred to teach another Sacred?"

My temporary relief was gone immediately. "But I'm participating as a Common," I said, frowning.

He arched his brow. "Are you telling me you haven't planned on using your powers at all?"

"Well, yes," I said, shrugging. "We agreed to keep my Sacred status a secret."

Ragnor gave me a stunned look. "It doesn't mean you can't use it if your life is in danger—which it will be."

He was right.

"Now, explain to me how your power works again," he said, watching me closely.

I sighed. "I can stop and resume time by will," I said, scowling, "though it hurts like a motherfucker when I do that, so I can only stop time for a few seconds, perhaps more if I train."

Ragnor nodded. "Let's try to work on that first: prolonging the use of your magic without the side effect."

"I do have a question, though," I said, cocking my head. "Did you get headaches after you found out you're Sacred?"

He gave me a somewhat cryptic look before he said, "Not exactly. Each Sacred has different side effects. You have headaches, while others could have pain in their joints or lose their sense of hunger, perhaps even feel completely parched right after using their powers. It varies with every Sacred.

"Having said that, Sacreds learn how to use magic with minimal side effects given enough time and practice," he continued, giving me a pointed look. "Two things we don't have a lot of at the moment. But let's do our best, shall we?"

I nodded, determined to do just that, and braced myself for action.

"When you're ready, stop time and count the seconds," Ragnor instructed. "Since I won't be able to help you, considering you'll stop *my* time as well, try to stretch yourself to the limit, which will give us a sense of your current maximum."

"Yes, sir!" I said, mock saluting.

His lips twitched again. "Let me know when you're done."

I nodded and closed my eyes. I took a deep breath before I focused on my will and thought, *Stop*.

The pain that followed told me I needed to start counting.

Gritting my teeth against the pain, I opened my eyes to slits and looked at Ragnor. For some reason, he seemed to move closer . . . which shouldn't have been possible. I'd just stopped time, after all. He was supposed to stop along with it!

"Aileen?" Ragnor suddenly said, his hands landing on my shoulders. "What's wrong?"

"I . . ." I said, and the pain grew stronger. "I've just s-stopped time, b-but y-you're moving!"

I managed to look up to see Ragnor's face, and his eyes rounded with shock. Slowly, he turned his head from side to side, looking around him, before his face slackened as realization brimmed in his irises. "Release the magic," he commanded.

With pleasure was my mind's response before I thought as forcefully as I could, *Resume!*

Immediately, the pain disappeared. A shuddering sigh left me, and I staggered back, almost falling before Ragnor caught me around my waist and helped me stand straight.

When my eyes met his worried ones, I gave him a reassuring smile and said, "The pain is gone. I'm fine."

He nodded somewhat stiffly and reluctantly let me go. "What's not fine is what we've just discovered," he said, the worry still written on his face.

Confused, I said, "The only thing we discovered is that for some reason, my power doesn't work on you. Which doesn't make sense," I added, frowning as I began to pace back and forth, agitated. "Back in the Auction, when my powers first presented themselves, no one moved, including Atalon and you, and it was like I was the only one in the world."

"Atalon?" Ragnor asked, bringing my eyes to him. His were narrow as fury rose to his face. "What does he have to do with it?"

I froze in place. I'd just realized I hadn't told him about what happened with Atalon back in the cell my former Lord had locked me in. The fact he knew everything there was to know about my past thanks to his own Sacred powers. And the really crucial fact was that, back in the gala event, when I stopped time, Atalon had managed to move then and take me to that cell right under Ragnor's immobile nose.

"Okay, so," I said carefully, walking toward him, "remember how back in the gala all hell broke loose?"

His face was set in a menacing scowl when he rigidly said, "Kind of hard to forget, yes."

Feeling like I was approaching a wild predator on the hunt, I kept my eyes on him and said, "I stopped time right before then. That's how Atalon managed to grab me and run; he somehow moved while time stopped, just like you did."

His eyes glowed neon. "Why didn't you tell me that before?" he growled, baring his teeth.

Wincing, I stopped right before him and cupped his face in my hands. "I'm sorry," I said softly, scanning his face. "It didn't come up."

His hand was suddenly on my throat, curled around it from behind in a possessive hold that made me tense. "I thought we were through with secrets," he said, our noses almost touching when he brought us close with his second hand slithering around my waist, plastering my front to his. "I thought you didn't hide anything from me anymore."

I could tell he wasn't talking just about this, but the other secret too. And yet I decided to pretend we were only talking about Atalon. "I didn't hide it on purpose, Ragnor. It's just so many things have happened, I didn't really think about it." Or the fact Atalon knew everything about me, including my ugly past with Logan, which I refused to share with Ragnor. I bet that would make him feel just peachy if he knew.

But he *wouldn't* know. There was no reason for him to. Atalon would be dead in less than a month anyway, and he would take my secrets with him to the afterlife. And Logan pretended I didn't exist, so there was no danger on that front either.

Perhaps I would be able to get away with never telling Ragnor about this side of me.

Ragnor's eyes dimmed a little, and to my shock, he put his head down on my shoulder and hugged me tightly. "It's fine," he said, and his voice sounded deeper yet somewhat weaker. "Just . . . I wish you would trust me, Aileen."

My heart lurched in my chest. "I trust you, Ragnor," I said quietly, hugging him back. "I do. Believe me."

He tensed. "Then why are you lying to me?"

Panic roared to life inside me. But before I could think of some excuse, something to say to divert the conversation away, Ragnor did me the favor by raising his head and stepping back, releasing me from his hold. His gaze was flat when he said, "In any case, your explanation about Atalon only cements one thing."

With my lips dry and heart racing, all I could do was ask, "What thing?"

He gave me a somber look. "Your power only works on those who are not aware of it. Which means keeping it a secret isn't just a temporary necessity, but the forever kind."

CHAPTER 9
AILEEN

I cried out as pain blasted through my entire body, until I screamed, "*RESUME*!"

My hold on time, on my magic, released like air out of a balloon, and the pain receded to a lingering soft pounding in my temples. Blinking my eyes open, I realized I was down on my knees, raindrops falling now that time had resumed, wetting my hair and my clothes.

Ragnor crouched before me, putting his hand on my shoulder. "Again."

A pathetic whimper escaped me. "I . . . I can't."

"Yes, you can," Ragnor insisted, forcing my head up with his fingers under my chin. His eyes met mine. "You held on for fifteen seconds this time. You need to keep on practicing so we can get to half a minute today."

"I said that I can't!" I snapped, glowering at him as I pushed his hand away from my face. "My head is fucking *killing me*, Ragnor! I can't take it anymore!"

His face contorted in cold anger. "I didn't take you for a quitter, Aileen."

I shook with barely repressed rage. We'd been at it for the past two hours, and I was cold, exhausted, and at my wits' end. My progress was so painfully slow, I was on the verge of having a frustrated meltdown.

Ragnor's sigh brought my eyes back to his face. He gave me a pitying look that did nothing to calm my fury. "Look," he said quietly, "in the Hecatomb, who do you think will win, Atalon or me?"

This was such a ridiculous, out-of-left-field question, I couldn't help but let out a humorless bark of laughter. "You, of course."

He nodded. "Yes, I'm stronger than him," he said, not out of arrogance but with cold self-assuredness. "Then what do you think the Atalon League participating members will do?"

I frowned. "What do you mean?"

The rain grew from a drizzle to a full-on downpour, and Ragnor grabbed my elbows and helped me up to my feet. Once we were inside, he threw me a towel and led me to the dining table, where he sat me down and seated himself right next to me. "There are six fights in total in the Hecatomb," he said then. "Five between the League members, and one between the Lords."

"I remember," I said, cuddling the towel close.

He nodded. "Since the battle between the Lords is the one to decide which League wins overall, do you remember what happens to the losing League's members if they lose in the members-versus-members fights?"

I recalled the piece of paper he had shown me a few days ago, back in his office.

In the event that League X wins more rounds, and its Lord wins the final battle, League Y's both Common and Gifted members will submit to be put in a special Hecatomb Auction.

In the event that League X wins more rounds, but the Lord of League Y wins the final battle, League X members have three choices:

1. Remain as a League and appoint a member as a new Lord

2. Initiate a Hecatomb Auction and dissolve the League

3. Become Leagueless

"Yes, I remember that too," I said now as I realized where he was going with it.

"Now," he said, "who do you think the Atalon League members believe will win?"

"You," I said without hesitation.

He gave me a brief smile. "Yes, me. Then who do you think is more motivated to win the members' rounds? My League, or Atalon's?"

Realization dawned. "Atalon League," I murmured, as things became clear. Ragnor was trying to tell me that even though everyone in both Leagues knew he was most likely to win the battle between the two Lords, when it came to the members' fights, the Atalon League had far greater motivation to win.

Meaning the Rayne League members had to give it their all, too, or we would end up dead.

Grimacing, I looked away and said, "I do wonder, though, if it's right for me to use magic when I'm signed up to the Hecatomb as a Common." I thought of Atalon, and my hands curled into fists. "You're not the only one who's aware of my powers, after all."

"That's what he wants, I believe."

I whipped my head toward him and narrowed my eyes when I saw his face turn somber. "You think Atalon *wants* me to use my powers against his League members?"

"Yes," Ragnor replied at once, "I believe that's exactly what he wants."

"But why?" I snapped, anger flooding me again. "It's not like he's going to live long enough to have me back in his League or whatever!"

Ragnor was quiet for a few moments after my outburst, his face grave, before he said, "That's why I think your, and everyone else's, assumption is wrong."

I froze. "What assumption?"

He was far too serious for my liking when he replied, "That I'll win."

The drive back to the underground compound was somber and silent. Both Ragnor and I seemed to be stuck in our own heads, and we didn't talk until we entered the League and parted ways near the cafeteria, where I planned to grab a bite of dinner before going back to the suite.

I was so lost in thought that when I grabbed a plate full of pasta and headed to a random empty table in the almost-deserted cafeteria, I didn't hear my name being called until a hand landed on my shoulder, making me snap out of my own head.

Turning around, I was surprised to see Bowen, in his kitchen uniform, standing there. My former dishwashing teammate seemed the same as always but for the dark bags under his eyes, indicating he hadn't had a good night's sleep in who knew how long.

"Hey," I said. "Sorry, I didn't hear you. I was . . . distracted."

He gave me a small smile that faded quickly. "Yeah, we all are," he said before he sat down at the empty table I now manned. "Can I ask for a favor?"

Surprised, I studied him. There was a tinge of desperation in his brown eyes. "What is it?"

He pushed his dirty-blond hair back, an act of discomfort, before he said, "Can you talk to Jada?"

I suddenly recalled what the platinum-haired Common participant, Yelene, had said earlier today, back in the meeting room. "I heard she won't come out of her room," I said, pushing the past aside and leaning forward, catching Bowen's eyes. "CJ never got around to telling me what happened."

Bowen looked around, as though he was afraid someone was eavesdropping on us—even though the only people in the cafeteria were sitting at a table on the other side of the room—before he said, "CJ and Jada are close. Closer than brother and sister. Closer even than lovers."

"Okay . . . ?" I said, baffled. I knew they were on good terms with each other, but I never suspected they had some sort of special relationship. In fact, every time we'd worked together, they bickered and teased one another in a way that seemed mostly friendly. Though I would be the first to admit I could be oblivious when it came to these things.

But the way Bowen talked about their relationship, one would think they were soulmates or something.

"Look, I can't go into details," he said curtly, "but ever since CJ left the kitchens and joined the Troop, he and Jada started fighting more often than not, and things reached a breaking point when CJ was voted into the Hecatomb."

"Why, though?" I asked, still puzzled over why Bowen was telling me this—but more so about the fact Jada and CJ had fought over such a thing. "I mean, CJ was a second-timer when Ragnor bought him. Joining the Troop is a huge promotion for someone of this status." I could only think of Isora, who'd been forced to become a blood slave thanks to the same status. That CJ managed to climb up the strict social ladder of the League system was quite a feat.

"But it also puts him more at risk," Bowen countered, scowling. "Even without the Hecatomb, the Troop members risk their lives on a daily basis. They are sent on missions outside the League and put their lives on the line if need be. While being a kitchen assistant might be considered bottom tier, at least it's safe."

"I agree," I said, meaning it, "but most vampires *want* to be as high as possible in the League's hierarchy—"

"CJ is different!" he cut me off in irritation before he took a deep breath and said more quietly, "He never wanted this. He liked having the dishwashing job. He liked working with Jada and me—though especially Jada. He never wanted this—and neither did Jada."

I was still confused. "Did CJ ask to join the Troop?" I asked, since this could be the only reason why Jada might be upset. Or the only one I could think of anyway.

When Bowen shook his head, though, I said, "Then why the hell is Jada upset? It's not like CJ could do anything about his job change."

"It's more than that," Bowen said, gritting his teeth. "Believe me, I want to tell you, but I'm under oath not to. So please, can you just do me this one favor and talk to Jada? Ask her to make up with CJ and come along with me to watch the Hecatomb and root for him?"

I wished I could read minds, because his words made no sense. "Let me get it straight," I said slowly, wheels spinning in my head, "you want me to talk to Jada, who, unjustifiably so, is angry with CJ for joining the Troop and now the Hecatomb, so she and CJ will make up?"

Bowen shot me an annoyed look. "I told you it's much more than that."

"But still—"

"Look, Aileen, are you going to do this or not?" he cut me off again, anger in his voice. Though I had a feeling he wasn't angry with me but rather with this whole situation.

I let out a breath and said, "Yes, I will." Because even if Bowen couldn't tell me everything—he was under "oath" or something, whatever the fuck that meant—Jada and CJ were important to me, along with him. I didn't like hearing Jada was hurting, and that by proxy, so was CJ.

So I ate quickly, bid a relieved Bowen goodbye, and went back to the suite to find the place empty, without a sign of Ragnor. And while this had been going on ever since the whole Hecatomb thing began, I couldn't shake the feeling of uncertainty that threatened to swallow me whole.

CHAPTER 10
AILEEN

Jada's suite was similar to the one I'd shared with Zoey and Tansy when I was first given the Imprint. It had a circular living room with three doors leading to three different bedrooms.

"She's in there," Yelene, one of the Hecatomb Common participants and Jada's suitemate, now told me, pointing at the door in the middle. She'd been surprised to see me when I'd first knocked on the door, and her bright eyes still had a bewildered look, as if she didn't know why I was even there. "Don't expect her to open the door, though."

"Thanks," I told her, attempting a friendly smile. She gave me a hesitant one back before leaving the suite.

I walked to the door and started with a polite knock. "Jada? It's me, Aileen."

No response.

All right, then. "Bowen is worried about you. So is CJ, and so am I," I said, raising my voice just in case. "All I'm asking you is to open the door and tell me you're okay."

Still no response.

"Jada," I tried again, "I understand you're upset with CJ for participating in the Hecatomb. But it's not his fault. None of it is."

I started becoming angry the more I thought about it. "You're being selfish here, Jada."

"Fuck you!"

The scream scared the bejesus out of me, since it was so close, as if Jada was pressed to the door on the other side. Evidently, she was listening, and something I'd said must've triggered her. Going out on a limb, I said, "Why? Because I called you selfish? Because I don't pity you? Sorry, but I have no time for this bullshit."

She became quiet again. With a sigh, I said, "What are you trying to achieve here, exactly? This protest of yours is pointless. It only hurts you and everyone around you—CJ in particular." Scowling, I added, "He's going to risk his life, and he might lose it if he's too preoccupied with whether you're okay or not. Do you really want that?"

Throwing the door open, a Jada I'd never seen before appeared, grabbing the front of my T-shirt. Her sunken gray eyes were glowing, and her muss of dark curls had a greasy sheen, telling me she hadn't showered in days. She seemed exhausted and ill. "This is exactly the problem," she snarled like a wild animal, glowering at me. "He's going to get killed and take me along with him! Now who's the selfish one?!"

I frowned. "Why will *you* die if he dies?"

She released me with a shove and went back into the room, grabbing the door as if to slam it in my face, but I caught hold of it just before she did. "No, Jada, you're going to explain to me what's going on with you two or I swear to God, I'll physically drag you out of here and lock you and CJ in the same room until you make up."

When she bared her teeth and unsheathed her fangs, her face, usually so light and open, took on a twisted expression, almost murderous. "I'd like to see you try," she said, her voice deceptively soft.

I gave her a humorless grin. "In case you haven't heard, I was chosen to participate in the Hecatomb," I said and saw her eyes widen. It appeared she hadn't heard. "I have a feeling I can take you."

Our gazes locked in a battle of wills. But Jada didn't know me well enough to realize it was futile. I was now far too invested in her issues to back off. In fact, I was dying of curiosity. I understood being upset over the fact her loved one was going to put his life on the line, but this was different.

In the end, as expected, I won, and Jada released the door and stepped into the room, sitting on the edge of the bed. She put her elbows on her knees and let her head fall, her curls gliding down her neck. "Close the door."

Once I did, I took in her room. Dozens of blood bottles were scattered across the floor, along with clothes and papers, among other things. Her bed was unmade, and the smell in the room told me it was in dire need of a good, in-depth cleaning.

Clearing a spot on the floor, I sat down facing her and said, "Tell me."

She looked at me, her eyes no longer glowing but rather tired and miserable. "What I'm about to tell you can't leave this room," she told me quietly. "Only Bowen and our Lord know about it."

My spine stiffened at the mention of Ragnor. I thought this was a Jada–CJ issue, with Bowen involved since he was their close friend, but if Ragnor knew about whatever this was, then that meant it was more than a fighting couple's matter.

She took a deep breath and let her head fall again. "CJ and I . . . we met a few decades ago. Before the . . . Imprint."

Interesting. "So you met when you were human," I murmured thoughtfully.

To my shock, she shook her head and raised her eyes to meet mine. There were thousands of things unsaid in the depths of her irises that caused me to freeze as a foreboding feeling spread through my insides. "*I* was human," she said quietly, "but he wasn't."

The way she said it gave me this nagging feeling she wasn't saying CJ had been a vampire back then. "What was he?"

She seemed slightly surprised that I caught on, but then she shook herself and whispered, "A being called Malachi."

And she lost me. "What the hell's a Malachi?" I already knew there were other supernatural races roaming among humans other than vampires—the Jinn, for instance. I never thought about what the others might be, because frankly, I was far too occupied with keeping myself alive.

But the way her mouth shaped the word Malachi, and both the reverence and fear on her face as she spoke that word, indicated that whatever this race was, it was very different from the Jinn. The Jinn incited horror without a shred of awe. Most of them were monsters, rising seven feet tall with horns.

Jada took a long few moments to give me an answer. "That's the name of the celestial species we humans usually call angels."

"Angels," I repeated, as though the word were foreign. "You mean the winged ones whose names end with *el*?"

"Just so you know, *el* means God in Hebrew," Jada murmured. "But yeah, basically."

For some reason, the only things I could picture were the cupids in that one Raphael painting. "So you're saying CJ was an angel," I said, imagining CJ with a pair of wings. It made me want to laugh for some reason.

"A Malachi," she corrected, her lips stretching into a somewhat wistful smile for a fleeting moment before it dissolved. "And yes. He used to be one."

Her gaze met mine. "He and I met when I'd just turned eighteen years old," she said, and when her face softened, I knew she was remembering. "I lived in New Orleans at the time. Fresh out of high school, I was trying to get accepted into the Mardi Gras marching band—I used to play the trumpet.

"But on the day of my audition, I received a call from my estranged mother," she continued with a grimace. "She told me she needed my help. Which I found hilarious, considering she left home years before, and I had to take care of my disabled, drunk father all by myself. And just when I finally thought I could maybe follow my dream and become the first woman—and a Black one too—in that marching band, I felt too bound by our blood ties to not help her."

She looked away. "She lived in the Boston area at the time, and so I spent my savings to go see her. And when I did, I found a winged man sitting in her small apartment living room."

"CJ," I murmured, entranced.

She nodded. "Yeah, Chanjomaron."

I frowned. "Excuse me?"

"His full name," she said, her face splitting into a nostalgic smile. "It's such a beautiful name, isn't it?"

I begged to differ, but I locked my lips and gave her a sharp nod. *I think CJ suits him far better than this weird-sounding mouthful of a name.*

"Anyway, my mother was in deep shit with the Malachi," Jada said, her face faltering. "There is an underground market—like the black market, only for races other than humans—and she was running an illegal trading business of forbidden substances. The Malachi caught a whiff of that and started an investigation."

There were many things to process here, but one thing confused me. "Why would the Malachi care?"

"Because the Malachi are in charge of interdimensional law enforcement," she replied matter-of-factly, as if I was supposed to know what that meant. She must've seen my confusion because she added, "This realm we know as Earth is in fact one of many that live in parallel to one another."

I was trying my hardest to swallow my many questions in favor of the most important ones, but this gave me a full stop. Not because it was hard to process, but because I was starting to connect pieces of a puzzle I hadn't believed actually existed.

I'd had this fleeting thought some time ago that maybe all the things written in the Tefat, the religious book of the Morrow Faith my father belonged to and had tried to instill in me, were actually true.

Since so many things were happening, mainly the Hecatomb and the shit it stirred up, I had put Eliza's threat from a couple of weeks ago in the back of my mind. It had been such a baffling encounter, and a somewhat scary one, that I didn't feel like thinking about any of it anyway.

But I remembered what she said. The words were engraved in my brain. *"Natalia Aileen Zoheir-Henderson, Child of Kahil. As a level-two threat to the Realm of the Living, you demonstrated powers that allude to you becoming a large-scale catastrophe; consider this a warning.*

"Under any circumstances, never again attempt to resurrect the Morrow Gods nor ever again visit Esheer or seek the Jinn. Failure to comply with these restrictions will lead to your demise."

In the Tefat, there was a short chapter about the Realms of Oon. Every time I read that chapter, I treated it like a fairy tale, or a mythological story, because it was far too whimsical to be believed (or had been before I knew about vampires and became one myself, that is). It explained that the Realms of Oon were once delicately interwoven with one another, until an incident had taken place and torn them apart, making each of them exist separately.

The Tefat didn't go into many details about the Realms of Oon, because only two mattered in relation to the Morrow Gods: Aderra, the Realm of the Living—or, as Jada plainly put it, planet Earth—and Esheer, the Realm of Fire . . .

"Aileen?" Jada's voice snapped me out of my thoughts, and I turned to look at her. She frowned at me. "Am I boring you so much that you had to drift off?"

"No!" I exclaimed at once, giving her an apologetic look. "Sorry, I was just trying to digest what you're telling me. Where were we again?"

"Why the Malachi needed to intervene in my mother's illegal trades," she said dryly, shooting me a questioning look before she resumed. "The Malachi usually avoid our realm for many reasons—unless someone in this realm is threatening the stability of others, including the Malachi's own realm, Haramon."

I nodded. "Got it. So that's why CJ was at your mother's? To arrest her? How did that go?"

Jada gave me a humorless look. "He was there to take her to Haramon to stand trial," she said quietly, her voice turning bitter. "She asked him to wait until I arrived because she wanted to make amends with me and say goodbye. As if that would fix all the damage she'd done."

At least your mother was willing to apologize, I couldn't help but think, my hands curling into fists. Most people who do bad things are aware of what they're doing—and do it anyway.

My father didn't think he'd done anything bad. He knew he was going against the law, that the things he was doing were considered crimes by any sane person, but his blind devotion to his cause, to resurrect the Morrow Gods, made him see them as means to an end. A necessity. He would never apologize for any of it.

"Yet my mother never got the chance to do that," Jada continued, and I returned my gaze to her. She was looking at the ground with a pained expression etched on her face. "Because the moment I set foot inside her apartment and my eyes met Chanjomaron's, everything changed."

I waited for her to continue, but her gaze seemed far away, as though she had been thrust into the memory and refused to leave. "Jada?" I asked, softly touching her knee. "What changed?"

She blinked, and I saw tears that made me go still. "One of the reasons Malachi don't meddle in our realm's business is due to a . . . *phenomenon* that can occur if they set foot here." She sucked in a breath. "A *phenomenon* called *Alara Morreh*."

Wiping the tears away, she said, "*Alara Morreh* is a human who was quite literally born to become a Malachi's soulmate."

Oh, shit.

"Every Malachi has such a human," she whispered now. "But it is forbidden for the Malachi and humans to even interact without a higher-up Malachi—a *Seraph's*—permission. And consummating with a human is not just forbidden, but outright nefarious."

She gave me a sad smile. "I was, and still am, until the day I take my last breath, Chanjomaron's Alara Morreh. And that means our souls are so connected that if he dies, while physically I won't die, my soul will forever be lost, leaving me an empty, walking shell."

CHAPTER 11

AILEEN

I never got to ask Jada all the questions I had because a knock on the door put a stop to Jada's story, and Yelene's voice came through, saying, "Aileen, the morning training is in five minutes."

Jada jutted her chin toward the door. "Go," she said, looking more worn-out than before with her tearstained cheeks. "You know most of the story now anyway."

"Jada—"

"Don't." She shook her head, scowling at the pity I couldn't quite hide in my voice. "I'll be fine. I'll get over him threatening to turn me into a fucking zombie somehow. So just . . . go."

I had nothing to say, so all I could do was give her shoulder a squeeze and leave for the training, hoping I didn't make things worse.

Everything that Jada told me, along with my own startling conclusions about the Tefat and the Realms of Oon, circled around in my head while George ordered us to do pull-ups. I was so out of it that I failed to complete the set first and thus was sent to run laps again.

Which was just as well, since I needed to clear my head, and a good jog was bound to do that.

At least, until George called for me to stop and said, "Today, you're going to duel one another."

I felt a headache coming. This was the last thing I needed right now.

"CJ and Zoey, you'll start," George said and motioned to the bench at the back. "The rest of you sit down and watch."

Once we were seated, George turned to Zoey and CJ and said, "You have five minutes. Use everything you know, every trick up your sleeve, to defeat one another. The loser will be determined by which one of you is forced to yield first."

When they started the duel, I was physically watching, but my mind had traveled back to Jada's room. And it seemed like I wasn't the only one unfocused on the duel, because next to me, Yelene leaned over and whispered, "You talked to Jada."

I glanced at her and nodded.

Yelene's face seemed to relax. "How is she?"

"Not fine," I murmured back. "But I hope it changes soon."

"She allowed you to enter her room," she said quietly. "That's progress."

I glanced at her again and saw her giving me a small smile before she returned her eyes to the duel. I did the same, and this time, I forced myself to focus on CJ.

I'd noticed it before in the mock battle during the talent show, but the way CJ moved was both graceful and swift. It reminded me of Tansy's ballet dance from the Auction on one hand and Ragnor's fighting techniques on the other. It was a strange mix of the two, but CJ executed his moves as if he'd done it hundreds of thousands of times before.

It made me wonder how old he was. Scratch that—if he was a Malachi, how was he a vampire now? Could Malachi become vampires? What was a Malachi's lifespan?

Whatever the answers were, Zoey stood no chance. The duel was over in less than one minute, with CJ's hands wrapped around Zoey's neck as he pinned her to the floor.

George nodded for them to part, and they did. "Zoey, your reaction time is great, but you leave yourself too open while you're attacking," he said now, pointing at her stomach, which she seemed to massage while wincing. "You might've landed that kick to his upper arm, but you got punched in the gut in exchange. If it was a Hecatomb battle, your adversary could've easily aimed for your chest and torn your heart out."

Zoey scowled but nodded.

"CJ," George said, turning his prying eyes to Chanjomaron (if the situation weren't so dire, I would've so made fun of him for this). "Flawless, as usual."

CJ's face was grave as he gave our mentor a sharp affirmative nod.

While Zoey shot CJ a dirty look, George turned to us on the bench. "Next up, Sulien and Aileen."

Again? I couldn't help but think when Sulien and I switched places with Zoey and CJ. Sulien, the same guy I mock battled in the talent show, was now standing in front of me, giving me an indecipherable gaze. I studied him more thoroughly this time too.

Sulien had a gentle face that didn't quite go with the athletic ridges of his figure. His eyes were a warm brown and in a tilted shape that gave him an almost pitiful look. Last time we battled, I had been so busy following his movements that I didn't pay attention to his face, but I really should have—because despite his naturally puppy eyed look, there was an almost wild feel to him. As if he wasn't quite civilized.

"Begin," George now said, stepping back.

I got into position, preparing myself, but to my surprise, Sulien raised his hand and said, "I'd like to ask Aileen a question first, if I may."

George glanced at me for a split second before he nodded. "Make it quick."

Sulien stepped closer to me, and I released my stance, staring at him. "What is it?" I prompted.

He stopped a few steps away. "Last time we fought," he said, "you used a technique I'm unfamiliar with. What was it?"

I probably shouldn't have been so surprised, and yet I was in shock. "Oh."

He frowned. "I don't believe my question is out of place."

"It's not," I murmured, slowly shaking myself from my stupor. "It's a type of martial art. That's all."

"That much I know," he said dryly. "I asked which one."

I was about to tell him it didn't matter and that he should drop it, but then I reconsidered. What was the harm of telling him the name? It wasn't like he could find any information about it anywhere. It was practiced by very, *very* few, if any at all.

"It's called Iovan's Imperium," I told him now. "Now can we go back to the duel?"

Sulien was about to speak, but George interjected. "Enough. In position."

Sulien seemed annoyed, but he finally dropped it and stepped back. When George said once again, "Begin," Sulien was on me like an animal taken off the leash.

This time, I refused to use Iovan's Imperium, despite George's instructions. I refused to give Sulien more food for thought.

Unfortunately, that decision led to my very quick loss.

When training ended, I followed the others outside and was about to head to the cafeteria when I saw a familiar man waiting near the escalator leading up. "Bowen."

"Aileen." He nodded toward me before he turned to look to my right.

I did, too, and saw CJ come to a stop right next to me. He was glancing between Bowen and me. "You having lunch together?"

Before I could respond, Bowen said, "Yes. You too."

CJ frowned but didn't object.

Thus the three of us walked to the cafeteria in complete silence. A silence that stretched until we sat down at an empty table, each with a plate full of food. Then, as if someone flicked a switch, Bowen spoke. "Aileen spoke to Jada this morning."

While CJ's head whipped toward me, I looked at Bowen, surprised. "How did you know?"

Bowen's eyes were dark. "She came to work and told me."

My lips parted, but CJ beat me to it. "What did you talk about?" he asked, voice insistent and strained.

I was about to speak but again was cut off before I could.

"Jada told her about you," Bowen said, voice low as he looked to the sides before his angry eyes settled on me. "Which is all fine and dandy, but she's now acting as if she's already *dead*."

Now I knew what he meant by *dead*. What Jada would suffer if CJ were to die was a fate far worse. It would be a different kind of death. A torturous one. "I didn't say anything, I swear," I hissed, agitated. "I just pushed her to talk to me. That's all."

CJ pushed his uneaten food away and rose to his feet. "Is she there now?" he asked, looking at Bowen. When the latter nodded, he stormed off toward the kitchens.

Bowen glared at me before he got up on his feet too. "I wanted you to talk sense into her, not make her relive everything that enforces her stupid decisions," he spit before he left after CJ.

Feeling sick to my stomach, I stared at the food for a few moments before I made the decision to go to the kitchens after them. I couldn't help but feel responsible for this, even though logically I knew I wasn't.

The kitchens were full of staff working on lunch. I could hear Lon, the kitchen manager, screaming at some poor assistant at one of the stations and quickly avoided running into him by entering the dishwashing area.

That's when I heard Jada screaming, *"I wish you were dead already so I could start my suffering now!"*

Great.

Taking a deep breath, I turned the corner and saw CJ and Jada facing each other, glowering. I'd never seen CJ glower before. He usually was such a chill dude, but now he seemed as though he'd been a sleeping volcano the entire time, and Jada was the trigger for his eruption.

"I'm so disappointed in you, Jada," CJ snarled now. "I didn't know you had such little faith in me. That you didn't believe in me. That you think I'm not strong enough to survive this. That tells me our entire relationship has been a sham."

Jada's face shattered and to my shock she slapped him. "*Asshole!*" she yelled, tears escaping her eyes. *"You ruined me, you ruined my life, you ruined EVERYTHING!"*

CJ's eyes glowed. "*You got it backward, Jada,*" he growled, grabbing her arms and shaking her. "*You* ruined *me*!"

"Stop, both of you," Bowen said, and when I turned to look at him, he seemed on the verge of hysteria. In fact, he stared at the two as if he'd never seen them before. "You don't mean any of those things, I know you don't—"

"*Stay out of it!*" Jada screamed at him before returning her cold glare to CJ. "If I could turn back time, I would've never come to Boston," she told him in a shuddering hiss. "Meeting you was the worst thing I ever did."

CJ released her and stepped back. "Couldn't agree more," he said bitterly.

A freezing silence stretched in the room, making my heart race and my blood chill over in response. *It's your fault,* a nagging voice whispered in my head. *You were the final nail in the coffin of their apparently broken relationship.*

But how could soulmates have a broken relationship? They were supposed to be *soulmates*. The whole idea of that, according to fairy tales at least, was to fall in love and live happily ever after.

I might've only learned about this earlier today, but clearly, the fact that Jada was CJ's Alara Morreh, or whatever it was called, was the actual source of all their issues.

So what was the point of having an Alara Morreh, a soulmate, if shit could still hit the fan anyway?

My thoughts went to Ragnor then, and suddenly I was filled with utter relief that he was no Malachi and I wasn't his Alara Morreh. Because if that was what being soulmates was all about, then I could do without it.

Ragnor and I were already going through some shit as it was, so having our souls bound to the point we became each other's life source?

It sounded like an absolute nightmare.

CHAPTER 12
AILEEN

Ragnor waited for me outside the cafeteria after lunch for our afternoon training session. He was leaning against the wall, talking with another man, a gorgeous bronze-haired, golden-skinned Adonis—his Lieutenant, Magnus.

Every vampire that passed them by on their way in and out of the cafeteria seemed transfixed by the sight of the Lord and his Lieutenant chatting casually out in the open. I felt almost embarrassed when I walked toward the two, sensing multiple pairs of eyes landing on me when I came to a stop before them.

"I'm here," I said lamely, drawing both men's attention. I flushed slightly as the feeling of being watched grew stiflingly worse. "Can we go now?"

Ragnor nodded impassively and said, "Let's go."

To my surprise, Magnus followed us toward the exit. He kept on following us even when we were already outside the warehouse, nearing Ragnor's SUV.

I paused then and turned to Magnus. "Are you coming with us?"

He gave me a blank look and said, "Yes."

My heart fell, and my stomach churned in disappointment. I wanted to have Ragnor to myself. I was barely seeing him with this whole Hecatomb shit as it was, and every time we did, we were arguing.

But after witnessing Jada and CJ going through a major relationship crisis, I realized how good Ragnor and I had it, and I wanted to make amends. I wanted us to go back to how we were before everything started going to shit.

Before I stupidly let him know I was still hiding something from him.

It appeared today would not be that day, unfortunately.

Magnus took the passenger seat, and I let myself into the back seat. When we hit the road, Ragnor suddenly said, "Aileen is a Sacred."

I froze.

From my seat behind Ragnor, I could see Magnus's profile. His face went slack with shock as he whipped his head toward me. "What did you just say?"

"You heard me," Ragnor said with a tired sigh. "The point is, you're coming along with us so Aileen can experiment using her powers on you."

Magnus's confused gaze turned to Ragnor. "How many people know?"

"Three, including me and you," Ragnor said, and I could feel his rising tension even without seeing him. "The other one is Atalon."

"Huh." Magnus leaned back, a deep frown on his far-too-impeccably-perfect face. "So. You're not going to tell me what power she has."

Ragnor shook his head. "Just like I won't tell her about yours."

Irritation made me speak before I could think. "You know that 'she' is right here, right?" I snapped, folding my arms as I turned to look at Magnus. "You're Gifted, aren't you?" I remembered someone telling me that the Lieutenants of every League were always Gifted.

But to my surprise, Magnus shot me a smirk and said, "I used to be."

"Used to?" I repeated, frowning.

His smirk turned into a Cheshire cat grin. "I know, right?"

"Stop toying with her," Ragnor murmured before he said, "Aileen, what I'm going to tell you must not leave this car."

"Don't worry," I muttered, feeling somewhat bitter when I added, "I'm good at keeping secrets."

Ragnor snorted. "Don't I know it," he said lightly, but there was gravity in his words. A heaviness both of us could feel. But he broke the slight tension by saying, "Magnus is a Sacred too."

Now it was my turn to be shocked. "Seriously?" I said, looking at him. "But doesn't that mean you have to become a Lord? Why are you still a Lieutenant?"

Magnus arched his brow. "Why are you not a Lady, too, then?"

I opened my mouth to speak before silently closing it, thoughts running through my head. Did my being a Sacred mean I had to be a Lady eventually? But Magnus wasn't, though I didn't know how long he'd been Sacred, since he said himself that he used to be Gifted, and I knew Gifted could become Sacred after a few centuries of living, but still . . .

"Aileen." Ragnor's voice brought my eyes to the top mirror. His gaze met mine before he turned it back to the road. "Not all Sacreds become Lords. While it is mandatory for a Lord to be Sacred, some Sacreds prefer to live under the radar, keeping their true status to themselves. Granted," he added, "almost no Sacred chooses this path. Most Sacreds would rather not have to answer to anyone, thus they become Lords of their own Leagues."

"I'm special." Magnus grinned and winked at me. "I'd rather have our Lord here order me around than have to be responsible for others in return for freedom. Can you imagine?" He widened his eyes comically.

A chuckle escaped me. "Yes, that sounds like a true nightmare indeed."

Ragnor scoffed. "I feel like you're taking a dig at me here," he said, before adding in a murmur, "Ungrateful brats."

Magnus snorted and teasingly pushed Ragnor's shoulder. "Shut up, old man."

"You're almost as old as me," Ragnor told him as he nudged his shoulder back with far more force. "So *you* shut up."

I burst out laughing. I'd never seen Ragnor acting so childishly. It was beyond refreshing. In fact, it made him seem the age that he appeared to be—in his late twenties. And Magnus too. I'd never talked to him like this, let alone seen him freely express his emotions not just in front of Ragnor, but me too.

Soon we arrived at Ragnor's town house, and we settled in the living room this time. Ragnor and Magnus pushed the two sofas to the walls, creating a spacious area for me to train in.

Ragnor turned to Magnus. "Once we start, you may feel certain pains you cannot fathom."

Both Magnus and I frowned, but before I could speak, Magnus said, "All right."

Ragnor then faced me. "When you're ready, do it."

I didn't need to be told twice about what to do. It was self-explanatory. So I closed my eyes, and with a force of will, shouted inside my head, *STOP!*

Pain exploded behind my eyelids, and I sucked in a breath, forcing my eyes open. Magnus stood there frozen while Ragnor walked toward me. "Hold on," he told me quietly, "and hit him."

I gritted my teeth as I willed my legs to move toward the Lieutenant. Once I was right in front of him, I raised a shaking fist and sent it into his midsection. He was immobile, the impact unseen.

Ragnor nodded and said, "Now kick him."

I didn't have the capacity to feel sorry for the helpless Magnus with all the pain pounding in my head, so all I could do was oblige. I shot a kick to his shin before the pain suddenly became unbearable and I lost my balance, falling down on my ass.

And just like that, time slipped out of my control, and without me even thinking anything, it resumed on its own.

Magnus grunted and staggered back, glancing between Ragnor and me with bewildered eyes as he cradled his stomach. "What the hell?"

Ragnor smirked. "I have to say, it's quite satisfying, seeing you so confused."

Giving him a filthy look, Magnus rubbed the places I'd hit and narrowed his eyes on me. "Whatever your power is, I didn't even see you moving," he said with a hint of awe.

Then he stretched his hand toward me, and I took it, letting him help me up on my feet now that my own pain had subsided. "Sorry for that," I murmured, massaging my temples. "But for what it's worth, I have to suffer when I use it too."

"And I guess you're not going to tell me what it is," Magnus said.

Ragnor didn't reply, and when I turned to look at him, I saw his gaze on Magnus, who was still holding my hand. Heart jumping in my chest, I shook Magnus off and quickly said, "So what now?"

As his eyes narrowed, swirling with emotions that made my heart race, Ragnor said, "Let's do it again."

Once Magnus and I were ready, I stopped time once more and bit my lip as the pain returned. Before I could move, Ragnor was suddenly in front of me, his hands cupping my face, forcing my eyes to lock with his glowing ones. "Keep holding on no matter what," he said, and before I could question him, his lips crashed against mine.

The kiss shocked me so much I froze. Thousands of thoughts exploded in my head, causing the pain to rage on even stronger. I groaned, needing him to step away so I could gather myself and keep holding on to time, but then his tongue flicked against my lower lip, causing me to gasp and him to deepen the kiss in return.

My entire body melted as I grabbed his shirt and kissed him back, heat burning every fiber of my being. The pain was a nuisance, but the more he kissed me, the less I could focus on the pain.

Lust poured through me as he ravished me, his hand fisting in my hair while the other arm grabbed me, pulling me closer and tighter to his body. I shuddered, melting against him as his kiss turned even more ferocious, as if he couldn't get enough and, in all frankness, neither could I.

It felt as if we hadn't touched each other in ages, and the sudden hunger I felt was all-encompassing.

But as abruptly as he started it, Ragnor ended it, stepping away from me, causing me to sway desperately forward, needing his hands on my aching breasts, flicking my pebbling nipples, cupping the blazing heat between my legs . . .

Then I saw his face, saw the anger and frustration there, and I froze once more. And when he said, "Don't ever let another man touch you," it was as if he poured a bucket of ice all over me.

My eyes widened as my lips parted. "What?"

But just then, with his touch gone, the pain returned with a vengeance, reminding me it was still there, and I cried out, pleading with it to be *released*.

Time resumed, and I fought for breath, needing some sort of reprieve. I walked to one of the sofas and sat down, wiping the perspiration on the skin of my forehead with my sleeve as I closed my eyes and leaned back, sighing.

"Um, I don't feel any pain this time?" I heard Magnus say, confused.

"Consider it your one pass," Ragnor murmured, his voice lowered, laced with a threat that confused Magnus but made tension spread through my body.

I had so many things I wanted to say in response to that, but I was utterly depleted of energy. I'd somehow managed to stop time for much longer this time. It had been at least twenty seconds, all thanks to Ragnor's distracting kiss, and now it took its toll.

But his words rang in my head as I recalled the look on his face when Magnus helped me up. What the hell was up with Ragnor now? Why was he so jealous all of a sudden? There was no reason for him to go all caveman mode on Magnus for daring to grab my hand. Did he really think I was interested in anyone else but him?

I opened my eyes and turned to look at the man in question. He and Magnus were chatting in quiet voices, their faces serious. I knew we were having a hard time right now when it came to trust and keeping secrets, but I thought that at least he had enough faith in me to believe I wanted him and only him.

I'd told him I loved him, even after everything he'd done to me, for God's sake!

I was reminded of CJ and Jada just then. Their fight back in the kitchens. How Jada felt about the looming Hecatomb and CJ's participation, and how this thing seemed to have ruined their relationship beyond repair.

While our situations were different, I couldn't help but think that the fate of my current state of affairs with Ragnor would not lead to a better outcome.

Perhaps the fact he considered me his, that he was crazy enough about me to get jealous, should've made me happy. But in the end, it only told me one thing.

Unless Ragnor knew all my secrets, he would forever doubt my loyalty.

CHAPTER 13
AILEEN

Ragnor was actively avoiding me.

The Hecatomb was just a little over a week away. The hovering threat of it was beginning to become far more present than before, and now Ragnor was avoiding me.

Before, he had given me the excuse of his being busy, which I'd accepted, since it sounded quite plausible with everything that was going on.

Now, unless it was during training, which now consistently included Magnus as my literal punching bag, he kept himself out of my sight and even vicinity. At night, when I came back to his suite, sore and aching from training all day, he was never there and left no notes as to where he was.

It reached a point when his sheets no longer smelled like him, he'd been gone for so long.

I had no idea where he spent his nights or where he slept. Since he always seemed no worse for wear when he came to pick me up for my individual training, I assumed he *was* sleeping.

Just not with me.

I'd thought he was going to go all alpha male on me after getting all jealous that day with Magnus, but instead, he raised a cold wall between us, reminding me of the first few weeks of our initial acquaintance. That did not make me feel good.

If only I had a room of my own to hide in rather than the suite I shared with him. Funnily enough, after our return from the altercation with the Jinn, Ragnor and I had begun living together in his suite without even discussing it. It was as if we both saw it as a natural course of events.

Now I realized it might've been too early in our relationship to move in together.

It seemed I wasn't the only one going through a rough time privately, though. CJ had been looking worse and worse with every day that passed to the point he looked as if he hadn't had a good night's sleep in ages.

To forget my own problems and try to help him with his, I offered to have lunch with CJ. He took me up on it but was very tight lipped during the entire meal, evading my questions.

Until I asked, "Is Jada at least coming out of her room now?"

That's when CJ looked away and said, "Yes."

And that was that.

Every day seemed to crawl by while the training sessions turned more and more brutal, until finally, the first week of training reached its end.

And the first day of the mixed training with the Gifted Hecatomb participants arrived.

"I've asked our Lord for his permission to attend the Hecatomb."

Zoey and I stared at Isora, while our forks were halfway to our mouths. "No," I blurted before I could stop myself.

Isora rolled her eyes. "Well, he agreed, so fuck you."

"Are you serious?" Zoey said, arching a brow. "The Hecatomb isn't some theatrical play."

She was right. According to the briefing we'd gone through on the first day of training, the Hecatomb was basically a battlefield. Depending on the assigned monitor, there could be some additional entertainment, but that was definitely not the point.

The point was to see who filled the arena with more gore and death.

Isora glared at her for a moment before taking a sip of her coffee. "Obviously, it's not. But my two friends are going to participate, so I have to be there."

Part of me was touched, but another, bigger part felt uneasy. "Renaldi is going to be there," I told her, eyeing her closely.

She gave me a serious nod. "I know. That's another reason why I want to go."

"To see *Renaldi*?" Zoey asked, her disgust palpable. "Why the fuck would you do that?"

Isora smiled cryptically. "I have some unfinished business to discuss with the asshole."

"I don't like it," I murmured.

"Lucky for me, it's not up to you to decide what I do or not," Isora retorted sweetly before rising up. "Don't you have training to get to?"

Before either Zoey or I could respond, she stormed off, evidently upset. Zoey and I looked at each other, and she said, "What did she expect? That we'll support her coming to see a bloodbath, along with her traumatic former Lord?"

Sharing the exact same sentiment, I could only sigh and massage my temples. After days of training my powers, the pain was constant even when I wasn't actively using my magic. It sometimes turned even more painful when something lay heavy on my mind, like the fact Ragnor actually approved of Isora coming to watch the Hecatomb.

Since I'd had it up to here with Ragnor, this was just another thing pinned to my mental board of what the hell do you think you're doing?

After quickly finishing our breakfast, Zoey and I left for training. It was to take place in a larger gym, and I wondered who our mentor was going to be. George had told us it was going to be someone different.

I just hoped it wasn't Ragnor, because I didn't think I could handle having him give me the cold shoulder during the morning session as well. It was hard enough as it was when it was just Magnus and us.

Unfortunately, when Zoey and I arrived at the gym, we found out who was going to be our mentor, and that vampire was the only vampire other than Ragnor I'd wished I wouldn't have to see in close quarters again.

Lieutenant Margarita Wallen.

The woman who first introduced me to the Rayne League when I became a vampire and then tried to sabotage me right before the Auction out of pure jealousy over Ragnor and Logan.

The same one who threatened me more than once to keep my distance from her two favorite men.

And she was supposed to train me so I would survive the Hecatomb. Sounded legit.

Margarita's auburn hair was pulled into a tight bun, her catlike green eyes on the man standing next to her as she listened to him speak.

Logan.

Right. He was also here, as a participant in the Hecatomb. Great.

"Wow," Zoey murmured to me, her brown eyes on Logan. "I forgot how good he looks up close."

"Yeah," I muttered, pointedly looking at the gym's entrance so as not to look at my ex-boyfriend. "He does. Though I would not make a move if I were you."

Zoey sighed. "Yeah, I wouldn't want to get on *her* bad side."

I whipped my head toward her and saw her glaring at Margarita, who seemed oblivious, as she was transfixed by whatever Logan was saying to her. "I can tell you from experience she's a hound dog, all right," I whispered. "It's a wonder she hasn't sought me out to torture me since I came back."

"You mean she's like that with our Lord too?" Zoey asked, eyes wide. "That's preposterous. He's our *Lord.* She has no say in whether he dates you or not."

My lips parted as I was about to say *we're not dating*, but then I clamped my mouth shut. What were we, then, if not dating? The whole one-month-trial thing was postponed until after the Hecatomb, sure, but what were we now, then?

Ragnor and I weren't friends, so we couldn't be friends with benefits. Hell, it'd been a while since we'd *benefited* each other as it was. Were we lovers, then? That would entail dating, too, and considering everything going on, it wasn't on the table at the moment.

I sneaked a look at Logan again. I knew everything there was to know about Logan. From the shallowest things, like which movie was his favorite, to the deepest ones, like what buttons to push to get my desired response.

With Ragnor, I didn't even know what his favorite color was, let alone what he was thinking most of the time. In fact, the only subject I was intimately familiar with where he was concerned was what he liked in bed. And that was that.

It occurred to me, not for the first time, that I was in love with Ragnor, but I knew absolutely nothing about him.

So was that truly love at all?

With Logan, things had been simple. I'd known the entire time we were together that I wasn't *in love* with him. I was infatuated with his good looks, sure, and liked his personality well enough, but that was the extent of it. What I'd felt about Logan was closer to possessiveness. I hadn't seen him as a man with his own mind and thoughts. I'd seen him as a thing that I considered mine and mine alone.

Which, I knew, was a whole bucketload of shitty. But unfortunately, that was the truth.

With Ragnor, I didn't even know how old he truly was. Hell, I didn't know anything about his past. Nothing about his human life.

Which, I also realized, was what dating was for: to get to know your partner better.

And yet . . . maybe, like with Logan, I wasn't really in love with him after all?

My thoughts went to Jada just then. I'd seen her briefly after breakfast, heading into the kitchens with her shoulders slumped and her head hanging low. The look in her eyes when she'd talked about CJ had been—despite the overwhelming pain—full of love, which had led to that despair in the first place.

Perhaps what I felt now, with Ragnor, was something similar to that.

Or was I deluding myself?

"Good morning, participants." Margarita's shrill voice snapped me out of my thoughts, and I focused on her. I realized a line had formed where Zoey and I stood with all other eight participants. "We're going to start with some basic warm-ups before Lieutenant Magnus and our Lord will join us for an assessment."

She looked us over, and I saw her eyes skip from Zoey on my left to Yelene, who stood to my right—avoiding me completely. We were off to a great start. "As you know, in the Hecatomb, you're going to fight in five pairs of one Gifted and one Common. Today's assessment will determine the makeup of the pairs."

CJ raised his hand. "What are the factors you'll take into consideration?"

Margarita glanced at him briefly before she said, "Mostly, it will be about who complements who, ability wise," she replied, almost uninterested in the question. "Some Gifted's Gifts might not be compatible with someone's combat style, so the review will be to assess what would be the ultimate pairs."

She clasped her hands behind her back. "Now, let's begin."

For starters, she had us running laps. It was a great way for me to think through what she'd said about the pairing-up situation. Out of the five Gifted participants, I was aware of the Gifts of three. Cassidy had her powerful voice; Logan had his enhanced legs, surely part of the reason he was a Commander; and Neisha, one of the Troop's Commanders, was the vampire version of a bionic woman. About the other two, Haneul and Oberon, who were also Commanders, I had no clue, but considering they were chosen for the Hecatomb, they had to have some insane Gifts.

I wondered who I was going to end up in a pair with. I hoped for Neisha. I would definitely feel safer with her by my side rather than Cassidy or Logan, whom I had prior relationships with.

After running laps, we were forced into a brutal warm-up session that, an hour later, left most of us fighting to catch our breath.

As I was lying on the floor, trying to get ahold of myself, I saw two men—Magnus and Ragnor—enter the gym, approaching Margarita. The three talked among themselves for a short while before Margarita clapped her hands. "Participants, sit down on the benches."

All ten of us took to the benches. Zoey settled next to me, still sweaty. "This gruesome training is going to kill me before the Hecatomb can even try to," she mumbled to me, groaning as she leaned back against the gym's wall.

"Just a friendly reminder that you *chose* this," I told her with a frown. "Though I still don't quite understand why."

Before she could respond, Margarita clapped her hands again, bringing everyone's attention back to her. "We'll start with two versus two mock battles. Every Gifted and Common will have a chance to fight alongside each other today, so make sure to give it your all for our assessment to be as accurate as possible." She paused and narrowed her eyes. "It's for your own good, after all. Anyway, first up—CJ and Neisha versus Logan and Zoey."

"Wish me luck," Zoey murmured as she took to the floor with Logan by her side. The two exchanged smiley greetings.

The mock battles had a two-minute time limit. Right after Margarita ordered "Start!" it was abundantly clear which pair would've won if the fight lasted longer.

CJ and Neisha moved together as if they could read each other's minds. They overpowered Logan and Zoey almost too easily, and not because either Zoey or Logan was bad, but they seemed almost clumsy in comparison. Logan and Zoey both focused on using their legs, that being their strongest suit (or Gift, in Logan's case), which gave them a large disadvantage against CJ and Neisha, who covered each other's weak spots seamlessly.

While the fight was happening, Magnus was scribbling things down in his notebook while Ragnor watched with a cool, impassive look on his face. But his eyes were following the movements, letting me know he was focused despite his expression.

The next battle was Cassidy and Yelene against Haneul and Sulien. Haneul, with a hawk resting happily on his shoulder, seemed like he couldn't hurt a fly, but when the battle started, his whole appearance changed. His hawk, too, changed as if a flip was switched.

Before Cassidy could even use her singing Gift, Haneul's hawk began attacking her with its talons. She cried out and tried to avoid it, while Haneul himself, as quick as lightning, came after her with his entire might, leaving Yelene and Sulien to fight it out between themselves. The battle was interesting in that I gathered Haneul's Gift must be connected to the hawk. Was he a bird whisperer when he was human, perhaps?

Once the fight was over—I concluded neither of those pairs was compatible—Margarita called, "CJ and Oberon versus Aileen and Neisha!"

Neisha gave me a big smile as we took to the floor. "I have a feeling we're going to nail it," she whispered to me. "So don't hold back. Oberon is one scary motherfucker."

I studied the Commander in the opposing pair. Oberon, with his massive tanklike body, indeed seemed like a force to be reckoned with. It was his first battle of the day, like mine, so I was curious to see what Gift he had.

Soon enough, I found two things.

Once Margarita called "Start!" Neisha and I moved together toward Oberon, both of us seeing him as the primary target. Unfortunately, that made it easier for CJ to flank our backs and attack Neisha with powerful blows that made her stagger back.

I focused on Oberon, who didn't move from his spot. He gave me a slow grin when I shot a fist to his head, and while my punch connected with his cheekbone flawlessly, I knew a moment later I'd made a mistake.

Because by then, vines were wrapped around my ankles, and with a simple flick of his wrist, Oberon had me hanging upside down from vines that sprouted out of the pockets of his training pants. I was utterly immobilized.

"First mistake, little Common," he told me, pulling out seeds from his pockets. "When fighting a Gifted, always focus on the surrounding area rather than the vampire himself."

I gritted my teeth because he was right. I was so focused on his intimidating muscle mass that I forgot Gifteds had all kinds of powers, and those powers didn't have to necessarily be connected to their actual limbs, like Logan's and Neisha's, or other parts, like Cassidy's vocal Gift. In fact, I should've realized it from the last battle, when Haneul utilized his hawk to attack unsuspecting Cassidy.

With a bitter feeling, I grated out, "Fine. I yield."

Oberon slowly let me down and even offered to help me up. With a glance at Ragnor that told me his eyes were on Neisha and CJ, who were still battling it out, I took Oberon's hand and rose to my feet. "Do you take vine seeds everywhere with you?" I grumbled.

The Commander gave me a big belly laugh that made him look like a heavy-lifting Santa. "I have all kinds of seeds with me," he said, wriggling his brows.

I couldn't help but laugh at that.

The fight concluded moments later, when Neisha had CJ in a choke hold, and I returned to the bench, sitting next to Zoey, who gave me a suspicious look. "What did you and him talk about?"

"Nothing, really," I replied, shrugging. "Why?"

"Because our Lord has been looking at you two as if he was ready to go on a killing spree," she murmured back, and I stiffened.

Slowly, I turned to look at Ragnor, but he seemed to be talking with his Lieutenants, his face as impassive as before. "Are you sure you saw right?"

"Don't be daft," she scoffed. "If the entire League didn't already know about you two, then the way actual smoke came out of his ears would've let them all know."

I couldn't even begin to comprehend her words when the next round was up—with Zoey and Cassidy against Yelene and Logan.

The next few battles proceeded as before. I found myself paired with Oberon next, and while we made a good team, Yelene and Haneul were far more compatible than we were, and they managed to overpower us with overwhelming ease.

Same went for my pairing with Haneul. He was a quiet man, and he seemed to rely mostly on himself, which had been great before when he supported the much weaker Yelene, but with me, it turned out to be a hindrance. I was more the long-enduring-battle type, while he was the kind to quickly finish off his foe. That made the battle very strenuous.

When it was my time to pair up with Cassidy, I was pretty tired. Cassidy didn't give me so much as a nod, and I barely managed to nod at her; I was barely standing on my two feet. And with our opponents being Oberon and Sulien, I was already feeling tired.

The battle was short-lived. Cassidy and I, much like in our relationship, were not compatible whatsoever. She was the stand-in-place-and-rely-on-her-Gift type. That made both Oberon and Sulien focus their attacks on her, and when I tried to intervene and attack them back, they were so much in sync, they managed to fend me off while still overpowering Cassidy at the same time.

After that fight, I was able to rest for a few more battles. Until Margarita said, "Final battle will be Neisha and Zoey against Logan and Aileen!"

CHAPTER 14
AILEEN

Logan's face was quite expressionless when I rose from my seat and headed toward him. But I knew him well enough to know he was giving me a mental scowl.

It was the twitch in his right eye. It was always that twitch whenever he was displeased about something.

I was not happy about it either. In fact, I felt as much displeasure as he did, only I had a feeling I hid it better.

But our personal feelings shouldn't matter. The Hecatomb was a week away. If we wanted to survive that damn thing, we had to put our differences aside.

"Hey," I murmured, feeling the energy seeping out of me as I came to a stop beside him, looking at Neisha and Zoey chatting animatedly with one another.

Logan did not respond. He didn't even glance my way.

Taking a deep breath, I made a split-second decision. "I know neither of us is happy about this *pairing*," I whispered, wincing at my own word choice and ignoring my rising anxiety. "But the Hecatomb is not a joke, Logan. So please, give this fight your all and work with me as best as you can, for both our sakes."

Because if there was one thing I was sure of, it was Logan's and my compatibility when it came to fighting styles. And while I did not like having to deal with him, especially after we had successfully ignored each other ever since I first became a vampire, my will to live was stronger than my ego.

And his will should be too.

Whether Logan accepted what I said or not, I wouldn't know, because Margarita immediately told us to be ready, and when she called "Start!" we were already on the defense against Zoey's and Neisha's immediate onslaught.

As Logan fended Neisha off by evading her attacks, I was doing the same with Zoey. My reaction time was just slightly better than hers, and it was enough for me to avoid getting beaten.

I hated being on the defense, though. I always felt safer when I was actively doing something in a fight rather than protecting myself. And while defense was important, offense was more up my alley.

So when Zoey tried to punch me next, I decided enough was enough. I grabbed her flying wrist and with grueling effort flung her across the room and away from me. She landed on her side, gasping in pain.

I didn't waste a moment and turned to Neisha. She and Logan were still in the same position, with him evading her powerful blows. She sniggered at him, since she could see what I saw: the sweat on his forehead from having to restrain himself.

He was actually refusing to fight. As if he didn't acknowledge that the results of this mock battle were so much more important than our shitty past.

That realization settled heavily in the pit of my stomach, and I snapped loudly, "Get a fucking grip, Logan!"

Both Neisha's and Logan's heads whipped to my direction. Using that momentum, I sent a kick toward Neisha and felt a surge of satisfaction when I felt my heel digging into her ribs.

She grunted and staggered back, Zoey rejoining her now that she was on her feet. I moved to stand next to Logan again. "Are you seriously going to fuck us both over?"

"You have no right to tell me what to do," he hissed back, his eyes, like mine, still on Neisha and Zoey, who were now standing in a defensive stance, as if to tell us it was time we stopped playing and took it seriously.

"I'm not trying to do that," I snipped back before I took a deep breath and prepared myself for what I knew would force Logan into action. Tension rolling over my body, I hissed, "Just stop acting like a wet blanket and start *fighting for your life*."

Before he could respond, I surged forward and sent a round kick toward Neisha. She gave me a grin as she blocked it with her arm, but I was already sending my fist to her face.

The moment my fist connected with her cheek, I felt Zoey coming from behind me, and I knew it was time I began.

So I launched the first Behest.

Ever so gradually, I slowed down my movements. At first, Zoey was still moving at the same pace as before, but before she knew it, she began mimicking my pace. And while I slowed everything down, I gathered my restrained, bubbling energy in the pit of my gut, readying myself.

And when the time was ripe, with Zoey attempting to punch my face, I exploded.

With my gut as the center of my energy for the second Behest, I shot forward into her fist and connected both my feet with her stomach, using my core to bring her down with one fast motion.

Zoey cried out as her back crashed against the floor, but I didn't stop moving. I swiveled around and found Logan executing his own second Behest on Neisha, bringing the Gift of his enhanced leg muscles into play when he practically kicked her into unavoidable submission.

With Neisha and Zoey down, Logan's and my heavy breathing were the only sounds in the room. We glanced at one another, and I gave him a nod that he did not return before he walked toward the bench full of wide-eyed participants, almost falling down on his ass as he was fighting to catch his breath.

Wiping the sweat off my forehead, I took back my seat on the bench as well. It seemed we didn't need to reach the time limit of our mock battle. With our successful synchronized attack of Iovan's Imperium's first couple Behests, it was clear which pair was superior.

And unfortunately, it was not Neisha and Zoey.

We took a lunch break before it was time for the pairing decisions.

At first, I thought it would be a lunch break like any other: I would go with Zoey to find Isora, the three of us would eat together and gossip about what was happening, and then we would part ways.

This time, however, was different.

"Stop," Ragnor called when everyone—us ten Hecatomb participants and his two Lieutenants—reached the cafeteria's entrance. Once he had our attention, he said with a blank face, "We'll all sit together."

Shocked murmurs broke out among the participants. Margarita and Magnus, too, seemed baffled as they shot Ragnor questioning looks he determinedly ignored.

When we entered the cafeteria with Ragnor at the head, every vampire in the room turned to stare. As we headed toward the tables in the middle, those damned tables that used to give me hell those first few months I worked as a kitchen assistant, my heart sank to the floor.

I'd never wanted to sit at one of these tables when I served them. I always saw those who sat there, Ragnor included, as elitist, entitled assholes.

I'd never thought of myself as one. Even now, when I was in a relationship of some sort with Ragnor, the head of those elitist assholes, I still didn't think of my standing as higher than before. If anything, I was the root of all problems coming this League's way.

I stopped in my tracks when everyone took seats around the party's arranged long table. Ragnor, who sat at the head, caught my gaze, and with a small movement of his chin, practically told me to get my ass over there.

But I refused.

Even if it was out of stubbornness only, I did not want to sit at table number one. It was a matter of principle, and while I didn't have many of those, this one was important to me.

Back when I was human, I worked as a cashier at the grocery store. It was a low-income job, with even lower respect levels, but I'd been proud of it. It was a normal occupation. Something anyone could do. There was no need for blood and gore and little girls screaming for help.

Then I became a kitchen assistant. While working in the Rayne League kitchen meant being subjected to Lon—the kitchen's head, who could give Gordon Ramsay a run for his money—and being forced to serve certain higher-ups-filled tables, it wasn't all bad. I'd met CJ, Jada, and Bowen there. They were the only vampires who'd been kind to me right from the start. They left me with good memories of that work, even if it had been Sisyphean and difficult.

In retrospect, I could say I was proud of that job too.

Participating in the Hecatomb, while not a job in the official sense of the word, was closer to the one I'd had many years ago, back in my hometown under my father's tutelage. At the very least, it was a far cry from a regular grocery store or kitchen work.

In that sense, I was the complete opposite of Zoey, who seemed to revel in her being voted in as a participant. She saw it as a stepping stone, like most vampires in her position did.

I saw it as the lowest of the low. There was no pride, no dignity, in fighting and killing others. And while I never claimed to be an altruistic pacifist, and I *was* ready to kill to save my own skin, I would never glorify it.

I'd stared death in the face, both as a perpetrator and a victim, more times than I could count. Most of the deaths I'd witnessed were so brutal, especially given the victims' ages, that it made me sick just thinking about it.

So while I wasn't a stranger to death, I never took pleasure in it, and even if I were in Zoey's position, I would've never done what she did.

So I gave Ragnor a small shake of my head and walked away toward the buffet, where I piled some rice, chicken wings, and salad on a plate and then took a seat at an empty table like the good old days.

"I must say, I like you, Henderson."

I whipped my head up with a mouth full of rice to see Oberon putting his own tray on the table and taking the seat across from me. He flashed me a grin and winked. "It seems we're both of the same mind."

For some reason, his smile coaxed one out of me too. "I saw you sitting down with the others earlier, though," I told him, arching a brow.

He dug his fork—which looked minuscule compared to his massively thick, muscular arm—into his steak and with one bite, demolished almost the entire thing. "It takes one's courage to say 'fuck the system' and propel others into action," he said wisely after he swallowed.

As if to prove his point, another person appeared at the table: Haneul, with his hawk on his shoulder. "May I join you?" he asked quietly, a slight accent to his voice.

"Of course, bud," Oberon said with a big, toothy grin, and patted the seat next to him. Haneul nodded and sat down, putting his own tray of food on the table. "I told you," Oberon then said to me, "all it takes is one person."

My smile grew as my heart warmed a little. But when I glanced at table number one, that fuzzy feeling dissolved as I saw Ragnor speaking to Margarita, his back purposely turned to me, while a trembling server tried to get their table's order.

I looked back at Oberon, who seemed to study me. "Why did you really follow me?"

Oberon threw me another shrug, but this time, his face was serious when he said, "Because I, too, have low regard for those who think they need to be served." He pointed his fork at me. "It would've been a different story if there wasn't a buffet and the cafeteria worked like a restaurant, but since it's not, I find it off-putting."

I didn't realize my shoulders were tense until they fell, relief filling me up. I suddenly felt so validated, and while I hadn't thought I needed this before, I realized I did. "That's exactly what I believe too," I said quietly.

The rest of the lunch passed in companionable silence that made me feel far less alone.

CHAPTER 15
AILEEN

A tense silence filled the SUV when Ragnor drove us to his town house for the private training.

After Margarita said that the results of the pairing decisions would be postponed until after private training, Ragnor and I met up at the entrance of the League, this time without Magnus, and neither of us spoke even one word.

I knew that he was angry at me for many things—most recently for refusing to sit with him and the others at table one. But there were other things he'd already been pissed off about before then, and he was no longer able to keep a straight face. Fury etched the sharp lines of his face, his eyes constantly glowing neon blue as he kept them on the road while driving through the city, his knuckles white as his fingers clutched the wheel so hard, it was a wonder it remained intact.

A small part of me wished we wouldn't speak of anything other than my training when we arrived at his town house. But the realistic part of me knew that was naive. The fact that Magnus hadn't joined us this time could only mean Ragnor wanted some one-on-one time with me—and not the thrilling, sexy kind.

Though to be fair, we hadn't had the latter in what felt like forever now. Could we even be considered in love anymore? It sure as fuck didn't feel that way.

And that thought was the most depressing of them all.

While we drove in that terribly tense silence, my thoughts drifted away to CJ and Jada. Before I was bought by Atalon, I hadn't thought the two were anything more than close friends. That had always been the vibe I got from them. However, learning of the true nature of their relationship wasn't surprising either.

Unlike Ragnor's and my issues, however, Jada's and CJ's were far more grave. They were Alara Morreh, after all. And seeing both Jada and CJ every day in passing, and seeing their faces grow darker and more somber the closer we headed to the Hecatomb, made me feel like sometimes, Ragnor and I were acting childishly in comparison.

Even if I were to die in the Hecatomb, Ragnor would live.

And in the unlikely scenario that Ragnor died, I would live too.

Yet despite our situation being far less dire than Jada's and CJ's, why couldn't either of us let it go?

By the time Ragnor parked at the town house, I was already a ball of unwound nerves. When he didn't make an attempt to exit the car, I grew still, bracing myself for whatever was coming for me.

To my shock, his whole body seemed to forcibly relax, and when he turned to look at me, his eyes were no longer glowing, and the fury in his face was gone, replaced by a look I couldn't read. "Next time, when I tell you to do something in public, you do it."

I stared at him, trying to read him and failing, which brought me far too much stress for my liking. "I thought you said we were equals," I said quietly.

"If or when we go public with our relationship, it would be a different story," he bit back, and I could hear, even if I couldn't see, the anger he was barely repressing. "But until then, you do *not* undermine my authority. *Ever.*"

My hands curled into fists as my own anger rose, overshadowing my brewing anxiety. "*If* we go public?" I repeated, glaring at him. "*If?!*"

His face remained unchanged at my rising tone. "It seems to me as though you're not really interested in having anything to do with me anymore," he said in an almost mocking drawl of a voice that made blood rush to my face. "You seemed far more receptive to Oberon's attention. You even sought Logan's back in the mock battle, for whatever reason."

My rage came to a startling halt as I gaped at him, speechless.

He didn't stop. "And yet when I try to get you to talk to me, aside from when you're forced to in our private trainings, to communicate what's on your mind, you're stonewalling me and ignoring me for days on end afterward, leading me to sleep most nights in my office in case I won't be welcomed again in my own fucking bed. So yes, Aileen"—his voice was rising now—"excuse me for thinking that perhaps we were nearing our end before we could even properly begin."

All I could do was stare at this man before me. It was a version of Ragnor I'd never seen before. A version of him I never even comprehended might exist. For me, Ragnor was this all-powerful, flawless being. He always had a perfect shield around him that made it seem like nothing could hurt him. He was beyond human, even beyond vampire or vampire Lord. He was the closest thing to a god I knew.

But the Ragnor here, in this SUV, was looking far too broken to be a god.

"Are you . . ." I started, voice dry, before I swallowed hard, cleared my throat, and said, "Are you, perhaps . . . jealous?"

Ragnor stared at me for a few moments, as if he needed to process what I'd just said, before he turned around and left the car.

I unclasped myself and rushed out after him. "You cannot be serious," I said, my heart racing as I grabbed his arm and pulled him to a stop. "You're not really jealous."

He whipped around, using my grip to grab my arm and pull me toward him until I was plastered against his front. "So what if I am?" he growled, eyes wild as they bored into mine. "Nothing I said is a lie."

I stared back at him, so fascinated by this man before me that all my previous anxiety and anger left me, replaced by pure wonder. "Ragnor," I whispered, his grip suddenly sending shock waves down my spine, causing me to press myself harder against him. "I've never wanted anyone or anything as much as I want you."

His face was like thunder while he wrapped his arms around me, his hand grabbing a fistful of my hair to force my head back, capturing my eyes with his. "Words and actions are two different things," he hissed. "I don't feel like you want me. If you did, you would've told me what your relationship with Logan is or why you barely look my way nowadays."

I shuddered at the rawness I could hear in his voice. With a deep breath, I cupped his face and leaned my forehead against his. "I didn't mean to neglect you," I said. "In truth, I thought you were the one avoiding me."

"It's all because I could feel you wanting distance," he murmured before he leaned back and narrowed his eyes, glaring at me. "I don't like it when you smile at other men. Or when you touch them, even by accident." His eyes suddenly glowed again. "I especially hate it that you have some sort of past with another man, a past you clamp up about when asked."

Staring at him, I couldn't help but feel a looming defeat. Did I really have no choice but to tell him about this part of my past? And if I did, then what about Ragnor? Would he tell me about *his* past if I asked?

That would require actually asking him, idiot, a little voice of reason inside me said.

But another voice, which was more like a gut instinct, really, insisted, *Do you really wanna know?*

And because I was an indecisive bitch, all I said was, "Logan is the son of my foster parents. Those who took me in after my father first went to jail."

Ragnor studied me, waiting, but when I said nothing more, his anger rose again. "And?"

"And nothing," I lied, pulling out of his arms, choosing to wrap my own around myself. "That's all there is to it."

In the end, I chose self-preservation.

I chose to leave things in the same tangled mess with Ragnor as they were before this conversation.

And when pure frustration made him glower at me for a few long moments before he stormed off into the town house, I knew he was realizing the very same thing.

After a tense training session followed by icy silence on the way back to the League, it was finally time to discover what pairing decisions had been made.

Margarita, the other contestants, and I congregated back in the gym after the private sessions. After a few words about the decision process, she finally said, "The pairs are as follows: Haneul and Yelene, Cassidy and Zoey, CJ and Neisha . . ." She paused, displeasure spreading through her face, before she continued, "Oberon and Sulien, Logan and Aileen."

She suddenly threw me a murderous look that lasted barely a second before she smiled professionally at everyone. The change was so instantaneous that I almost thought I'd imagined it, but knowing Margarita, I doubted it. "Now that this is settled, starting tomorrow, you'll have your morning session in your assigned pairs for the last week of training. The afternoon private session shall remain unchanged. Dismissed."

As the participants began to depart, my eyes found Logan's. His were thunderous when they met mine, and before I could approach him, or call his name, he stormed off, not unlike Ragnor had done earlier that evening.

My blood ran cold, and I could feel myself growing pale. Logan's behavior wasn't a surprise, but it just hammered in the point that he might be willing to kill himself in the Hecatomb rather than cooperate with me.

The Hecatomb was a mere few days away. We did not have time for this. And yet, despite my fears, I could never reprimand Logan. I did not have that right.

When minutes later I arrived at Ragnor's suite door, I suddenly found it impossible to bring myself to unlock it and let myself in.

I couldn't stay in his suite until we mended things—*if* we mended things at all. Perhaps Ragnor *was* right, and I did need space more than I'd realized. Perhaps I had also unknowingly projected it.

In the end, it was about more than our scuffle from before or my past with Logan. It was about the fact that this whole Hecatomb was my fault and that I might've dragged people to their deaths.

Just like I had years ago with my father.

As Logan had once predicted, once a monster, always a monster.

PART III

CHAPTER 16
LOGAN

My life could be split in two: before Aileen Henderson—and after.

When I was a mere thirteen-year-old boy, my altruistic parents decided to join the foster care system. Being young, but not *too* young, I understood what it meant, and I did not like it. Not one bit.

"Am I not enough?" I asked Mom once, tears in my eyes, a few days before the fateful phone call that would change my entire existence. "Why do you need another child?"

"Logan," Mom said softly, pulling me close for a tight, loving hug. "You're enough. You'll always be enough. But your father and I . . . we always wanted to give you a little brother or sister. A sibling to be there for you when we're not."

My shoulders slumped as I hugged her back. "I don't need a sibling," I whispered. "All I need is you."

Back then, I didn't understand my parents' concerns. I'd been their "surprise" baby, born to my mother when she naturally conceived at the ripe age of forty-seven. They loved me and cherished me so much, so they never wanted me to end up alone at a young age when they died.

It was a pessimistic thought, inconceivable for a little boy who'd known nothing but love and happiness his entire life.

My opinions as a naive child fell on deaf ears, and four days after that conversation, Mom's phone rang. We were in the kitchen, and I was eating breakfast before heading off to school. I saw Mom answer the phone, and her eyes widened as multiple emotions filled her face.

Shock. Hope. Exaltation.

Intuitively, I knew. But when Dad sent me off to school with a kiss to my forehead, while Mom was still on the phone, I refused to believe what my instincts were telling me.

Normally, I was a model student. I liked school. I liked studying and hanging out with my friends from the soccer team during breaks. I especially liked playing soccer after school, with Coach Cohen never failing to lift my spirits and tell me I was bound to become the next soccer superstar. The Ronaldo of America, he called me.

That day, I could not concentrate in any of my classes. I couldn't answer my teachers' questions, to their surprise. Even the coach's normally uplifting words in the after-school soccer training, preparing us for the upcoming regionals, couldn't help me because of the state I was in.

When I finally came home, I remember standing outside, staring at the wooden front door of our New England historical town house, terrified to set a foot inside and find out if I was right.

So I took a different approach. Sneakily, I headed toward the kitchen window and hid beneath it, out of sight. I could hear murmurs from inside—the house walls were not very thick—and that made my heart leap. Then, I put my hands on the outer ledge and pulled myself up, peering inside.

What I saw made me momentarily freeze.

A girl my age was standing there, face inscrutable, as she listened to my parents talk to her in low, soothing voices. I could only see her profile, but that was enough to make my heart stop in my chest.

Up until that moment, I had never been interested in girls. I was barely out of the "ew, girls" stage as it was. Before, they had just been in the background, harmless and not worthy of my attention.

But the moment I saw that girl, with her brown wavy hair gliding down the slope of her back to her curvy waist, my body reacted before my brain could compute what was happening.

All the blood rushed south, causing an irritating, uncomfortable feeling in my body.

Flushed, I wriggled around, trying to get rid of that sensation, but then I saw her turning to look at the window and I got a full view of her hauntingly beautiful face. Heart shaped with high cheekbones, lush, peach-colored lips, and stunning hazel eyes that, I belatedly realized, had found mine.

I let go of the ledge and crouched down, my heart pounding in two places at once: my chest . . . and the aching tightness between my legs.

Since I wasn't a complete idiot, I finally realized what was happening to my body and had to take a few more minutes to calm down. Then, when I felt like I could breathe, something akin to compulsion drove me to enter the house and head to the kitchen, where I got the view of her back.

My mom said, "There you are, Logan. Please meet Aileen Henderson, your new foster sister." I couldn't take my eyes off the girl who turned around to look at me.

And with a parched throat and dry lips, I approached her and offered her my hand. "Hi there. I'm Logan. Nice to meet you."

Then she took my hand, her skin touching mine, gave me the faintest, smallest of smiles that made the painful tightness reappear in my pants, and said, "I'm Aileen. It's nice to meet you too."

And from that moment, I was a goner. She caught me hook, line, and sinker.

For the first time in my thirteen years of living, I had a crush. And it was on my new foster sister.

Little did I know that was the beginning of my misfortune.

From the moment Aileen set foot in my school as the new girl, she was the object of many rumors—especially since everyone knew my parents were the ones who took her in.

I was quite popular at school for being the star soccer player and also a straight A student, along with good looks I was unaware of at that time, so the fact that it was *my* family who fostered the new girl was quite the news.

Unfortunately, that put a target on Aileen's back.

"She's so scary," I heard one of the girls, Olivia, say during an English class. Aileen was sitting on the other side of the room, looking outside the window, and thankfully couldn't hear what was said about her right behind me. "I heard from Jenna that she overheard the principal talking to Mrs. Travers about how that girl's parents were in jail or something."

"Oh my God." The other girl, Danielle, gasped. "So she's, like, a delinquent? I know it's a public school, but shouldn't she be in, like, juvie or something?"

I couldn't help but get angry. In the past week, I'd avoided Aileen at all costs—not because she did something. It was rather because my body's reaction whenever she was around terrified the shit out of *me*. But I did hear my own parents talk, and I knew that Aileen's father was in jail, leading to her current situation.

And it irked me, those stupid girls talking shit without an ounce of understanding about how the world worked. While I wasn't that much better, I at least knew, from the few meals I'd shared with my new foster sister, that she was the last person I would call either scary or a delinquent.

So I turned around to the girls behind me and whispered, "Why don't you mind your own business?" And, because I couldn't help it, I added, "Also, *she* didn't do anything, so why should *she* be sent to juvie?"

Both girls blushed and looked away, mumbling something incoherent. Scowling, I turned back around and glanced at Aileen. She was no longer looking outside the window. Instead, her eyes were on me, as unreadable as usual but perhaps with a bit more warmth than before.

When we returned home that day, Aileen caught me before I went into hiding in my room. "Thank you," she told me, her unique voice, lower than most girls', reaching parts of me that threatened to wake a bigger, more physical part of me.

Desperately trying to get ahold of my own emotions, I pretended to be oblivious and said, "For what?"

"You know what," Aileen said, shooting me a small, faint smile that hit me right in the gut. "I just wanted to thank you."

I nodded, deflated, and said, "You're welcome," before turning around and attempting to head back to my safe haven.

But Aileen's hand caught my wrist, drawing me to a stop and forcing me to face her again. She was about my height back then, before I had my growth spurt, and so our gazes linked in a direct line.

Her hold on me loosened as she stepped closer to me, invading my space. Then, before I could do anything, she pressed her lips against my cheek.

Frozen, all I could do was *feel*. I could *feel* her body a hairbreadth away from touching mine. All my thoughts—my entire being, really—were hyperfocused on the spot where her lips made contact with my skin. The fruity smell of her shampoo tingled my nose, making me want to lean into her, close the small distance that was left between us, take her head in my hands, and kiss her.

But before I could act on those instincts, she let me go and stepped back, giving me another look I couldn't decipher before she walked away.

After that, in the privacy of my room, my sexual awakening reached its peak.

CHAPTER 17
LOGAN

I don't know how it happened, but a couple of months after Aileen first joined my family, we became close.

It was a gradual process. At first, I'd been taking the food to my room for dinner every night. Then, I started attending dinners with my parents and her. The conversations were mostly about school, but they were pleasant nonetheless.

Then, at some point, Aileen and I started spending time watching movies in the living room after dinner. We never spoke much throughout the movies, just sat there eating microwave popcorn and getting used to each other's company.

Before I knew it, we started eating lunch at school together. Or rather, I let Aileen join me at lunchtime with my friends. She didn't speak to them much, or even me, but just sat there, listening to us as we talked about soccer and new superhero movies.

The turning point came a few weeks before my fourteenth birthday. I remembered it vividly: It was a Thursday night, and Aileen and I were waiting for the popcorn to be ready. My parents were out for the night—they had a weekly date every Thursday, which I found utterly disgusting back then—and so it was only Aileen and me at home.

"I'm so happy I got the Blu-ray from Dave," I told Aileen while we waited. I was excited to see the movie; it was the third one in an epic fantasy saga I was completely into at the time.

Aileen smiled at me, and while I wasn't immune to that smile, and it still made me feel things that confused me, I'd finally managed to get ahold of my newfound hormones. "The second one wasn't as interesting as the first, so I hope this one's better."

I chuckled and almost jumped when the microwave announced the popcorn was ready. We grabbed the bag and settled in the living room next to one another, the movie already waiting for us to press play.

For the first twenty minutes, we simply watched the movie in silence, as we always did, munching on the popcorn. But then I felt her hand brushing against my thigh.

Freezing, I thought she didn't do it on purpose and scolded my body for reacting to such a fleeting touch over my jeans. But then it happened again, and again, until suddenly her hand was on my thigh.

Blood rushing in one direction only, I swallowed hard and glanced at her. Her eyes were on the TV screen, but her thumb started making circular movements on my thigh.

Taking a deep, shivery breath, I tried to focus on the movie, but my efforts were in vain. My entire being was hyperfocused on the spot Aileen touched.

When the bag of popcorn was empty, Aileen put it away and, to my shock, closed the gap between us and cuddled up to my side, leaning her head on my shoulder, while her hand was still on my thigh.

My heart raced, and my face felt flushed. Everything disappeared but the feel of her body so close. I'd never had a girl this close to me before. I didn't know what to do. I was dumbstruck by the unfamiliar, yet not unwelcome, situation.

"Logan."

Her voice speaking my name made it hard to breathe. Slowly, I turned my head toward her, and she pulled her head back from my shoulder to stare at me. Her eyes were more brown than green in the dim light of the living room, and the way she looked at me, as if I were the answer to all her questions, made me feel a rush of feelings I couldn't identify.

"Aileen?" I said, scanning her face, trying to figure out what it was she was trying to do.

Then, before I could process anything, she leaned forward and pressed her lips against mine.

At that point in my life, I knew nothing about sex, or intimacy, or anything to do with the subject of romance. I'd been sheltered, with soccer being my whole life before Aileen came along. I had always avoided watching the porn videos some of my friends sent me, since they didn't really interest me yet. I saw them as vulgar and boring, so I didn't bother clicking on any of those links.

But when Aileen's maddening scent tingled my nose, followed by the soft touch of her lips, I was suddenly in a territory I had never dared broach before. Because, for the first time in my life, I felt desire. Lust, even.

For her.

Only for her.

The kiss was chaste—a peck, really—and when she leaned back, I found myself instinctually leaning forward, trying to follow her touch.

Because it wasn't enough.

"Aileen . . ." I said, staring at her. Entranced by her very existence. "Why . . ."

"I like you, Logan," she said, so bold that she rendered me speechless. "I really, really like you."

My throat grew dry as all I could do was look at her while a sudden epiphany landed on me.

I realized then what it was I was feeling toward her.

"I . . . I l-like you . . . too . . ." I mumbled, flushing at how uncool I was being, and cleared my throat. "I . . . I mean—"

She cut me off with another kiss, and this one was different. She pressed herself into me, her hands grabbing my shoulders, and I didn't know what to do with my own hands. Where did I put them? What should a boy do in this situation? I was lost in lust and confusion.

She leaned back only an inch to whisper against my lips, "Open up for me, Logan."

I opened my mouth to speak, and she took advantage of that, giving me my real first kiss.

And since I liked the girl, all I could do was let her ravish my lips with hers as much as she wanted to, the movie long forgotten.

After the first kiss, Aileen and I spent all of our time together.

We never spoke about what we were, but it was clear to both of us that we were more than friends.

After all, every night, once my parents went to sleep, Aileen would sneak into my room, and we would make out until neither of us could breathe and I would feel the aching need in my gut, in my *pants*, growing to a breaking point.

I started sitting next to her in classes and spent my lunchtimes with her only. We spoke about mundane things, like our favorite colors and music or debating the existence of aliens. Our conversations flowed naturally, as if we'd been friends our entire lives.

Then came the night before my fourteenth birthday.

We had dinner like every night with my parents before we headed to our rooms. I waited until I could hear Dad's loud snoring and counted to ten before I heard a knock on my door, followed by Aileen tiptoeing into my room, closing and locking the door behind her.

A huge, almost goofy smile spread over my face as I stretched my hands from my seat on the bed. "Hey."

"Hey," she whispered back before straddling me and burying herself in my body. My arms closed around her, and I took in her mesmerizing smell, enjoying the feel of her body against mine. I loved feeling her so close.

She felt *right* in my arms.

Then she said, "Let's have sex."

Bewildered, I was sure I didn't hear her right. I turned to look at her and saw her staring at me, her hand playing with my hair. "What?"

"Sex," she said, shrugging, though a small smile appeared on her face. "Let's try it."

My lips felt dry as my heartbeat quickened. "But . . ." I murmured, looking away from her as I felt my cheeks flushing. "Isn't it . . . like . . . I don't know . . ."

She chuckled softly. "Everyone does it," she said, her voice luring my eyes back to her. A wicked glint flashed in her eyes when she added, "I bet your parents do it all the time."

I couldn't help my disgust when I exclaimed, "Ew!"

She rolled her eyes. "Oh, come on. It's not like you didn't learn about how babies are made, Logan," she said before poking my cheek and flashing me another wicked smile that filled my stomach with knots. "Although you did look squeamish when Mrs. Holden said she was going to assign you that baby doll to take home and take care of."

I opened my mouth and closed it like a fish, lost for words. She pushed. "Come on, let's do it."

Something a lot like panic made me snap, "But what if we make a baby?" Then, I thought about it again and blurted, "Don't we need c-condoms?"

She grinned. "We don't need condoms, silly," she said, cupping my cheek and causing my already haywire heart to palpitate. "I haven't gotten my period yet, meaning I can't get pregnant. Besides, I think we have to do it, like, a lot to get pregnant."

Even back then, despite my naivety and lack of knowledge, I knew there was something amiss in what she was saying. I didn't know about her past at that point in time. I didn't understand where she was really coming from. All I knew was that something about it did not sit right with me.

Taking in a deep breath, I said, "Maybe we can just like . . . fool around." I swallowed hard, feeling a bit sick. "You know, like touch each other—"

For the first time since I'd met her, I saw fury filling up her beautiful face. "Everyone else is doing it. Everyone's having sex!" she snapped, leaning back and glaring at me. "We're not babies! Besides, don't you want to have sex with me? Isn't that what boys want?"

Suddenly, I knew I had to tread carefully, or this conversation could sour very fast. Narrowing my eyes, I struggled to choose my words. "I . . . yes, but . . . but I feel like maybe we are going too fast—"

"Too fast?" she cut me off, her eyes flashing dangerously. "We're thirteen, Logan! I know girls who have already had sex and who are way younger than we are!" She grabbed my shirt in anger. "Don't you think about doing it? Don't you want to know how it feels? What's it like? If you love me, you'll want to do it with me."

My breath got stuck in my throat. I'd never said those words before. I'd never told her I loved her. But she felt it nonetheless. She knew it before I even did.

I loved Aileen Henderson.

I loved her so much that all the alarms in my head became background noise I paid no attention to.

All I wanted was to see her smile. This angry Aileen was beautiful in her own way, but I wanted the Aileen I knew back. I did not want to argue with her—it was our first disagreement, and I hated it. I just wanted her to be . . . happy. To love me as I loved her.

So I grabbed her hands, locked her gaze with mine, and asked, "Will it make you happy if we do it?"

She squeezed my hands back and resolutely answered, "Yes."

I let out a sigh of defeat, cupped her cheek, and kissed her before I said, "Then let's do it."

The night before I turned fourteen, Aileen and I lost our virginity to one another in the quiet darkness of my room.

It was the first time in my life I'd gone against my instincts for another person. Because the truth was, I wasn't ready. I had barely realized my feelings for Aileen, barely managed to understand my body's reaction and how to deal with it, and sex should've come much later, when I was more emotionally ready.

But I loved Aileen. I fell in love with her at the tender age of thirteen, and that love blinded me to everything else—even to my own feelings.

So I let her take the lead in our relationship. I let her have her way with me every night after that first one we spent together.

We had sex every day until, before I knew it, I couldn't go a day without her in my bed.

And as my desperation and need for her grew, my love for her turned more twisted and obsessive with every touch and every word we exchanged.

CHAPTER 18
LOGAN

For three years, Aileen stayed with my family.

During those three years, we started dating in public once we turned fifteen. It was partly because I hated hiding our relationship from my parents but mostly because my possessiveness of her reached new heights, and I wanted the entire world to know she was *mine*.

Because when Aileen turned fifteen, she started attracting much more attention than she had before. I caught our classmates, and even juniors and seniors, staring at her when she passed through the high school corridors, their eyes scanning her from head to toe. I even heard some of my soccer team members talking about her while they rated the level of fuckability of all the girls in our grade. They rated her too high.

It drove me up a wall, having to keep our relationship a secret. I didn't want to anymore. I wanted to snarl and growl like a fucking animal at everyone who dared look at her. I wanted to show her off.

So to do that, I had to let my parents know.

Unfortunately, that conversation didn't go as well as I'd hoped.

"Aileen's your *sister*!" Mom said after I sat her and Dad down to tell them the news. I wanted to do it alone, without Aileen, because I feared something like this might happen, and thank goodness I did that.

"*Foster* sister, Mom," I countered, folding my arms. "It's not like you adopted her. She's not legally my sister."

Dad looked at me with concern. "You know we adore Aileen," he told me in his calm way, "but I believe what your mother's afraid of is that a relationship between you two at such a young age is bound to end badly."

"I know we're only fifteen," I said, getting angry. "But Aileen is the one for me. I'm going to marry her when we're old enough."

Mom and Dad stared at me as if they'd never seen me before. "Logan, honey . . ." Mom said, eyes wide. "Relationships at such a young age might not go too far."

"You have no right to say that," I snapped, now furious. "You and Dad met when you were our age! So what's the difference?"

They couldn't say anything back to that. So reluctantly, after a tense conversation, they gave Aileen and me their blessing.

And the next day, I held Aileen's hand the entire time we spent at school and glowered at anyone who dared think they could steal what was mine.

Because I wasn't kidding when I told my parents I planned to marry Aileen. It was the truth. The absolute truth.

I refused to let her go, no matter what.

Until I was forced to, the day her father got out of jail and took her away.

Even after Aileen was no longer a foster child, we arranged meetings in an old shed in the backyard of the small house Aileen's father rented after he was released.

At first, I didn't understand why we had to meet in that shed. Why couldn't she introduce me to her father? Why did we have to hide as if we were doing something wrong?

Aileen had been tight lipped and resolute about her decision, though. All she said was that her father wouldn't approve and left it at that, no matter how much I tried to push her for answers.

I knew she was hiding secrets. She wouldn't talk about her father—I'd learned he was in jail through my parents, not her. I wanted to know what he did time for—I believed that after three years of dating I deserved that much—but Aileen refused to tell.

It drove me insane, but I forced myself to be patient. I believed she'd come around and tell me when she was ready.

Even at sixteen, I was still naive enough to think that I knew Aileen at all.

It gutted me that I couldn't just see her every day like I had when she lived at my house. What made it even worse was the secrecy she forced on our relationship once more. It was only at school when I was allowed to show her affection—thankfully, her father allowed her to stay in school and not go back to being homeschooled, as she had been before being fostered by my parents.

But even that wasn't enough.

Nothing was enough when it came to Aileen. I wanted everything. I wanted her to submit herself entirely to me.

Because that's what I did. I was hers. Completely, utterly hers.

And I couldn't help but feel like she wasn't mine. No matter how much I tried.

It became more and more obvious when we had sex. When we first started screwing around, I knew we both felt the same. We both felt pleasure. We enjoyed it equally.

But once she returned to her father, things started going awry in that regard.

Suddenly, every time we had sex, she stared at me and faked her orgasms.

She'd never faked them before.

I knew Aileen's body. I knew what it felt like when she truly came. But suddenly, she wasn't feeling it. In fact, it almost seemed like she was *bored* every time we did it.

And that hurt.

It hurt so fucking much.

So one time, when I sneaked into the shed, I decided it was time to find out what the hell was going on. Because I wanted her to be the Aileen I knew, who enjoyed my body as much as I did hers, who didn't feel like she had to fake her orgasms to make me feel good or something.

Little did I know that day would be my ruin.

Because the moment I went in, she didn't even say hi; she wrapped her arms around me and kissed me long, deep, and wet.

Since I was in love with the girl, all I could do was respond in kind. I was desperate to feel wanted and needed by her, and so I let her do whatever she wanted to me.

The moment we were on the short mattress in the shed, stopping our kiss to catch a breath, I said, "Tell me what you want."

She looked at me with her beautiful, mesmerizing eyes and said, "I don't think you can handle it."

I felt affronted by her assumption. "I can, Leenie," I said, calling her by the nickname I'd given her years ago. "Anything you want, just tell me."

Studying me, she said nothing for a few long moments. Then, she said, "Okay."

At first, it was nothing I couldn't handle. She tied my hands to the bars attached to the shed's wall and then straddled me, caressing my body until I struggled against the shackles.

By the time she reached for my hardness, I was drowning in lust, and all I could do was plead with her. "Leenie . . . please . . ."

She let go and caught my gaze. "This is what I want you to do to me," she whispered as her hands closed around my neck, her nails digging into my skin so painfully, I couldn't help but gasp, excitement and fear warring inside me.

And then she strangled me.

At first, I didn't realize what she was doing exactly. I knew Aileen had some kinks, even though most of our sex was more fumbling than anything else. But the moment I'd asked her to all but let go, it seemed I allowed a dark side of Aileen to show. A side of her I was faintly aware of but never gave too much thought to.

I thrashed against the restraints as I felt the air leaving me. It was impossible to breathe. Tears clouded my vision as I begged her with my eyes to stop. But when I saw the euphoric look on her face, I realized something I should have figured out a long time ago.

Alarms went off in my head as I thrashed harder against her. It was only when I felt myself growing limp, my consciousness threatening to leave my body, that Aileen finally released the pressure and sat straight.

Breaths coming in short, wide eyed, and full of fear, I stared at her. I was reminded of the few times Aileen had taught me some of the martial arts she knew. It was a particular martial art called Iovan's Imperium, and I remembered how delighted she was when she executed the Behests on me under the guise of showing me how it worked.

She had the same exhilarated look on her face then as she did now, seeing me in pain.

"More," she whispered, pressing her lips against my cold ones. "I need you to do this, and more . . ."

Before that evening in the shed, I'd never known what real pain was. Growing up in a somewhat sheltered environment, I'd never experienced pain as a part of my life.

But when Aileen showed me the horrors that she wanted me to do to her, it was the first time I knew true pain.

The strangulation was almost child's play in comparison to what she later did to me.

I begged her to stop. I begged her to show mercy. To see that I hated what she was doing to me. That she was right—I couldn't handle the things she wanted.

But every time I saw her elated look as she inflicted pain worse than anything I'd ever felt, my fear trembled under the weight of my love for her. I loved her so much that seeing her so happy made me want to make her even happier.

And because I was so gone for her, it reached the point where I passed out and later woke up in a hospital bed, the painkillers barely numbing the thudding ache I could feel throughout my entire body.

My parents didn't let me see Aileen after that. If I were in their position, I wouldn't have let myself see her either.

But I was still a confused seventeen-year-old boy who was deeply in love, despite everything, with a girl. I wanted to see her, *needed* to see her, and get some answers. Because by that point, I knew Aileen was not the fragile little girl I'd always perceived her to be.

By that point, I knew about the crimes Aileen's father committed. I knew what he'd done, and what Aileen had had to go through her entire childhood. And yet I always refused to see what she truly was because I wanted to believe people could change. That blood didn't dictate shit.

It took me a few months, until just before I turned eighteen, to finally reach out to her and ask to meet. I was terrified of seeing her. There was a discrepancy in my mind between Aileen, the girl who hurt me so badly I had to stay in the hospital for a few weeks, and Leenie, the girl I was in love with, whom I wanted to protect and cherish.

She'd tried to text me, call me, approach me in any sort of way she could. But I didn't know what I would feel the first time I saw her after what she'd done to me. I was scared to find a monster in place of the girl I loved so much.

It took everything in me to finally agree to see her. We settled on meeting at her home, in the backyard, but not in the shed. I couldn't handle the shed.

The moment I walked into the backyard and saw her was a moment I would never forget.

She was sitting on the grass, staring at the woods beyond the yard, her dark hair falling over her shoulder. She seemed so small and dainty, her olive skin pale under the moonlight, as if one gust of wind could blow her over.

She did not look like a monster.

She looked like the girl I wanted to hold in my arms and never let go of.

Gritting my teeth, I settled down next to her. She obviously knew I was there, but she kept her gaze fixed ahead, wrapping her arms around her folded knees.

Taking a deep breath, I blurted, "My parents don't want me to see you anymore."

When she turned to look at me, I averted my gaze, unable to withstand the full shock of her face after so long. It was already hard just sitting there next to her, longing for her, feeling my body humming in her presence as if she hadn't caused it the worst pain of my life.

"I want to touch you," she said, and I could hear the genuineness in her words. This was Leenie, the girl I loved, talking. Not Aileen the monstrous torturer.

Feeling my heart breaking at what had become of us, I couldn't help but say the truth. "I want to touch you too." But I couldn't—or rather, I wouldn't. How could I, after everything?

She was quiet, and I felt my breaths grow haggard as tears filled my eyes. Suddenly, words bubbled in my throat, and I had to get them out. "I love you, Aileen," I whispered. "I've never loved anyone before, and yet . . ."

From the corner of my eye, I saw her raising her hand, as if to console me. And even though my body was drawn to her along with my mind, my instincts made me recoil, unable to allow her to touch me. Hating this, hating myself, I turned to face her, eyes wide and full of desperation.

"Why did you have to do that?" I asked accusingly. "Why did you have to . . . to—"

She cut me off. "It's what I know, Logan." Her voice cracked, and her eyes seemed shattered and broken. "It's the only way I know how to show you I love you—"

I snapped. "When you love someone, you don't send them to the hospital!" My voice rose. "When you love someone, you make sure they're safe, that they're . . . they're—"

"I was lost!" she cried out, her body trembling. "I was stupid, and lost, and goddammit, Logan, it happened right after everything went down with my father—"

"We're not fucking kids anymore, Aileen!" I shouted, all the confusing emotions inside me bursting out. "You're acting like you're still Daddy's little lost girl—"

"Don't you dare," she hissed, glaring at me. "You don't know what happened—"

"Then why don't you ever tell me anything?" I couldn't help but scream. Because it was the truth; she never told me a thing. Everything I knew about her was because of my parents or some newspaper articles. She never opened up to me fully, never shared what she truly went through. "In the past four years I've been dating a fucking ghost. A ghost, Aileen!" My voice trembled. "I know nothing about you or your circumstances—heck, I only know the dry fucking details because I fucking googled it! And you never told me shit! What did your father do? What the hell happened before you were brought over to our house?"

Her eyes filled with pain that drove me crazy. "Teach me how to love you properly, and I promise you," she said, almost begging, "I will tell you everything."

How dare she feel pain? How dare she beg me to stay with her, to "teach her how to love me" after everything she'd done? The audacity . . . the selfishness . . . And yet, despite it all, I couldn't hate her. I just *couldn't.* Because all I could feel when I saw the pain in her eyes, even after everything, was the need to love her and protect her. "Love should come naturally, effortlessly," I spit out, disgusted with both her and myself. "It should never be forced or taught. That you wish for it to be this way . . ."

Her eyes widened with fear. "Don't leave me."

I barked out a bitter laugh. "That's what you don't get about love, Aileen. Even though I'm so fucking angry with you, and even though you hurt me more than anyone else in this world, I will never be able to leave you. This is love in its most honest and brutal form."

And then, I gave in.

I pushed her down on the grass. I kissed her, ripped her clothes off, and buried myself inside her moments later.

Nothing was solved. And yet the staggering need I felt for her overpowered any sense of logic and rationality.

Little did I know it would be the last time I would see Aileen for years to come.

CHAPTER 19
LOGAN

The day after I slept with Aileen, she disappeared.

My calls and texts didn't get through, as if she had deactivated her number. I even went to her house only to see a **FOR SALE** sign that hadn't been there before.

Aileen had disappeared without a trace.

The only piece of information I had came a couple of weeks later in the form of an article about the arrest of Amir Zoheir-Henderson, Aileen's father, for the second time. He was arrested, apparently, the very same night I'd visited Aileen.

Whether it was a coincidence or not, I wasn't sure. All I knew was that Aileen was gone.

And I was left to deal with the gaping hole she left behind.

It was a hot summer day when my life took a sharp turn yet again.

Like every day ever since Aileen left, I spent most of my time practicing soccer in preparation for college. It was summer break, and staying inside wasn't an option for the person I'd become post-Aileen.

So I trained until I was out of breath and my clothes soaked with sweat. I trained until I was on the verge of passing out from pure exhaustion. All so I wouldn't have to think about her. About the woman who'd ruined me physically and emotionally.

That day, there was only one difference. My parents wanted to take me to dinner outside town at my favorite restaurant.

I'd been stonewalling them for weeks, refusing to leave my room when I was home and only giving them half answers when they asked me questions. I put distance between me and everyone around me, not just my parents; my friends, too, received the cold shoulder.

And the night before, I heard my mother cry. She hardly ever cried, and yet in the last few months, she'd cried more than I'd ever seen in my entire lifetime.

All because of Aileen.

So that morning, when she all but begged me to be available for dinner, I wasn't heartless enough to say no.

When I got into my father's car that evening, Mom turned to me from the passenger seat and smiled. "How was practice, sweetheart?"

Her smile did not hide her bloodshot eyes, however.

Swallowing my guilt, I replied with a shaky smile of my own. "It was okay."

She grabbed my hand and turned back to face the road, squeezing my palm so tight, I was afraid the blood flow would stop.

Dad cleared his throat before he asked, "Did you practice with Jace and Hamilton?"

My heart ached at the question. Because it just blatantly showed me how distant I'd grown from my parents ever since Aileen waltzed into my life. But I didn't want to remind him of that, so I lied with a simple "Yes," even though it had been years since my relationships with Jace and Hamilton fell apart.

A moment after the lie left my mouth, Mom let out a sudden piercing scream, and before I could comprehend what was happening, a bus crashed into the front of the car, shooting it off the road.

The next thing I knew, I was in a burning car, upside down, with the seat belt suspending me from the car's roof. In the front, I saw my parents in similar positions.

Only, unlike me, their eyes were closed, their bodies still.

Terror hit me then as I fumbled with the seat belt until I clicked it open. I wriggled out of the belt and hit the ground, when I saw a pool of blood that had to be mine soaking my clothes. But I was too numb with shock to feel anything. All I could see were my parents.

"Mom," I murmured, trying to crawl toward her and failing when I realized my legs did not obey my orders. Trembling, I tried to reach her and Dad, to help them, to get them out of there . . .

The door of the car was torn open just then.

Sure, I was hallucinating. All I could do was stare as a tall, muscular woman threw the tin aside as if it weighed nothing. Next to her, a pretty woman with long auburn hair and green eyes walked toward me, her eyes fixed on mine.

She crouched before me, her hand gently pushing my hair away. "Neisha," she said, and the muscular woman reappeared next to her. "Call our Lord."

The muscular woman, Neisha, looked at the redhead with wide eyes but walked away.

The redhead gave me a soft, sad look. "I'm sorry," she whispered. "I'm so, so sorry for your loss."

My consciousness was quite foggy by then, so I could barely keep my eyes open. The last thing I remembered was her soft, gentle touch, soothing me, as I slowly succumbed to the inevitable darkness.

The next time I opened my eyes, I was already a vampire.

PART IV

CHAPTER 20

RAGNOR

He'd given her time. More time than he would've given anyone else.

But when Aileen refused yet again to tell him about the nature of her relationship with Logan Kazar, Ragnor was through.

If she didn't want to give him answers, then he'd seek them out on his own.

Now, he stared as Logan walked into his office, his posture stiff as he closed the door behind him. He moved toward the desk and took a seat on the other side, facing Ragnor. "Good evening, my Lord."

Ragnor nodded as he studied the boy. He was barely out of high school when Ragnor gave him the Imprint. More than three years later, he was now a full-fledged Gifted vampire of Ragnor's League, one of the top Troop members, and a decent man all around.

Ragnor's hand clenched into a fist under the desk as he cut to the chase. "You and Aileen Henderson share a past."

At once, the cautious soldier before him transformed. Logan's turquoise eyes widened, his skin paled, and he looked down, his shoulders tense. "Yes," he grated out.

The reaction made Ragnor wary, but he kept his face blank as he continued. "She mentioned that your parents fostered her for a while."

Logan gave a jerky nod, still looking down at the floor, hiding his expression from Ragnor.

Leaning back, Ragnor made a calculated decision. He pushed his inner ire aside and used his magic. Spreading out his aura, he made sure to keep it as calm as possible, like a still lake in the middle of a forest. He channeled the calmness surreptitiously, so as not to raise Logan's alarm.

Moments later, Logan relaxed and raised his head to look at him. Ragnor peered at him closely and said, "Tell me about your relationship with her."

Despite the effects of his aura, Ragnor could see Logan tensing up. "I was under the impression that once you become a vampire, your human life should be left in the past."

"It's true," Ragnor said carefully, "when it comes to new vampires who need to acclimate to the vampiric society. However, you're long past that phase."

Hearing Ragnor's meaning, Logan took a deep breath and looked away. "Aileen and I were in . . . in a relationship," he said, almost spitting the words out, his voice was so bitter.

While Ragnor had suspected this was the case, the impact of Logan's words made an ugly, unwelcome feeling crawl inside him. It made him want to tear Logan's head off. It also demanded he go and reclaim what he believed was his.

But with things as they were, Ragnor did everything he could to maintain as much composure as he could.

Even if his insides felt raw and bruised.

"How long?" he asked before he could think twice about it.

Logan's gaze slowly turned to him, and to his irritation, Ragnor saw realization dawn on the boy. "Four years," Logan responded quietly, cautiously. "Excuse me for asking, my Lord, but are you, perhaps . . ."

Before Ragnor could stop himself, he growled, "Yes."

Logan froze, eyes wide and glowing neon green. "Please pardon my impudence, but I feel compelled to tell you the following," the boy said, speaking far too formally for Ragnor's liking. When his subjects spoke in that manner, it usually meant they were trying to overstep.

And of course, as Ragnor predicted, that was what happened next.

"Whether your relationship is purely physical or emotional as well," Logan said, a soft tremor in his voice, "Aileen is . . . she's a mons—I mean, she's . . ."

"You wanted to say 'monster,' didn't you?" Ragnor asked, voice deceptively soft. Because he almost couldn't believe his ears, and if he wasn't careful, his spread-out aura would change from soothing to the complete, horrifying opposite.

Logan clamped his mouth shut and looked away, trembling. "I apologize, my Lord, but I believe you should hear this because I respect you. She might look pretty and innocent, but don't let her fool you, my Lord."

Ragnor's growl erupted out of him, making Logan flinch and pale further. "Do not talk about her like this, Logan," he snapped. "I won't allow it."

Shaking from head to toe, Logan attempted to meet his gaze and looked away at once, swallowing hard. Still, he did not bend under Ragnor's pressure and said, "With all due respect, my Lord, you don't know her as well as I do." He whispered, "The terrible things she did to me . . . Those things couldn't have just disappeared. She's . . . she's a *demon*."

Ragnor's aura shifted, and he immediately drew it back before Logan could suffocate under his uncontained rage. He was on the verge of asking him what exactly Aileen had done to him when a part of him told him to stop.

You've heard enough, the voice of reason murmured in Ragnor's head. *If you ask any more than that, you'll truly betray her trust by going behind her back.*

But hadn't she broken his trust first by refusing to tell him any of it in the first place?

Gritting his teeth, Ragnor rose to his feet and rounded the desk. "I understand," he said, with his back to Logan's trembling figure as he headed to the door. "You may leave."

He got out and slammed the door shut behind him, feeling angrier at Aileen Henderson than ever before, but also feeling pity.

What the hell had she done to Logan?

Ragnor would've asked her, but he knew she would not give him a proper answer.

A notion that sent him spiraling all over again.

When he arrived at his suite, prepared for an ugly fight with his Alara Morreh, he found it empty.

Thinking she might come back later, he took a quick shower that did nothing to soothe his anger, sat down on the sofa, and attempted to read a book while waiting.

But as the hours passed, there was no sign of Aileen. More confused than angry, he left the room and searched for her. First in the Troop gym, then at his office, the infirmary, and even the greenhouse.

She was nowhere to be found.

Until the next morning, he saw her walking into the cafeteria with her two friends. And he finally realized Aileen had chosen to sleep elsewhere.

And his anger with her reached a breaking point.

CHAPTER 21
AILEEN

My body's discomfort woke me up.

When I opened my eyes, it took me a few moments to remember where I was, not only because the surface I was lying on was that of a sofa rather than a bed, but also because the living room I was in was smaller than the one in Ragnor's suite . . .

Right. Last night, I crashed at Isora and Zoey's place.

Cuddling the comforter close, I stared at the ceiling, wishing I could disappear, if only for a short while.

Because today, I had to start training with Logan, my now partner for the Hecatomb. And if that wasn't enough, I would also have to see Ragnor in the afternoon for the private training.

Every fiber of my being rebelled. I didn't want to see either Ragnor or Logan. The mental fortitude required for dealing with both of them was beyond me at the moment.

I was too tired and felt too guilty to be able to face both the demons of my past and the sad reality of my present.

But the Hecatomb waited for no one. And overruling my other emotions was the steadily rising anxiety about it being so soon and my feeling so underprepared.

And I had to remind myself that at least my situation was far less miserable than Jada's.

I heard a door creaking open followed by approaching footsteps. Then Isora's face popped up, her cobalt eyes peering at me. "Good morning," she said, giving me a concerned look.

"Morning," I retorted and forced myself to sit up. "Slept well?"

She nodded, and I could feel her eyes follow me as I put on my sneakers and rose to my feet. With a sigh, I turned to her and gave her half a smile. "Thank you for letting me crash."

"Anytime," she said quietly just as another door opened, revealing Zoey's haggard look. "Morning, Zo."

Zoey yawned and gave both of us a nod. Then, as we'd done many times before, we went to the cafeteria together for breakfast.

Unfortunately, I had barely put a spoonful of bacon and egg in my mouth when a familiar redhead made her way toward me, her eyes fixed on my face.

Swallowing the food hard, I ignored Isora's and Zoey's looks as Margarita stopped right next to me, her expression disdainful. "Come with me," she barked.

My first instinct was to refuse. But something in her catlike green eyes made me clamp my mouth shut and rise to my feet. "Lead the way," I murmured, grimacing as I felt many pairs of eyes peering at me from across the cafeteria.

As I followed Margarita to the exit, it felt as if I was being led to the guillotine. I mean, it was Margarita, Ragnor's Lieutenant, who'd hated my guts almost since day one. In fact, she had tried to sabotage me multiple times during those horrid times before the Auction, when I was still a newbie.

She'd also threatened me to stay away from Logan and Ragnor. Which made me wonder if that was what this was all about right now.

While Ragnor and I were being discreet about our relationship, I doubted she wasn't at least a bit aware that something was going on between us. It wasn't like we were purposely hiding; I had been staying in his suite ever since I came back to the Rayne League. It would've been weird if she, and others, hadn't noticed something.

If she was bothered about it, she could've easily said something before. So that left only one option.

Margarita led me to a small storeroom not far from the cafeteria. Once I was inside, she closed the door and locked it behind us.

Tense, I leaned against the wall and folded my arms, my eyes glued to her as she leaned against the wall facing me. She also mimicked my stance, folding her own arms and giving me a bitter look. "Logan told me the gist of it, you know."

I braced myself for what was soon to come.

"He hates you," she told me almost conversationally. "So much, in fact, that last night, he came begging to our Lord to pair him up with someone else."

Narrowing my eyes, I tried to pretend I wasn't panicking inside. Not because Logan wanted another partner—that much I knew, for obvious reasons. Rather, it was because *Ragnor* now had absolute confirmation that something bad had gone down between Logan and me in the past.

The one part of my past I really, *really* didn't want Ragnor to know about. Which had led to our current stalemate, which had also led to our recent arguments and fights.

"Our Lord and Magnus were adamant, however, that this is the right decision," Margarita said, not hiding her disgust. "So you and Logan are going to remain partners after all."

She glared at me as if this decision was my fault and said, "I'm warning you, Henderson. Do not interact with Logan more than need be for the training sessions and the Hecatomb. If you do . . ." She gave me an ugly smile. "You'll find out exactly what I'm capable of when you hurt what's mine."

Her words made my already-shit mood sour. "Despite what you and Logan think," I said through clenched teeth, "I have no intention of hurting him in any way. In fact, this whole Hecatomb is about ensuring we all come back in one piece—both mentally and physically. So this threat is quite redundant."

Margarita sneered. "Let's hope you're right," she spit. Moving to the door, she turned the key sharply and pulled it open violently before storming off.

I leaned my head back and took a deep breath. I knew *I* was going to be on my best behavior, but I couldn't say the same about Logan.

Our last fight from many moons ago still rang in my head. "*After all this time, I expected some sort of decency from you,*" he'd growled. "*Shame on me for believing that you had changed. That you might be different. But I was stupid, and that's on me. You are a* fucking *monster. You are exactly what your father made you. And you* can't *change because it's who you are.*"

Facing that kind of attitude, I had a feeling I was in far more danger than he was.

When I entered the allocated training room for me and my Hecatomb partner, Logan was already there, doing push-ups. He didn't look up when I closed the door behind me, nor did he say anything as I took off my shoes and began doing some stretching myself.

A loaded silence spread through the room as we warmed up for far longer than was normally needed. I was reluctant to be the first to make a move. The tension in the room was already severe as it was. I could feel myself freezing up, too, as not-so-irrational fear spread through me. Not just because of the Hecatomb and what our relationship meant when it came to a life-or-death situation but rather because of what our relationship entailed.

Watching him moving up to jumping squats while continuing to ignore me, I felt an old pain flare in my chest. A memory hit me of a time when we were human and we were training together, joking and laughing about, shooting the breeze without a care in the world.

I'd felt so much love for him then. Love I now knew was not really romantic love but love from one human being to another. I'd cared for him. I'd needed him.

Just like I needed him now if I was to survive the Hecatomb.

Each pair had its own trainer. I knew from Zoey that Magnus was her and Cassidy's trainer. It made me wonder if Margarita and Ragnor were also going to be trainers and if one of them was going to be assigned to us.

I was not happy about either of these options.

When the door finally opened, my worries were proved to be justified.

Ragnor strode inside, kicking the door shut behind him, and shrugged off his trench coat as he headed to the front of the room. He threw the coat aside, kicked off his shoes, and focused his midnight blue gaze on Logan.

Logan straightened and gazed back, his face set in a bitter yet resolute expression.

"Let's make sure all three of us are on the same page," Ragnor said without preamble, still not looking at me as he leaned against the wall. "Logan, you're aware of Aileen's expertise with Iovan's Imperium."

It wasn't a question. It was a statement that I felt was directed as a dig at me. I inwardly flinched while Logan bobbed his head once sharply.

Ragnor's eyes flashed neon so suddenly, I couldn't help but outwardly wince. "Then this will make it easier," he said almost sarcastically. "Logan, since you're Aileen's partner, then you must know the following detail." He barely glanced at me before fixing his gaze on Logan again. "Aileen is Sacred."

Logan stared at Ragnor with an impassive look for a few long moments before it seemed Ragnor's words finally computed. His lips curled downward, and he reluctantly turned to glower at me, as if it were *my* fault. "Is she now?" he snarled.

I looked away, shaking with anger. Ragnor actively ignoring me did not bode well. Neither did Logan's reaction to the news Ragnor shared *without* consulting me. Then there was the tension thick in the air, suffocating me.

"She can stop time," Ragnor now said offhandedly. "I don't recommend she use it during your round, but it will be good if she has it ready just in case. Now that you know, her time stopping won't work on you."

"Time stopping," Logan murmured, glowering at the floor. "Of course she just had to be different . . ."

Ragnor's face turned murderous.

And I was through. "Can you not talk about me as if I'm not in the room?" I snapped, fury rising inside me.

Ragnor and Logan ignored me. "Let's focus on general training for now," Ragnor said, his voice as angry as he looked. "In two days, we'll start the group training, and you'll sharpen your cooperative skills while facing the other pairs in mock battles. So for now, let's start with the basics of Iovan's Imperium."

Logan scowled. "Can't we use another method?"

"Since you're versed in it to a certain degree, I believe this method to be best," Ragnor said. "Of course, we won't neglect other methods. But let's start with this one as the basis of the strategy we need to develop for you to use in the Hecatomb."

Logan's dissatisfaction was evident. I, too, was growing angrier as the minutes ticked by. Part of me wanted to leave the room and escape this suffocating tension. Another part wanted to hit both of them for ignoring me and acting as if I were nothing but air.

But I forced myself to practice patience. This was too important to let myself stoop to their level of pettiness. So even if they wanted to act this way for the entire training, I had to be the bigger person and swallow my anger.

So for the rest of the training, while Ragnor basically instructed Logan, with both of them avoiding talking to me at all costs, I gritted my teeth and focused on the training only.

Despite the evident animosity between the three of us, we managed to outline some sort of strategy for the Hecatomb. With Ragnor's chilly suggestions and Logan's monosyllabic responses, we at least managed to communicate, albeit poorly.

I'd been on my best behavior. I'd taken the high road. But the moment training was over and the two men got ready to go, I couldn't restrain myself any longer.

"You really want me to die, don't you?"

Both men stopped what they were doing.

Furious, I walked toward them. "I allowed it for this session," I said quietly, my hackles rising, "but next time you decide to act like I don't exist, or like I'm public enemy number one, I'm not going to stay silent."

Ragnor was the first one to look at me, his eyes devoid of emotion. I glared back. "I know you both feel wronged by me. I'm deeply sorry for that. But that doesn't excuse your behavior. You two should know better. Especially you," I snapped at Ragnor. "You're supposed to be older than dirt, aren't you? Then act your fucking age, old man."

I turned my glare to Logan, who was now staring at a spot beyond my shoulder. "And you, Logan," I said, my voice trembling. "I know you have issues with me. But please put them aside until after we make it out alive in the Hecatomb. After that, you can go back to treating me like I don't exist, but at least until then, treat me like your Hecatomb partner."

I didn't wait for them to respond. I took my leave before either of them could speak, feeling a wave of exhaustion draping itself over me.

But beyond all that was hurt. Not because of Logan, though that hurt in its own way, but because of Ragnor. Because despite everything we'd been through, he'd never behaved like this before. He'd never utterly ignored me.

And that scared me far more than the prospect of dying in the Hecatomb.

CHAPTER 22
AILEEN

That afternoon, Ragnor wasn't the one who waited for me near the cafeteria entrance. Instead, Magnus was there, drawing attention from most female—and some male—vampires, who openly salivated over his admittedly godly looks.

When he saw me, he waved his hand and I approached him, feeling my anger from before blooming again. "Hey," he said when I stopped before him. "I'll be training you today."

"I figured," I murmured, clenching my hands into fists. "Where's Ragnor?"

Magnus seemed pained. "Look, I don't know what's going on with you two," he said quietly, "but whatever it is, I recommend you fix it sooner rather than later. We're heading to the Hecatomb in a few days," he added, "and you should really not let your issues be your undoing."

With those eerie words, and my distress already rising the closer the Hecatomb got, Magnus took me to Ragnor's town house, and the training commenced.

Knowing Magnus was right, I decided to see Ragnor that evening. I was still beyond furious with him, not to mention extremely hurt by his behavior, but the Hecatomb was almost upon us. I had to make sure things were at least amiable between us if not fixed entirely.

So instead of heading straight to the suite, I went to his office. His secretaries, however, told me he wasn't there.

I looked for him in the cafeteria, but he wasn't there, either, so I headed to the Troop gym, hoping to find him there.

And I did find him there.

Just not alone.

Hiding behind the wall, I did the mature thing and eavesdropped.

"You can talk to me," Margarita said to Ragnor in the training room we'd been in that morning. "You've always talked to me before."

Her pleading, whiny voice made my fury worse. I really couldn't stand that woman.

"This is different, Margie," Ragnor said, and the fact he called her by a nickname made pain hit me deep. He hardly ever called me by a nickname. Perhaps he called me "baby" once or twice, but he never gave me an actual nickname.

Asshole.

"What's so different?" Margarita asked, frustrated. "She's just another lover for you. I know you, my Lord." Her voice turned bitter. "When things get complicated, you leave. So why don't you leave her now?"

A deep sigh followed before Ragnor said softly, "I don't think I can talk about this with you, Margie, of all people."

His words gave me pause.

"My Lord," Margarita whispered, and I could hear the hurt in her voice. "Tell me. I can take it. You talked to me about Ilona all those years ago. And about Parvati, and Naima . . ."

My heart rate picked up.

"Those times were different," Ragnor murmured. "Look, I don't need your help. Thank you for worrying about me, but I can handle this on my own."

I could hear Margarita growl. "I don't get it!" she snapped. "Why her? What's so special about this woman that two powerful men are going so crazy over her?!"

"*Two* men?" Ragnor inquired, and I could feel my heart come to a chilling stop.

"Yes, my Lord, it's not just you that this . . . this *woman* is manipulating," Margarita hissed. "She also leads Logan on as if she owns him. In his training with me earlier today, he was so angry, he almost hurt himself!"

I felt myself shaking at her words, almost unable to compute what she was saying. When the hell did I "manipulate" either of them?

"Margarita," Ragnor said quietly, "do you know about her relationship with him too?"

My throat clogged as my fury quickly changed into pure, undiluted panic.

"Of course I do," Margarita said haughtily. "Logan told me *everything*. That woman is a fucking nightmare, my Lord. The things she did to him . . ."

I couldn't listen to this anymore. I pushed myself off the wall and was about to leave when I suddenly lost my balance on a stair and fell down, causing quite the noise. I hadn't noticed before, but that conversation made me weak in my knees in all the wrong ways.

Before I managed to lift myself back up to my feet and get the hell out of there, I heard footsteps behind me. "Aileen?"

Tears clouded my eyes as I stood up, my back to Ragnor. "So it's not okay when I don't tell you something, but it's totally fine when you hide things from me too?" I couldn't stop myself from saying it. "It's good to know just where we stand."

"Aileen—"

I whirled around and glowered at him, not caring that Margarita was right there behind him. "Did you ever plan to tell me you and your

Lieutenant had been in a relationship once?" Because that's what it was. That's why Margarita had been so possessive of him before. Why it took me so long to realize that, I didn't know. "And what about those other girls she mentioned? What about *your* past? Did you ever plan to tell me more about it?"

Ragnor's face contorted in anger, but I didn't care. "Save it," I sniped before I walked away.

Unfortunately, he didn't just let me leave, because he followed me and grabbed my wrist to stop me when we were outside the Troop's gym. "Let's talk," he said, forcing me to look at him with his hand grabbing my chin. "We can't keep talking in circles like this—"

"I don't want to talk to you anymore," I cut him off with a snarl and swatted his hands away from me. "You're a piece of shit, Ragnor."

He grabbed my hand again, and this time he forced me to follow, not letting me go. When I saw he was leading me to his suite, I felt as if an invisible pressure had locked itself around my neck.

I didn't want to go back there.

But Ragnor manhandled me into his suite and closed the door behind us.

Caging me.

"Aileen," he said, grabbing my shoulders when I tried to put some distance between us. "We've got to talk."

To my horror, the tears fell on my cheeks. I was in pain. So much pain that I couldn't think straight.

Any rationality I'd had before was gone.

Talking? There was no need to talk anymore. I knew exactly where we stood now. What else was there to talk about?

"You don't love me, Ragnor," I told him with a hollow feeling that made me cry harder. "I refuse to believe that this is how you express your love."

Ragnor's eyes flashed in fury. "Like hell I don't love you," he growled, grabbing my face. "It's because I love you that you drive me fucking insane, Aileen."

Everything I'd been feeling in the last week and a half surged inside me, causing any lingering rebellious spirit to leave my body, replaced by numbness. "I can't do this anymore," I whispered. "I can't, Ragnor."

"I can't either," he said, leaning his forehead against mine. "Please, Aileen . . . Let's stop this futile fight."

"How?" My voice broke. "How can we stop when we can't seem to see eye to eye?"

"Because I love you, and you love me," he said plainly. "Isn't that all that matters?"

I laughed bitterly and leaned back, staring at his eyes. "Do we *really* love each other, though?"

His eyes glowed as he growled, "We do. Or at least, I know *I* do." He paused, peering at me with what looked almost like panic. "Don't you?"

Did I?

Did I love this man, who broke me almost beyond repair and yet built me up in a way no one else ever did?

Did I love this man, who wanted me to strip myself bare while remaining clothed and yet offered comfort and warmth when I was most vulnerable?

Did I love Ragnor Rayne, who'd forced me into my vampiric existence, sold me to the enemy at the Auction, and yet all but begged me to take him back? Who was willing to go to war for my sake?

And suddenly, all the arguments and fights we'd had in the past few days, all the disagreements and disappointments—it all diminished when I looked at everything in the grand scheme of things.

My shoulders slumped and my head fell. "I do," I whispered, the fighting spirit leaving me. "I love you." *So much that it hurts.*

His arms wrapped around me as he embraced me close, cradling my head against his chest. "I love you, Aileen," he murmured into my hair, squeezing me tight. "I'm sorry. Let's drop this whole thing, Aileen. We don't need to know everything about each other's past—not if it risks our relationship."

He was right. I knew he was right. And I also knew I would live to regret it if I didn't stop it from going further.

Just earlier today, I'd seen Jada crying on Bowen's shoulder. I'd also watched CJ between trainings, and he seemed to grow more gaunt and worried the closer the Hecatomb got. The relationship between the two of them seemed all but over.

Instead of spending the time they had left until the Hecatomb together, in each other's arms, they spent it by avoiding each other at all costs.

And while I couldn't judge them, since I was not in their shoes, I could judge myself and my own relationship.

Would I be able to live with myself if I headed to the Hecatomb without ever patching things up with Ragnor?

And I had my answer.

I squeezed him back at his rare apology. "I agree. I'm sorry too."

He leaned his head back, stared into my eyes, and caressed my cheek before drawing near and closing his lips over mine.

The soft yet rough touch of his kiss made me shudder and sigh, as if it was all I'd been waiting for this past week.

I deepened the kiss, wrapping my arms around his neck, pressing my chest against his and giving in to the abrupt, strong desire thrumming through my veins. And when he responded in kind, his hand grabbing the nape of my neck while his thigh shoved between mine, his knee rubbing against my clothed crotch, I was suddenly desperate for him.

Silently, we shrugged off our shirts and pulled each other's pants down, as if battling over who could get the other naked first, while our kiss grew deeper, faster, and far more furious than before.

Our frustration with each other, which we might've agreed to bury, burst out the moment his unsheathed, hardened length pressed against my entrance. A switch flipped inside us, and we were suddenly grappling with one another, each of us trying to get on top of the other.

As our tongues danced, his hands found my breasts and squeezed, making me gasp into his mouth. That gave him the leverage he needed to push me onto my back, forcing my legs apart in such a rough way that it made my already dripping pussy even wetter, and thrust hard and deep inside me.

I moaned, and he used the momentum to bite my lower lip, hard, almost bruising it, as he began to move inside me, his hands gliding over my thighs as he pushed my legs up toward my head, giving him the full view and access to my most intimate part.

And when he leaned back, finally letting my lips go, his grip on my thighs tightened, and he began to really move.

It was fast, rough, and hard. All I could do was lie there, immobile, as he fucked me into oblivion and beyond, my eyes rolling up in abysmal pleasure as I moaned loud enough to wake the dead, the tension inside me rising, pulling at my stomach, and building up to my quickening heart.

And when I finally shattered, the orgasm rippling through me so strongly I spasmed, Ragnor had no choice but to growl as he emptied himself inside me for many long moments.

When he pulled out, I could feel his cum dripping out along with my own juices, and when I saw his midnight blue eyes, now neon with his recent release, watching the trail of cum out of my pussy, I spasmed again as a mini orgasm hit me out of nowhere.

His face grew ravenous, and when my eyes dropped to his beautiful dick, I could see he was hard again, precum creaming the head.

For the next few hours, all we could do was fuck. I was on my hands and knees, then riding him, then lying with my back pressed to him as he entered me from behind, and yet the desperation we had for one another, mixed with things we'd left unsaid, made it feel as though there weren't enough orgasms in the world that could be enough to satiate this infinite hunger.

In the end, what forced us to stop was sheer exhaustion. With the room smelling heavily like sex and the sheets damp from all the coming we had done, he hugged me close to him, bare chest to bare chest, and we fell asleep like that together, clinging to one another.

Nothing was really resolved; that much I knew. But after the night we had, I felt like maybe we could get past this issue and find peace as a couple again.

CHAPTER 23
AILEEN

I felt the stares as Ragnor and I walked into the cafeteria the next morning. It wasn't because we were seen together but because we were holding hands.

When Ragnor grabbed my hand after we left the suite, I had been startled, but I said nothing. Now, as Ragnor took me to an empty table (thankfully not in the served area), I realized that he'd decided to officially go public.

Before yesterday's fight, I would've been angry at him for making this decision all by himself without consulting me. But now, after spending the night in his arms and waking up to see his beautiful face smiling at me, I was actually flattered.

Because it meant Ragnor was through with us being discreet and wanted to show the whole world I was his, and he was mine. And that made me feel all kinds of warm and fuzzy inside.

When it came to Ragnor, I was far too easy.

Once we settled on our table, Ragnor turned to me with his pretty eyes and said, "Care to brew me some coffee, dear?"

I arched an eyebrow. "Dear? Really?"

He grinned, looking more relaxed than I'd seen him in a while. "Please?"

Sighing, I shook my head and let go of his hand. "Fine. Anything else, oh dear husband from the sixties?"

Chuckling, he placed his coat on a chair and said, "I'll get us some food. Eggs and bacon?"

I couldn't help myself, so I stood on my tiptoes and kissed his cheek. "You know me so well, darlin'."

When I was about to head to the coffee station, he pulled me toward him and, with a smirk, pressed his lips against mine. Butterflies filled my stomach as electricity shot through my veins, making me weak in the knees and need to hold on to his shirt for balance. His hands grabbed my waist, making me shudder slightly.

I heard whistles and catcalls all around us, and while I wished I could deepen the kiss and have a full-blown make-out session with him, this was neither the time nor the place. So I pulled back, flushed and a little too excited, and smiled at him. "Later," I promised, pulling out of his grasp.

He grinned before he headed to the buffet.

I took the time making coffee to collect myself. I was of half a mind to go back to the suite and change into dry underwear, but that would've been overkill, I guessed.

When the coffee was ready, I walked back to the table and saw Ragnor sprawled over his chair and nibbling on a piece of bread as he looked at me. Why did I find that hot?

Forcing my reawakened libido down, I cleared my throat and handled the coffee carefully as I grabbed my seat on the other side of the table. "They were out of O minus, so I put O plus instead," I told him when I pushed the mug toward him. "Hope that's okay."

He frowned at me, and for a moment I wondered if the change was that drastic, until he suddenly moved to the chair next to mine. "I don't like you sitting so far," he murmured almost petulantly as he grabbed the mug and sipped, his arm spread over the back of my chair possessively.

Feeling giddy at his uncharacteristic boyish, immature behavior, I did my best to keep my cool exterior as I ate my breakfast.

It didn't help that Ragnor pushed his thigh against mine under the table constantly while his hand behind my back played with my ponytail.

After so many days of going to sleep alone and being ignored and avoided by him, this situation almost felt like a dream. But I was determined not to let my bitterness fester.

We needed to get a handle on the Hecatomb situation first before we let ourselves work through our relationship issues.

Once breakfast was over, Ragnor said, "I'm heading to the office for a bit. Please start training with Logan until I arrive."

I nodded, and when I saw the worry in his eyes, I cupped his face and gave him a soft, chaste kiss. "Thank you," I said, holding his midnight blue gaze. *For not asking me any more questions about Logan.*

He gave me a somewhat pained smile in return. "I learned my lesson," he said somewhat sadly before giving me another kiss and leaving in the direction of his office.

When I arrived at the training room, Logan was already there, only this time, he wasn't doing stretches. Instead, he seemed to have been waiting for me, seeing as he was leaning against the wall with folded arms, his eyes on me the moment I walked through the door.

Before I could even close it behind me, Logan said, "You were right."

Immediately alert, I cautiously stepped toward him. "About what?"

"We need to work together if we don't want to die," he said bluntly, scowling. "Though I can't deny that I hate that we were paired up."

I nodded slowly, heart racing. "I understand."

His eyes flashed and I froze in my place. "You understand?" he said, voice dropping an octave. "*You* understand?"

Fuck.

"Logan," I said, attempting to sound calm despite my voice growing small and tense as anxiety covered my skin with perspiration. "I meant to say that I understand why—"

"You understand shit," he snapped, cutting me off, as he pushed himself off the wall and strode toward me menacingly. My instincts told me to step back, but I held my ground, even when he was all but in my face. "Just looking at you takes my entire mental capacity to deal with. Hearing your voice is even worse. It feels like I die inside every fucking time, and if this goes on, your mere presence will finish me off before the Hecatomb has a chance to."

His words cut deep, right at the guilt I would forever feel when it came to him. I began to shiver, distressed, as I whispered, "Logan—"

"And now I have to see you acting all lovey-dovey with our Lord?" he said incredulously, laughing humorlessly. "What a fucking joke."

I flinched, and he leaned forward, his nose almost touching mine. "So I thought hard about how I can fucking cooperate with *you* for the sake of the Hecatomb," he snarled, turquoise eyes glowing a bright neon green. "And I decided there is only one way."

Sudden dread filled me as I saw the intent in his eyes, followed by his hands grabbing my face roughly, making me grit my teeth. "I need to give back as good as you gave me over three years ago," he said, and before I could get over the shock, his lips crashed against mine.

Motherfucker, I thought in panic as he bit my lip to force my mouth open and let his tongue in. My dread transformed into pure hysteria as I grabbed his shoulders and tried to get him off me, shaking with anger and fear.

But Logan was strong and shoved my hands away, wrapping his arms around both my body and arms. I tried to press my lips together and refuse him entry a second time, but then I saw him unsheathing his fangs and lowering his head to my neck, his fangs grazing against my skin.

"*Stop*!" I screamed, trying to shake him off, thrashing against his almost unbreakable hold as tears welled in my eyes. *"Logan, stop!"*

His fangs tore my skin, and I screamed in rage as I felt him take a sip of my blood.

And so the only thing I could do was scream in my mind, *Stop him!*

A soft pounding in my head, followed by Logan's sudden immobility, made me suck in a breath.

Did it work? Did I manage to stop time, along with Logan, who knew about my time-stopping ability?

Seeing as Logan wasn't moving, I decided to ask questions later. Wriggling out of his hold, I shoved him away and released myself from his fangs and clutches. My hand went to my neck, feeling the blood still trickling, while I looked at Logan. I was both terrified and furious.

What the hell had just happened?

Pain slowly built in my head, but I knew I could hold on for at least twenty seconds more, thanks to my training with Ragnor. So I held on while I tried to figure out the situation.

Did Logan think that by assaulting me back, he would be relieved of his trauma?

The fury exploded inside me, and I had to hold myself back from striking him. Because deep down, beyond my anger, I knew I deserved it. He was a victim of *my* past choices.

Everything in me wanted to respond in kind. To attack him back. To tear into him for what he'd just done.

My instincts and emotions battled with rationality. Because the rational part of me knew I had to let it go if I were to work with him and survive the Hecatomb.

But could we really do this? What if Logan did it again? What if this was a warning that he would abandon me when the actual Hecatomb happened?

Taking a few deep breaths, calming my racing heart and forcing my anxieties down and away, I cautiously thought, *Release,* and watched as Logan fell on his knees, fighting for breath, whipping his head up, looking so inhuman with glowing eyes and fangs still coated in blood.

He was no longer the Logan I knew.

Just like I was no longer the Aileen he knew.

"Did you get it out of your system?" I asked, unable to hide my disgust but successfully masking my own fears.

Logan growled in response, slowly rising to his feet, eyes flashing as if to say, *Hell no*.

I braced myself, preparing for defense against an attack. Because I wouldn't let him get close to me a second time. There was a limit to how much I could sacrifice and suffer to make him feel better.

But suddenly the glow in Logan's eyes dimmed and he sheathed his fangs. Confused, all I could do was stare at him, fearing it might be a tactic to get my guard down, until I heard the door open.

Wiping the blood on my hand with my black shirt and pulling my ponytail over my shoulder to hide the bite mark, I turned around to see Ragnor entering. His eyes narrowed, probably feeling the unbearable tension in the air. "What's going on?" he asked at once.

"Nothing, my Lord," Logan answered immediately. "Aileen and I were just discussing optional techniques that we could use in our strategy in addition to Iovan's Imperium."

I had to physically stop myself from gaping at him. The Logan I knew couldn't think of lies to save his life. This shocked me far more than it probably should have.

Ragnor glanced between Logan and me a few times in silence before he nodded and said, "All right, then. Tell me what you were thinking about."

For the next twenty minutes, Logan laid down what seemed to be an extremely well thought-out tactic that made me realize he'd thought about it prior to our training. All I could do was stand there, unable to look at either of the men as I was still reeling from what had just happened with Logan, and listen as he detailed the idea.

I did manage to gather that this strategy, in essence to divide and conquer—keeping my powers under wraps until a case of emergency, if either of our lives was at risk—was probably the best we could come up with when it came to fighting together in the Hecatomb. We still needed to work together, but at least we would each be facing another foe instead of standing together.

Nearing the end of the training, though, I began losing my focus as Logan's assault took over my mind, and I was so out of it, Ragnor kept sending questioning looks my way.

But Ragnor asked me nothing. Not when we had lunch together, nor when we went to his town house for private training. In fact, he followed my act of "business as usual" right up until it was late at night, when we were in his suite.

That's when our fragile peace threatened to break.

CHAPTER 24
RAGNOR

Ragnor traced Aileen's figure with his hand as the two lay in bed, facing each other silently. Ragnor could tell she was on edge, even though she was in his bed, showered and supposedly relaxed. There was caution in her hazel eyes that had been there the entire day, ever since the morning training with Logan.

He'd debated whether he should broach that topic. Talking about her relationship with Logan had become a minefield. Ragnor did not want to go back to the way they had behaved before making up the night before.

But he also knew this couldn't go on.

"Talk to me," he murmured, drawing her eyes to his, his hand stopping on her waist.

She grimaced. "Ragnor . . ."

Her hesitation made a spark of anger light up inside him, but he pushed it away. "We can make an exchange," he offered. "You tell me about Logan, and I'll tell you about . . ." This time, he hesitated, before he forced out, "Yulia."

Just uttering the name made him feel all sorts of things, but he was determined. Because Aileen had been right. It had been unfair of him to ask her to tell him everything, when he refused to offer anything in return.

He could only hope that this would be enough.

Aileen stared at him for a few long moments before she said, "Logan and I dated for four years when we were in school."

Since he already knew as much, the news didn't come as a surprise. What made him tense was the fact that he had a hunch where this was going, and he didn't know if he was truly ready to hear.

But when Aileen huddled closer to him, resting her head against his chest, and told him about this part of her convoluted history, all he could do was wrap his arms around her, lean his chin on top of her head, and listen.

"I've never been in love with him," she told him quietly, "merely infatuated with his good looks and naivety. When the two of us met when we were thirteen years old, he was as ordinary as every boy while I . . . was not."

Squeezing her tightly, Ragnor remained silent, listening as Aileen finally opened up about the secret she'd been hiding for so long.

CHAPTER 25
AILEEN

I told Ragnor everything.

How Logan took my side when other kids at school attempted to bully me for my father being in jail at the time. How I practically forced him to have sex with me at too young an age. How our relationship deteriorated into the realms of dysfunctionality and toxicity.

And then, I told him about that one night that changed everything.

"I tortured him," I whispered, burying my head in his chest, unable to look at his face as I shared this next part. The part I'd been fighting not to talk about. The part I wished I could bury and forget forever. "There's no other word for it, really. It was torture. And I was . . . I was *excited*, Ragnor. I was so sick that I *loved* him giving me this power to mentally, physically, and sexually torture him."

"Aileen," Ragnor murmured, hugging me tight but somehow not tight enough for me to feel safe from my own past mistakes.

I shook my head. "I know what I did. I'm not stupid. I acted the same way I'd seen my father act numerous times. I acted like the monster Logan now sees me as. The same monster I know, deep inside, I truly am."

The monster Logan kept claiming I was, and rightfully so.

"You're not a monster, Aileen," Ragnor said, leaning back so he could cup my face and raise it so I would look at him. "What you did was wrong. I won't deny it. But you grew up in a horrible environment that showed you these things were okay. That's the only reason why you turned out the way you did. You have to show yourself some mercy."

I gave him a small, bitter smile that made Ragnor's arms squeeze around me. "I might forgive my actions when I was far too young to understand things properly," I said quietly, "but I was seventeen when I did that to Logan. I can never, *ever* forgive myself for that, nor do I intend to."

My words lingered for a few long moments in the air before he pressed his lips to my forehead, his touch gentle and warm. "I'm truly sorry you had to go through that," he murmured against my skin. "I'm sorry I didn't find you sooner."

I leaned back to look at him with sudden caution. "Logan still bears a lot of resentment toward me," I murmured, pained, "which I don't have the right to blame him for. But he . . . tried something earlier."

Ragnor stilled, gaze sharpening. "What did he do?"

Looking away, I sucked in a breath and said, "He . . . well, we fought, and he . . . kissed me."

He tensed, gaze turning into a full-on glare. "Did you kiss him back?"

I shook my head vehemently and cupped his face. "No, Ragnor, I didn't," I said hastily, "and I'm only telling you this so you know I don't hide anything from you. But please don't make this into a big deal. I plan to deal with Logan on my own. He's *my* problem."

I could tell Ragnor hated hearing this, thanks to the little twitch in his eye. "He touched you against your will," he bit out, glowering at my lips. "And you expect me to let it go?"

"Please," I whispered and pressed my lips against his softly. "Do this for me. *Please.*"

Please have faith in me. Trust me. Believe in me, I begged silently. *Please.*

CHAPTER 26
RAGNOR

Her lips taunted him, and he couldn't stop himself from grabbing her hair and crashing his lips deeper against hers, biting on her lip to gain access inside her mouth, to entangle his tongue with hers. She gasped, her hands grabbed his shoulders, and Ragnor felt his cock grow hard.

Because he was going to fuck her tonight hard enough that he'd leave a mark.

A mark Logan wouldn't be able to *not* see the next day.

Feeling a vicious kind of arousal, Ragnor pushed Aileen onto her back and devoured her mouth while his hands roamed under her flimsy tank top, cupping her bare breasts. She moaned, her legs almost automatically spreading to cradle him between her thighs, and Ragnor's cock threatened to tear through his sweatpants.

He tore her top off and released her lips in favor of her hard nipple, which he took into his mouth and sucked on. She gasped, her back bowing as if she wanted him to suck harder, which he gladly did.

And while he fondled that breast, he quickly got her shorts and panties off, revealing her gloriously slick pussy, just waiting to be ravished by his mouth and cock. Unable to allay his craving, Ragnor pushed her thighs up, bringing her pussy to his mouth, and gave her a long, languorous lick, from her tight entrance to the pebbled clit, where he closed his teeth carefully around the bud and sucked.

Aileen screamed and thrashed against his unbreakable hold, which made Ragnor feel quite triumphant. He then wondered how she would react to some vampiric play in bed. Deciding to test it on a whim, he unsheathed his fangs and, as carefully as he could, sank them into the sensitive skin around her clit.

Her hands were in his hair as she screamed yet again, a flood spraying right into his mouth as she came, shuddering and shattering under his hands and mouth.

Ragnor couldn't help but smirk. It seemed his sexy Alara Morreh loved some blood play in bed.

And that turned him on even more than he was before.

He released her only so he could quickly get rid of his pants before he was looming over her, his hands fondling her plump, smooth breasts, as he settled his aching dick against her wet entrance. Her eyes were partially lidded as she looked at him, lips parted, fighting to catch her breath.

That look was so arousing, he almost came right then and there.

But Ragnor refused to end things so quickly. So in one thrust, he buried himself to the hilt inside her warm, silky pussy that fit him like a glove, and felt like he'd just come home.

And as he fucked her hard and rough, he sank his fangs into the areola of her breast, causing her to moan and thrash against him, needy and sweet and oh so delectable.

She felt so good—too good to be true, almost—that he wanted to keep fucking her forever, not letting her go even once.

But when he shoved himself inside her one last time, he couldn't help but come, pouring his seed into her pussy, claiming her as his yet again, but not enough to appease the slumbering beast inside him.

So before she regained her composure and they were forced to talk about another uncomfortable topic, Ragnor claimed her again, and again, and again, until the clock showed it was morning already, and there was no time left to completely satiate his endless hunger when it came to Aileen Henderson.

CHAPTER 27
AILEEN

My entire body ached—and not just from another day of training.

Last night, Ragnor had fucked me as if it was our last night on Earth.

And I'd loved every moment of it.

Unfortunately, it meant we hadn't slept a wink, and so I was already exhausted when it was time for the morning training session, this time with the rest of the participants.

Thankfully, Logan acted as if nothing happened yesterday and treated me coldly, if at all, as usual. I did notice him glancing at my neck a few times, though, where Ragnor had given me a huge hickey that practically told the world I'd just been relentlessly pounded the night before.

Which, in all honesty, I didn't mind. Even if Logan's face grew dark every time his eyes rested on that spot.

That afternoon, Ragnor brought Magnus along for the private training session, which went fine enough, considering I was far too tired to be able to exert mental prowess over my time-stopping powers. Magnus was a great help, as always, and Ragnor was in such a good mood, everything went smoothly.

Until Magnus left earlier than usual, leaving Ragnor and me to drive privately together back to the League.

Part of me wanted to keep this heady feeling of being in love and thoroughly fucked. It put both Ragnor and me in the best moods we'd been in for a while.

But I didn't forget that he owed me something in return for me telling him about Logan, and about another dark part of my past.

So despite my reluctance, I glanced at Ragnor, who was driving with a small smile on his face I was sure he wasn't aware of, took in a deep breath, and said, "Tell me about Yulia."

And just like that, the air in the SUV filled with spiky tension.

My words wiped Ragnor's smile off his face, replaced by a somber look that made me wish I hadn't spoken in the first place. For a few moments, I thought he might not speak at all, maybe dismiss it or try to delay the inevitable, but to my utter relief and dread, Ragnor said, "All right."

Instead of continuing the drive, Ragnor parked on the side of the road and turned to me. "Keep in mind it's a story of a time before I became a vampire," he told me quietly, and I stilled. I didn't think Ragnor had ever spoken to me of his time as a human, and a sense of excitement reverberated through me.

He let out a breath and said, "It's been more than a millennium," he said, "around the time of an era humans call the early Middle Ages, not long after the fall of the Western Roman Empire in the year four seventy-six."

The fact that Ragnor was old was never a question, but it suddenly occurred to me just *how* old he was.

"I met Yulia in one of the tribes that settled north of the Black Sea, a region that we know today as southern Ukraine, though back then it was home to several tribes and trade routes rather than an established state," Ragnor said, and while he looked at me, I could tell his gaze was faraway. "Yulia was an outcast in the tribe for being barren. She was used solely for the pleasure of the tribesmen and nothing more, because of her immense beauty."

My chest ached a little at his words, but I ignored it and asked, "How did you two meet?"

Ragnor gave me a wistful smile. "I was . . . passing through the trade route near the tribe," he said quietly, "and I saw her from afar, collecting herbs in the field, dressed in rags. She was very hard to miss." His smile disappeared. "I was young then. Barely out of my juvenile years. And she was the first woman I'd ever seen. I thought no one could ever compare."

I felt self-conscious then as I wondered just how beautiful Yulia was for him to practically wax poetic about her.

He looked away. "When I saw a tribesman grabbing her just as I was about to pass, tearing her clothes for all to see and attempting to rape her under the cold sun of winter, I couldn't stand idly by. I saved her then, and when my eyes met her beautiful silver ones, I was done for."

Returning his gaze to me, his face grew serious. "There were many reasons I won't get into as to why a relationship with a . . . woman I met on the road was not exactly good for me," he said, voice lower than before. "But when I met Yulia, I lost all sense of reason and, for the first time in my life back then, defied my core rules.

"We ran away together and lived in hiding."

I opened my mouth, with so many questions running through my mind, but he shook his head, telling me it wasn't the time for questions just yet. Clamping my mouth shut, I anxiously waited to hear the rest.

"Yulia and I only spent one year together," Ragnor said, leaning back against his chair. "But that year was the happiest in my life at the time. She was everything I wanted, everything I wished for, and she was in love with me just as fiercely too."

Ugly feelings rose inside me, but I was determined to ignore them as I listened.

"But all good things come to an end, and ours was no different," Ragnor said with a hint of sorrow that made me feel as if he'd sucker punched me. It took away my breath. "Her people found us, and so did mine. We were physically torn apart."

He lowered his gaze. "Later, I learned that Yulia was executed, and when I went to search for her, unbelieving that this was the truth, I found her corpse hung from a tree, as if to warn the tribespeople of what their end would be if they rejected the tribe's rules."

When he turned to look back at me, the sorrow in his eyes was even more prevalent than before. "I've never loved anyone after Yulia," he said quietly. "I was infatuated and attracted to other women, sure, but love was beyond me. The terror of losing the one thing that meant something to me, and in such a brutal, horrible way, left its scar, a scar I never tried to take care of, and I let it fester."

He grabbed my hand then, threading his fingers with mine. "Until you came, Aileen."

My very soul shuddered at his story, at his words. I'd never expected that something so terrible happened to Ragnor when it came to love. And while I had many questions, none of those mattered when I saw the truth in his eyes.

He meant everything he'd said.

I leaned forward, grabbed his face, and gently kissed him. "Thank you for telling me," I said, meaning it. I knew that it must've taken a significant effort for him to show me this vulnerable side, and I appreciated that he did it in spite of himself, just to keep his word.

And especially, I was relieved that he trusted me enough to share his past with me, no matter how hard and tragic it was.

CHAPTER 28
RAGNOR

That night, as Aileen lay naked in his arms after he'd had his wicked way with her, Ragnor felt a pang of guilt that didn't allow him to sleep.

While the essence of what he'd told Aileen about Yulia was true, he'd altered the details and lied.

He knew he was being a hypocrite, after she'd bared her soul to him and asked for the same in return, which he adamantly refused to do. But part of it wasn't simply for Ragnor's self-preservation, but rather for her own good too.

If Aileen knew the full truth of his past, of who he used to be when he met Yulia and what Yulia had truly meant to him, there would be no going back.

He loved Aileen. He loved her so much that he wanted to protect her from his own dark past. Which he knew Aileen would argue couldn't be much worse than hers. About which she would also be right.

But the restrictions he had were nothing in comparison.

Because he knew far too much for a mere vampire, even a vampire Lord. If he were to share what he knew, even with Aileen, his lover, his Alara Morreh, then he wouldn't be the only one to suffer the consequences.

He hated that his only way to protect Aileen from dangers beyond her understanding was to lie.

But seeing as she was already in hot water because of her status as the last Child of Kahil, he knew adding to it wouldn't just be unwise but utterly dangerous.

And so Ragnor had to live with his guilt as the cost for keeping his loved one safe.

CHAPTER 29
AILEEN

Ragnor's entire demeanor changed.

I didn't notice it at first, since the day after our talk, Logan and I, along with the other Hecatomb pairs, joined together for an ensemble training session, practicing mock battles and honing our cooperation skills.

Since the cojoined sessions were overseen by Magnus and Margarita rather than Ragnor, I didn't see him until it was time for my private session that evening.

He acted the same as he always did and was affectionate enough to sneak in kisses and some fondling in between practice rounds, but I couldn't help but feel he was keeping a measure of emotional distance.

Perhaps it was because he'd told me something extremely private about himself and he didn't know how to acclimate to feeling vulnerable, or perhaps he regretted telling me in the first place. Whatever it was, it made me feel uneasy.

And unfortunately, my being uneasy showed.

"Fuck, Aileen," Logan growled at me as I landed on my ass after Neisha easily dodged my attack and sent me flying. "What the hell is wrong with you today?"

"Nothing," I snapped at him, scowling as I climbed to my feet. "I'm fine."

Logan glowered at me, eyes glowing. "I thought you wanted us to put our past behind us," he hissed at me quietly enough so only I could hear. "But now you're acting as if I don't exist? Very mature."

His words irked me to no end. In fact, Logan's entire attitude since he'd forced a kiss on me two days prior had been grating on my nerves. I'd done my best to move on from that because we genuinely had no time for such scuffles when the Hecatomb was right around the corner, and yet he acted bitter and cynical every time I dared speak to him.

So now when I wasn't, he suddenly cared? What the fuck was that all about?

"You know, not everything in this world is about you, Logan," I hissed back at him and walked to the table at the far end of the room to grab a bottle of blood.

He followed me. "Then at least be professional and put whatever it is out of the training room," he sniped, as if he were itching for a fight.

And since I wasn't calm enough myself to put a stop to it, I whirled around to face him, only to find he was barely an inch away, his body plastered to mine. "Back off, Logan," I growled in warning, and it wasn't just about the physical proximity.

"No," he said in a low voice, eyes holding mine. "I think it's time we talked and cleared some things up so you won't act like a little bitch."

His sheer *audacity* helped me to momentarily forget Ragnor and focus solely on him. "*I'm* acting like a little bitch?" I said, shocked. "Who's the one that ignored me first? Who's the one who *forced a kiss on me* as if it would get rid of his fucking trauma?"

His face turned thunderous. "*And whose fault is it that I have this trauma?!*" he yelled at me, hands grabbing my shoulders. "*The very least you could do is take fucking responsibility instead of acting as if* I'm *the one at fault!"*

An animalistic growl escaped my throat as I completely lost it. Before I knew what I was doing, I punched his face.

He gave me a humorless, wild smile in return and punched me in return.

Ignoring the pain on my cheek, I screamed in rage and pushed him to the floor, straddling him as I sent my fists flying at his face one after another, seeing red.

Suddenly, someone grabbed me from behind and forcefully took me off him, while I saw Neisha helping Logan to his feet as he spit blood.

I struggled against the hold. "*Let me go!*" I shrieked, thrashing around.

"You've got to calm down, Henderson." I heard Oberon's voice in my ear. Apparently, he was the one who held me. "You don't want to make more of a spectacle out of it than it already is, do you?"

His words made me grow still, fighting to catch my breath, as I was suddenly aware Logan and I were surrounded by the other participants, along with the two Lieutenants.

Fuck, fuck, fuck.

"Let me go," I said breathlessly.

Oberon released me, and I glared at Logan, who was glaring at me back with enough hatred to fill a continent.

A clap of hands drew everyone's attention to Magnus, whose face was grim. "Let's take ten, everyone," he said, glancing briefly at me before he said, "And while I know tensions are high with the upcoming Hecatomb just a couple of days ahead, please do try to restrain yourself and work together with your partners rather than against them."

I looked away, furious with Logan, Magnus, Oberon, and everyone, really—but mostly with myself.

I'd let Logan goad me. And I had no one to blame but myself.

As everyone left the gym, I reached the table and grabbed a blood bottle, drinking its contents almost in one sip. My heart was beating hard in my chest, and I was still feeling the adrenaline from before, along with the need for violence, but this time, I did everything I could to push it all down.

Unfortunately, my efforts were in vain.

"Aileen."

I turned around and felt my barely contained fury threatening to explode when I saw Margarita standing there, her face carefully blank. "Yes?"

"Come with me," she said and turned around, heading to the exit of the gym.

Since I knew ignoring her wouldn't solve whatever this was, I threw the now-empty bottle away and followed her out.

She took me to an empty training room and shut the door behind her before turning to me. I was about to speak when she slapped me.

The violence within me still hadn't dissipated, and I was tempted to succumb to it once more when Margarita's eyes glowed and she said, "It seems you really don't take my warnings seriously."

Cupping my bruised cheek, I glared at her. "This is none of your fucking business, *Lieutenant*," I snarled.

"Logan is my business," she hissed back, "and you dared mar his face with your dirty whore hands."

I barked out a humorless laugh.

Her face grew angry. "Since words don't seem to get through to you, I'll start moving to actions."

"I don't care," I told her truthfully. "So do your worst, Margarita, but don't forget that whatever happened just now with Logan, he still needs me as his partner." When her eye twitched, I grinned. "So I wouldn't recommend roughing me up, if only for his sake."

She growled, but I ignored her, moving past her and outside the room, heading back to the main training facility.

I was done with letting people think they could do whatever they wanted with me. I'd been lenient with Logan for a long time, and for a good reason, but now that it was coming to bite me back in the butt, I could no longer ignore it.

The same went for Margarita. I was through with having others intimidate me as if I were their little lackey.

So for now, I would do everything I could to ignore them and just focus on the mission, which was to survive the Hecatomb.

Anything else could wait.

CHAPTER 30
AILEEN

The cafeteria transformed.

Gone were the buffet and the tables and chairs, and in their stead were a few high-top party tables filled with blood-mixed champagne glasses. Music streamed through a couple of monitors, overseen by one of the League members, who seemed to have been a DJ in his human past. The floor was filled with vampires talking and dancing under decorated letters that dangled from the ceiling, creating the words **GOOD LUCK IN THE HECATOMB!**

"They really went above and beyond, didn't they?" Zoey said from where she, Isora, and I stood near one of the champagne tables.

"It is the last night before you head to your possible doom, after all," Isora said with a shrug, "and many high-profile members are going, like Oberon, Neisha, and Logan."

Isora was right; many members seemed to cluster around the aforementioned three. I knew Logan was popular in the League, but I hadn't realized just how much until now.

Zoey sipped from her glass before she said, "Perhaps I should go mingle as well."

I couldn't help but smile at her words. "Already preparing the ground for when you return victorious?"

She snickered. "Well, I do plan to become a full-fledged member of the Troop once we win this thing, and if possible, I would like to become a Commander."

To be fair, Zoey's ambitions weren't that far-fetched. I heard the talks among the Hecatomb participants during our last few training days. She had the potential to develop a Gift as she grew older in her vampire years. She was just that strong, for a Common.

My eyes went back to Logan, who was smiling and laughing with a few members as he drank a glass of beer. He seemed so young just then, and it occurred to me that he'd once told us in the newcomer course that he'd been given the Imprint three years ago—or a bit over it now, since it had been about seven months since then. Either way, it meant he'd been eighteen at the time, which meant not long after I had left him, Ragnor had given him the Imprint.

I couldn't help but wonder how he even got the Imprint in the first place. Was he on the Waiting List, like all other vampires?

"Hey," Isora said, nudging me with her elbow. I turned to look at her, and her eyes flickered to a point behind my shoulder emphatically. "Someone is coming over."

I turned around to see Jada heading my way. It'd been a while since I last saw her, and it seemed as if it had been years. Her black skin, which normally shone with health, was now completely ashen. Her brilliant gray eyes had sunk into her face, her lips were cracked and dry, and she seemed to have lost too many pounds for a mere week, causing her to look so small under her now oversize clothes.

"Aileen," she said when she approached me after dragging her feet as if she had no energy left in her limbs. "Can we talk?"

Seeing her in this state made my heart race in something akin to panic. "Of course."

"I'll leave you to it," Isora said, taking her glass, and left after a look of concern toward Jada. She didn't even know Jada, but even a stranger could tell the situation was dire.

Jada's sunken eyes peered at me, lacking their usual mischievous glow—or any other emotion, really. "I would like to ask you something," she said in a drawn, lifeless voice.

"Yes," I said, glancing around the room. Where was CJ? Why was he letting his soulmate, or "Alara Morreh" as Jada had told me she was called, off his radar when she looked like the walking dead?

"If CJ dies," she said, making my eyes snap back to hers in shock. She did not seem remotely startled by her own words as she continued. "Please kill me."

My mouth fell open. "I . . . what?" Had I just heard her right?

She shrugged, as if we were talking about the weather. "If a Malachi dies, their Alara Morreh will continue to live in suffering. I want to avoid that. So please kill me if it comes to that."

I was at a loss for words. I did not want to kill Jada, no matter her circumstances. She had no idea what she was asking of me—or of anyone, really.

But even though I wanted to refuse, to object, to tell her I wouldn't do it, the look in her eyes made me come to a searing, unbearable pause. Because I recognized that look. I'd seen that look too many times in my past.

She looked like the girls my father tortured.

Utterly hopeless.

And so the only thing I could say was, "All right." Because back then, I couldn't give those girls the peaceful death they deserved. And while Jada's circumstances were vastly different, her eyes told me she was feeling just as tortured, albeit a different type of torture.

Jada nodded and then walked away; conversation done.

I wished I knew how to reach out to her and make it all okay. I wished I could tell her that CJ wouldn't die, that he would prevail, that this promise was redundant.

But I knew better than most that words were empty, and actions spoke far louder. And I couldn't promise CJ, or anyone else but Ragnor, would make it out alive.

Ragnor was packing when I entered the suite later that evening. I had already packed earlier, so I simply sat in the living room and watched as he neatly folded his clothes and put them in the open backpack.

"How was the party?" he asked me with a small smile. Ragnor had made a brief appearance at the beginning of the party just to say a few words but had disappeared to his office right after to tie up a few last things before he left his secretaries in charge until his return.

"It was all right," I said, thinking about Jada. The truth was, it wasn't. Nothing about it was all right.

I felt as though I'd neglected my friend, the first person in the Rayne League who'd welcomed me with open arms. I'd been so busy training and sorting shit out with Ragnor, not to mention Logan, that all thoughts about Jada's and CJ's circumstances had been put in the back of my mind.

But now that Jada already looked as if CJ had died, and especially now that she had made her request, I was suddenly overwhelmed by everything I'd failed to pay attention to—and not just Jada either.

I hadn't visited Tansy once since training started. I knew from Isora, who was by her side most days, that she was still in a coma, so there wasn't anything new in that regard, but it didn't mean I hadn't neglected caring for someone when I was partially responsible for her state.

There was also Isora herself, who was going to be at the Hecatomb and potentially come face-to-face with Renaldi, the Lord who'd tormented her before she was bought by Atalon. I'd been so wrapped up in my own shit that I hadn't even asked her how she was dealing with this whole situation.

I was a shit friend.

And, looking at Ragnor, I also knew I was a shit lover.

In conclusion, I was a shit person, and I felt like absolute shit about it.

Ragnor finished packing and zipped up the bag before he came over to sit next to me on the sofa, wrapping an arm around me. "You okay?" he asked, squeezing me to him.

I was tempted to succumb to his warmth, but I couldn't. Not when I was feeling like I'd let down everyone around me.

But I was curious about one thing. Something I had wanted to ask Ragnor but never got the chance to, thanks to my self-absorption. "Do you know about the Malachi?"

Ragnor's response was not what I'd expected.

He retracted his arm and leaned back, looking at me with eyes gone blank, his shoulders tense, his jaw locked. "The Malachi," he repeated, as though the word were foreign.

I frowned, not understanding his stiff reaction. "Yeah," I said quietly. "Jada told me about them. That they are a celestial species like angels. I figured you probably knew." It would be very strange, after all, if he didn't, considering one of his League members used to be one.

Ragnor's eyes glowed, making me tense, but I couldn't read him. I had no idea what emotion was riding him hard enough to make his eyes glow. His face was completely indecipherable. "I see," he said, and offered nothing more.

I had the sudden nagging feeling that Ragnor was telling me without telling me to back off. That this subject was taboo, for whatever reason. It wasn't just his expressionless face, but the tension drawn in his shoulders. The sudden distance he put between us, as though his latest emotional distance now showed in the physical sense.

Since I had trouble with doing what I was told, especially when it came to Ragnor Rayne, my first instinct was to push. But looking at his glowing eyes, I had the sudden feeling that pushing him right now would be a mistake.

Whatever his deal with the Malachi was, it seemed I had stepped on a landmine.

So I plastered on a fake smile and said, "Never mind. Forget it," before rising to my feet and walking to the bathroom to take a long, calming bath.

Fighting with Ragnor the night before we headed to the Hecatomb would not be wise.

Not for him, and certainly not for me.

CHAPTER 31
RAGNOR

That night, Ragnor lay in bed, eyes open, staring at the ceiling, while Aileen slept soundly next to him, her soft breaths filling the room.

He couldn't sleep. Not after Aileen had dropped such a bomb on him a few hours ago. Because she shouldn't have known about the Malachi. She shouldn't even utter that name.

That she was his Alara Morreh was a fact he intended to hide. For eternity, if possible.

And yet she knew about the Malachi, or at least that they existed.

She said Jada had told her about them. Meaning Jada told her about Chanjomaron's true identity. Otherwise, Aileen shouldn't know about them.

Meaning Jada had also told her she was Chanjomaron's Alara Morreh.

A ripple in the air above him made Ragnor grow still. As if he had been summoned by Ragnor's thoughts, or Aileen's earlier words, a tall man appeared, hovering over the bed with his silver wings spread out. His tousled black hair was slicked back, and his jungle-color eyes peered at Ragnor, almost glowing in the darkness like a vampire's.

Grimacing, Ragnor got off the bed and motioned silently to the Malachi to follow him out. He obliged, and Ragnor led him outside the suite, toward his office. He did not want to risk anyone, especially Aileen, catching sight of him.

Once they were in his office, Ragnor locked the door and turned to face the Malachi. "What brings you here, Luceras?"

Luceras's eyes, which were usually cold and unfeeling, seemed a bit less so. In fact, Ragnor noted that while he appeared relaxed and emotionless, there was tension in him that wasn't usually there.

"I came to collect a favor you owe me," Luceras said.

Ragnor had dreaded this moment ever since he used Luceras to find out the location of the Jinn's headquarters a couple of months ago. And yet he didn't expect for the Malachi to come and collect the favor so soon. "Tell me."

Luceras's eyes sharpened. "When you reach Houston tomorrow, go to a motel called Alby's, room 204," he said with a sense of urgency Ragnor scarcely ever heard from him. "You'll find there a certain someone you know."

Ragnor didn't have to guess, and his hands curled into fists. "Eliza?"

Luceras nodded. "You are to take her to the Hecatomb and protect her until this ordeal is over with," he said in a commanding tone that ruffled Ragnor's imaginary feathers in the wrong way. "Then you are to bring her to your League for protection until further notice."

Ragnor took two things from Luceras's words: One, Eliza, for whatever reason, was in hot water and in need of rescue and protection, meaning she couldn't use any of her various connections to protect her. And two, that Luceras was going against the Malachi's wishes.

Ragnor had hosted Eliza in his town house a few weeks ago, after she'd done something to enrage a Seraph, one of the Malachi top dogs, though what it was that she had done, Ragnor didn't know.

But after they fought over Aileen's fate, and Eliza's threat to end Aileen's life if she dared to overstep the boundaries reserved for the

Children of Kahil—the followers of the Morrow Gods—Eliza left, and Ragnor had not heard from her since.

Ragnor knew that Eliza could protect herself from the Malachi—even from a powerful Seraph like the one she'd messed with. But the fact that Luceras was telling him now that she needed help told him it wasn't simply the Malachi who were after her.

Meaning that, for whatever reason, Eliza could not use any of her connections, not even the one entity she directly served, to save her.

And while their relationship wasn't what it used to be after they did not see eye to eye when it came to Aileen, Ragnor couldn't ignore the fact that one of his very few friends was in danger, even without it being a favor for Luceras.

"I'll do it," Ragnor said and couldn't help but add, "though not because you asked me to."

Luceras visibly relaxed. "Good," he said, "then I'll leave her in your care. Consider it one of two favors done."

Ragnor did not like the reminder that he had yet another favor he owed Luceras, but for now, he put it at the back of his mind and said, "I accept."

PART V

CHAPTER 32
AILEEN

I looked outside the airplane window at the green view of the United States' countryside as we made our way to Houston, Texas, for the Hecatomb.

The entire airplane was reserved for the Rayne League participants and spectators, along with the two Lieutenants and the Lord, of course. I'd asked Ragnor before we boarded who was left in charge of the League while all the higher-ups were gone, and Ragnor replied that since the Hecatomb only took three days in total, it wasn't a long enough time to appoint someone as temporary Lord, or to leave the Lieutenants there.

He did say he left heavy security behind, though.

Now, Ragnor was sitting at the front of the plane with his two Lieutenants. The business cabin was reserved for the Hecatomb participants, while the spectators were sitting in the economy cabin. Every Hecatomb participating pair sat next to one another.

Meaning Logan was sitting right next to me.

After our physical fight a couple days ago, it seemed like we had made a silent agreement to only interact when absolutely necessary. Our training sessions since then had been about going through mock battles silently and without needless chatter.

That was fine with me, to be honest. I was sick and tired of having every conversation with him turn into either a verbal or physical fight. Thankfully, our mutual silent treatment seemed to appease Margarita as well, since she hadn't tried to threaten me since that last time.

Unfortunately, I had almost five hours of flight time to spend next to Logan until we reached Houston.

Not so unfortunately, Logan seemed to be asleep.

At least until an hour later, when the plane wobbled a tad too violently for my liking, waking Logan up from his slumber.

Once the plane settled, Logan stretched and glanced at me. Before I could look away, our eyes met.

He scowled and snapped quietly, "What?"

"Nothing," I quickly replied, looking away.

I expected that this would be the end of it, but to my shock, I heard Logan take a deep breath before he said, "We need to talk."

Slowly, cautiously, I turned to look at him again. He glared at the back of the seat before him.

In truth, I feared talking to him. I didn't want another fight. But I also knew avoiding talking to him until the very last minute when we had to fight for our lives might not be a wise decision. "All right."

He tensed before turning to face me. "I will forever resent what you did to me three years ago," he said, cutting right to the chase. "But for what it's worth, I apologize for the way I handled our last physical . . . encounter."

My spine stiffened in response. "Thank you," I said, trying not to sound as if I was forcing the words out. "I appreciate it. And I'm sorry too."

Jaw locked, Logan nodded and looked away. "Let's just focus on the Hecatomb from now on."

"Agreed," I said at once, feeling an odd sense of relief and regret. I just wished things between Logan and I weren't so uncomfortably, provokingly loaded.

The rest of the flight went by in a relatively more relaxed silence. I dozed on and off for most of the time, and when I didn't, I stared at the view outside the window.

When we landed at George Bush Intercontinental Airport, Margarita, who was in charge of arranging transportation for the Hecatomb, led us outside the airport, where a large bus awaited.

The bus trip took about half an hour to get to Midtown Houston. Margarita took us to the back of a fancy building, where we all waited by an old wooden door. She knocked an odd number of times, like in Morse code, before the door moved aside automatically.

Wide concrete staircases leading into a dark underground. We followed Margarita silently into the gloom; the only sound echoing in the space was our footsteps. At some point, the stairs grew wider and wider until they turned into a spacious, long hallway with tall ceilings, all painted black with candle lights all over the walls.

It all felt quite stifling, but I swallowed my discomfort and hurried after Margarita and the rest.

The hallway ended in a desk occupied by two tall men wearing butler uniforms, as if to match the Gothic Victorian-era atmosphere. It was even more pronounced when one of the butlers said in a heavy English accent, "Welcome. Tell me the name of your League."

"Rayne League," Margarita responded, and I frowned, suddenly looking around me. Where was Ragnor?

The butler wrote something down with a fancy quill and straightened, moving around the desk. "Follow me."

The passage we'd come through split into two curved hallways, one leading to the right and one left, as if to surround a larger circular room. The butler took us through the right corridor, which was just as dark and candlelit as the main hallway.

We arrived at a door, which the butler opened. It led to a large lounge, painted red, gold, and black, with antique couches and sofas, dark wooden tables, and a kitchen in the corner that seemed as if it had been taken from *Downton Abbey*.

"The two doors lead to the male and female residences," the butler said and gave us all a polite bow. "For any questions, you may find me at the front desk."

Once the butler was gone, Margarita turned to look at us. "Go get settled," she said. "In fifteen minutes, all participants should meet back here."

It was already so late at night that I just wished I could call it a day and sleep like the Rayne League members who came as spectators—like Isora—could do. But with the Hecatomb officially starting tomorrow, I knew I'd have no such leisure.

The female residences were filled with bunk beds, hammocks, and only a couple of queen beds. Margarita claimed a queen bed for herself, and I saw Yelene, Zoey, and Cassidy arguing over who should take the other.

Since I did not want to fight over a fucking bed, I claimed an upper bunk, while Isora, throwing a smile in my direction, took the bed under mine.

Once I was done in the room, I returned to the lounge, where CJ and Neisha were already waiting.

When I joined them, their conversation stopped and they turned to look at me. Since I had a feeling I had just interrupted a private chat, I felt somewhat nervous when I said, "Hey, sorry, but have you seen Ra—I mean, our Lord?"

Neisha and CJ exchanged glances before returning their gazes to me. "No, not really," Neisha replied with a shrug. "I assume he's in his room?"

CJ shook his head. "I saw him saying something to Margarita before we left the street. He disappeared after that."

Meaning I wasn't hallucinating, and he really wasn't here. The question was, where was he then? "Thanks," I murmured and sat down on the couch.

"So how are you doing?" Neisha asked, swiftly changing the subject. "I mean, things have been quite tense between you and Logan lately . . ."

Thinking back at how public our fight had been made my cheeks flush in embarrassment. "Yeah, we're fine now," I responded, looking down at the marble floor. "Sorry for making things . . . weird."

"It's all good," CJ said with a smile that didn't reach his eyes. I wondered how things were with Jada now. She'd come along as a spectator, and every time I glanced at her, I had to look away. Her misery was far too hard for me to process, given everything else that was going on.

That and the fact she requested that I kill her if things with CJ's battle went awry.

Looking at CJ, who was now chatting about what would happen tomorrow, I wondered for the first time if I should tell him about Jada's request. She was his soulmate, his *Alara Morreh*, as Jada called it. I had a hunch that he would want to know.

But I knew this wasn't my call, or even my business, really, so all I could hope for was that CJ survived and, consequently, Jada did too.

A few minutes later, all participants gathered in the lounge, and Margarita took us out of our League's dormitory and back to the eerily dark corridor. The butler from before awaited us near a door on the inner wall, which led to yet another dark candlelit corridor that ended in a tall gate.

The moment I stepped beyond the gate, my jaw dropped. Before me was an actual honest-to-God Colosseum-like arena. Its floor was white marble, surrounded by multiple seats like an actual stadium.

Margarita raised her hand to draw our attention to her. "This is where the Hecatomb will take place," she told us. "Take a few minutes to get accustomed to the feel of the arena, the floor, and everything else. Because after today, the next time you'll set foot here will be for your battles."

Everyone spread out then, looking around in wonder. I couldn't help but stay in place, wondering about the marble floor. When I tapped my foot on it, it felt slippery. That wasn't very safe. Didn't arenas usually have sand?

"What do you think?" Zoey asked as she came to stand next to me, her eyes sparkling in excitement.

"This is going to be tricky," I told her, and she turned to look at me in surprise. "The floor is far too clean and slippery. Your feet will have no grip in even the best of sneakers. But fighting a battle barefoot is also not optimal . . ."

Zoey's surprise faded into a chuckle. "You worry too much, Aileen," she told me, squeezing my shoulder. "It's going to be okay. We'll all make it, slippery floor or not."

I stared at her, even more worried by her confidence bordering on arrogance. I remembered the marble floor back in my father's basement. A few girls had tried to escape—Tansy being the only successful one—and the one thing that got them was how slippery the floor was. It caused them to fall down, alerting my father to their attempts.

Crouching, I pressed my fingers to the floor and slid them across it. I grimaced when my fingers slipped, making me press my palm against the marble.

The bad, ominous feeling accompanied me all the way back to the residence, where I settled in my bunk bed, covered myself in the blanket, and wished it could be three days later already.

CHAPTER 33
RAGNOR

Calling Alby's a motel was quite the stretch. The old vine-wrapped building seemed more like a haunted house from horror movies than anything remotely close to being inhabitable by actual people.

Bracing himself, Ragnor pushed the almost-unhinged entrance door and went into the motel.

Surprisingly enough, the inside wasn't as bad as the outside. Sure, it was dusty and in dire need of cleaning, but it was orderly, with a front desk staffed by a woman wearing a suit.

The woman peered at him as he approached the counter. "Vampire," she drawled, startling Ragnor. "It's been a while since I last saw one'a y'all."

Sniffing the air, Ragnor realized why she knew what he was. "Nymph," he said quietly, studying the woman's face. She wasn't pretty enough to be a tree nymph—a *Dryad*—or a water nymph—a *Naiad*. Which left one option. "Of the Oreads, I believe."

The nymph shot him a toothy smile that made her seem more like a goblin than an actual nymph. "Formerly," she said, "but true. You must be one of them Lords, then."

Ragnor decided to neither confirm nor deny, so instead, he said, "While seeing a nymph in the middle of an urban area is definitely an intriguing mystery, I'm here on business."

She arched a brow. "Get on with it, then."

"Point me to the direction of room two oh four." Ragnor cut to the chase.

The nymph grinned. "That girl's sure wild," she cackled. "First, that hottie Malachi, and now a sexy Lord vamp. What a naughty girl."

Losing his patience, Ragnor simply asked, "Well?"

She nodded toward the elevator doors near the counter. "Take those to the second floor," she said and pushed an old rusty key toward him. "The room's right there. The girl's probably knocked out, so here ya go."

Ragnor took the key, nodded to the nymph, and reluctantly approached the elevator. When he pressed the button, the elevator made odd sounds that made Ragnor think that perhaps he should take the stairs instead.

But he knew there was a reason the nymph had directed him to the elevator and nowhere else. Now that he was here, Ragnor realized this was one of those alleged "sanctuaries" for the supernatural. These places were rare, especially in large cities like Houston; they were usually hidden in the countryside or along abandoned roads, pretending to be normal inns.

All for the sake of survival, of course.

These places, however, were also home to some dangerous supernatural species. That might've been the reason why he probably couldn't take the stairs.

The elevator doors opened, revealing a tiny compartment that barely fit him. He had to hold his breath the entire rocky ride to the second floor. An eternity later, the door opened again, and Ragnor stepped out, relieved.

The corridor was dark and ominous, not to mention stinky and dirty, with cobwebs evident even in the dim lights. Thankfully,

Ragnor didn't need to go far to get to room 204, since it was right near the elevator.

Ragnor didn't bother knocking; he shoved the key into the hole, and the door clicked open. He pushed it and, ignoring the strong smell of mildew, entered the room.

It could've passed for a proper motel room had it not been for the heavy dust in the air that made Ragnor want to both sneeze and cough. Waving the dust away, he squinted his eyes to peer into the room, trying to figure out where the bed was through the dust-filled fog.

He found the bed and Eliza lying on top of it, as the nymph had predicted, passed out.

Ragnor couldn't help but feel sympathy for her, despite everything. Usually, she looked like a healthy woman in her twenties (despite being double that age), with a pretty face. The only out-of-place thing about her, normally, was the eye patch over her left eye and the scar running down to her neck from beneath that patch.

But lying in this dump, she looked far younger and more vulnerable than Ragnor had ever seen her.

He knew now why Luceras wanted to retrieve her. The last time they'd met, he had already been aware she was on the run after committing some sort of a crime. But seeing her now, so exhausted that her guard was completely down, he knew things had gotten even worse for her somehow.

Grimly, he gently put her unconscious body over his back. He then looked around the foggy room until he found her dirty, worn-out satchel she took with her everywhere and put it over his shoulder. Then he left, ordering the elevator yet again.

It arrived with a concerning creak, and he entered it, barely fitting himself, the satchel, and Eliza in the minuscule compartment. But with effort he managed—though he was squished against the disgustingly dirty door—and the elevator descended back to the lobby.

Unfortunately, when he stepped out, he saw three men with brightly colored wings spreading out of their backs standing at the counter.

Ragnor recognized them at once. They were the Seraphim guards, the elite soldiers of the Malachi who were chosen to protect the Seraphim, the leaders of the Malachi.

He couldn't help but wonder, not for the first time, what the hell had Eliza done that warranted such a persistent hunt from the normally unflappable Malachi?

The guards swiveled their heads toward him simultaneously, and deadly tension filled the air.

Ragnor knew running would be futile. As much as he hated to admit it, the Malachi were faster. That left him one option, which he really did not like.

"*Deveran*," the Malachi in the middle said, staring at him emotionlessly despite having just used a derogatory term. "Hand over Eliza Wains."

He glanced at the nymph. She seemed curious about what was going on yet unafraid of the possible fight that could come. *Forever loving gossip, those nymphs,* Ragnor thought in disgust.

Returning his gaze to the Malachi who'd spoken, Ragnor said calmly, "Not going to happen."

The Malachi stared at him impassively as he commanded, "Get her."

The moment the other guards jumped toward him, Ragnor's decision was made. And before they could reach him, Ragnor reached for the aether and drew the one power he had left from a time he'd rather have forgotten.

He managed to see the guards' eyes rounding in surprise before everything blurred, and he, along with Eliza and her satchel, were phased into a dark hallway that opened toward a desk with two men wearing butler suits.

Before he could forget, he murmured, "Take us to my room." Before the exhaustion following caused him to succumb to oblivion.

CHAPTER 34
AILEEN

It was odd seeing Magnus, out of everyone, cooking breakfast in our League dorms' kitchen when I woke up the next morning.

I was the first in the lounge other than Magnus, who seemed as if he'd been there for quite a while.

"Good morning," I said, walking toward him. "Coffee?"

Magnus shot me a warm smile. "You've got the machine on the other side of the room. As for blood, you have all types in the fridge here."

"Thanks," I said, smiling back sleepily as I grabbed a bottle of AB plus and headed to the coffee station. With a hot mug ready, I rejoined Magnus in the kitchen and said, "I could help you, if you want."

"Nah." He shrugged. "I like cooking. And besides, you have a Hecatomb to worry about. Leave the cooking in the next couple days to me and the others."

That made my smile widen. "If I didn't have Ragnor, I would've fallen for you right here, right now."

"Fallen for who?"

Sleepiness evaporating, I whirled around to see Ragnor entering the room from a different door than the male and female residences—meaning he probably had his own room, being a Lord and all. Despite that, however, he seemed far more tired than I'd ever seen him, with heavy bags under his eyes and paler skin than usual.

Worried, I put aside the coffee and strode toward him, grabbing his face. "What's wrong?" I asked, a sense of urgency making my heartbeat quicken.

He gazed at me and, to my shock, pressed a soft kiss to my lips. "All's well, baby," he murmured, wrapping his arms around me and squeezing tight.

Unsure what to do with this sudden public display of affection, I hesitantly hugged him back and held him. When I felt him growing heavier, and his breaths turning deeper, I realized he had just fallen back to sleep while draped over me.

"Magnus, a little help?" I squeaked as I attempted to hold myself still and not cave under his weight.

With a sigh, Magnus helped me put Ragnor down on the sofa. When I stared at his sleeping face, I couldn't help but murmur foul-temperedly, "What did he bother waking up for?"

Magnus returned to the kitchen with a scoff. "He obviously wanted to see his honey bunny."

I scrunched my nose. "Don't ever say 'honey bunny' ever again, Magnus. It's unbecoming."

He chuckled while flipping omelet after omelet on a pan. "Blimey, Miss Henderson," he said with a fake, exaggerated British accent. "I know the decoration is rather inspiring, but do please contain yourself, and do not speak posh words like *unbecoming*."

I choked out a laugh despite myself. "It's not a posh word, you dolt."

Grinning, Magnus did not reply and resumed his cooking. In the meantime, I sat on the sofa next to Ragnor and, in a split-second decision, put his head over my thighs and caressed his face, combing his unruly hair.

Slowly, the League members trickled into the room. I felt their eyes on Ragnor and me, but I didn't care; I loved touching Ragnor and comforting him as he slept, and if anyone thought anything about that, I couldn't care less.

I saw Jada walk into the lounge some time later, joining Magnus in the kitchen to help with breakfast, along with some other spectators who jumped in. She still seemed emotionlessly weary, but it was nice to see she could at least function well enough to move around and even cook.

A large dining table, which had been pushed to the wall up until now, was placed in the middle of the lounge, surrounded by chairs and set for breakfast. When it had filled up with Magnus's and his impromptu cooking crew's dishes, I knew it was time to wake up my boo. "Ragnor," I murmured, leaning down so I could kiss his temple. "Breakfast's ready."

He squeezed his eyes shortly before his lids rolled up, revealing his stunning midnight blues. His sleepy gaze focused on me and a soft, sexy, and almost boyish smile stretched his lips. "Hey."

My heart fluttered at the sight. "Hey," I whispered back, unable not to smile back.

He rolled to his side, burying his face in my abdomen and wrapping his arms around me. "Give me five minutes."

As if to reply, my stomach growled, causing him to chuckle. Flushing a bit, I gently rolled him back to his back. "I don't think I can wait that long," I said sheepishly.

He grinned, stretched, and sat up. "All right, then. Breakfast it is."

We sat down at the table, and I was still aware that most members were openly staring at us. Though their gazes were piercing, I did my utmost to ignore them as I piled some eggs and bacon on my plate.

Despite the tension of the looming Hecatomb, breakfast was surprisingly relaxed. I chatted quietly with Isora, who sat next to me, while Ragnor, who sat on my other side, spoke with Magnus about making a cooking schedule for the next three days.

Once breakfast was over, it was time for us to head to the arena. And the relaxed, almost familial atmosphere from before shifted immediately.

By the time we entered the arena to head to our assigned gallery, most seats were already occupied by spectators from other Leagues. I looked around as Margarita, following the butler, led us to our assigned seats.

"Participants," the butler said when we arrived, "you shall occupy the first row in your participatory pairs."

Following that instruction, we participants sat down next to our assigned partners. Ragnor took the seat at the end of the row, with Magnus and Margarita right behind him.

A movement from the opposite side of the arena made me raise my eyes. More vampires trickled in, and when I squinted, trying to see who they were, I saw a spot of platinum-colored hair that made my heartbeat quicken.

It was the Atalon League.

"Bastard," Logan murmured, glowering at the Atalon League members. "I never liked Lord Atalon, but even I didn't think he would be so petty as to take his rivalry with our Lord this far."

For a moment, I thought he was talking to Oberon, who sat on Logan's other side, but when he glanced at me, anger in his eyes that, for once, wasn't directed at me, I realized he was actually making conversation with *me*.

Clearing my throat to hide my surprise, I said, "Atalon is fickle and cunning. He was biding his time until the right occasion presented itself."

Logan *tsk*ed and returned his angry glare to the Atalon League gallery. "Fuck him."

I couldn't agree more.

The crowd suddenly cheered, and when I scanned the arena, I saw a familiar figure, accompanied by two more I recognized, entering to the sound of celebratory music. As if the Hecatomb were a frat party rather than an actual fight to the death between two Leagues.

Lord Renaldi, along with his two Lieutenants, looked like he took his role as Hecatomb moderator and, apparently, a host, to the extreme. He wore a loincloth that seemed like a miniskirt, which barely hid his essentials and only emphasized how thick, long, and muscular his legs were. His wide, overtly toned chest was completely naked, and he wore a deep red cloak tied around his broad shoulders. His dark, tousled hair seemed to be in even more disarray than I remembered, and his feet, sporting golden sandals, walked steadily on the marble floor until he reached the middle of the arena.

Zoey, who sat to my right, scoffed. "I can't believe he dressed like a fucking gladiator."

"Not even a historically accurate one," I murmured in response. He looked as if he'd tried to mimic the look of the warriors in *300* or something.

When the cheers died down, Renaldi's Lieutenant, whose name was Stefan, handed him a cordless mic. "Welcome to North America's twenty-second Hecatomb!" Renaldi called into the mic, grinning toothily. "The first one to occur in over twenty years!"

Everyone cheered again. I didn't, and neither did the other Rayne League participants. Because in truth, there was nothing to cheer about.

Renaldi spread his mic-less arm and slowly turned to face the other side of the arena. "This Hecatomb is going to be between the oldest League in North America—the Rayne League—and the most illustrious League in the United States—the Atalon League!"

A large spotlight suddenly shone over our gallery, and the two large screens at the top of the arena blinked to life, with the right one showing our League's gallery and the left, the Atalon League's.

"Now give your grand applause to this Hecatomb's participants!"

The spotlight now shone solely on the first row. I squinted at the blinding light, while the cheers in the arena grew deafening. The Rayne League's screen showed the participants, and I couldn't help but think that I looked almost constipated on that screen.

"Today, we'll finally uncover the five battles that will take place tomorrow!" Renaldi said with an abundance of excitement I couldn't for the life of me relate to. "But before that—let's introduce the participants!"

I stilled, feeling a wave of anxiousness go over me. With everything that had been going on in the past several weeks, I hadn't given any consideration as to who Atalon League's participants would be. I thought of Eleanor, Oz, and Fareez, the three vampires who'd been purchased by Atalon along with Isora and me during the Auction four months ago. I wondered if they were here, about to spectate this clusterfuck, and hoped not.

"From the Rayne League, we have . . . Oberon Grimes, Sulien Salvador, Neisha Barnes, CJ Maron, Cassidy Jones, Zoey Rittman, Aileen Henderson, Logan Kazar, Haneul Kang, and Yelene Yarnikova!"

It almost felt like we were players in a football game being called one by one. It was even more unnerving that the spotlight moved from each one of us to the next as our names were called. We all looked quite stoic and somber on the screen, which, I believed, was the appropriate response on this occasion.

"And now, from the Atalon League, we have . . ." Renaldi said as a drumroll echoed in the arena. "Fareez Goshenan, Demetria Holsten, Eleanor Simmons, Jebediah Ackerman, Oz, Laurenia Olivers . . ."

I stopped listening, feeling sick to my stomach.

Because all I could hear echoing in my head were the names *Fareez, Eleanor, Oz.*

And when I saw their faces on the screen, my heart dropped, and I realized I had heard right.

The three vampires, other than Isora, whom I'd been on good terms with, maybe even friends with, while being at the Atalon League, were put here to be pitted against me.

CHAPTER 35

AILEEN

Dancers filled the floor of the arena for an intermission, but I hardly watched any of their routines.

Because on the other side of the arena, I was watching my former League mates, a feeling of dreadful terror filling up my stomach.

How did Eleanor, Fareez, and Oz end up participating in the Hecatomb? That made zero sense to me. They were relatively new members of the Atalon League. There was no reason for them to be chosen as participants to represent the Atalon League as a whole.

Of course, the fact that Ragnor had decided to let his members choose their participants didn't mean that Atalon did the same. I had a miserable hunch that Atalon had brought them here for one reason only.

To show me who was really in control here.

I didn't want to end up facing any of them. I didn't want to kill them.

But even if I didn't, someone else would. Because this was the Hecatomb, and while surrender was an option other than death, in reality, it really wasn't.

Someone tapped my shoulder and slowly, as if through a dream, I turned around to see Ragnor sitting right behind me. He must've switched places without me noticing, since I was still reeling from the shock of finding out who was going to face us, and probably die in the process.

"What's wrong?" he asked in a murmur, leaning forward so his voice would reach only me.

I parted my lips, but no sound came out. I couldn't speak. I had nothing to say. Too many things were wrong with what was going on here. Where could I even begin?

Whatever he saw on my face made him grimace. "Atalon is going to pull all kinds of tricks while the Hecatomb is underway," he told me quietly, guessing correctly what was on my mind, as the music of the intermission slowly faded, indicating its pending end. "Don't let it get to you. Don't get distracted. You can't afford to be."

I gave him a jerky nod that meant basically nothing. Don't let it get to me? How?

Isora appeared next to Ragnor. "My Lord," she said quietly, her face pale, which made her blue eyes paler than usual. "Three of the people on Atalon's team were the newcomers bought with Aileen and me in the Auction."

Ragnor's face darkened. "I see," he said, before turning to me. "It doesn't surprise me that he would do something like that. Still," he added, jaw hard, "my words stand."

He nodded to Isora before rising to his feet, walking back to his designated seat.

Isora gave me a grave look. "You have to protect yourself first and foremost," she told me, putting her hand on my shoulder. "Don't try to be a martyr, Aileen."

"And now, ladies and gentlemen, it is time to decide which pairs are going to fight to the death tomorrow!"

Renaldi's disgustingly cheery voice brought my attention back to the arena. The dancers were gone, and the floor was taken by Renaldi and his Lieutenants, along with a large, round object that held a few notes. It looked like those lottery machines used on TV.

"Let's start, shall we?" Renaldi grinned from ear to ear, his face spread across the arena's screens as he relished the situation, as if it was all a mere game.

When Renaldi played the lottery orb, I felt Logan tensing next to me. Zoey, on my other side, went very still too.

"Drumroll, please!" Renaldi called with a flick of his fingers, and a dramatic drumroll played in the arena, reaching a stop in the crescendo when he pulled a note out of the orb. As he cleared his throat, his grin widened, and I almost felt as if he was looking in my direction when he said, "Logan Kazar and Aileen Henderson! Let's see who they are against, shall we?"

My heart beat so loud, I didn't even hear the second drumroll until Renaldi pulled out a second note and made my heart stop.

"Eleanor Simmons and Jebediah Ackerman!"

"This has to be rigged," I said, pacing back and forth in our League dorms' lounge. "There's no other explanation as to why I'm going to face Eleanor out of all the Atalon League participants. My luck is shitty, but it can't be *that* shitty."

Isora, who was sitting miserably on the sofa, watched me with tears in her eyes. "You know," she said quietly, voice shaking, "I thought that after Renaldi, no other Lord could be as cruel. And yet Atalon seems to contend for the grade A asshole spot."

I stopped my pacing and buried my face in my hands, taking a deep breath. "I have to come up with a plan," I said, mind reeling. "I . . . I can't kill her, Isora. I'll have to . . . to surrender, or—"

"No, Aileen," Isora cut me off, angry. "You are *not* going to surrender—"

"*Then what do you want me to do?!*" I snapped, seething. "What the fuck should I do, Isora? Kill yet another innocent person with my own fucking bare hands? Is that what you're suggesting?"

Isora clamped her mouth shut and looked away, tears trickling down her face.

A door opened, and I saw Logan coming out, wearing sweatpants and a tank top similar to mine. He watched me and Isora, as we were the only ones currently in the lounge, and seemed taken aback. But then he said, "It's time for our training."

Of course we had to train, since tomorrow was the day we'd been preparing for. But what a day would it be, if I ended up killing a friend?

"Yeah," I said bitterly, "let's go train."

The arena's training rooms were not far from our dorms. They were smaller than the ones at the Rayne League and were obviously not designed for long-term training sessions.

When we arrived at the room, Logan started stretching, obviously expecting a rigorous last session before the money time tomorrow, but I had a different plan. "Logan," I said, drawing his attention, "we're going to change our plan."

His lips curved downward, showing his evident displeasure. "And what do you mean by that?" he asked in a dangerously low tone.

"Instead of taking the pair together, we're going to split the duties," I said, my voice resolute. "I'm taking Eleanor. You'll take Jebediah."

Logan glared at me. "And why, dare I ask, would you want to do that?"

Instead of skirting around the truth, I decided, for once, to be up-front about it. "Eleanor is a friend," I told him, capturing his gaze with mine. "I'll decide what to do with her, not you."

It seemed my words struck a nerve. "It's not up to you to decide," he hissed, walking toward me. "We're supposed to be a *team*, Aileen. After you berated me all those times about putting my issues with you aside to take this on, now you want to go back on your words?"

My hands curled into fists. "It has nothing to do with you."

"It has *everything* to do with me!" Logan snapped, reaching me and grabbing my arm. "You don't get to change the plan at the last minute because of a personal issue. You're supposed to cover my fucking ass,

Aileen. What if your 'friend' comes after me? Will you let her kill me because she's more of a 'friend' to you than I am now?"

I threw his hand off me. "She can't even harm you, Logan," I snapped, my emotions getting the better of me. "You're *Gifted*, for God's sake, and she's a mere Common!"

"Unless she has great teamwork with her *Gifted* partner!" he snapped back, grabbing my shoulders now. "Whatever she means to you, I refuse to let you fuck me over because of your personal feelings!"

"Let me go!" I yelled, grabbing his arms and attempting to throw him off me again, but he persisted.

"Not until you come to your fucking senses!" he seethed, and I suddenly realized he was in my face, and my back was touching the wall. "It's not just about you or even me, Aileen! We're representing the Rayne League members! We're representing our Lord! The very Lord you mess around with!"

I glowered at him. "This has nothing to do—"

"Jesus, Aileen, *everyone* has *everything* to do with this shit show!" he cut me off with a growl, leaning so close his nose touched mine. "I don't care if you decide you have morals. I don't care if she's your friend. The Hecatomb isn't just about you. We all have to survive this fuckfest, and that means we need to fight tooth and nail to get out alive!"

He released me so hard, I flailed for a moment before balancing myself, watching him as he headed to the middle of the room. "Now, stick to the fucking plan, Aileen, so we can both get to see another day."

CHAPTER 36
RAGNOR

The last thing he wanted was to stay in his room, but Ragnor's sense of duty and friendship, despite everything that had happened between them, didn't let him leave Eliza's side.

She'd been sleeping for who knew how long, and yet Eliza refused to wake. Ragnor would've been worried had it not been for the visit he received from Luceras in the night prior.

Luceras, whose expressively colorful junglelike eyes usually expressed nothing, had peered at the sleeping Eliza with what Ragnor would've called concern had Luceras been any other species but a Malachi.

Ragnor had pretended not to see when Luceras reached out to Eliza, caressing her hair once, before he nodded to Ragnor and left.

Now Ragnor was saddled with the uncomfortable feeling that if harm came to Eliza, he would make an adversary out of a powerful being.

So despite his gnawing worry over Aileen and her upcoming battle the next day against a vampire she considered a friend, he couldn't leave Eliza's side.

The spectacle of Renaldi's hosting of the opening ceremony rested heavily on his mind too. But that was neither here nor there. Nothing he could do about it now.

"Eliza," he said, weary of all the troubles that seemed to pile up without an end in sight. "I know you're strong enough to wake up from . . . whatever this is. I need you to tell me what's going on." Maybe then, at least, he would be able to resolve one of his many problems.

To his surprise, Eliza stirred. Then, slowly, her single eye opened. She turned her head to where he sat on the chair near the bed, and her eye widened. "What . . ." she croaked, shock written over her face.

Ragnor gave her a humorless smile. "Are you hungry? Thirsty? I can get you something if you want."

She pushed herself into a sitting position and looked away. "I don't . . ." She swallowed hard before peering back at him. "Where are we? This isn't the Rayne League."

"The Hecatomb arena," Ragnor replied simply, watching as another wave of shock caused her to freeze.

"Oh," she said, frowning. "Shit. Is the Hecatomb happening now? How long have I been asleep?" She paused. "Why am I here? I was supposed to be recuperating at Alby's . . ."

Ragnor almost genuinely smiled at her confusion. He wondered how she would react if he told her Luceras wanted to get her out of Alby's and under Ragnor's protection. He had a feeling he would have had a good laugh at whatever expression she would've made.

Unfortunately, humor wasn't an emotion he was capable of at the moment. So instead, he said, "I got you out of Alby's and here. I'm under the impression that you got yourself into some deep shit, Wains."

Eliza snorted, as if to say, *You don't even know the half of it.* But instead, she asked, "How did you even know I was there?"

Luceras's words from last night echoed in Ragnor's head. "*Don't tell her it was me*," he'd told Ragnor. *"Come up with an excuse. I don't want her to know I was involved in any way, shape, or form."*

So Ragnor replied ambiguously, "I have my own ways of finding things out."

She shot him a look that told him she didn't buy it. But thankfully, she let it go and instead said, "You mentioned food?"

Ragnor folded his arms. "I'll bring you some—for a price."

"Wow," she said dryly, "and here I thought you were simply being altruistic toward an old friend. How very optimistic of me."

Ragnor shrugged. "Think of it what you will," he said, "but it won't change the fact I need to know what happened to make you go into a deep slumber for God knows how long."

He saw her eye tick in irritation. "Fine," she said, angry, "but food first."

Ragnor rose to his feet and gave her a mock bow. "As you wish, my Lady."

She stared at him, suspicious. "You're being too nice to me, considering how we parted ways last time we met."

Deciding against answering her question outright, Ragnor simply sent her a thin-lipped smile and left for the lounge to grab something for his old friend, whom, despite everything, he had missed.

And once she had eaten and told him her story of what had happened to her in the past few months since they'd last seen one another, his whole world tilted on its axis.

CHAPTER 37
AILEEN

The arena was filled to the brim. Vampires of many Leagues came to watch the "show," and there seemed to even be bets going on, according to some conversations I heard here and there.

"Why does it feel like we're at a festival?" I asked no one in particular as Logan and I took our seats in the Rayne League gallery.

"It's better for the monetary gain," Logan murmured in response, staring around the arena in disgust. "It feels like we're in that movie. The one where kids kill one another for the entertainment of the upper class."

Zoey, who came to take her seat next to me, gave the two of us an excited smile. "I don't know what you're talking about," she said. "It gives me an adrenaline rush like nothing ever did! I love this electric air here."

Both Logan and I stared at Zoey in apprehension. The fact she actually seemed as exhilarated as she claimed made me feel sick. "Zoey," I said quietly, "this is an illusion. Don't let this illusion be your undoing."

She shot me an almost reckless smile. "Don't worry, Aileen," she said, eyes glowing gold. "I'll be fine. The pair pitted against Cassidy and me doesn't seem to be much trouble."

Her overconfidence made me dread it all even more.

I turned to look at the arena again, or rather, to the gallery on the other side. The Atalon League vampires had taken their seats as well, all wearing matching red-and-black tactical garb.

We wore the same type of tactical garb, only in navy blue and gold, the Rayne League's official colors. It was made up of a pair of trousers made from a stretchy material, a skintight top, and combat boots that were easy to move in.

I saw Eleanor, Fareez, and Oz wearing those clothes, and it made my stomach churn.

As if on instinct, I looked to the side, searching for Ragnor. We hadn't spoken at all since yesterday. He'd been cooped up in his room the entire night and this morning too. We'd even left for the arena without him.

I'd wanted to knock on his door and demand to know what he was up to, but something, a sixth sense maybe, told me to let him be. That he would find me when it was time.

Still, I could've used a long embrace and a few encouraging words to tell me everything was going to be all right.

Especially since my battle was the first one out of the five.

"I heard from Magnus that our Lord is preparing for his own battle." Logan's voice drew my eyes to him. He watched me carefully, his turquoise eyes almost sympathetic. "You might not see him before our battle."

Knots filled my stomach. "But Ra—our Lord doesn't need to prepare," I said, frowning. "He's *the* Ragnor Rayne, after all. He can take Atalon in his sleep."

Logan shrugged. "Perhaps he doesn't want to take any chances."

Great. Now I had more anxiety than before. Because Ragnor, while cautious, was never paranoid. That didn't sound like him.

The crowd suddenly cheered and whistled, and I turned my gaze to the arena, where Renaldi walked in, wearing an actual Greek white toga with a leaf band around his head, with his Lieutenants. It did nothing to soften his overly muscular body.

"Welcome, vampires, to the official battle day!" he now called into the mic, spreading his arms theatrically.

The cheers were deafening. My anxiety loomed over me, growing worse with every passing minute.

"Soon you'll watch the Leagues battling it out!" Renaldi said with a wild smile. "The order of the battle is now on the screen!"

Seeing my name and Eleanor's in the same line made me want to empty my stomach.

Logan suddenly took my hand and squeezed. I looked at him and saw he was still staring at the arena, at Renaldi. "We're in this together, Aileen."

His words warmed me so much that tears welled in my eyes. I would've never thought I'd hear such words from Logan, of all people. The man I'd hurt so much in the past, both physically and mentally. And he was able to get over it to be there for me.

"Thank you," I whispered back, wiping the tears from my eyes. "Thank you, Logan."

He kept holding my hand throughout Renaldi's entire opening speech.

Logan and I were led to the waiting room by one of the butlers while a dancing intermission took over the arena to entertain the onlookers before the battles.

Much like the design of the arena's corridors and rooms, the waiting room was also decorated in a Gothic style, with candles hung on black walls and extravagant sofas that seemed to belong in the Palace of Versailles. They were plush and comfortable, though.

As Logan and I waited silently in the room, the door opened and both of us turned to look as Ragnor walked inside.

My heart skipped a beat, though not because I hadn't seen him since yesterday. Rather, it was his state that took me by surprise:

His wavy dark-brown hair was disheveled, his midnight blues were bloodshot and sunken with lack of sleep, and his face was grave, with a growing scruff, as though he'd forgotten to shave.

He seemed as if he'd aged, which was biologically impossible, considering he was a vampire.

His eyes found me, and there was a flash of something in them I couldn't quite decipher. In less than a second, he was in front of me, grabbing me into a tight bear hug, his face buried in the nook of my neck.

"Aileen," he whispered, voice barely audible. "Aileen . . ."

Dread filled me at his tone. He sounded almost desperate. So un-Ragnor-like. "Hey," I said softly, hugging him back, startled. "What's . . . what's wrong?"

He didn't reply, just hugged me tighter.

We stayed like that for a few long minutes. From beyond Ragnor's shoulder, I saw Logan looking determinedly at the wall, probably trying to give us some semblance of privacy.

Finally, Ragnor let me go just enough so he could cup my face. "I love you," he said suddenly, catching me off guard.

My lips parted, wanting to ask what had brought this on now, of all times, but when I saw his eyes and the unreadable look in them that made me feel even more dread than before, all I could say was, "I love you too."

"Miss Henderson, Mr. Kazar, it's time."

Ragnor let me go, and I looked behind him at the butler, who was now at the door, looking at us.

Logan rose to his feet and gave me a nod. I turned to look at Ragnor, whose face now contorted in rage that I knew wasn't directed at me but made me question who it was directed at. "Good luck," he said, voice somewhat stifled, before he stepped back and left the room just as abruptly as he appeared.

Feeling uneasy for far too many reasons, I followed the butler out along with Logan, through the corridor, toward the entrance of the arena.

Before he left, the butler told us to wait in the entrance until our names were called. That's when Logan grabbed my arm, forcing me to look at him, and said with a grim yet determined look, "Whatever that was about, put it in the back of your mind. We have a battle to win now. You can talk to him after."

Knowing he was right, I nodded, and then we heard Renaldi's voice echoing in the arena, calling, "Please welcome the Rayne League's Aileen Henderson and Logan Kazar!"

"Here we go," Logan murmured, letting me go, and we both stepped into the arena.

The cheers were even stronger than before, full of vehement bloodthirstiness that made me feel even sicker than before. I looked up to see my face filling the large arena screen. It was pale and etched with trepidation. I looked like I was about to pass out at any moment.

Unable to look at myself anymore, I averted my gaze.

Logan and I stopped in the middle of the arena, and once we did, Renaldi called, "Please welcome the Atalon League's Eleanor Simmons and Jebediah Ackerman!"

From the other entrance across the arena, Eleanor and Jebediah walked in. The closer they got, the better I was able to see Eleanor. I realized she was thinner than I remembered and that her tactical gear, while the same as other participants', was covering a turtleneck shirt. It made no sense to be wearing anything under this skintight tactical top, especially since it was humid and warm in the arena.

It gave me an ominous feeling I wished I didn't feel. Especially when I saw Eleanor's face and how emotionless it looked. As if she was operating on autopilot.

Jebediah, on the other hand, looked no worse for wear. I'd seen him around the Atalon League but never knew his name. All I knew about the blond-haired, green-eyed man that had an athletic build similar to Logan's was that he was Gifted, though I had no idea what his Gift was.

Eleanor and Jebediah stopped across from us in the center of the arena. And then, Renaldi, from his spot at the host's cabin, said, "Let the battle begin!"

And the battle I wanted the least to fight started.

CHAPTER 38
AILEEN

Before Jebediah and Eleanor could move, Logan and I attacked.

Both of us launched ourselves at Jebediah. Logan used his Gift, his enhanced strength in his legs thanks to his years as a soccer prodigy, to shoot a kick, which contacted, at Jebediah's midsection. Before Jebediah could respond, I came from behind him and chopped the nape of his neck with an intense precision.

A normal human would've passed out from my chop, but Jebediah was a vampire—and a Gifted at that. So all it did was give him a momentary concussion that made him stagger in place.

As Logan used the momentum to launch a set of kicks at Jebediah as if he were a punching bag, I turned around toward Eleanor. All she did was stand and stare at what was happening with dead, dark eyes, her body immobile.

Why wasn't she fighting?

Why was she only standing and staring as if she was simply awaiting her turn?

Something was wrong.

And without thinking twice about it, I closed my eyes and thought, *STOP!*

The soft pounding in my temples, along with the sudden silence, told me time had listened to my command, and I opened my eyes and looked at Logan, who gave me a quizzical look. "What's wrong?"

Part of our plan was to use my time-stopping power only in an emergency, in case one of us was on the brink of death, so as not to exhaust me. But this was a different emergency. "Eleanor is acting weird," I said quickly, knowing I had less than thirty seconds to talk to him. "You've got a handle on Jebediah, so let me handle her by myself."

Logan's face contorted in rising anger. "Aileen, we agreed to stick to the plan of doing everything together—"

"I know!" I snapped, cutting him off, pointing at Eleanor. "But she's not even moving! Let me handle this on my own." I sucked in a deep breath and said, "Please."

Logan looked at Eleanor for a few precious, long seconds. The pain rose in my head steadily and angrily, ready to take me under unless I released my hold on my power soon.

He then let out an angry breath. "Fine. But keep some of your attention on me in case I need your help."

Relieved, I said, "Noted," and thought in my head, *RESUME!*

The noise of the audience returned with a vengeance, and I approached Eleanor, while Logan continued his onslaught on Jebediah, who now seemed to get ahold of himself and began to fight back.

"Eleanor," I said when I was right in front of her, my hands on her shoulders. "Talk to me. Please."

She stared at me, but I could tell she wasn't really seeing me. She did not speak.

Heartbeat quickening, I gave her a shake. "Please, Eleanor, talk to me," I said, feeling so helpless. How could I possibly *fight* her, let alone *kill* her, when she was like this?

The ground suddenly shook. Heart lurching to my throat, I whipped around to see Jebediah had come to his senses and seemed to be activating his Gift. He was the one causing the ground to shake somehow, making Logan lose his balance momentarily.

Jebediah then rocketed toward Logan and shot a punch to his gut that made Logan reel back and cough blood.

Fuck.

Letting Eleanor go, I ran toward Jebediah and sent a kick to his knees. But Jebediah must've sensed me coming this time because he evaded me almost too easily and punched my ribs so hard, I fell down, out of breath, as pain bloomed where he'd punched.

What the hell was this man's Gift?

But there was no time to figure it out, because Jebediah was now on Logan, pinning him to the floor seemingly without effort and punching his face over and over again. Logan thrashed, trying to release himself from under Jebediah, but Jebediah was somehow strong enough to hold him down.

Adrenaline rushed over me, and I was about to climb to my feet and head over there when a cold, metallic thing suddenly pressed against my throat.

A knife.

Held by Eleanor, who somehow came from behind me.

"Don't move," she whispered in my ear, her voice lower and far more deadly than I remembered it. "Or I'll cut your head off."

And it was then that I remembered something crucial. Something I'd forgotten.

Eleanor used to belong to the Renaldi League. She used to do bloody, dirty work for Renaldi under the pretense of being a prostitute.

She was taught how to kill. To assassinate, to be more precise.

Whatever was going on with her now, I realized she could actually kill me if she wanted. And it seemed she did want to do just that.

Meaning I had underestimated her and put Logan and myself in danger.

No, I thought determinedly, closing my eyes. *We can make it. STOP!*

This time, the pain was so unbearable, I could barely open my eyes. But I did, watching as Logan struggled to wriggle out from under Jebediah's frozen weight.

"Goddammit, Aileen!" Logan now yelled, face bloody and almost disfigured.

Through the pain, I took the knife from Eleanor's hand and pushed her hand away. According to Ragnor, weapons weren't common in the arena, for the vampires strived to show their powerful abilities without relying on external factors. So the fact that Eleanor brought a knife could only mean one thing.

She wasn't here for show.

She was here to kill.

I walked toward Logan, fighting the pain, as I helped him up to his feet. "Let's take him out," I said, wincing both because of the pain and Logan's furious glower. "Berate me after we finish this, please."

Logan spit blood and gave me a single, angry nod.

Resume! I thought, and the pain receded, leaving a wave of weariness I could've really done without.

Before Jebediah could act, Logan and I attacked him together. He shot a kick to his head, while I aimed my own kick to his knees. Both our kicks connected together, making Jebediah cry out.

I glanced behind me to see Eleanor looking at her hands, not making a move at us. She looked almost robotic, as if she were operating under direct orders, and she wasn't to move until further commands.

Whatever the reason for Eleanor's strangeness, it gave me time to focus on beating Jebediah.

Jebediah tried to kick at Logan, but Logan recoiled slowly, too slowly for Iovan's Imperium to take effect. Gritting my teeth, I ran toward Jebediah and grabbed his shoulders, shooting my knee to his back. Jebediah swiveled around, but I jumped away . . . and slipped.

I fucking *slipped* on the marble floor.

Jebediah's eyes flashed in victory as he came at me full force, somehow causing the floor to shake and rumble, making it hard for me to try and get up.

He aimed a kick at my head, and I could barely roll away from him. By then, Logan reached from behind, wrapping his arm around

Jebediah's neck. "Aileen, use it!" Logan screamed at me as he struggled to keep Jebediah immobile with his hold, as Jebediah thrashed and struggled against him.

The floor stopped shaking, probably thanks to Logan distracting Jebediah, so I managed to climb to my feet, the adrenaline numbing the ache in my ribs.

Knowing there would be hell to pay later, I closed my eyes and, for the third time, thought, *Stop!*

Time barely obeyed my command this time, and I knew we had only seconds before my control would slip. "Do it!" I screamed at Logan through the silence in the arena.

Logan didn't hesitate; he pushed Jebediah to the floor and, with one foot on his back, Logan raised his other foot, and with power and strength no human could hope to have, he stomped down on Jebediah's neck, cutting through the skin, meat, and veins, ripping through until his foot touched the floor itself, severing Jebediah's head from the rest of his body.

I could barely see Logan's face turn to shock when I felt my hold on time slipping before I could even command it to resume.

The cheers returned, but the crowd suddenly turned silent, as if not understanding what was happening. Which made sense; for them, one moment Logan was barely holding onto Jebediah, and in the next blink, Jebediah was on the floor, dead, blood pooling under him.

Before the exhaustion could kick in, I forced myself to rise up and turn around to face Eleanor.

But Eleanor wasn't there.

And when I looked for the knife I'd taken from her, I didn't find it anywhere.

Then I heard the crowd collectively gasp, and I slowly turned around.

Eleanor was right before Logan, holding the knife in Logan's chest.

My heart stopped, and I couldn't move as Eleanor, using strength I didn't know she was capable of, twisted the knife and curved it before taking it out, a beating heart impaled on its sharp, bloody edge.

Eyes wide, Logan fell to his knees, looking down at his gaping chest. He then turned to look at me, his face slack with shock, before, to my utter dismay, he smiled.

Then Logan crumbled to the floor into a puddle of his own blood, dead.

CHAPTER 39

AILEEN

Nothing made sense.

Logan couldn't be dead. He was a Gifted, an elite vampire. He was a Commander in the Troop. He couldn't possibly die.

Especially not at the hands of a Common like Eleanor.

"I'm sorry, Aileen."

I tore my eyes from Logan's body to look at Eleanor, who looked at me with that lifeless expression on her face. She still held the knife with the heart, no longer beating, lodged on it.

I tried to speak, but I couldn't. I had no words. I couldn't even feel anything other than shock.

Ever so casually, Eleanor slid the heart off her knife until it fell with a sickening splashing sound on the floor. Then she walked toward me, leisurely, as if she hadn't just killed Logan. Killed my ex-boyfriend. My old friend. The one person I didn't think would ever die, especially not like this.

"It's what this is all for, isn't it?" Eleanor now said, her eyes glued to me, face blank.

I couldn't move as she stopped before me, as if she'd cast a spell on me. "It's not possible for both of us to get out of this alive," she told me quietly, and for the first time I saw her face crack. Agony flashed in her eyes, causing them to glow. "So kill me, Aileen."

My shock multiplied. I was almost unable to comprehend what she was saying.

"If you don't, *he* will, even if I kill you," she whispered, and I froze. "I don't want to kill you. Please," she begged me. "He's going to control me soon—"

And just like that, her face was wiped of all expression once more, turning deadly and lifeless.

She attacked.

My body moved automatically, avoiding her knife and evading all of her attempted attacks. She was ferocious and fast, unrelenting in her pursuit, and I had a hard time keeping my attention intact to make sure she didn't get a hit in.

You have to kill her, a voice inside me urged. *You must. There is no other way.*

She'd just killed Logan. She'd also begged me to take her life. I had all the reasons I needed to kill her—even her own consent.

And that's when I knew I could not get out of this without doing just that.

So as she attacked, I started slowing my movement and began to attack back, sending punches and kicks her way, which she evaded. Gradually, the pacing of our fight grew slower and slower, so much so that despite whatever control she was under, she couldn't help but match my pace.

Once we reached the ultimate pace, I moved from the first Behest, *Gradus Diminutio*, to the second, *Propero Incrementum*, and I accelerated my pace immediately, connecting my punches with every part of her body I could reach. The impacts made her stagger back, gasping in pain as I relentlessly and rapidly went on the complete offense.

Then, I moved to *Crura Implacabilis*, the third Behest. Letting my upper body rest, I pushed all the power and momentum to my legs and kicked her over and over again, not letting her take the offense, no matter how much she tried. She was completely under my dominion, thanks to Iovan's Imperium.

The next Behest, *Coactus Impetum*, was all about spreading the power evenly throughout the body and using certain sets of attacks to goad her into attacking me in a certain way I wanted. It worked almost too well; Eleanor was like a rubber band, snapping into action once she saw the openings I carefully created using the Behest. She aimed for my sides, her knife brushing against my skin and drawing blood.

I continued to compel her to attack the places I wanted her to, and she fell into the trap over and over again, unaware she was exhausting herself in the process. And it was only when I saw her knife hand starting to shake that I moved to the fifth and final Behest: *Perniciosius Finis.*

I concentrated the entire power I'd gathered and grew throughout the fourth Behest in my hands and arms, and when she almost slipped on the floor due to her tired state, I rushed toward her, grabbed her head, and using every bit of power, strength, and energy I had left, I closed my eyes and pulled.

A sickening tearing sound reverberated through me as I felt my balance tipping, and I fell back on my ass, feeling her hair in my hands and the wet blood dripping down on my clothes.

I was terrified to open my eyes to see the carnage I'd created, but I forced myself to. Eleanor's head was in my hands, her face turned to me, her eyes glassy. Her neck . . . her neck was nonexistent. It was all a mess of torn flesh and veins.

It was then that it occurred to me everything was silent. The crowd did not make a sound. All I could hear was my own heartbeat, quick and uneven.

And suddenly, I couldn't hold on to the severed head anymore. With a sudden wave of rage, I threw it away and pulled my knees to my chest, burying my head there as my entire body shook with fury mixed with agonizing sorrow.

When Renaldi cleared his throat and said in a cheery voice that made me sick, "And the winner is . . . Aileen Henderson of the Rayne League," I couldn't hold it in anymore.

I turned my head and vomited.

A butler led me out of the arena just as Renaldi announced there would be a fifteen-minute break before the next battle.

Right at the exit, I saw Ragnor was waiting. I couldn't look him in the eye. Not after the shit show I'd just pulled. Not after I'd basically killed one of his prized Gifted vampires.

But Ragnor didn't seem to care about any of it. Instead, he pulled me into his embrace, stroked my hair, and murmured that everything was all right now.

And yet nothing was all right. Nothing was okay. Because of me, Logan was killed. Because of my incompetence and overconfidence. Because I was an idiot.

Distantly, I wondered if Atalon had noticed when I'd stopped time. He must've been watching just like Ragnor, and he knew of my ability. Did he just let it all play out without intervening?

Ragnor squeezed me tight, and yet even his embrace did not bring me comfort. Nothing would, really.

"Do you want to go back to the dorms?" Ragnor asked me after a long silence.

Even though I was exhausted, my head was pounding, and every fiber of my being begged for rest, I couldn't. There were four more battles to be fought—perhaps not by me but by people I cared about. I needed to see this through, even if I felt like my whole world was falling apart.

So I shook my head and said, "Let's go back."

But the moment I tried to walk, I suddenly lost all strength and my knees buckled. Ragnor caught me around my waist, and only with his help was I able to somehow make my way back to my seat in the gallery.

I felt eyes following Ragnor and me from the crowd—and the spectators of the Rayne League. Once Ragnor helped me sit down and took the seat next to me, where Logan had sat just an hour ago, I felt all the energy leaving my body and leaned against Ragnor, wishing I could turn back time instead of simply stopping it.

If only I'd stuck to the original plan . . .

"Hey." Isora's voice made me flinch. But then I felt her hand on my arm, and I turned to look at her. She had exchanged seats with Zoey and was now sitting on my right, her face worried.

I couldn't look in her eyes, too. Not after I'd just killed Eleanor, who'd been her longtime friend since the two became vampires.

She kept holding my arm, refusing to let go, even though I was in no state to talk. I was grateful for her worry but also ashamed.

Because I didn't deserve it.

As Ragnor and Isora sat by my sides, like two supporting pillars I didn't deserve, the break eventually came to an end, and the next battle began. This time, it was between Oberon and Sulien against Oz and Laurenia from the Atalon League.

Unlike my battle, this one was quick and short. Oberon easily overpowered Laurenia, another Gifted I knew in passing back at the Atalon League, using his Gift of plant manipulation, causing the seeds in his pockets to grow and wrap themselves around her before she could even attempt an attack.

"Surrender," Oberon demanded, aiming a sharp vine tip at Laurenia's bare chest.

Laurenia shook her head.

So Oberon carved her heart out.

On the other side of the arena, Sulien was trying to get a hit on Oz, who moved around evasively, not even attempting to go on the offense.

It was like Oz was biding his time until Laurenia was defeated, because once Oberon killed her, Oz raised his arms and said loudly, bored, "I surrender."

The crowd *boo*ed but the rules were absolute. Once he surrendered, the battle was over, with another win for the Rayne League.

Isora sighed. "Thank God Oz surrendered," she said quietly, and I turned to look at her. "I wouldn't have wanted Oberon and Sulien to die."

Confusion cut through my numbness. "But Oz is Common," I said quietly.

Isora gave me a small smile. "Yeah."

She didn't elaborate, and I didn't pry. To be fair, I didn't really care about anything as long as I didn't have to see another person I knew die.

Unfortunately, my slight relief was short-lived.

CHAPTER 40
AILEEN

"Please welcome Zoey Rittman and Cassidy Jones from the Rayne League!"

I watched Zoey and Cassidy step into the arena to the noise of the crowd's endless cheers. They seemed confident and self-assured, which should've made me relax but had the opposite effect.

"Are they good?" I asked Ragnor just when Renaldi announced, "Welcome Fareez Goshenan and Demetria Holsten!"

Ragnor nodded. "They are good," he said, face set in a dark expression. It seemed as if he was restraining himself from saying anything more.

It did not give me the assurance I desperately needed.

When Renaldi started the battle, I was almost too afraid to watch. But when Cassidy and Zoey moved seamlessly together, creating openings and attacking with full force, I relaxed a little. Maybe they *were* good. Maybe I was worried for naught.

Those were my thoughts until Demetria used her Gift.

From the entrance where Demetria and Fareez had stepped into the arena, two large mythological monsters appeared. They were live sculptures, made of marble, of a large griffin and an eight-foot-tall Minotaur.

Demetria's Gift was to bring the sculptures she made to life.

And those sculptures had the exact properties of the mythological creatures they were crafted after.

The Minotaur, holding a mace, charged at Cassidy, whose green eyes were wide with shock and terror. She held her hands up over her face to brace for impact, knowing she didn't have enough time to move away—the Minotaur was too fast.

It crashed into her, throwing her a few feet away.

In the meantime, the griffin flew through the arena in circles, its eyes on Zoey, who was now locked in a battle with Fareez, who not only held his own but gave as good as he got. The griffin probably watched for an opening to attack.

My heart beat hard in my chest as I saw the Minotaur cornering Cassidy against the arena's wall. *Sing,* I willed in my head. *Sing, Cassidy, before he it—*

The Minotaur raised its halberd to the side of Cassidy's head.

I watched in horror as it cut in a precise horizontal line, literally cutting her head in half.

Her severed head rolled to the floor.

Cassidy couldn't use her singing Gift anymore.

The Minotaur roared in victory.

It didn't compute.

None of it.

Why didn't Cassidy sing? Why didn't she fight back when she had an opening?

"NO!"

I whipped my head to Isora, who jumped to her feet, watching the arena with terror. Slowly, I returned my gaze to the battle and saw as the griffin flew down on Zoey, who'd slipped on the floor and found herself down with her chest far too bare for an attack.

And the griffin used that to dig its talons into Zoey's chest, making her back arch as blood trickled down from her mouth, and it plucked her heart out.

This couldn't be happening.

It made zero sense.

Even when Renaldi announced, "And the winner of this round is the Atalon League!" none of it felt real.

Zoey and Cassidy couldn't be dead.

How could they be dead when just this morning, Zoey talked and laughed with everyone?

How could they be dead when just earlier, I saw Magnus give Cassidy a pep talk?

Ragnor's hold on me tightened. "You can leave," he told me quietly, face grim. "You don't have to watch the rest of it."

I shook my head. I needed to watch. If my friends were dying, bearing witness was the least I could do. I couldn't look away.

I had to watch, even though it killed me that Logan, Cassidy, Zoey, and Eleanor were dead.

All in the span of a couple of hours.

All because of this Hecatomb, because of Atalon and Ragnor.

And because of me.

The fourth battle was between two vampires of the Atalon League I didn't recognize called Petra and Caleb, and the Rayne Troop Commander Haneul Kang and Yelene, the Common Troop member.

The battle started like any other. Petra and Caleb were on the offense, moving together to separate Haneul and Yelene from one another. But Haneul, whose Gift was his deep connection with his hawk, made the bird attack the Atalon League pair while he put some distance between them and him.

While Petra and Caleb were distracted by Haneul's hawk, Yelene launched an attack on Caleb, targeting him specifically, which told me he must've been the Common in the pair. Haneul made his hawk focus only on Petra while Yelene battled with Caleb, fighting for who got more punches and kicks in.

Then the tides changed.

Petra, who'd been trying to get the hawk off her up until then, suddenly jumped.

And didn't land.

She kept on climbing upward, as if she'd just jumped on an extremely springy trampoline instead of hard, cold marble.

Haneul pointed at her almost floating figure, and his hawk flew toward Petra, but to my shock, it was too slow; Petra was already falling back down, and not back to her previous place, but rather forward, toward Yelene.

Seemingly realizing what she was trying to do, Haneul began running to cross the arena, but he was too late. Petra landed on top of Yelene, her hands in Yelene's hair, preparing to sever her head.

That's when Haneul suddenly screamed, "We surrender!"

And just like that, we lost that round.

But we didn't lose more people.

There was another fifteen-minute break before the final battle of the day. At that time, with Ragnor still by my side, Haneul approached Ragnor. "I apologize, my Lord," he said with a blank face that seemed to feel anything but apologetic, "but after the last few rounds, I deduced this would be the best outcome."

I looked at Ragnor. He looked even more exhausted than before all of a sudden. "You made the right call," he said in a rough, grave voice. "Good work, Haneul."

Haneul bowed. It was a straight-backed, arms-to-the-side kind of bow that meant the utmost respect.

"Ragnor," I whispered once Haneul returned to his seat, "we have to win the next round."

He hugged me to his side. "I know."

He didn't say we would win. That I had nothing to worry about. In fact, he seemed even more somber than before. He didn't even seem surprised that we were in this position.

It was as if he'd predicted this part of the Hecatomb would go wrong.

And that made me feel sick again. Because if Ragnor lacked faith, then how could I have any?

This dreadful feeling in my gut grew to impossible proportions when the break was over and it was time for the last battle between Neisha and CJ and the Atalon League's pair, which I was unfamiliar with, named Azaz and Thorne.

When the battle started, I found myself looking at Jada. She was sitting a few rows behind me, her large gray eyes glued to the arena in something akin to a trance, as if she was compelled to look by some external force.

I returned my gaze to the arena, where Neisha and CJ worked together to take down Azaz, who seemed to be the Gifted one in the pair. He was agile, though, and he managed to avoid every attack by Neisha and CJ. He instead managed to get some kicks in on CJ.

Neisha must've realized this was going nowhere when she suddenly lifted CJ as if he weighed nothing and, quite literally, threw him like a pitcher would at the pair.

CJ stretched out his hands and landed on Thorne, his hands wrapping around Thorne's neck. With what seemed to be minimal effort, he tore Thorne's head off.

The crowd cheered, and I even relaxed a little, seeing the good shape Neisha and CJ were in.

But I relaxed too early.

Because when Neisha was attempting to take down Azaz, Azaz instead rushed at CJ, who was still holding Thorne's severed head, and with his bare hands, Azaz managed to tear into CJ's chest from his back, his hand creating a hole in CJ's torso. When he pulled his hand back, he opened it and pieces of red, bleeding meat fell to the floor.

CJ's heart.

Crushed to literal bits.

Two screams filled the arena just then.

Neisha's was wild and furious, and she was immediately on Azaz, tearing his head off as easily as if she was squashing a fly.

And behind me, Jada's was that of a woman who had just lost the most important, precious thing in her life.

Her soulmate.

Her Alara Morreh.

I moved before I could even comprehend what I was doing. Ragnor and Isora called after me, but I climbed the stairs to the row where Jada lay on the floor, her endless screams both heart wrenching and terrifying.

Crouching before her, I tasted my own tears as I pulled her shaking body into my arms. She thrashed against me, screaming and crying, seemingly unable to stop.

"Jada," I said, my voice breaking, and she stilled. "I'm . . . I'm here."

She looked up, her eyes so pale, shattered, and broken, they made my own tears multiply, clogging my throat. "Do it," she begged, clinging onto my shirt. *"Do it."*

I knew what she wanted me to do. What I'd promised her I would do if the worst came to pass, which it just did.

When I saw light in her eyes dim, she released my shirt, as if she couldn't hold on anymore, her screaming coming to a stop. I saw what Jada had talked about before. And why she asked me to kill her.

Jada's face grew devoid of emotions, her body becoming limp like a rag doll, the vitality of what made Jada *Jada* disappearing right before my eyes.

Moments later, Jada was gone and in her place was a breathing body with no soul.

As if when CJ was killed, so was her very own self.

He was her literal soulmate. Without him, Jada practically ceased to exist.

A hand, belonging to Ragnor, landed on my shoulder. "It's over," he said, looking at Jada with both devastation and unbearable pity. "Let us return to the dorms."

I picked Jada up. She didn't even resist. It was as if in the span of seconds, she'd become devoid of any agency.

My chest squeezed, aching, as the events of the last few hours passed through my head, while walking back to the dorms along with the remaining Rayne League members.

The realization of everything that had happened threatened to seize control over my mind. Threatened to make me crumble and fall right there and then.

But I couldn't fall apart yet. I had a deadly request to fulfill.

A sob escaped my lips when we entered the lounge and I laid Jada on the sofa. "Bring me a knife, please," I said to Ragnor, voice hoarse.

He didn't ask me why. He simply went to the kitchenette, grabbed a knife, and brought it over to me.

Shaking, I sat next to Jada, who stared, unblinkingly, at practically nothing. She didn't even move. She was comatose with her eyes open.

Ragnor, Isora, and others surrounded Jada and me, as if they were all aware of what was coming. They might not have known the details, but they'd all seen what had just happened to Jada when CJ died.

It was as if everyone just instinctively *knew*.

So it was silent from the moment I forced myself to dig the knife into Jada's chest until the second I carved out her heart.

Jada, in her vegetative state, didn't seem in pain as she passed.

The knife fell from my hand, along with the heart, to the floor. "I'm sorry," I whispered in the awful silence, endless tears escaping me. "I'm sorry . . ."

Isora sat next to me and pulled me into her. "Don't be," she said, her own voice breaking as she began to cry too. "It's not your fault. None of it is."

Gently, Neisha, whose own face was smeared with tears, picked Jada's body up. "I'm going to store her in another room until we depart," she said quietly. "She deserves to be buried back home."

Home. The Rayne League.

Ragnor's League.

My League.

The very League that had just lost some of its finest members.

Ragnor took the seat to my right and pulled me to him softly. "Rest, Isora," he said quietly. "I got her."

Isora obliged and left for the dorms along with everyone else, giving us space.

And when it was just Ragnor and me, just the two of us, it all finally hit me, and I let myself fall apart in his arms.

CHAPTER 41

AILEEN

Before the battles, we had planned to celebrate tonight if—or when—we won.

And yet, while we'd won, the losses we suffered had been too severe. Nobody was in a festive mood.

So instead, everyone went to sleep early, and Ragnor invited me to spend the night with him in his room.

It wasn't very spacious, but it was much cozier than the packed dorms. It also had a private washroom.

Once Ragnor locked the door behind us, he pulled me into his arms. "Let's go wash together," he said, squeezing me tight.

I nodded, leaning back a bit to look at his face. He seemed exhausted. But he still pressed a kiss to my lips and engulfed me in his heat.

The washroom included a bathtub large enough for two. So once it was filled with water, Ragnor and I entered the tub together, with me sitting with my naked back to his bare chest.

His arms wrapped around me as he leaned his head on my shoulder. "Don't blame yourself for what happened," he said suddenly, making my sore throat and eyes almost burst out in another wave of uncontrollable sobs. "Death is inevitable in the Hecatomb."

I leaned deeper into him. "Logan died because of my own stupidity," I whispered, and saying these words out loud made it feel even more real than before. So real that a fresh wave of tears fell down my face. "I insisted on changing the plan. I underestimated Eleanor. I was a fucking idiot, Ragnor."

He took a deep breath. "There was nothing you could've done better," he said. "You've done the best you could, considering the circumstances."

"But it wasn't enough," I hissed, turning to look at him. "Logan died because of me. That's the fucking truth."

Ragnor caught my tears on his finger, his face grave. "Blaming yourself won't bring him back to life, Aileen," he said softly, cupping my cheeks. "So grieve him, mourn his death, take as much time as you need, but once done, do not dwell on it."

I leaned into his hands, wishing I could redo everything. I never knew how much it hurt to lose so many people I cared for in one day.

Was it karma, finally catching up to me? Was it God's way of retaliating after I'd helped my father take so many innocent lives?

"Hey." He raised my head so my eyes would meet his. "I'm here. You're not alone in this."

And just then, I knew exactly what I needed.

So I leaned forward and kissed him.

He kissed me back at first, but when I came to straddle him, feeling his hard cock under me, he paused and pulled back, looking at me with unsure eyes. "Aileen, maybe we shouldn't—"

"Please," I whispered, caressing his face as I pressed my lips against his throat. "Just for tonight, help me . . . help me forget it all."

Ragnor did not deny me again. Instead, he pulled me into a long, deep kiss that left me heady with desperate desire.

I placed my pussy over his erection and shoved myself down on him at once.

We both cried out at the friction, and my heart thudded in my chest as electricity filled my body, making me clench around him, causing him to groan.

Then I moved, riding him, taking him inside me over and over again, while he fondled my breasts and sucked on my nipple, and I held on to him by his messy wet hair.

He filled me up so completely, so good that all I could think was *his heat, his touch, his lips.*

But it wasn't enough.

I wanted—no, needed more.

So I pulled back and got out of the bathtub. He followed me, and, as if he knew exactly what I needed, he pressed me against the wall, grabbing me under my knees, and buried himself back deep inside me.

Crying out at the feeling, I held onto his shoulders as he pounded in and out of me with power and strength that belied his former state of exhaustion. In fact, he seemed far more alive than before, vigorously fucking me into oblivion.

And when I finally reached the peak, my orgasm causing me to spasm all over him, he groaned and came inside me, filling me up with his warm seed.

Yet despite the fact we'd both just come, neither of us was nearly satisfied. It was as if we'd taken the lid off a pot that had boiled for too long.

Ragnor took me back to the bedroom and threw me unceremoniously onto the bed. Then he pushed my thighs up and covered my entrance with his mouth.

I cried out as he sucked my clit and fucked me with his tongue. I thrashed when he bit his fangs into the skin around my clit while pushing three fingers into my pussy. Another orgasm tore through me, making me see pretty stars and causing me to feel a hunger for him like I'd never felt before.

I pushed his shoulders, and he lifted his head from my pussy, licking his lips. It was so sexy I almost moaned, but I wanted to taste this time. So I pushed him to his back, grabbed his beautiful long, thick cock, and put my mouth over the head.

He buckled under me as I sucked his cock, pumping at the base with both my hands. He made sexy sounds as I licked and sucked and tasted every inch of his sexy cock, enjoying having him under my control, consumed by his desire for me.

The Lord of the League.

The Ragnor Rayne.

And he was letting me ravish his cock like there was no tomorrow.

His hands were suddenly in my hair. He attempted to pull me off him, but I persisted, and eventually, he had no choice but to come into my mouth.

I drank every drop of semen he let out like it was water, not letting go until I sucked him dry. Only then did I raise my head and look at him, mimicking his earlier stunt by licking my lips and making a pleasure noise.

That was Ragnor's undoing.

With an animalistic growl, he pulled me toward him and flipped me so I lay on my stomach. He straddled me from behind, one hand on the nape of my neck while the other locked my wrists behind my back. Then, with a renewed erection, he slid into my slick, wet heat.

And fucked me while holding me absolutely immobile, at his mercy.

I came again. And so did he, but he didn't stop fucking me, growing hard again as if his stamina knew no bounds.

He slapped my ass as he fucked me, over and over again, the pain giving me waves of pleasure I was addicted to. "Harder," I croaked out, needing him to mess me up, to do to me everything I wanted.

And Ragnor obliged at once.

He pulled me up with my back to his chest as he kept on fucking me, his hand on my throat, choking me hard. Exhilarated, I came just from the anticipation of what he was going to do to me.

He rubbed my clit as he sank his fangs into my throat, his cock pounding restlessly in and out of me, all the while holding me still by choking my throat.

I shattered around him all over again, unable to stop spasming with pleasure.

He bit me harder, making the tiny muscles in my loins clench around his deliciously hard cock, and he came inside me, moving his hand from my clit to my ass, taking it in a bruising hold.

He held me still as he emptied himself inside me, and yet somehow, it still wasn't enough.

And it seemed it wasn't enough for him either.

Neither of us was ready to stop, and so we didn't.

For most of the night, he fucked me, roughing me up, biting me everywhere, taking everything he wanted, and giving me everything I needed.

And even when we fell onto the bed in a pile of absolute mush, neither of us having any liquid left inside to spill onto one another, I still needed more. Wanted more. And I could tell he did too.

But it was late into the night, and I realized that tomorrow was Ragnor's turn to fight against Atalon.

"You win tomorrow," I told him, breathless, on the verge of falling asleep, "and I'll let you fuck my ass."

He didn't grin. He didn't say anything. Instead, Ragnor fell asleep, exhaustion taking him over, and I soon followed suit.

CHAPTER 42
RAGNOR

He watched Aileen sleeping for a few moments after he'd pretended to have fallen asleep, before he rolled out of the bed and got dressed.

Then, Ragnor left the room and the dorms, heading toward a training room, where he found Eliza.

She was sitting in a cross-legged position, meditating. But she sensed his arrival because she opened her eye and turned to look at him. "I didn't find it," she told him, her face filled with agony. "I'm sorry, Ragnor."

He hadn't had hopes for her to find it in the first place. Atalon was smart, after all. Far smarter than he'd let on. Atalon had a genius, cunning mind. He always thought ten steps ahead, while Ragnor could only think of eight.

"Will you watch?" he asked her now.

She rose to her feet and walked toward him. "I will," she said quietly, "and I'll do what you asked. I promise."

He nodded, unable to speak anymore.

His only hope was that Aileen would not come to hate him again.

Yet he knew it was a futile hope.

CHAPTER 43
AILEEN

I woke up after a restless sleep in an empty bed, and it was only when I entered the lounge that I realized where Ragnor was.

"The Lords have to be isolated in the waiting room for an hour before the battle," Magnus told me in the kitchenette, handing me a plate of breakfast. He looked as if he hadn't slept a wink, much like everyone else in the Rayne League. "It's some sort of old Hecatomb rule. There used to be a reason for it, but I can't for the life of me remember what it was."

Nodding to him in thanks, I took the plate and sat down next to Isora. The mood was bleak, the recent losses hanging over everyone's heads. Plates remained half eaten, if touched at all. I could barely take a bite of my eggs and bacon.

No one spoke when it was time to leave for the arena. We all walked in silence, taking our seats in the gallery.

Like yesterday, the arena filled up entirely. It wasn't every day, after all, that vampires got to see two Lords battling it out. And these weren't just two Lords, but the famous Ragnor Rayne and Orion Atalon.

Unlike yesterday, I didn't feel nervous when it came to this battle. I knew that Ragnor could take Atalon in his sleep.

I was still worried, though. I didn't want even a hair on Ragnor's head to be harmed.

When Renaldi, now wearing a penguin suit that made him seem somehow even more extravagant than when he wore that stupid toga yesterday, entered the arena with his Lieutenants, everyone cheered, knowing what was to come. "Ladies and gentlemen!" he called into his mic. "You know what's on the menu today, don't you?"

The audience's response was deafening.

"Then without further ado, let us get to the main course!" Renaldi grinned toothily. "Please welcome Lord Ragnor Rayne and Lord Orion Atalon!"

I clapped along, watching as Ragnor and Atalon entered the arena from their respective entrances. Ragnor was wearing a simple uniform of jeans, combat boots, and a black tee. Atalon, on the other hand, was wearing fancy white pants that did not seem fitting for combat, a far-too-tight leather shirt painted dark red, and surprisingly old, beaten sneakers.

He also wore oddly shaped earrings colored gold.

Renaldi stepped back and said into the mic, "You know the rules: You either die or you win. Surrender isn't an option. It's time you settle this for once and for all."

Once he was on the outskirts of the arena, along with his Lieutenants, he said, "Let the battle begin!"

Neither Lord moved. They were both staring at each other, their faces blank.

Tension rose in the air as the audience, which went silent, waited with bated breath for either of them to make a move.

As the minutes ticked by, and with no change in the arena, I grew more and more confused and anxious. Why wasn't Ragnor attacking? He could take Atalon. That shouldn't be a problem for him, especially since I knew what he was capable of.

Ragnor had the magic of manipulating his aura. He could use it to force any emotion he wanted into Atalon, rendering him utterly helpless and easy for the taking. But as it looked now, Ragnor wasn't doing anything of the sort.

And it wasn't just Ragnor, but Atalon too. He just stood there, his hands in the pockets of his fancy pants, staring unblinkingly back at Ragnor.

But then, just as I was watching Atalon on the big screen, I saw his face change ever so slightly. It was a minuscule change, barely visible to those who didn't know him.

His lips twitched, as if he was pulling back a smile.

My heartbeat quickened as I turned my gaze to Ragnor. His face was still blank, but his eyes . . . those midnight blues looked strange. Unfamiliar. Vacant.

An awful memory of my battle yesterday came to me just then. Eleanor, with her dead eyes, operating like a robot under the command of another . . .

"No," I blurted, slowly rising from my seat. "Ragnor, *no*—"

Atalon moved just then.

He walked leisurely toward Ragnor, as if he had no cares in the world. His face broke into a smile as he got closer to Ragnor, and the look on his face was triumphant. He didn't speak as he pulled out a knife, a knife he was allowed to bring to the fight of the Lords, and pushed it into Ragnor's chest.

As though he was frozen, unable to move due to some sort of external force, Ragnor simply stood there and *let* Atalon carve his heart out.

And my own heart stopped.

As if in slow motion, I watched Ragnor crumbling to the floor while Atalon walked away with his heart impaled on the knife.

And then, the pain came.

Pain like no other I'd ever felt.

It was as if someone was carving *my own heart* out.

And the pain was so agonizing, I screamed.

And screamed.

Nothing mattered.

Ragnor was gone.

And my soul was being sucked out of my body, as if it had just lost the one thing that kept it in place.

PART VI

CHAPTER 44

ELIZA

I was used to worst-case scenarios in my line of work. When one's job includes taking deadly risks, preparing for the worst outcome was a must, or you'd go insane.

But no amount of preparation could've braced me for the chaos that ensued in the Hecatomb arena.

From my hidden spot near the exit of the arena, I watched as the scenario I feared most came to pass.

Atalon killed Ragnor.

My friend. One of the few people on this damned planet I actually trusted.

Despite our recent arguments, and many differences, I cared for Ragnor deeply. He was like family. Like the brother I never had.

He was also one of the strongest men I'd ever known.

And yet he was killed right before my eyes.

And unfortunately, the disasters only kept coming from there.

A scream cut through the air. It was bloodcurdling and full of agony, as if the woman who screamed was dying.

I whipped my head in the direction of the scream, seeing Aileen Henderson in the gallery, standing, seeming as if she was being killed over and over again.

Instincts took hold of me just then, and I burst into the arena, running at full speed toward Aileen. A bad, ominous feeling filled my stomach, as if my senses caught on to something my mind didn't, and I knew better than to think twice.

But before I could reach the gallery, Atalon was there, taking hold of Aileen so fast, no one could stop him. I saw some of Ragnor's vampires trying to move into action, but Atalon was unnaturally faster, holding Aileen—who'd stopped screaming and now lay in his arms, too still for my liking—and running toward the exit.

Changing direction, I ran after him, wishing I could be faster, but I was no vampire, and certainly not a vampire Lord.

I chased after Atalon as he exited the arena through the dark corridors, but I lost sight of him soon enough. Still, I didn't relent, the foreboding feeling propelling me forward, telling me that if I didn't get Aileen away from him, the thing I'd been trying to prevent would come to pass.

But even after I ran out of the arena, Atalon was nowhere to be found, Aileen gone with him too.

"Fuck!" I snarled as I ran through the streets of Houston, trying to look for any trace of Atalon, but to no avail.

It was all in vain.

So at some point I stopped, fighting to catch my breath, dread cascading through my body.

I had to do something, but what could I do? My own powers were still depleted after I'd overexerted myself. I was in danger too.

And yet, if I didn't find Aileen, if what my instincts were telling me was true, then soon, none of it would matter.

Because the world as I knew it would be over.

CHAPTER 45
ELIZA

Four months ago

I was completely stuck.

In the depths of Oregon's Washington County, I was faced with a dilemma. The cleft to my right seemed to lead up an uncommonly traversed mount, while to my right, there was an entrance to what seemed like a long-abandoned mine.

One of two would lead me to my destination; that much I knew. But the other might leave me lost between realms for who knew how long.

This was the problem with portals. Finding them was tricky enough as it was, but knowing to which dimension they would lead was almost impossible.

Oregon was one of the few places on Earth filled with an abundance of portals leading to many different realms. Normally, encountering two portals in the same place was a rarity, but in recent years, in such places as Oregon, it was starting to become the norm.

Which made my job a lot harder.

With a grimace, I covered my good right eye with my hand and took the patch off my left. Bracing myself, I put two fingers over the eyelids and forced my eye open.

Pain ricocheted through every cell of my body. Biting my lip hard enough to taste blood, I heaved my breaths through the nose and attempted to focus on the blurry vision before me. It was black and white, like an old film, with only two spots of color—orange where the cleft was and blue over the abandoned mine.

Before the pain could become unbearable, I let go, and my eyes closed shut. Slowly, the pain subsided, leaving the left side of my face feeling numb.

Letting out a sigh and wiping my forehead with the sleeve of my jacket, I fixed the patch over my left eye and poured some water from my canteen over my hand, placing it on my bleeding lip.

Usually, I wouldn't use my left eye if I could help it. The pain was one thing, but the following aftereffects were just not worth it. If I used it for too long, the entire left side of my body would become temporarily paralyzed for different amounts of time. That's why I relied on my other power more. But when faced with two routes, one of which could risk my life, I had no choice.

Putting the canteen back in my pouch, I headed to the abandoned mine, knowing for sure now that this was the right direction.

Passing through portals was quite the experience. The moment I "entered" the mine, the portal activated, sucking me in like a vacuum cleaner, blurring my sight and making me feel as though my entire body was shrinking, before it spit me out in a different realm altogether.

Seeing the clear blue sky and the bright-green grass leading toward a ravine, in which sat an impossibly enormous palace made of shining crystals and other minerals, I knew I had arrived at the right place. Despite the damage it caused, my left eye never disappointed.

I trod the plane of grass, my sneakers crushing the grass far too loudly for my liking. Taking them off, I hung them by the laces on the strap of my pouch and breathed far more easily now that the noise was gone.

Quickening my pace, I jogged through the grass until I reached the large courtyard, filled with all kinds of greenery, from palm trees to strawberry bushes, a few thin streams of water slithering around colorful flowers and plants. It was like a well-cared-for jungle.

Not planning on traversing the yard, though, I only stuck to the sideline, hopping over the water as to not make even the smallest splashing sound. When I finally saw a pretty crystal wall ahead, I slowed down and crouched.

As if on cue, the flapping of wings echoed right above me.

Covering my mouth, I jumped into the nearest bush, ignoring the immediate itchiness that followed. Through the thicket, I saw two tall, winged figures landing not far from where I was hiding.

They spoke in a language I didn't understand, using hand gestures and annoyed facial expressions. They were obviously scouts, going by the tags pinned to the pockets of their cargo pants, but seeing how expressive they were, they must've been quite young.

The older the Malachi, the better they were at masking their thoughts. And those who mastered the art of stifling their emotions completely were the Seraphim, the most highly ranked Malachi.

These two were most likely very young Malachi, since Cherubs, the youngest, couldn't enlist. And with scout being the starting position of every Malachi, it made it easier to identify their place in the Malachi's hierarchy.

When the two walked away toward the jungle yard, I took a deep breath and let myself out of the bush. Irritated by the itchiness, I tore the leaves and twigs off me before I quietly made my way in the opposite direction, looking for an entrance into the large palace, or any other way to get to its top floor.

I highly doubted I would find a Seraph milling around the lower floors. They might've gotten rid of their emotions, but they were still proud.

When I reached the end of the wall, I finally saw an archway. That was the good news. The bad news was that a few Cherubs were hanging around the entrance, and while they were practically babies with wings, I also knew their intelligence was already at the level of a young adult human.

Another bit of bad news: Aside from grass, there were no plants or trees anywhere around here. Meaning no place to hide—or climb—to get to the upper floors.

The Cherubs' foreign chatter tingled my ears as I debated whether I should retrace my steps and climb one of the trees I saw on the way instead. It didn't seem likely the Cherubs would go anywhere, seeing as how they practically manned the archway.

Gritting my teeth anxiously, I pulled away and walked back in the same direction I'd come from. When I reached the first tree in my way—thankfully, not a palm tree but a solid oak—I didn't hesitate and immediately climbed the trunk.

By the time I reached the uppermost branch, I was huffing and puffing, sweat sticking to every part of my still-itchy skin. Parched, I took out the canteen and sipped water before putting it back in the pouch and focusing back on the palace wall.

With how tall the palace walls were, I'd only managed to scrape the second floor. And luckily, there was a small balcony not too far ahead. It wasn't quite within jumping distance, but I could definitely reach it with a good throw.

Crawling toward the end of the branch, I pushed away the leaves and scanned the area. I could hear the distant wing flaps, meaning there were still some scouts patrolling above, but as for the ground, it looked like the coast was clear.

Pulling out a grappling hook, I took a deep breath, stared at the balcony, and threw.

It missed.

I pulled it back using the attached rope and aimed once more, throwing it with all my might.

And missed again.

Come on, Eliza, I thought, annoyed. *You managed far trickier throws in the past. You've got this.*

Gritting my teeth, I threw one more time, and the third time was definitely the charm, because the grappling hook clung to the balustrade beautifully.

Wiping the new wave of sweat off my forehead, I tied the end of the rope to the branch and tightened the knot as much as possible so it would create a sturdy tightrope.

Then I mounted the tightrope.

It had been many years since I learned the art of tightrope walking. Normally it would involve holding a balancing rod and taking the time to center one's balance. But since I was in a hurry, I chose the risky method.

With a deep, calming breath, I propelled myself forward and ran.

Or rather, hopped.

I used long-distance jumps, restoring my balance when I landed on the rope by digging my toes into it before immediately jumping right afterward.

It took four jumps to get to the balcony.

Once I climbed over the balustrade, I could finally breathe. Cutting the rope and hanging the grappling hook over the iron hook of my belt, I knew I should really hurry up now. It wouldn't take long for the scouts—or someone else—to find the rope.

Thankfully, the Malachi did not believe in windows, because all I needed to do to enter the second floor was step through the archway of the balcony. I took a very short moment to take in my surroundings: a large open space with translucent walls and glass-made musical instruments. No sign of stairs, or even an elevator.

The realization hit me too late, making me feel so dumb, it was almost as painful as forcing my left eye open. The Malachi didn't need a stairway or an elevator. They could simply fly to the upper levels.

Great. Now what?

Heartbeat speeding now as anxiety spread through me at the sudden dead end I was facing, I quietly lurked around the floor, hiding behind a large grand piano, despite the floor being completely empty. There had to be a way up without using a pair of wings. Staircases were an inseparable part of architecture. What building wouldn't have them?

A building of a species that didn't need them, obviously.

Still, I couldn't lose hope that I might be wrong. So I hovered around the entire floor, preparing to hide myself the moment I encountered any Malachi, but it seemed that no one was here. Even in the room I entered, which seemed to be residential, no one was around.

Was this floor deserted?

Either way, when I reached the other end of the floor, my wish was granted. A spiral staircase disappearing into the tall ceiling greeted me in an empty hall. Relief washed over me, and I ascended the stairs quietly and quickly, my feet extra soft against the crystal steps.

When I reached the third floor, another spiral staircase awaited, in a similar empty hall made of crystals. Perhaps this was one tall stairway to the upper floor? If so, I would be very lucky.

As long as the halls these staircases were built in stayed empty, that was, since I had no place to hide here.

But the more floors I climbed, the more sure I became that no Malachi used these halls, or staircases, leaving them completely abandoned. Which, of course, made me wonder why they built them, then.

I reached the final floor accessed by the spiral staircase. Seeing no more stairways, I walked toward the exit arch of the hall when I froze in place. Because through the archway I could see a row of Malachi wings, as the Malachi themselves sat with their backs to the archway, looking ahead at something.

Then I heard a distant male voice speaking in plain English.

"We will now begin the trial of Felleya, daughter of Murdoch."

The Malachi's Court of Justice was now in order.

CHAPTER 46

ELIZA

In my forty-some years of living, I never thought I would visit Haramon, the Realm of the Malachi, in my lifetime. But even in my wildest dreams, I didn't think I would actually witness a Malachi *trial.*

Yet here I was, in a large amphitheater made of pure crystals all around, on the tenth floor, placed under the clear blue sky, about to watch a sight an outsider like me should never behold.

Anyone who interfered in Malachi business, and this counted as one of the highest-level businesses the Malachi had to offer, had only one fate: death.

Which was why I was hiding at the very back of the amphitheater, behind a silky white curtain near the archway I'd entered through.

About a thousand Malachi sat in the audience, all wearing the traditional Malachi gear, meaning no shirts and different types of bottoms. Unlike other intelligent races, the Malachi embraced nudity, even seeing it as part of their right, because of their wings. So that female Malachi hung around topless, with their chests on display, mattered shit not.

The Malachi were far more progressive than either humans or vampires, that was for sure.

At the bottom of the amphitheater was a long desk, behind which sat twelve winged figures—six men and six women—who made up the Malachi's Court of Justice. They were also the highest-ranking Malachi—the Seraphim. The ones who ruled over the rest of the Malachi.

And in front of them, on her knees, was a woman with her back to the audience, her ankles and wrists cuffed to the floor in chains. Her feathery wings, colored a deep crimson, hung loose on the ground, her long platinum hair gliding between them.

"Felleya, daughter of Murdoch," said one of the Seraphim sitting at the desk, his voice echoing clearly in the open air, thanks to the absolute silence, "Seraph Cadriel has charged you with the following crimes."

Another Seraph at the desk rose, holding a scroll as she read, "Unauthorized visit to Aderra, unauthorized association with multiple outlanders, unauthorized usage of aether, usage of aether against other Malachi, an attempted offense against a Malachi guard while awaiting trial, and sexual relations with an outlander."

Those were some serious allegations. First of all, the Malachi had to ask the Seraphim for special approvals for almost everything. They couldn't leave Haramon without approval, and special approval was required for them to legally travel to Aderra, or rather the Realm of the Living (planet Earth for short). They also couldn't contact "outlanders" as they called them—which basically meant anyone who wasn't Malachi—without the Seraphim's consent.

Some charges were far more severe than others, though. Controlling the aether was an ability all Malachi were born with, and while they could use it freely in this realm, it was a different story when it came to other realms. Worse than that was controlling the aether with the intent to attack a fellow Malachi. That was a very big no-no. Same went for attacking a Malachi guard.

But the worst offense of them all was the Malachi having sex with an outlander. That went beyond a simple crime; it was a downright *sin*.

Meaning this Malachi, Felleya, was fucked.

"Do you have anything to say for yourself before we proceed?" a male Seraph now asked.

While I was pretty far from the stage below, I could still tell Felleya was trembling. She didn't utter a word and simply shook her head slowly, her hair glistening with her movements.

"Then we shall pass the judgment now," a female Seraph said, and all twelve Seraphim stood up before she continued. "We hereby declare you a sinner and order your expulsion, effective immediately."

A cry left Felleya.

No one spoke as two Malachi, not Seraphim, went onstage and stood at Felleya's sides. At first, I thought they were going to release her from the chains and drag her away, but what they did next made me sick to my stomach.

Each Malachi grabbed a wing, and with a sudden forceful movement, tore them away.

Felleya's screams of agony as blood trickled from her wingless back were too hard for me to bear. I looked away, squeezing my right eye shut, and shakily put my hands over my ears.

The cruelty of what I'd just witnessed, the absolute horror of tearing a Malachi's beautiful wings away . . . I'd seen my fair share of terrible things throughout my life. But somehow, watching those men rip Felleya's wings apart from her shoulder blades took its place as one of the top five most horrible scenes I'd ever witnessed.

I didn't know how long it took for the screams to subside, but when they finally disappeared, I lowered my hands and opened my right eye, turning to look back at the stage. The Seraphim were still at the desk, but Felleya was gone.

Yet a pool of blood, as red as her former wings, still remained.

My target was a Seraph named Theorius.

As I hid behind the curtain, watching the Malachi leaving the amphitheater by flying upward toward the clear sky, not looking back to see if there was a Peeping Tom (because why would they?), I wondered how I could locate Theorius.

From the dry details I had acquired, I knew he had the Seraphim's trademark white wings, blond hair, and eyes so bright, they were almost white. I studied the six male Seraphim who still lingered at the desk down on the stage. They were all different shades of blond. I was too far away to see the color of their eyes.

When the amphitheater was empty but for the Seraphim, who were now talking near the desk in their foreign language, I decided to try and get closer. Lowering myself on all fours, I hid behind the empty chairs in the audience and made my way through the rows as carefully as I could.

After coming so far, the last thing I wanted was to get busted so close to completing my mission.

The Seraphim's voices grew louder the more I progressed. I just wished they would speak in English again so I could understand what they were saying. Unfortunately, it seemed English had been reserved only for the trial.

When I reached one of the front rows, I peeked through the rift between the seats in front of me. The Seraphim were still talking to one another, but I could finally make out more of their features.

And I easily found my guy.

Theorius was standing in front of the desk, leaning his side against it, giving me a full view of his profile. And when he moved his head at one point to look upward, I managed to see his eyes.

They were just like their description. The irises were almost white, as if they were glowing like a vampire's.

Another thing that helped was that the Seraph who was talking to him said something that sounded suspiciously like "Theorius."

With my eyes locked on him, I simply watched and waited until the Seraphim dispersed. It was fascinating in its own way, seeing them interact, this aloof, arrogant, emotionless people. As they chatted in their native tongue, their faces looked as though they were carved in stone. Not even a hint of expression. And while I didn't understand their language, the tone of their voices was oddly empty of lilting gestures. They spoke almost as monotonously as robots.

By the time the Seraphim began to fly away, I was fully anxious. Thankfully, Theorius was still here, talking to another Seraph, only the two of them remaining in the amphitheater. And yet what would I do if he flew away like all the others?

Think, Eliza!

I looked down at my grappling hook. The only idea I had was suicidal—if it succeeded. Which was what I needed, obviously.

Biting my lip, I saw the two Seraphim were starting to make motions of ending the conversation. Before I could think twice about what I was about to do, I grabbed the grappling hook and tied it swiftly to a rope.

A moment after I was done, Theorius and his friend took flight.

With an internal scream of pure fear, I threw the grappling hook.

And it latched onto the hem of Theorius's pants.

Gripping my end of the rope as strongly as I could as I sat on my ass, I pulled my entire weight to my core, weighing myself down as much as possible.

At first, Theorius didn't seem to realize what was wrong. He flapped his wings strongly, making my biceps groan in pain as I tightened my hold. When he realized something else was preventing him from flying away, he looked down.

His eyes met mine.

He shot downward, straight to me, and I let go of the rope and pushed my hands forward, palms up, just as he was about to crash into me.

His naked chest hit my palms.

And at the same time, I lowered my mental walls and opened my mind.

CHAPTER 47
ELIZA

Everything disappeared as an invisible tether bound Seraph Theorius and me together, snapping into place tautly, creating a momentary connection.

My mind invaded his, and images came through, pouring into my head with an intensity that shook me to my core. There were so many images, so many memories and experiences this Seraph had gone through, it made me feel small and young.

Theorius had lived a very long life, and I now had to search for a tiny needle in this endless haystack.

Thankfully, I had already mastered my ability, so all I had to do was mentally whisper *Euphorrey's Relics*, and every memory and all knowledge Theorius had that was associated with these two words streamed into my head through the channel I had opened. I let it pour, rushing in, knowing I would have time later, when I was safe, to sift through it all and find what I wanted.

When the last image entered my mind, I severed the link between Theorius and me with a simple mental slash. My vision returned just in time to see Theorius stumble back before he fell on the floor unconscious.

Normally, when I used my psychometry on humans or vampires, they were out for a good ten minutes, sometimes even longer, so their minds could rebuild their mental walls. But I'd never used it on a Seraph, one of the strongest creatures in all realms.

Meaning he could wake up in less than a minute for all I knew.

Which didn't leave me much time to get out of here, but it would have to do.

Rising to my feet, I started to run.

I ran through the rows, not caring if I was seen now that no one was here, and reached the stairway hall. I then ricocheted down the stairs so fast I began feeling dizzy, thanks to the spiraling pattern, but eventually reached the second floor.

When I was making my way to the balcony I'd entered the palace through, I started hearing voices and the flapping of wings. My heart jumped out of my chest with the realization I was being chased now and that, like I predicted, Theorius had recovered faster than anyone else I'd ever used my powers on.

Just as I reached the balcony, I heard voices echoing right behind me, telling me they now had their sights on me. Which was less than ideal, yet I could do nothing about it.

All that mattered was that I got the hell out of there.

Forcing any hesitation away, I pulled myself up on the balustrade and jumped.

Feathers fell around me as my feet hit the grass, sending reverberating shocks up my calves. I swear I heard my leg's bones crack.

Whether it was the truth or not, adrenaline took care of any pain I might've felt, and I started running toward the junglelike courtyard.

By now, the sounds of flapping wings and calling voices were all around me as I was pursued. I didn't bother looking anywhere but straight ahead, though; all I needed was to get to the portal, and I would be in the clear.

I broke through the jungle and onto the plane of grass. Malachi started appearing in my vision, which told me I was close to being caught, but I refused to let it happen. Not now, when I'd gotten what I needed.

With my heart beating loudly and quickly in my chest, perspiration covering every inch of my skin, and breaths coming out of my throat short and raspy, I saw the area where the portal was, marked by a little ripple in the air unseen by the untrained eye.

And just when I felt a Malachi's hand scraping against my forearm, I forced myself with a jump through the portal and landed on the other side, hitting the ground with a loud *thump!*

I whipped my head back and saw the ripples in the air dissolving around a few Malachi hands that attempted to reach forward before the portal sealed itself completely, becoming a null.

Thank whatever divine being that's up there that portals could only be used twice: for entrance and for exit.

Because that law of realm crossing had just saved my sorry ass.

My apartment in Portland, Oregon, was the furthest thing from neat, tidy, and welcoming. Dusty, full of cobwebs, with barely hinged doors and a creaky, sticky floor, it would easily fail any biohazard test with flying colors.

Gently putting my bag on the least-dirty surface—coffee table, of all things—I limped into the shower. As the water cascaded over my head, surprisingly warm despite the state of this place (and the water heater), I checked my left ankle. An ugly blue-and-purple spot blossomed on the skin, which told me it probably was broken.

Grimacing, I quickly washed my skin and rinsed it, grabbing a clean-enough towel to wipe myself dry before I limped to the dank bedroom naked (but with flip-flops, because I wasn't that careless). When I tried to open the ancient closet, the left door came loose, and I had to put it on the floor.

Evidently, this apartment needed more than a simple cleaning. But since I was tight on money at the moment, it would have to wait. It wasn't like I used this apartment a lot anyway.

Getting dressed in fresh, surprisingly dustless jeans and a V-neck shirt, I put on my beat-up sneakers and went to the little balcony at the back of the apartment. Funnily enough, the chair and table there were less dirty than the ones inside.

Sitting down, I looked at the road below, where many homeless people set up camp. This neighborhood was one of the worst when it came to homelessness and increased crime rates, which would be a problem for a regular person. Thanks to my abilities, I was able to take care of myself in that regard.

Leaning against the chair and closing my eyes, I used one of my aforementioned abilities to sift through the data I'd just risked my life a few hours ago to get.

Psychometry is the power to read an object by creating a point of contact—even the slightest touch would do. That's exactly what I did when my palms touched Theorius's chest. I created a link, a channel for my mind to reach out to his, or in that case to force myself inside and take what I needed.

Now, I was going to use the other aspect of psychometry—called *cognokinesis*.

I fell into the depths of my mind, though more specifically into the mental chamber where the memories I collected gathered. It was shaped like a neat warehouse filled with wooden shelves stocked to the brim with glowing white orbs. There were so many orbs now, after my encounter with Theorius, that the orbs filled the floor.

I sighed. There was nothing more tedious than organizing this chamber. It always left me utterly exhausted, which staying in the space within one's mind tended to do. But organizing could wait.

I sent my mental hands toward the orbs on the floor. Picking them up was the same as trying to hold air, only this air was solid enough for me to lift. I then peeked into the memory-filled orbs, looking for the relevant information.

This process took some time, since when I first used my psychometry on Theorius, the memories I took were all over the place with no concrete theme. It was only when I precisely looked for the keywords-affiliated memories that I received what I needed. However, finding the latter was quite the task.

But I had all night to do this, so I took a physical breath and got right into it.

The first memory orb I activated took me into the amphitheater at the palace in Haramon. It was Theorius's most recent memory of the trial I'd witnessed, only in this memory, I saw it from his point of view.

And when I saw the Malachi Felleya's pretty face looking so lifeless, it made my stomach churn.

But Theorius's emotions remained silent. He was a Seraph, after all. He was as emotionally detached as the rest of them.

The next memory was of Theorius speaking to a few Cherubs. I heard him using the language I didn't understand, probably teaching the Cherubs something, if I went by the classroom setting.

On and on, I delved into Theorius's memories, looking for my objective. It wasn't until I was about halfway through when I finally found it.

The memory began with Theorius walking through a snowy forest. His wings were nestled together with a ribbon wrapped around them, probably so they wouldn't get dirty or something like that.

It also told me this forest must not be in Haramon. Otherwise why would he bother walking and not flying? Much like vampires, the Malachi and other supernatural races preferred to keep their existence a secret from humans. A flying Malachi would definitely get attention.

Though some rare Malachi had the power to turn invisible, which made flying without being detected much easier. Specifically, I knew exactly one Malachi who could do that.

Internally shaking my head so I wouldn't think about *him*, I returned my attention to the memory.

Theorius reached a small town. It seemed European in style, like those off-the-grid countryside villages in eastern Europe. Maybe Hungary? Or perhaps Kosovo? It could definitely be somewhere in the Balkans.

Either way, Theorius lingered at the edge of the town, obviously waiting for someone. When a figure walked out of one of the houses and headed toward us—Theorius and me seeing this from his point of view—I knew this was the person we were waiting for.

The person, a small, bald man with crystal clear eyes, smiled up at Theorius. "It is good to see you, Malachi," he said in perfect English. Rare for these parts to find someone who spoke English, let alone without a hint of accent.

It told me two things.

First, this man must not be native to this town. And second, this was before Theorius became a Seraph, meaning it had to have occurred more than a few centuries ago.

"Arphiase," Theorius said in return, and for the first time since I'd started prodding his memories, I could feel his emotions. He was curious and even a little excited. Expectant. Hopeful. That was quite the range of emotions.

The man, Arphiase, smiled at Theorius. "Would you like to come inside?"

The two walked back to the house Arphiase had come out of. As Arphiase offered to make Theorius a drink, I couldn't help but study the little man. The name *Arphiase* was not native to eastern Europe, that much I knew. Maybe Greek? *Arphi* could come from the word *arche* in Greek, which meant "beginning," or "origin."

Whoever this man was, one thing I knew. He was definitely not human. Because no human moved the way Arphiase did: elegant and smooth, flitting from one spot to another as though he were walking on soft clouds.

I got my answer when Arphiase poured himself a cup of red liquid from an oddly shaped container. That was definitely not wine.

Meaning Arphiase was a vampire.

When the two settled at the dining table, Theorius jumped right into it. "You know why I came," he said, unable to hide the excitement in his voice. "Do you have it?"

Arphiase sipped his drink and gave the Malachi a short nod before he took out a half-burned piece of parchment and handed it to him. "I took great risks to find this information," he said quietly. "The people of Euphorrey are dangerous."

Theorius studied the parchment, and so did I. It listed what seemed to be ingredients. Names of some types of irons and gems along with prices.

Theorius deflated, bitter disappointment rising inside him. "I wanted concrete proof," he said, glaring at Arphiase. "This tells me nothing."

"It tells you what kind of material they ordered," Arphiase argued. "Material that, mind you, they have never asked for from the blacksmiths in Cairo before."

Suddenly, the memory became an indistinguishable blur before it sharpened again. We were no longer in Arphiase's house, but instead watching from a highway, which told me this memory had to be from recent years. Quite the time leap, but I didn't complain.

Theorius flew through the overcast sky, using the clouds as hiding spots from human eyes. He was following a van heading into a large city. I had no idea where we were—the road signs were too far away for me to read, and I didn't recognize this area.

It wasn't until the van stopped near a building in the downtown area of the city that I realized what was happening.

A few normal-looking people got out of the van, the driver handing the key to the valet for parking. None of that would've raised my suspicions if the driver hadn't turned around for a moment, showing me his face, which, thanks to Theorius hiding in a nearby tree, I could make out.

He was one of the Jinn. I recognized him.

Theorius waited for what felt like forever before, some time later, the valet returned the van to the front entrance. Then the Jinn came out, though they seemed to be missing a couple, and, joined by another hooded figure wrapped in a blanket, drove out of there as if their asses were on fire.

Interestingly enough, Theorius didn't follow them. Instead, he jumped into the air, quickly hiding behind the clouds, before he landed on the rooftop of the building. Once there, Theorius and I waited again until the rooftop door opened and a man walked out.

This man I recognized too.

Because he was a vampire Lord. Lord Orion Atalon, to be exact.

And while his face was thunderous, his eyes were triumphant. Because in his hands was exactly what I was looking for. Or at least, part of it.

The Tears of Euphorrey.

CHAPTER 48
ELIZA

Two days ago

"After my break-in to Haramon," I told Ragnor, watching him closely, "I had two missions: first, to avoid being caught by Seraph Theorius and the Malachi who were hunting me down, and the second, to somehow get the Tears of Euphorrey from Atalon."

Ragnor rose from his seat and paced back and forth in the room. It hadn't even been ten minutes since I woke up after my weeklong recuperating slumber, and yet I was already a bundle of nerves.

Because soon, Ragnor would know the true meaning of Euphorrey's Relics, and what it meant that Atalon had one.

"I thought Euphorrey's Relics were practically a myth," Ragnor murmured after a long silence. "According to what I was once told, the Relics siphoned the Morrow Gods' powers after their deaths and mixed them with the blood of the dead of the Massacre of Euphorrey, which created an overpowering magic in each of the Relics."

I grimaced. "Yes," I said, "that's exactly it." I took a deep breath. "There are five Relics altogether. Out of the five, the Tears of Euphorrey is the most dangerous Relic. Because it gives its owner the power to . . ."

I hesitated, reluctant to share the horrible truth. But Ragnor shot me an impatient look, and I knew he had to know. He had to prepare. So I looked away, clenching my hands into fists, and spit it out. "The power to control any living being with a single thought."

Unsurprisingly, Ragnor scoffed. "That's it?" he said, and when I turned to look at him, he gave me an almost incredulous look. "I mean, it's a bad power, but you know my mental fortitude is unmatched—"

"What if I told you that more than one Seraph had fallen victim to the Tears of Euphorrey?" I cut him off, a grim, dark feeling settling in the pit of my stomach.

He stared at me for a few long moments before he said, "Are you talking about the case of Garroth's disappearance?"

Garroth used to be one of the strongest Seraphim in the world—until two hundred years ago, when he suddenly disappeared off the face of the realms. "Not only Garroth," I said, "but Michael too."

Ragnor seemed to see where I was going with this, and he suddenly grew wary. Michael had been a *known* Seraph—he was considered an angel in multiple religions. He was just that famous. But Michael, despite the stories and legends surrounding his existence, had disappeared more than two thousand years ago, never to be seen again.

Theorius, I knew, was a Cherub under Michael's tutelage. That was the reason he was ardently looking for Euphorrey's Relics. Because while he no longer had emotions, he still wanted to solve the case of Michael's disappearance, even if only out of a sense of obsessive duty.

"Both Garroth and Michael were known for their mental fortitude, which far surpasses yours, no offense," I said now, monitoring Ragnor's face carefully. "Theorius, the Seraph I got this information from, and another, vastly different source, believe the Tears of Euphorrey was the culprit—or rather, its owner at the time."

Ragnor shook his head slowly. "It makes no sense," he said, sitting back down on the chair. "A mere Relic couldn't possibly hold enough power to take down a Seraph. Where is the evidence of that?"

"This is the thing, Ragnor," I said quietly. "When a Seraph dies, what do they turn to?"

He knew exactly what I was talking about, and his face went slack as finally, my point seemed to hit home. "They turn to ashes."

"Exactly," I said, feeling a dark resolution rising inside me. "I'm going to try and infiltrate Atalon's dorms and find the Tears."

Ragnor's eyes were filled with dread as he looked at me. "According to what little I know about the Relics," he said, voice tense, "they can bind themselves to their owner."

"That's one thing you don't have to worry about," I said, grimacing. "The Relics won't be able to be bound to anyone else other than the descendants of the Morrow Gods—or rather, the Children of Kahil."

Ragnor didn't seem relieved at the information. And he shouldn't have. Because the fact was, Atalon had the Tears of Euphorrey. Somehow, the Jinn had gotten their hands on that Relic, and, for whatever reason, they gave it to Atalon, a vampire, of all people.

But Atalon being in league with the Jinn was the least of our problems right now. Because in two days, Ragnor would have to face Atalon in the final Hecatomb battle, and if Atalon got to control Ragnor's mind . . .

It would be the end of him.

In the end, even though I managed to infiltrate the Atalon League dorms while everyone was away watching the Hecatomb League members' battles, I did not find the Tears of Euphorrey.

And when I tried to find a way to sneak up on Atalon in his League gallery, the vampire Lord was surrounded by his powerful League members, the seven-pointed-star gold earrings dangling from his ears.

He was always wearing the Tears.

After weeks of using my powers to hide myself from the Malachi, moving from one state to another, barely sleeping, trying to keep myself alive, I was still recharging, my powers so depleted, I could use none of them.

My uselessness had cost Ragnor's life.

And perhaps Aileen Henderson's too.

PART VII

CHAPTER 49
AILEEN

Fire surrounded me. Endless, furious fire that seemed to take over everything, creating a suffocating, yet smokeless, hell.

In this hell, I was somehow able to exist, formless and shapeless, as if I was part of that fire, only with a mind of my own and a sense of sight.

I had no idea how I got here. In fact, I couldn't even remember anything. Who was I? What was my name? *What* was I? I had no answers to these very basic questions. I had a sense of self, but no idea what that self was.

So all I could do was float around in the fire and watch it flickering all around me.

Until I heard an odd sound, which told me I could also, in fact, hear.

I looked around, trying to find the source of that sound in the middle of the flames, and I saw something rippling in the fiery air. Something that took on a form from the fire, growing into a shape that seemed to be like that of a bird. A very large bird that could've passed for a chameleon, what with its colors mimicking those of the flames it was born from.

A pair of yellow orbs flashed in the fire-shaped head of the bird. They were eyes, I realized, as I felt those orbs staring at me. Eyes that flashed with contradictions: violent yet gentle, wise yet unassuming, warm yet impossibly cold.

The fire-bird's beak parted, and a voice came out. It was a surprisingly human voice, only it was soft yet chillingly clear.

"Let us make a deal."

A deal? I wondered, baffled. Wanting to ask what it was talking about, I tried to speak, but it seemed like I had no mouth, or even vocal cords.

Yet the fire-bird, whose name I suddenly recalled from the fog of my memories was Bennu, or rather, the Phoenix, seemed to read my shapeless mind. "You do not belong in this realm, Child of Kahil. You should return to the Realm of the Living."

Its words stirred yet another memory. I was a Child of Kahil, a descendant of the Morrow Gods, daughter of a follower of the Morrow Faith. It was a knowledge deeper than that of my name. It was engraved in my very essence more than any other identity ever could be.

The Phoenix spoke again. "I'll return your soul to your body in the Realm of the Living," it said, "in exchange for you releasing me when the time comes."

Release you? I thought, knowing it could hear me. *From where?*

"From here," the Phoenix replied plainly.

Isn't it your home, though? I wondered as I recalled another memory from the mud that was my mind. It was of a story I'd read in a book called the Tefat. A story of the birth of Bennu the Bird, later named the Phoenix by the Grandmaster, the creator of the world. Bennu was a lost, aimless Spirit born in Esheer, the Realm of Fire. It was meant to serve as Esheer's guardian, never to leave this place.

But Bennu had found a way to escape when, eons after its birth, three human men somehow found themselves in Esheer. So Bennu had struck a deal with the men: It would return them to Aderra, the Realm of the Living, where they came from, and in return, the men would summon Bennu and release it from the eternal hell of Esheer.

The three men were greedy, though. They wanted more out of Bennu. They were drawn to its powers and demanded some be given to them. After eons of being stuck alone in this hellish place, Bennu knew nothing about humans. It had no concept of what greed was. Bennu, too naive for its age, believed their demands to be valid and agreed to their terms.

The three human brothers each got one of Bennu's powers. Neser, the eldest, received its power of fire. Desher, the second eldest, received Bennu's ability to manipulate ash. And the youngest, Ankharen, got Bennu's power to control the flow of time.

Once the three brothers returned to Aderra, the Realm of the Living, they displayed their powers to the humans and were perceived as Gods. They gathered a following, created a faith with them as its central Gods, and believed themselves to be the most powerful beings on Earth.

So much so that they forgot about their promise to Bennu.

But while Bennu might've been naive, it wasn't dumb. As it waited for the brothers' summons that never arrived, it realized the humans wouldn't keep their part of the bargain. So Bennu bided its time for the right moment, when it brought about the brothers' demise.

So went the story of Bennu and the Morrow Gods.

And it seemed I was faced with the same opportunity as those Morrow Gods from the myth, if I were to believe the fiery bird before me was, indeed, Bennu, the mythological Phoenix.

I believed it, though. How could I not, being in this hellish place, with a fiery bird peering at me with bright yellow eyes?

You really like striking deals, I commented almost wryly as I considered its proposal. In the Tefat, I recalled, every story had some sort of moral to be learned. In the Morrow Gods' story, it was how greed and broken promises could bring about one's misfortunes.

If I were to go by that story, I would have to keep my end after getting out of here, no matter the cost.

"Deals are the only way for two parties to receive equal results," the Phoenix now said, answering my nonquestion. "But unlike the story you know, I now have a way of making sure you keep your promise."

I would've been disappointed if you didn't learn your lesson, I couldn't help but think. After all, Bennu the Phoenix was one of the very few beings created by the Grandmaster itself. It had the standing of a being beyond a god. It always struck me as strange that such a being showed such naivety in the first place.

If that's the case, I thought, *then I would like to ask for another thing.*

I could swear the Phoenix sighed before it said, "Ask away."

Carefully choosing my words, I thought, *When I return, I want to have the option to call upon you, releasing you from here, on my own terms. Even if you feel it's not the right time yet.*

The Phoenix didn't speak for a while. It seemed my request took it by surprise, which made sense; I doubted anyone before wanted to voluntarily release the Phoenix for their own use. The Morrow Gods had been afraid of the Phoenix, even though they went back on their promise. So were other creatures whom the Phoenix had struck deals with throughout the stories in the Tefat.

I, too, was afraid of the Phoenix. But I'd also read the Tefat and knew exactly what the Phoenix was capable of. Rather than hoping the Phoenix would never appear, like those before me, I wanted to have the chance to perhaps use it.

And it would satisfy both the Phoenix and me.

It seemed the Phoenix came to the same conclusion, because I could swear its fiery beak stretched into a flame-filled smile. "I accept your request. And so the deal is made."

Before I could say, or rather think, anything else, the fire consumed both the Phoenix and me, and my vision turned pitch black.

CHAPTER 50
AILEEN

I opened my eyes, short of breath, sweat covering my skin.

For a few long moments, I was disoriented, memories pushing their way back into my head. I remembered my name. Remembered who and what I was. Remembered the last few days. Remembered Logan, Zoey, Cassidy, and CJ. Remembered Jada.

That's when my disorientation turned into absolute horror. But the memories did not stop.

Because I also remembered the Phoenix and the promise I'd made.

But the latter didn't matter. I couldn't dwell on it even if I wanted to, because I remembered Ragnor.

I remembered Atalon carving his heart out.

Ragnor's heart.

Ragnor was dead.

Agony made me suck in a breath and put my hands over my chest, where the pain was most unbearable. I couldn't breathe. I couldn't even cry. I was in a state of shock, panic, and utter pain.

It felt as if a vital part of me was missing. As if my heart was cut in half.

I'd thought my soul was crushed before. It felt that way when I watched him getting killed right before my eyes.

And yet now, my soul was somehow still here, barely intact, holding on by a thin last thread, but here.

I almost wished it wasn't. I wished I could be like Jada. That once the pain became too hard to bear, I would simply become . . . nothing.

But I was still here.

My soul, however flimsy, was still here.

And the agony refused to stop.

Because Ragnor was dead.

He was dead.

"Good morning, Aileen."

The voice was familiar, and it made my despair come to a screeching halt. Because that voice . . . it belonged to a very specific individual. And how could it be *here*?

That's when I realized that I was no longer in the arena. I was lying in a queen-size bed, still wearing the jeans and tee I last wore. There was natural light in the room, though, coming from a nearby window. I was no longer underground, meaning I was no longer in the proximity of the arena.

Slowly, I turned my head to the side and saw a familiar man sitting in the chair near the bed. He had tousled black hair, pale gray eyes, and a handsome face that was sadly attached to a tall, lean body. He wore black clothes, along with an affectionate smile that made me want to hurl.

Wode's smile widened when he saw my eyes widen in shock. "Missed me?" he asked, cocking his head as his smile turned almost boyish. "I know I did."

"You . . ." I spluttered, unable to find the words as panic rose inside me. "Where am I? Why are you here? What—"

"Easy," he cut me off softly. "I'll answer all your questions, don't worry. But first, I need to check something."

The Jinni who'd once kidnapped Isora and Zoey and fought Ragnor and me all those weeks ago, stretched his arm toward me. I flinched, not wanting him to even breathe next to me, but he touched my temple despite my evident recoil.

"Interesting," he murmured, withdrawing his hand. "It seems you somehow retained your sanity, despite losing your Alara Morreh."

The shock returned with a vengeance, only this time, it was multiplied by the thousands.

He didn't just say *Alara Morreh*, did he?

"That definitely makes things easier for me," Wode said, smiling again, just as the door behind him opened, followed by what seemed to be a maid holding a tray. "Ah, food is here. You must be hungry. I also got some blood for you. I hope B plus is all right."

Wode took the tray from the maid and shooed her away before he put it on the nightstand. "Come on now," he said. "Sit up and eat. You look like you haven't eaten in days."

I wasn't hungry. I wasn't even thirsty. I was too shocked to even register such unimportant needs.

He sighed. "You either sit up by yourself or I make you," he said, giving me an almost pitying look. "What will it be?"

Beyond the shock, the thought of him, or anyone else, touching me was distressing enough that I sat up, took a spoon, and ate the porridge on the tray.

"Good girl," Wode murmured soothingly, "you'll need all the energy you can get for the next few days."

I had no idea what he was talking about, and I didn't care. I had to get out of here, so nothing else mattered.

Wode kept quiet until I finished the food and drank every drop of blood. Only then did he say, "Let's talk."

Ragnor's face suddenly flashed in my head, and the pain in my chest doubled, making me sick to my stomach. Seemingly aware of what was happening, Wode got a bucket from God knew where and gave it to me. I emptied the entire meal right into it, heaving until nothing was left.

"That won't do, Aileen," Wode said with another sigh. "As I said, the next few days are going to be hard on you. The process of removing an Imprint is quite hard on the body."

I froze, raising my head to stare at him, eyes wide. "What did you just say?"

Wode grinned sinisterly. "Ah, yeah, that caught your attention, didn't it?"

"What did you say?" I repeated, my heart beating so hard, it was almost deafening.

He leaned back against the chair and crossed his arms behind his head. "As I said, we have a lot to discuss. Let me tell you some dry details first."

He spread one arm to gesture over the room before he returned it behind his head. "We're in our new headquarters in Vegas. I know," he added when he saw shock slamming into my face yet again, "it's kind of like we're closing a circle. We met here for the first time a few months ago, after all."

"How long have I been out?" I said, fear now replacing the shock. How could I be in Vegas, when I had just been in Houston? I couldn't have been out for more than a few hours . . .

"It's been three days," he said, shrugging. "You were unconscious for a while, which makes sense, since you have just lost your Alara Morreh."

I began to tremble. "You keep saying my Alara Morreh," I said, voice shaking just as much, "but I have no such thing."

Wode's eyes widened. It seemed now *he* was shocked. "Didn't Rayne tell you?"

My trembling grew worse as a foreboding feeling settled in my gut. "Tell me what?" I asked, feeling tears welling in my eyes. I knew what he was going to say before he did, and I didn't want to hear it.

I couldn't take hearing it.

But Wode was merciless, and he said the thing I feared most. "You were Ragnor Rayne's Alara Morreh. '*The one who's promised*,' as those winged assholes call it."

Shaking my head slowly, all I could say was, "No."

He arched a brow. "You seem to know what *Alara Morreh* means, so that means you know about the Malachi," he said, "but it appears you didn't know that way before he was a vampire, let alone even a human, Ragnor was a Malachi."

It made no sense.

None of it did.

Ragnor, a Malachi? Like CJ?

How?

"It seems Rayne hid some important details from you." Wode smiled, as if it was the best news he'd heard all day.

My head couldn't compute. Everything stood still at his words. I didn't know what he was trying to say, and I didn't bother trying to understand. Because I felt as if everything I knew was suddenly false.

Ragnor had lied to me by omission.

He never told me he used to be a Malachi.

When I tried to talk to him about it before, he'd changed the subject.

Why didn't he tell me? Why didn't he clue me in to the fact I was his Alara Morreh?

Why did I have to learn about this all after he was . . . he was dead?

"Let me tell you some crucial things you need to know, sweetheart," Wode said, and I whipped my head toward him, bile in my throat at the fond way he called me fucking *sweetheart*. "Do you know what vampires truly are?"

"I don't care," I spit, hugging myself. My trembling just wouldn't stop.

"Oh, but you should care, considering I plan on removing your Imprint and turning you back into a human," he said, smiling like a Cheshire cat. "Do you know what an Ekimmu is?"

I knew. It was a creature from the Tefat that served as a medium between species. Like a spiritual being, almost. But what did any of it matter? "I said I don't care," I growled, anger filling me up. I clung onto it. It was easier than feeling the agonizing pain.

"*Ekimmu* is an old name for a vampire." Wode spoke as if I didn't say anything. "And it explains what a vampire truly is. It's a form that brings out the hidden potential in humans, thus you have the Gifted, and even the Sacreds. It's a medium that allows mere humans to use more than just ten percent of their brains. The downside of that, of course, is the fact that the power that allows this, Lifeblood, forces you vampires to drink blood every day to replenish it, or you will suffer from Bloodlust."

My trembling came to a stop.

"The Ekimmu is also a species that can bridge between different supernatural species," Wode continued. "Say a human and a supernatural being birth a child. That child will be born human, never able to fulfill their supernatural potential to the max, unless they are given the Imprint and turned into a vampire. Only then their full potential, perhaps even a special Gift or magic, would come to fruition. The same goes for Malachi who fell from grace—fallen angels, basically, who were kicked out of the Malachi ranks. Like your precious Ragnor Rayne."

I stilled.

"Yeah, Ragnor Rayne committed a grave sin when he was a Malachi." Wode grinned. "He got his wings torn off and was banished from Haramon, the Realm of the Malachi. A banished, wingless Malachi no longer has access to their Malachi powers. They are practically humans—though punished to live as an immortal in their human form.

"But Rayne was given the Imprint and managed to access some of his Malachi powers back," Wode said. "That's the true power of the Ekimmu—of vampires."

I could barely process any of it. Just the knowledge that Ragnor hid so many things from me, that I had to hear about it from Wode, who somehow knew all of it despite being a Jinni and thus an enemy . . .

"And that brings me back to you, sweetheart." Wode gave me another of those maddening smiles, and I flinched. "Why do you think you're a Sacred?"

I froze. "How . . ."

"How do I know you're a Sacred?" He asked the question for me, since I couldn't. And he immediately answered. "Well, let's just say Atalon and I are on good terms. He told me all about your magic. What an interesting power you have."

I suddenly remembered a couple of months ago, when Atalon locked me in that cell with Isora, and the Jinn came to visit, taking Isora and me in exchange for some sort of object Atalon wanted. How did I forget about this? How could I be so stupid as to forget that Atalon and the Jinn had some sort of alliance going on?

Another mistake to add to the never-ending pile.

"But that's not the point here," Wode said, making my eyes snap to him. "You see, you're not simply a Child of Kahil, one of the mere followers of the Morrow Faith, but rather, you're a direct descendant of one of the Morrow Gods themselves."

The story I recalled while in Esheer suddenly came back to me. *Neser, with the power of fire. Desher, with the power of ashes. And Ankharen . . .*

"So you becoming a vampire actually brought you closer to your ancestor," Wode said with a sigh. "And while that is truly a wonder, a curious case to be studied, it unfortunately cannot be part of the plans."

Plans?

Wode smiled again, and something about this particular smile was especially twisted, and it made me freeze yet again. "See, long ago, we Jinn were promised a bride. A descendant of the Morrow Gods, to be exact."

My heart dropped as that foreboding feeling from before returned with vengeance.

"To summarize a long, tragic story, the birth rate of pure-blooded Jinn is close to nil," he said, smile gone. He looked the most serious he had been so far. "Our numbers have been dwindling for centuries. There are only a few hundred of us left."

"What the fuck does that have to do with me?" I bit out, a sense of panicked urgency making my heartbeat quicken.

Wode didn't beat around the bush. "Once every few centuries, a Sultan is born," he said, his gaze locking mine in an unbreakable hold. "Once the Sultan sets his sight on a Hemet, a bride of his choosing, no matter the bride's race, he can impregnate her over and over again and have her give birth to Jinn just as pure blooded as the others."

"No," I said, realizing where this was going now.

He nodded with a somewhat wistful look. "The moment I saw you here in Vegas that first time, I sensed you were my Hemet, Aileen. You're the most perfect Hemet I could find: a descendant of the Morrow Gods, a bride we were promised many centuries ago. It all fits—but for one thing." He paused. "You're a vampire."

And vampires were infertile.

"No," I insisted, feeling as though hives had risen all over my skin.

"This is why I'm going to conduct a ritual to get rid of this Imprint you were given by Rayne," Wode said and gave me an almost fond smile. "And then, once you're human again, I'll make you my Hemet."

I wanted to flee, but Wode had anticipated it. Because the moment I got out of bed and put distance between us, shaking from head to toe, he smiled and said, "I drugged the blood. You'll be fast asleep again soon."

And as if on cue, I sank into the darkness once more.

CHAPTER 51
AILEEN

It was nighttime when I woke up, back in the bed from before.

And despite the fact I'd slept enough to rest for a lifetime, I was utterly exhausted and numb. So numb that I could no longer feel a thing.

Pain? Agony? Shock? Disgust? I had no energy to feel any of it.

I was just . . . tired. So fucking tired.

I just wanted someone to carve my heart out and kill me. Because apparently, it was either that or become a broodmare for the Jinn.

Should I call the Phoenix? Should I use that last resort? What else could I do?

The door opened, drawing my attention to it. Into the room walked a man that made me think only violent thoughts. He was even worse than Wode.

Atalon smiled at me as he took the vacant seat next to my bed. "And here I thought you would've run away already," he said by way of greeting. "I guess Wode charmed you despite everything."

Since I had no energy to even speak, thanks to whatever drug Wode had put in my drink, I did the only thing I could.

I spit at him.

Atalon *tsk*ed as he wiped the spit from his cheek. "How crude," he said, "but why should I expect anything else from you?"

I bared my teeth, unsheathing my fangs. If only I could move, I would tear his head off. But aside from my head, I couldn't move a limb. Great.

"Anyway, I won the Hecatomb, fair and square," he said with enough nonchalance to stir awake the slumbering rage inside me. "So you should really respect the rules, don't you think?"

Fuck you, I thought, wishing he could read my mind like the Phoenix.

But apparently, he didn't need to, since it was written all over my face, if his smirk was any indication. "Now, now," he said, "I've been waiting for this moment for months. Don't ruin it for me."

The need to kill him was so strong, frustration gnawed at me and my inability to move.

"See, Wode and I have been planning this for a while," he said, grinning at me. "Ever since Rayne kidnapped you from my League, to be precise. The Hecatomb was a very useful camouflage."

Here we go with his fucking monologue. Atalon loved hearing himself talk, and he loved even more to reveal his smarts when the time was ripe. Especially if it was to rub it in an adversary's face.

What a fucking snake.

"Don't worry too much, though," he said. "After Wode has no more use for you, I'll give you back the Imprint. You'll become a full vampire of my League. So don't miss the vampiric life too much."

Move! I yelled inwardly at my body. *Kill the fucker!* But it refused my demands. What the hell was that drug that could affect a vampire to such a degree?

Atalon stared at me for a few moments, as if waiting for some sort of response, but all I could do was glower at him futilely. He seemed to realize this and smiled. "I think I like this silent version of you best," he said. "Before I make you a vampire again, I'll definitely cut out your tongue. That would bring us both much needed peace, don't you think?"

Asshole. Conniving, slimy asshole.

Atalon's eyes narrowed. "What did you just say?"

I realized then that I had just spoken my thoughts. When I opened my mouth, my voice finally returned. "I'm going to kill you," I told him conversationally. "I'm going to remove your arms first. Then, I'll castrate you, just for an added bonus, before vivisecting the rest of you. Only after you lose your voice from screaming in agony will I end your miserable existence. Your demise would be the least you could do for killing Ragnor—and for being a disgusting, inhuman creature."

He stared at me for a few long moments before he burst out laughing and rose to his feet. "What a detailed description," he said, amused. "Very bold claims out of someone who can barely move her toes."

"It's only temporary," I told him, the conviction ringing in my voice. "Just like your existence."

His humor dissolved into a bored expression. "So vulgar," he murmured. "Well, in that regard, you make a perfect match for Wode. Beasts often go well together."

He turned around and reached for the door, but just before he left, he turned to look at me one last time. "I'm looking forward to seeing you as a measly, pathetic human, Aileen."

It was only after he left that I knew what I had to do.

"Phoenix," I said out loud, "Bennu. I release you from Esheer and summon you to Aderra. I offer you freedom."

At first, I thought I'd said the wrong words, because nothing happened. But then pain exploded behind my eyes, and I had to bite down on my lip so I wouldn't scream.

Tears streamed down my face as the pain seemed to only grow worse and worse, until I thrashed in bed, my mobility returning along with the pain.

The pain suddenly faded, and heat filled me from the inside out. My body grew hotter and hotter until I had to kick the blanket off me, and I rolled to the cold ground, trying to cool myself as the heat turned intolerable.

And just when I thought I was going to be burned alive from the inside out, a clear voice rang within my head. *I am here, Child of Kahil.*

The heat slowly disappeared, and I fought to catch breath, trying to wipe the sticky sweat off my skin. *You're where?* I thought, trying not to panic as I figured out what was going on.

A Spirit cannot appear in Aderra as is, the Phoenix said, *so you will serve as my host.*

A host, I repeated, my panic growing. *You did not mention anything about me being a host!*

It is irrelevant, Child of Kahil, the Phoenix said, almost as if it was scolding me. *For now, we need to get you out of this predicament.*

"That's why I called you," I murmured as I forced my heavy limbs to straighten as I climbed to my feet. "How do I get the fuck out of here?"

That will not be enough, the Phoenix whispered in my head. *There is another way. A better way.*

"Enlighten me, then," I hissed, impatience and a hysteric sense of urgency burning inside me.

The Phoenix was quiet for so long, I grew antsier and antsier. I stretched my sore, numb limbs, trying to get myself in some sort of shape in case I had to run for my life in my current pathetic state.

But then the Phoenix said, *You have the power of time, Child of Kahil. Use it.*

"What the hell could stopping time for thirty seconds help me with?!" I growled, angry. "In my current condition, I wouldn't be able to make it a few steps out of the door, especially with the effects of using that power—"

I stopped my rant as the meaning of its words sank in. The Phoenix didn't tell me to stop time. It told me to *use* time.

Heart racing with sudden hope and excitement, I held my hands together, closed my eyes, and fervently, desperately, thought, *I wish I could go back to that moment. I wish I could stop him from going to that fight. I wish . . . I wish to save him—*

Another wave of pain exploded in my head, making blood trickle down from my nose. This time, I couldn't stop myself from screaming. My vision turned white as the pain increased, and I wasn't able to hear, see, or even feel anything other than pure, undiluted agony.

And just as suddenly as it hit me, the pain was gone.

Slowly, the white in my vision dissipated, blurring, before sharpening and showing me I was no longer in that stifling bedroom.

Instead, I was in the Hecatomb arena. In the Rayne League's lounge, to be more specific.

I was sitting on the sofa, with Isora at my side, holding on to me, and Ragnor on my other.

And I realized I'd done it. I'd actually done the impossible.

I'd turned back time.

CHAPTER 52
AILEEN

If I'd let myself, I would've grabbed Ragnor's face right there and then and just kissed the hell out of him.

I would've stripped him naked right in front of everyone and rode him to oblivion, feeling his warmth. Consoling myself that he was alive. That perhaps it was all a bad dream, and the final battle hadn't happened.

But when I looked at Ragnor and saw his exhaustion, the resignation in his eyes that I'd seen before my own battle, I realized something crucial.

Ragnor had gone into the battle with Atalon knowing he wouldn't make it.

And that meant yet another secret Ragnor had hidden from me up until the very end.

I had questions. So many fucking questions. I wanted to kiss him and shake him at the same time so he would spill everything. How did he know he would lose to Atalon? Why didn't he tell me he used to be a Malachi and that I was his Alara Morreh? Why didn't he confide in me, after I'd given him everything I had to give?

But those questions would have to wait.

Because the most important thing was to ensure we both survived the Hecatomb this time around.

I rose to my feet, startling both Isora and Ragnor. "I need to breathe," I said, urgency in my voice. "Ragnor, can you take me out?"

My beautiful Ragnor frowned, confusion temporarily wiping that awful resignation I could now recognize from his face. "Why?"

"Please," I said, holding his gaze, my body aching to jump on him, to feel him, to reassure myself that he was alive. That his heart still beat in his chest. But there was no time for that. "Just for an hour."

Whatever Ragnor saw on my face, he nodded and stood up. "Let's go now, then."

I had no complaints whatsoever.

For everyone else, the present I remembered didn't exist.

They didn't know Ragnor had died and I was kidnapped. For them, it had only been earlier today when the Hecatomb participants fought to the death and we lost important League members because of it.

The reason I was able to deduce that much was that everyone acted the same as they had when this day played in my memories. No one seemed the wiser about the fact we were now in a completely different timeline.

Because in this timeline, I knew what was going to happen, and I would do everything to stop it.

I would not lose Ragnor Rayne again.

Ragnor and I didn't speak as he took me out of the arena and back to the streets of Houston. It wasn't until we hit a main road when I said, "Where is the closest pharmacy?"

He looked at me, utterly baffled. "Why do you need a pharmacy?"

"Because I don't think I'll be able to sleep tonight," I told him, which was actually the truth. "I know there are certain sleeping pills that work on vampires." I'd once seen Isora take them, since she had trouble sleeping.

Reluctantly, Ragnor nodded, his look reeking of suspicion. But I didn't care what he suspected—it would never be what I actually planned anyway.

Ragnor led me to the closest CVS, where I went to the pharmacy counter and asked for a drug called Sunnight, which I knew was the name of the pills Isora was taking. She was given those pills by Leah, the infirmary nurse. Thankfully, I didn't need a prescription for these.

Since I had no money, Ragnor paid for the pills—an irony that was not lost on me—and we returned quickly to the arena. That's when I told Ragnor, "I'm going to make some food. Want anything?"

"Hey." He suddenly put his arms around me, and my body ached, wanting to lean into him to allow his warmth to envelop me. "Why aren't you talking to me?"

I made the mistake of staring into his midnight blue eyes. I almost surrendered to the worry within them. I almost broke down crying. *You died, Ragnor!* I wanted to scream. *You left me before you could even tell me everything about yourself!*

But there was no time. I had less than twelve hours until the final battle.

"I'm just tired, Ragnor," I said, forcing myself to leave his arms and head to the kitchenette. "It's been a long day."

He didn't touch me again but kept close to me. "Let me make you something," he offered.

"No," I said, insistent. "I'd rather make it myself." When he went silent, I glanced behind me to see he was looking away, folding his arms, obviously irritated. Regret filled me, along with an overwhelming amount of love I had to shove down for now. "I need to keep busy," I lied, "so just let me."

He nodded and sighed, raising his beautiful face to stare at me. "Let's eat together in my room, then."

I nodded, gave him a wobbly smile in an attempt to reassure him that all was well, and returned to work.

I wasn't much of a cook, but I knew how to make one thing pretty well, and that was pancakes. As long as I had the ingredients, my pancakes always turned out pretty fucking tasty.

And I needed them to be as tasty as possible right now.

Looking to the sides, seeing that no one was lingering around the lounge—everyone had retired early, I remembered—I plucked out ten white Sunnight pills and ground them into thin powder. I added that powder to the batter and made five perfect pieces.

Putting some chocolate on them, I grabbed the plate and went into Ragnor's room. He was sitting on the bed with his back to the door, his face buried in his hands. He seemed so defeated, hunched over like that.

But not for long.

"Hey," I said, closing the door behind me and heading to him. "I got some pancakes."

He turned to look at me with a weary look that made my weak heart want to wrap my arms around him and tell him everything would be okay. "They smell really good."

I put the plate on an empty chair. "Usually, I would say let's eat them while they're hot," I said, sitting down on him, startling him into wrapping his arms around me, his look surprised. "But I'd rather have you first."

Ragnor's eyes widened, and finally, *finally*, I let myself succumb to my wishes and planted my lips on him.

My entire body trembled when I felt his tongue dancing with mine. I wanted to cry in pure relief when his hands cupped my breasts through my shirt. When I released his cock from the binds of his pants, I was already so wet, needing him inside me. Needing to feel him as close and as intimately as humanly, vampirically, possible.

Shoving my pants and panties away, I took him inside in one swift movement that caused us both to moan in beautiful pain and pleasure.

"Fuck, Aileen," he growled, grabbing my ass in a bruising hold, pulling me up and shoving me down so fiercely, I could feel his dick rubbing my womb.

This was heaven. There was no other word for it. Ragnor, inside me, all over me, his lips on my throat, his hands forcing me up and down his length, my hands in his silky, disheveled hair . . . Pure heaven.

Heaven I had lost.

Heaven I planned to never, ever lose again.

No matter the cost.

Ragnor and I lay naked in his bed, cuddling together, his hand caressing my arm almost absentmindedly.

We'd spent the last few hours fucking each other ferociously, and both of us were spent. If I didn't know what was going to happen, I would've fallen asleep like I did this very same night, before I'd turned back time.

But this time, things were different.

"Let's eat," I declared after some time, sitting up and wincing, seeing as how I was sore all over.

As if it was an accomplice in my plans, Ragnor's stomach growled. "Yeah," he murmured, wearily sitting up. "Should we heat it up?"

"Nah, it's still tasty," I said, grabbing the cold pancakes and handing them to him.

He frowned. "Don't you want some? You said you were hungry."

I forced a grin on my face to hide my rising nervousness. "After eating you up, I feel quite full."

He barked out a surprised laugh, eyes twinkling a bit before they dimmed back to their previous, resigned expression I couldn't wait to wipe off.

To my utter relief, Ragnor practically inhaled the pancakes, unsuspecting that I might've added something to them. It warmed my heart that he trusted me at least that much. Ironically, that would also be his undoing.

When the plate was empty, Ragnor licked his lips. "That was fucking good," he said, and pulled me into his hug, lying back on the bed after putting the plate away. "Thank you, Aileen."

I buried my face in his chest, hugging him tightly. *I'm sorry,* I thought grimly. *I'm sorry, Ragnor.*

Slowly, I heard his breaths becoming even, his chest rising and falling at a monotonous pace. I counted the breaths, heard his heart calming down but beating, alive, in his chest.

Minutes later, Ragnor was asleep.

Gently, I pushed his arms away and sat up, watching him sleep. He seemed so serene and peaceful, as if he had no cares in the world. As if he hadn't hidden anything important from me. As if he hadn't died and left me all alone, almost tearing my soul away and leaving me to a brutal fate, similar to Jada's.

As much as I loved Ragnor, and as much as I was exhilarated that he was alive again, that I'd succeeded in turning back the clock to make things right this time, I couldn't help but feel resentment.

Just why did you never tell me anything?

I sat on the bed and watched Ragnor as the minutes turned into hours. I didn't sleep. I couldn't afford to. I had to keep an eye on him until the very last minute to ensure he wouldn't wake up before he needed to.

Being in an almost trancelike state, staring at Ragnor's sleeping face, I jumped when the bedroom door suddenly opened, revealing a familiar face I hadn't seen in a while.

Eliza looked at me, her right eye wide with the same shock that I felt at this moment. "Aileen? What . . ."

Her gaze went to sleeping Ragnor, and I could tell a million thoughts went through her head; about just as many passed through mine. "What are you doing here, Eliza?" I asked, quickly pulling on my shirt and jeans from before, so as not to talk to her stark naked.

"I . . ." she started, then paused, frowning, before turning to look at me. "You know."

I narrowed my eyes. "Know what?"

Eliza walked toward me. "About the Tears of Euphorrey."

Tears of Euphorrey? For some reason, that term sounded familiar, but I couldn't quite pinpoint why. "I have no idea what you're talking about," I told her frankly, deciding on a whim against dancing around the truth, feeling as though we had the same agenda. "But I do know Ragnor will die tomorrow if I let him fight."

She sat down on the chair. "Yes, he will," she said, grimacing. "But he must. There is no other way."

"But there is," I told her, watching her closely as she whipped her head up to stare at me, her good eye unblinking. "You know about the rules of the Hecatomb?" I asked, and when she reluctantly nodded, I smiled. "The rule is that the final battle will be between two *Sacreds*."

Her eye widened just then. "Aileen," she said slowly, "you can't possibly think—"

"I'm going against Atalon," I told her, smiling wider. "So please, in case it's related to that, do tell me about these Tears of Euphorrey."

CHAPTER 53
RAGNOR

Ragnor, far more groggy and confused than he should've been, woke up in his bed and stared at the ceiling.

Aileen had been acting strange.

She was strange when she'd asked to go to a pharmacy for sleeping pills.

She was again strange when she'd insisted on cooking.

Then, she was strange—though in a way Ragnor enjoyed—when she'd quite literally jumped his bones.

Now, he was trying to remember how the hell he'd fallen asleep. He was supposed to stay awake while Aileen fell asleep and go meet Eliza, to see if perhaps she'd created a miracle and managed to get the Tears of Euphorrey from Atalon.

But he'd ended up falling asleep instead.

Which meant Aileen had used those sleeping pills on him. In the pancakes, specifically.

Alarmed at that last thought, Ragnor got out of bed and dressed as fast as he could before he left the room.

The lounge was empty. So were the corridors when he hurried to the arena. But before he could reach it, a hand grabbed his wrist, drawing him to a stop.

He turned to see Eliza, staring at him with a look he couldn't quite read. "Follow me," she said quietly.

"I need to get to the arena," Ragnor insisted, shaking her off. "The Hecatomb—"

"Come with me," she cut him off, voice strained with worry. That's when Ragnor saw the drops of sweat on her forehead, the tightness of her lips, that evident stress in her right eye.

Eliza seemed on the verge of a meltdown.

But why?

"Where's Aileen?" he asked, having a sinking feeling that she was the source of this uncharacteristic anxiety displayed by Eliza.

She grabbed his wrist again. "Please, Ragnor," she said, pleading with him, which made Ragnor freeze. "Please, just once, don't ask questions."

Heart pounding loudly in his chest, he ignored the terrible feeling creeping into his gut as he followed Eliza. She took him to the Rayne League's assigned gallery entrance, where they entered and reached the seats occupied by his League members.

His members, much like him, were confused that he was there. "My Lord?" Margarita said, her eyes bloodshot, staring at him in confusion. "What are you . . ."

"Oh, shut up, Wallen," Eliza snapped, and Margarita whirled around to look at her, narrowing her eyes when she saw who had just spoken. Eliza ignored the other woman's glower and pointed at the arena. "Just watch."

Renaldi's voice suddenly echoed in the arena. "Welcome to the battle you've all been waiting for!" he called giddily into the mic. "Without further ado, please welcome Lord Ragnor Rayne!"

To his horror, Ragnor watched as a familiar figure walked into the arena. Aileen's blond hair glinted as she headed to its center, followed by stunned silence from the audience.

Renaldi, too, seemed stunned from his position on the outskirts of the arena. "Err . . . umm . . . Miss Henderson?" he asked, chuckling weakly. "This is . . . um . . . You know your battle was yesterday, right?"

On the screen, Ragnor saw Aileen smiling. "I'm here as acting Lady of the Rayne League," she said.

Ragnor was struck dumb.

"Acting . . . Lady?" Renaldi seemed puzzled. "Henderson . . . I mean, you are merely a Common member . . ."

Another figure appeared in the arena. From the opposite entrance, Atalon walked in, wearing a pleasantly surprised smile. "Never mind that, Renaldi," he said, drawing everyone's attention to him. "I'll happily battle Henderson here."

Ragnor stiffened. "Eliza, let me go," he said, gritting his teeth.

Eliza's hold on his wrist tightened. "Trust her," she whispered. "Trust *me*."

Trust Aileen? But—

It suddenly hit him. Two days ago, when Eliza told him about the Tears of Euphorrey, she said the only people it wouldn't work on were the Children of Kahil. The Morrow Gods' descendants.

In other words, Aileen.

And yet—"Eliza, the Tears aren't the only dangerous thing about Atalon," he said, staring at the arena with fear as Atalon took his place across from Aileen. "Atalon is a *double*."

Eliza stilled. "What are you talking about?"

Ragnor's heartbeat quickened as he shook off her hold. "It means that Atalon has more than one type of magic!" he snapped, panic suffocating him.

Before Ragnor could jump into the arena, Renaldi suddenly said, "All right, then. Let the battle begin—between Orion Atalon and Aileen

Henderson!" He then turned to look directly at Ragnor. "Interference will result in an automatic win to the opposing side."

Ragnor bared his teeth, growling. Because now he couldn't intervene. If he did, Aileen's life would be forfeit, for there was only one way to win the Lords' battle in the Hecatomb.

And Renaldi had just declared it in front of everyone.

Rendering Ragnor useless.

"If she dies," he said, voice low, "I'll kill you."

Eliza tensed, hearing the true threat in his words.

And with that, Ragnor was forced to watch his Alara Morreh battle for her life in his stead.

CHAPTER 54
AILEEN

I could feel the bloodthirstiness filling my veins when I watched Atalon enter the arena. His smirking, snakelike face, his pitch-black eyes glinting in sickening delight, reminded me of what he'd told me just twelve hours ago, before I had turned back time.

He might not know about the promise I'd made back in that awful, stifling bedroom, but I did.

I would kill him.

And I would make it *hurt like all fucking hells.*

The moment Renaldi announced the beginning of the battle, followed by his warning to Ragnor, whose eyes I could feel boring holes in my head all the way from the Rayne gallery, I braced myself.

Atalon put his hands in his pockets, his gold earring, the Tears of Euphorrey, glinting.

And I felt it. What Eliza had warned me about.

It felt as if someone was putting pressure on my skull. It was a pain similar to the one I felt when using my time-stopping powers, but also vastly different. This pain was probing, searching, invasive.

"What a valiant girlfriend you are," Atalon murmured as he began walking toward me, probably thinking he would soon take control over my mind. "I doubt Rayne would appreciate your efforts, though. Especially since you'll die here."

That was actually hilarious to me. "I thought you wanted me alive," I said through gritted teeth, fighting the pressure that kept on increasing on my skull.

Atalon cocked his head. "Why would you think that?"

Even though just breathing hurt, I forced a smirk onto my face. "I . . . thought . . ." It grew difficult to speak, but I refused to give in. "That after . . . I b-became . . . a broodm-mare . . . for the J-Jinn . . . y-you wanted me . . . to be g-given . . . your Imprint . . ."

Atalon paused, his own smirk wiped off his face, eyes glowing that shadowy glow only he seemed to have. "Who told you about this?" he asked, eyes no longer delighted but rather dead serious.

That made me grin wider, even as I winced with the never-ending pressure that made it hard to even move my lips. "You."

He snarled, enraged and aghast in equal measures. He was probably thinking that I was lying, but joke was on him, because I was speaking the absolute truth.

Even though that truth was only for me to know.

The pressure grew impossibly worse until I had to cry out, as if that would relieve some of it. But all it did was somehow make it even worse.

"No matter," I barely heard Atalon murmur. "Soon, you'll be helpless, and then, I'll—"

"HA!" I barked out the laughter through the pain. "Y-your Tears . . . won't . . . work on . . . m-me."

"Shut your mouth," he snarled, and I realized he was a few steps away. "The Tears will work!"

He seemed to be growing angrier, which made the pressure worsen with every passing second, so much so he didn't even bother questioning me about how I knew things I shouldn't have.

But it was also good for me. *Get even madder, Atalon.*

"Fuck!" Atalon growled, seeing as I could still laugh while he attempted to infiltrate my mind. *"Fuck!"*

"T-Time . . . for p-plan . . . B," I sputtered, grinning widely.

All of a sudden, the pressure was gone, as if it had never been there in the first place. "Cursed wench," Atalon spit, glaring at me. I could see him better now that my vision wasn't blurry from the pain. "Why? Why won't it work?!"

"You should know better than anyone," I said, finally able to speak normally again. "I'm a Child of Kahil, remember?"

Atalon's eyes widened with the belated realization. Apparently, even Atalon had his dumb moments. And this one had just cost him.

Because according to Eliza, using the Tears of Euphorrey took a toll on its owner's mind. And the longer the usage, the worse the damage would be.

Face contorting in fury, Atalon growled before he came at me full force.

And fast.

So fast I almost didn't avoid his punch and didn't manage to evade his kick to my already bruised ribs. Gritting my teeth, I kept myself at full attention, seeing the moment when he aimed for my legs and sidestepping his kick, but unfortunately, that meant his fist crashed into my gut, throwing me back a few steps.

He didn't leave any openings or any room for rest. Atalon was fast, relentless, and powerful as he came at me over and over. I had to keep my reaction time at top condition, or he would literally beat me to a pulp. And that wasn't an option.

Knowing my time stopping wouldn't work on him, I didn't bother attempting that. He didn't even leave me time to try and get into the first Behest of Iovan's Imperium, and I had a hunch that even if I succeeded, it wouldn't work on him. He was too fast and too ferocious to fall for any trap, and Iovan's Imperium was all about setting traps.

So I had no choice but to keep being on the defense, trying to come up with some sort of plan, seeing as he wasn't slowing down anytime soon, and I was growing wearier the longer the fight continued.

I had to change the tides somehow.

He suddenly stopped his onslaught and stepped back, smirking when he saw I was short of breath. "If you thought the Tears were your only obstacle, then you were sorely mistaken," he murmured, voice as silky and smooth as a snake's scales.

Wiping the sweat off my face, I stared at him long and hard. He was a vampire Lord all right, but I knew the nature of his magic. I'd witnessed it myself. He could create paintings that captured a scene from a person's past, present, or future, and once that person looked at the painting, they absorbed it, and it created a mental link with Atalon, allowing Atalon to learn everything about that person.

While it was a very powerful magic, I couldn't see a way for him to use it in combat.

That is, until Atalon grinned and said, "We played long enough. It's time to get serious, don't you think?"

And after he uttered those words, the arena, Atalon, everything distorted, growing blurry, darkening, before sharpening yet again, creating a new space.

A familiar space.

A room.

Basement full of little tiny bodies.

Bleeding, disfigured bodies.

I stared at the sight, unable to process what I was seeing. Because I'd just been in the arena, in the middle of a battle of nerves with Atalon . . .

But now I was back . . . home?

No.

I couldn't be back there.

This had to be an illusion.

Looking behind me, I saw the stairs leading up and away from the awful basement filled with the stifling stench of burning flesh. Without thinking twice, I climbed those stairs, realizing I could move as if I was really there.

Don't think, Aileen. Just act.

I burst through the door to the living room of my old home. I strode to the front door, pulling at the handle.

But it was locked.

Shaking, I looked around me. The house was the same as the last time I'd seen it. Meaning the layout had to be similar.

I walked to the kitchen, then behind it to the door leading to the backyard, where the river full of dead girls' ashes was.

Don't think about it, Aileen. Don't fucking think.

The door was unlocked, and I exited, but instead of being in the backyard, I was suddenly in a hospital room.

Before me, in a bed, lay an eighteen-year-old boy wearing a hospital gown, with a bandage around his bruised neck.

His turquoise eyes were open, staring at nothing.

Logan.

I knew it was an illusion. That this wasn't real. It was a memory that Atalon somehow forced on me, mixed with the reality that Logan was . . . was *dead.*

Trembling uncontrollably, my breaths turning short and panicked, I retrod my steps, and once I was through the door, it closed right in my face.

I turned around then and saw I was no longer in the hospital or my old home. Instead, I was in a filthy, messy apartment I faintly recognized.

On the floor of that apartment lay Cassidy, her eyes closed, her face the most serene it had ever been.

It was her old apartment she'd had with her abusive ex-boyfriend, Austin.

And Cassidy, like Logan, was . . .

"Get me out of here," I murmured, running through the apartment to reach the door that led me not to the hallway of that old apartment building but rather to the grocery store I used to work in.

I was at the storage room, and I frantically ran to the front of the store. I pushed myself through the aisles, attempting to reach the entrance, when I saw yet another body lying on the floor.

Zoey.

But Zoey didn't belong in the grocery store. So far, all the people and places matched, so this made no sense . . .

Until I saw her body was wearing black clothes, and a pistol was in her hand, blood trickling from her chest.

My heartbeat became deafening. It was a scene from that one time I was working when there was an armed robbery. I'd wrestled with one of the robbers when the pistol went off, the bullet hitting the robber in the chest, causing his partner to run away.

But that robber's death wasn't my fault, I couldn't help but frantically think, looking down at the dead body of Zoey with horror. Was she a representation of that awful day? Why? Why *her*? I didn't . . . I didn't kill her!

But you feel like you did, don't you? A voice murmured in my head. A very unwelcome, intrusive voice that made me break out in a cold sweat.

Keep going, I urged myself, forcing my feet to move over Zoey's body toward the grocery store's entrance. *Don't look. Don't think. Just keep on moving . . .*

I pushed the doors open . . . and ended up in the alley behind the Banner Bar, where Ragnor had given Cassidy and me the Imprint.

There, in the dumpster I had hidden behind what felt like ages ago, were the bodies of CJ and Jada, hugging one another, their faces peaceful.

Trembling all over, I stepped away and turned around to see a silhouette heading my way. The silhouette was that of a man with shoulder-length hair and a trench coat, and I knew it was Ragnor.

But the silhouette also had a pair of large, feathery wings.

The silhouette suddenly froze, and between one blink and the next, it was replaced with the body of wingless Ragnor lying in a puddle of blood on the asphalt, a gaping hole in his chest.

"No," I said out loud, needing to hear myself, "this is not real, Aileen. This is not real. *This is not real!*"

Let me, Child of Kahil.

I froze. "What?"

You are too young and inexperienced to deal with this magic, the Phoenix murmured in my head. *Let me handle this for you, Child.*

Tears falling down my face as I stared at Ragnor's dead body, his eyes glassy, breaking my heart for the second time, I knew I had no other choice.

My knees lost their power, and I fell to the floor. "Just . . . make him pay," I said quietly, defeatedly. "Do to him what I promised I would do."

The Phoenix did not respond.

Instead, I felt its warmth taking over my entire body, heating my blood, my bones, everything, until I was nothing but fire and flames.

CHAPTER 55
RAGNOR

Ragnor saw his fears come to life when Aileen ran across the arena frantically, pale with eyes full of tears, seeing things only she could see. Things that Atalon dug out of her memories and used against her. To weaken her. To beat down her will.

Because unlike many others, Atalon would not be satisfied by a quick kill. He could've killed her at any moment since he used his magic on her to force her into this trance. But he wanted to break her first.

Only then would he complete the hunt.

"You can't interfere," Eliza said over and over again, her own voice pained as she, along with the entire audience, watched Aileen crying and running around like a madwoman. "You can't take all the Lords together. The Association will hunt you down for breaking the rules. You're not above the law, Ragnor."

"My Alara Morreh is going to die!" he snarled, holding the railing so hard, his knuckles turned white. "She's going to die, and I'm just standing here, letting it happen!"

"Please, Ragnor," Eliza begged, wrapping her arms around him. "Please!"

Ragnor could not stand it anymore. He pushed Eliza off him and away, climbed the railing, and prepared to jump—

But then Aileen suddenly stopped. She stood in the middle of the arena, frozen.

Then her eyes rolled, showing the whites.

Ragnor's heart dropped.

And Aileen exploded.

Out of thin air, fire erupted, engulfing Aileen's body. The smell of smoke filled the arena, as ashes and flames circled around the tornado of fire that took over Aileen. The temperature in the arena rose in response to the fire sucking up the oxygen, and Ragnor could feel it was becoming harder and harder to breathe.

Atalon coughed, stepping back, staring, like everyone else, at the fiery storm that had taken over the arena. His eyes grew impossibly wide when the tornado suddenly disappeared, revealing not Aileen, but a giant bird made of fire.

"The Phoenix." Eliza's whisper made Ragnor's skin crawl.

But as much as he wanted to deny what Eliza had just said, he knew it to be the truth.

The Phoenix was here.

Not in Esheer, the Realm of Fire, where it belonged.

But here.

And it had taken over Aileen's body.

"Fuck," Ragnor growled, the tiny hairs on the nape of his neck rising. "It's . . ."

"A level-five threat to the Realm of the Living," Eliza murmured, and this time, Ragnor turned to look at her. He saw her right eye fixed on the Phoenix, and her left, under the eye patch, glowing green.

The situation had just turned from the worst to an utter disaster.

"Eliza," Ragnor said, jumping down from the railing back to the gallery, grabbing her stiff body. "Fight it. Fight *them*."

She didn't respond.

When the audience collectively gasped, Ragnor whirled around to look back at the Phoenix, and he saw a scene out of the depths of hell.

The Phoenix danced.

It spread its left wing, and flames took over Atalon's left arm, cutting it off from the rest of his body.

It spread its right wing, and flames took over Atalon's right arm, burning it to ashes, which then wrapped around his crotch.

Then the Phoenix raised its head, and as if that was the command, the ashes severed Atalon's penis.

Atalon screamed.

And continued to scream as the Phoenix continued its horrible dance.

Atalon's left foot was soon burned to a crisp.

Then his right foot twisted in an unnatural way and was severed by the Phoenix's command.

Bit by bit, the Phoenix cut Atalon into literal pieces, but did not sever the head. As if it was enjoying the torture. As if it was intent on making his death as painful as possible.

Then the Phoenix bowed, finished its dance, and a sickening sound sliced through the air as Atalon's screams were cut off by his final beheading.

And with his limbs spread all over the floor, while others were burned to ashes or disfigured beyond recognition, Lord Orion Atalon died.

But Ragnor was not able to feel any sense of relief. For the Phoenix was here, and next to him, Eliza was about to be taken over by as frightening a being, if not more so, as the Phoenix.

That's when the Phoenix burst into flames, its horrible croak reverberating through the arena, and burned, revealing Aileen beyond the ashes, naked and full of burns.

This time, Ragnor didn't think twice; he released Eliza and jumped into the arena, laser focused on his Alara Morreh.

The moment he reached her, he pulled her into his arms, cradling her, making sure she was alive, that despite her injuries she was well.

Her heavy breaths told him she was asleep.

As if she hadn't just summoned the Phoenix, one of the three major catastrophes that were forbidden from setting foot in the Realm of the Living.

As if she hadn't just cemented Eliza as her enemy with no way to turn back.

As if she hadn't almost stolen herself from him forever.

CHAPTER 56

AILEEN

My body felt as though it had been through the wringer.

Everything ached. My muscles were sore beyond belief, my burns were tender and painful, and all I wanted was to keep sleeping.

But according to Isora, who had been sitting by my side in the infirmary back at the Rayne League when I woke up earlier, I'd been sleeping nonstop for days, and enough was enough. I couldn't agree more.

Now, I watched the bed across from me, where Tansy was sitting up, reading a book. Apparently, in the time I was training, fighting in the Hecatomb, almost dying, turning back time, then almost dying again, Tansy had woken up from her long comatose state.

And acted as if she remembered nothing of the last few months.

It had been an hour since I woke up. While I'd sent Isora to get some sleep, since she looked as if she hadn't slept for as many days as I'd been sleeping, I tried to talk to Tansy, but the woman didn't answer me.

So now I was waiting for Ragnor. And to pass the time, I tried to jog Tansy's memories.

"What's the last thing you remember?" I asked her.

Tansy shrugged. "Dunno."

How talkative.

"Don't bother her anymore, Aileen," Leah, the nurse in charge, scolded me, pulling the curtains around Tansy's bed. "She needs rest and a calming environment."

I had nothing to say to that, so I lay back in bed and stared at the ceiling.

Too much time passed before the infirmary doors opened, revealing Ragnor. He made a beeline to my bed, and before I even sat up, I was in his arms.

"Hey," he said quietly, embracing me tightly.

"Hey," I said back, hugging him just as tightly.

We didn't let go of one another for a while, and neither did we speak. There were so many unspoken questions lingering between us, many things that needed to be said, but it was as if there were so many, neither of us knew how to even start that conversation.

In the end, Ragnor broke the silence first. "Are you well enough to stand?" he asked, leaning back so he could cup my face and scan my eyes.

"I think so," I said softly, my love for him suddenly overwhelming me, despite everything that we had yet to say.

"Then let's go," he murmured, his thumb caressing my cheek. "The funerals are about to start."

It took me a few moments to understand what he was saying, but when it hit me, it hit me hard.

Logan, Zoey, Cassidy, CJ, Jada.

Their funerals.

Any relief I'd felt when I saw Ragnor disappeared, replaced by sorrow that threatened to suffocate me. "Oh."

Softly, Ragnor pressed a kiss to my forehead. "You don't have to come."

"I want to," I whispered, feeling tears welling in my eyes. "I have to."

So, with Ragnor's help, we made our way to the Rayne League greenhouse, where we left to the field outside, where Tansy had almost taken her own life. Dozens of League members were already there, surrounding what seemed to be five coffins.

My sorrow transformed into unbearable guilt and shame. *Perhaps, if I'd gone back one more day, I could've saved them,* I thought for the first time since . . . everything. *Perhaps, if I hadn't been so narrow minded, so locked on saving Ragnor only . . .*

But the rational part of my mind knew it to be a futile thought. I might've been able to save Logan, but what about the others? I couldn't have fought Cassidy's, Zoey's, and CJ's battles for them. I couldn't have prevented Jada's soul being ripped apart by the death of her Alara Morreh.

And yet, I could've saved Logan.

But I didn't.

And even if I were able to turn back time again, I had a gut feeling I wouldn't be able to. As if my power knew something that I didn't.

It didn't take away from my guilt, or the shame.

Ragnor sat me down on one of the few chairs in the field, drawing my attention to him. "I'm going to give a eulogy," he told me quietly. "Will you be okay here for a few minutes?"

I could barely nod, buried under the weight of the misery. But Ragnor was still the Lord of this League. He had his duty to uphold. I couldn't ask him to stay with me.

They didn't deserve it.

Ragnor pressed another kiss to my temple and walked away to the closed coffins colored plain black. And after he raised his arm, drawing everyone's attention, he spoke.

"Logan Kazar, Zoey Rittman, Cassidy Jones, Chanjomaron, and Jada Moore," he said in a quiet voice that rang clearly in the silence of the field. "They were our League members. Our brothers and sisters. And they gave their lives so our League would thrive. For that, I will be eternally grateful."

The tears fled my eyes, trickling down my face.

"For almost four years," Ragnor said, "Logan was a pillar of support to many of his fellow members. He was loved and respected, a strong Gifted individual the League will miss.

"Zoey and Cassidy were given the Imprint around the same time, seven months ago," he continued in a softer voice. "They both made their places known in the vampiric society and in the Rayne League, as both Common and Gifted respectively. They fought side by side for this League, and they died side by side, valiantly and bravely.

"Chanjomaron—CJ . . ." Ragnor paused, and for a moment I thought I heard his voice shake a little, when he said, "He's been here for many decades. A good friend, a good worker, a good man."

Someone sobbed in the crowd, and when I turned to look, I saw Bowen. The last remaining member of the dishwashing team.

My shame tripled. They were his closest friends, and yet . . .

"The same goes for Jada," Ragnor continued, and his voice cleared. "She was a vital piece of the League's ecosystem. A good friend and a good woman."

Ragnor took a deep breath and straightened. "I will never forget the sacrifice they made, and I hope you won't either."

He walked back toward me and grabbed me in his arms, sitting down with me cradled on his lap. I cried quietly, and I could see tears brimming in his own eyes.

That startled me the most. Because Ragnor never cried. *Never.*

So when one after another, people who were close to the five took to the front to say their own eulogies, I whispered to Ragnor, "Who?"

"CJ," Ragnor responded, tightening his hold on me. "Chanjomaron. He's . . . he's been an old friend. Someone I cared for."

I never realized, but knowing that CJ used to be a Malachi, and knowing that Ragnor, too . . . It all suddenly made sense. "I'm sorry," I said, voice breaking, "If only . . . if only I'd thought clearer . . ."

"It's not your fault, Aileen," he whispered. "None of it is."

But it is, Ragnor, I thought, unable to utter words. *You don't know that in a different timeline, you died. That I saved you, when I could've maybe saved the others too. You don't know that I know you were a Malachi. You don't know that I love you so much, too much, that I can't tell you any of it.*

Ragnor and I sat in silence for the rest of the funeral, grief resting heavily on our shoulders.

"Where is Eliza?" I asked Ragnor when we were back in the underground compound. He was taking me back to the infirmary, or at least planned to, but I wanted to know that first.

"She's here," he said, not elaborating, which made me come to a stop, forcing him to stop as well. Seeing my determined look, he sighed and pinched the bridge of his shoulder. "She's not . . . well."

I frowned. "What do you mean, not well?"

He shook his head. "It means you shouldn't . . . or rather, can't see her." He gave me a meaningful look. "Not now that you've transformed into . . . the Phoenix."

My heart beat like a drum. *Is it time already? Is it time for the big talk?* "Ragnor," I said quietly, "I . . . I don't know where . . ."

"I know," Ragnor said quietly, caressing my cheeks. "We don't have to talk about it yet. But we will. When we're both ready."

Feeling my throat closing up, I nodded and hugged him tight. "Okay."

"Let's go back to our room, then," he said quietly. "It's been a long day."

More like a long month.

And so we went to Ragnor's—no, *our* room, and lay together in bed, holding onto one another, terrified that if we let go, then we'd both simply disappear.

Tomorrow, we could talk about everything.

But tonight, we just needed to make sure we were alive.

EPILOGUE

ELIZA

Doors rose from the misty, stony ground, encompassing the space and surrounding me from every direction. All doors were made of wood, and each had, or didn't have, a certain appeal. I'd already learned the nature of four doors from many years of traversing Lonaria, the Realm of Dreams.

The door directly to my left, which had a serene yet somewhat tense feeling, would lead me to Aderra, the Realm of the Living—which were all big words that meant planet Earth.

To my two o'clock, a door wearing a faint smoke was bound to a certain person's subconsciousness. I'd mentally bookmarked that door, knowing I would use it often in the near future.

Directly behind me, there was a door with a soft halo that was both gentle and blood-chillingly dangerous. That was a door that, unlike the other three I'd memorized, I only used once, when I was younger and much more reckless.

That was a mistake I would *not* repeat.

The fourth door, out of the dozens that had appeared around me, that I was intimately acquainted with was right in front of me. It was the simplest door, not giving off any sort of feeling, which had tricked me, once upon a time, into thinking its inhabitant was harmless.

I'd learned the hard way that, like everything in my life, anything that seems innocent never really is.

I steadied myself, preparing for what I was likely to find, before I pulled the door open and stepped through the threshold into searing brightness. Squinting, I kicked the door shut behind me and allowed my eyes to adjust. Once they did, I blinked and stared.

No matter how many times I came here, I could not get used to the sight. It wasn't that the scenery was interesting; the place was like a large ballroom, with marble floors and walls and iridescent chandeliers dangling from the dome-shaped ceiling. It was that in the center of the ballroom, on a throne made of bronze leaves, was a sight no living being should behold.

At first glance, it looked like a human man. He had pearly white hair trickling like a waterfall into a pool on the floor. He was tall and slender, with unblemished skin the color of deep indigo, and he sat draped in a toga-like silk cloth almost as white as his hair.

If that wasn't enough to make this manlike existence seem ethereal, then the eyes did the trick: The sclera was as black as the night, the irises the color of pure lavender, and its pupils entirely silver.

No matter how many times I saw the Spirit of Providence, I was always dumbstruck, needing to process what I was seeing, for no human had skin nor eyes like his.

"Hello, Eliza," the Spirit now said, my name a song on his lips. He tapped on the floor with his bare feet. "Come sit."

Obediently, I walked toward him and pulled myself down to my knees on the marble floor at his feet. With my arms resting at my sides, I bent my torso forward and said, "Greetings, Marduk."

Marduk wriggled his toes, motioning for me to straighten. I did, and stared into his inhuman eyes, holding my hands near my belly. His unusually ethereally beautiful face split into a wide smile. "You must wonder why I called for you," he said in a deeply masculine voice that, had he been a real human man, would've made me think dirty thoughts.

But that was far from the case with Marduk, and with a being like him, one is advised to take caution. He was the most intelligent being I'd ever encountered. He didn't alter his tone of voice just for the heck of it. Everything he did was a calculated move meant to bring him the advantage in every social setting.

Even though I'd known him my whole life, I had yet to figure out how to navigate the labyrinth of Marduk's mind.

He crossed his legs and gave me a look that, on anyone else, I would've said seemed like urgent concern. But I'd learned that with Marduk, assumption wasn't just the mother but the entire damned family of all fuckups.

"The Phoenix has appeared in the Realm of the Living," Marduk now said, and even though I'd witnessed it myself, the shock of his words, of my own memories, stiffened my spine. "You must eliminate its host."

I knew it was coming, and yet the words still came like a fucking wrecking ball. I'd told Aileen Henderson that once her threat progressed beyond two, she would be in danger. At first, I thought it would be because she would resurrect the Morrow Gods.

But Aileen Henderson went and did something even worse: She became a Spirit's host, and not just any Spirit—the Phoenix, a being that, if it so wanted, could bring destruction to the Realm of the Living.

"We can't let the Phoenix have free rein in Aderra, Eliza," Marduk said, probably sensing my consternation. "I shouldn't have to tell you how much is at stake here."

He was right. The Phoenix was a literal catastrophe. Back at the Hecatomb arena, just seeing it made my *other* self rise, putting a target on the Phoenix with the awful, terrifying label, *enemy*.

I'd also witnessed the dance of the Phoenix, though in its smaller, less brutal form. It used it singularly on Atalon, but it could just as easily use it to massacre hundreds of thousands if it so wished.

There were five levels of threats in the Realm of the Living. The first level included regular supernatural creatures, like vampires, Dryads, Malachi, and the like. The second level involved more complicated cases, like Aileen Henderson, being the awful Morrow Gods' descendant. Level three usually pertained to supernatural creatures who developed extremely dangerous powers. Ragnor Rayne was such a creature, but since he had no ambition to use his powers for mass destruction, his threat level was considerably lower.

The fact that the Phoenix was level five, the highest of all levels, was enough to cause a collective apoplexy among the shadow leaders of the Realm of the Living, with Marduk being their spokesperson in this instance.

So I had no other choice but to say, "I understand."

Marduk was quiet for some time, giving my face a long look that made me fidget before he suddenly asked, "How is your eye?"

It took everything in me not to flinch. He was talking about my left eye. The one that was sewn shut by a long scar. "Fine," I somehow managed to grit out. It had been years since he mentioned my left eye. Why now?

He grinned knowingly, and it made my stomach churn in warning. "How about this?" he murmured. "If you eliminate the Phoenix's host within the next six months, I will give you back your eye."

I stared at him, confused. It took me a full minute to comprehend what he was saying. My lips parted, and sweat trickled down my temples. I should've been happy; having my left eye back was the one thing I wanted more than anything else in this world.

But in all forty years of servitude, not once had Marduk promised me such a thing. Until now. And that fact could only mean one thing.

If I kill Aileen Henderson, he will kill me.

Why? Why did Aileen have to summon the Phoenix from Esheer? Why couldn't she just stay put and act like a normal fucking vampire? Why was she insisting on making Ragnor my enemy?

Ragnor, the man who was like the brother I never had. A man I trusted with my life—but not with the knowledge I held.

Before Aileen appeared in Ragnor's life, I had no trouble. I did my job. I acted like a good apostle of Marduk. I made sure to keep the *other* in check. My left eye barely even itched.

Now, my left eye itched constantly, as if to warn me of what was to come. The *other* took control over my body, pushing *me* into my mind, unable to leave my mental chamber but for visiting Marduk, like I did now.

And the worst thing yet was, I was now considering betraying the being that was my everything. The being that had been there for me. That had hurt me and built me up. The being I served with my own entire fucking being.

How could I betray him? How could I betray my god?

Yet how could I possibly kill Ragnor's Alara Morreh?

Sucking in a deep breath, I dared attempt a different way. A different path. I asked, "What if I manage to banish the Phoenix back to Esheer without harming its host?"

Marduk looked at me with his horribly beautiful face frowning in evident disapproval. "I did not expect my most excellent apostle to question my command. Especially not with the promise of a long-sought-after reward."

"Please," I blurted, looking down and bowing yet again. *Don't give up, Eliza. You have to try.* "Let me punish the Phoenix directly, not its innocent host."

"Innocent?" Marduk's voice was incredulous, and I winced but kept my bowing position, despite the uncontrollable trembling of my body. "The host has summoned that *fiend*. Nothing about them is *innocent*."

"The end result would be the same," I said, voice shaking. "The Phoenix will be removed from Aderra, and . . . and we'll prevent a death—"

"You dare go against my words?" Marduk's voice suddenly grew, making my trembling worsen. *"Your insolence knows no bounds!"*

I couldn't do this after all. I just couldn't. "Forgive me," I whispered, crying at the terrible aftershock of his words. "Forgive me, Marduk. I did not mean to be insolent. It was a suggestion—a bad suggestion. Please . . ." I bowed deeper, tears falling to the floor. "Have mercy."

Marduk made a hissing sound that made my trembling even worse. "The only mercy you will receive is by bringing me the host's head," he said in a smooth, silky voice that made shivers cascade down my spine. "There is no other *suggestion*." He spit the word as if he didn't even want to utter it. "My word is law, Eliza. You will do as I say, like you always did. You will not question my motives. You will not make any other *suggestions*. You will do what you are told as my chosen apostle."

His words were laced with venom and authority. There was no room for negotiation. As he said, his word was law.

And I was a mere apostle. A half-human hybrid who was forced to submit to her maker. Her destroyer. Her everything.

I wouldn't be able to save Aileen Henderson after all. And neither would Ragnor Rayne.

My life as I'd known it, the life I'd worked to cultivate outside of my role as Marduk's apostle was officially over.

Grief tore me apart from the inside. Grief for the life I thought I could have. The life I thought I deserved. The life I thought I could make for myself.

What a fool you are, Eliza Wains.

And so I did the only thing I could. I bowed again, staring at the floor, and in a barely audible whisper, forced out, "Yes, Spirit of Providence."

ABOUT THE AUTHOR

Sapir A. Englard is the author of the massive digital hit The Millennium Wolves. Published in 2019 on the Galatea app, the twelve-book series has amassed more than 125 million reads. The series is also available in French from Hugo Publishing. Englard's success has been documented in *The Boston Globe* and *Forbes*, as well as on TechCrunch and other websites. A graduate of Berklee College of Music, Sapir is a full-time writer and musician.